The
Fault
Beneath Us

ROSE CLAYWORTH

BALBOA.PRESS

A DIVISION OF HAY HOUSE

Balboa Press books may be ordered through booksellers or by contacting:

Balboa Press
A Division of Hay House
1663 Liberty Drive
Bloomington, IN 47403
www.balboapress.com.au
AU TFN: 1 800 844 925 (Toll Free inside Australia)
AU Local: (02) 8310 7086 (+61 2 8310 7086 from outside Australia)

Print information available on the last page.

ISBN: 978-1-9822-9461-8 (sc)
ISBN: 978-1-9822-9462-5 (e)

Balboa Press rev. date: 08/14/2023

Contents

Prologue

Rose, an English woman born and educated in the UK, has moved from her senior management post in English language tertiary education in the Middle East to a teacher development job at a university in New Zealand's North Island. Although the location is beautiful and her new colleagues are kind and helpful, the salary is not even half of what she was earning in her previous position and there is also income tax to pay. Despite this change in her financial situation the beauty of this quiet, peaceful country with a small population outnumbered by sheep and cattle, suits this stage of her life very well. She is hoping to achieve the much vaunted 'work life balance', something that has so far evaded her for various reasons.

Because of her new economic situation and decision to become resident in New Zealand Rose has had to sell her bijou penthouse apartment on the South Coast of the UK. Her brother Bill and his wife supervised the packing and export of her personal possessions and furniture in a forty foot container by sea from the UK. 15 years after the container's arrival in New Zealand Rose still has to unpack some of the boxes. As she does so, she comes across some of her diaries and picture postcards sent to Mum and Dad (saved by her now deceased parents) from her years as a married woman in Kuwait and begins to read them.

Now retired from teaching students (ESOL) and training teachers (TESOL) and happy as a New Zealand citizen, she decides to reflect on what she discovers in her diary entries and the memories they trigger, so as to come to terms with her decision to marry and leave the UK for Kuwait almost 50 years earlier.

Glossary

TESOL is now the preferred acronym for Teachers or Teaching English to Speakers of Other Languages. It has taken the place of **TEFL** (Teachers/Teaching of English as a Foreign Language) and **TESL** (Teachers/Teaching of English as a Second Language) which attempted to distinguish between the status of English in the location of teaching as a second, or as a foreign language.

fault (n), in geology, a weakness in the earth's crust; the cause of an earthquake

fault (n), an error, a mistake, with blame attached

Wisdom

"Life shrinks or expands in
proportion to one's courage."
— Anais Nin

"Life is a comedy to those who think,
a tragedy to those who feel."
— Jean Racine

"It may be unfair, but what
happens in a few days, sometimes
even a single day, can change the
course of a whole lifetime."
— Khaled Hosseini, <u>The Kite Runner</u>

"Our life is what our thoughts make it."
__ Marcus Aurelius, Meditations

Acknowledgements

With deep gratitude and thanks to my technical,
photographic and emotional support team:

L.R. Hutt, J.J. Hutt and C.D. Howell

Tuesday, 24 August, 1976, London

Dear Diary,

Another hectic day, but finally all the preparations for the big day tomorrow are finished. The weather's hot so the evening BBQ party and buffet lunch in the garden should go OK. I am SO tired. Thank goodness everything is done!

This short diary entry instantly triggered Rose's memory of her wedding. The day had finally come when Rose would change her legal status, her personal identity as inscribed on her passport and her single life by marrying Nabeel Fareed Fardan. Was it a happy day, even though she'd never anticipated it? Was it what many brides consider to be the best day of their lives? Negative in both cases, Rose now realised. She had never considered marriage to be an option, given her experience as a child of divorced parents. It was certainly not her childhood dream. In fact, she had enjoyed lifting plastic Prince Charming in his smart military uniform off his clockwork musical base and watching plastic Cinderella waltz in her pale blue ballgown alone, rather than in Prince Charming's embrace. Instead, Rose was following through on a carefully considered decision. After three months of inner debate and discussion with family she had eventually agreed to Nabeel's marriage proposal.

The logic on which she had based her decision to marry him was simple. They were both hard workers, so would be able to succeed in life together. She remembered the old adage: The world is your oyster. She hoped it would be. They had lived together for six years, had fought and argued over various topics, but they got along well otherwise. They both loved dancing and going to the cinema, theatre and concerts as often as possible. They enjoyed travelling. They both spoke fluent French and had lots of friends of different nationalities, giving parties and going to parties often. Their sex life was not astounding, but it was satisfactory given Rose's limited experience and her biological clock was ticking loudly at 29 years old. Although she'd never wanted marriage, she now enjoyed the companionship of being a couple and hoped they would have a family later. However, she also prayed that their combined DNA would be sifted by some merciful omnipotence to ensure that any offspring had the best of both their looks and personality. A child with her small eyes and his big nose would have the worst start in life, whereas his big eyes and her smaller nose would be a better endowment. In terms of personality, a child would probably benefit from Rose's more serious nature rather than Nabeel's capricious temperament.

Having triggered the episodic memory trace Rose recalled more details of that busy day. It was a bright, warm summer morning. There was no sign of the famous footballer, Georgie Best, at the Registry Office, though according to the Registrar he was supposed to be getting married on the same day. Bill, her younger sibling by two years, drove Mum, their teenage brother John and the soon to be 'happy couple' to Pelham Registry Office in his bright yellow Ford Escort, before returning to the flat to collect his partner and three older London friends, an upstairs neighbour, and two of Rose's mature students at the Adult Education Institute (AEI) in North London where she worked. The small number of other guests attending the civil ceremony, all close friends, would walk the short distance from Knight's Court to North End Road, through a bustling London street market.

Before Mum's severely disabling rheumatoid arthritis (RA) had crippled her hands she had been a skilled dressmaker, able to use complex sewing and knitting machines. She was also talented in crochet and her work had been displayed at an exhibition in the local Centre for Disabled People where she worked as a voluntary Secretary for the UK Arthritis Association. Rose had learned sewing skills from Mum and frugal as ever had made two dresses for her wedding day: a white satin short sleeved midi dress for the civil ceremony and another in ecru coloured silk, with a frilled neckline which could be worn off the shoulder. It was perfect for the BBQ party later that evening. Saving money was necessary and important.

In a week's time they would take a flight to Egypt for their honeymoon. Six days after that they would fly to Kuwait to start their married life together. For that trip with the help of Mum she'd made her first lined suit, in beige linen, with a Chanel-style jacket and a wrap-over skirt, from a sewing pattern at the height of fashion.

She hoped to create a good impression with Nabeel's family on her arrival. Over the past six years Rose had already met his four brothers and two sisters, so she knew Asma, the oldest sister, was chic and fashion conscious. Nabeel's parents were deceased, his mother having died in childbirth in Palestine. His father, after bringing up his seven children as refugees in Lebanon, with no right to return to their home in Palestine once Israel had been created, had passed away in exile.

Rose's father, Jack, and his wife and daughter were absent from the ceremony because of his divorce from Rose's mother. Rose's parents had separated when she was 13 and Bill 11. Their mother and father had never met since that day, but each had found a new partner and had another child. Mum had John, while Dad had Janet. The two younger children were close in age but separated from their older siblings by a gap of 15 years. Rose hadn't known what to do for the best with regard to the wedding, but given the situation, she had invited Dad's new family to her flat in Knight's Court a month before the wedding. They'd had a week visiting the tourist sites in London, and getting to know each other better. Nabeel hadn't been there as he was establishing his own business with his brothers in Kuwait. He had only arrived for the wedding in the nick of time, one week before the big day, because he claimed he was doing well in his business and found it difficult to get away from the office.

Rose had had her doubts about his late arrival but was of course pleased to see him, relieved that her plans for the day would be realised and their wedding day would be a happy occasion despite her initial reluctance to take

4

Nabeel's proposal seriously. The past six years spent together as a couple in London had been the background for her decision to marry, but she had never expected that marriage was on the horizon for them, given their different cultures.

Dear Diary, Fingers crossed all goes well tomorrow. I can't do any more - it's in the hands of the gods now! At least the bridegroom is here at last.

Wednesday, 25 August, 1976, London

Rose cast her mind back again to the scene in the wood-panelled room that morning. Chairs were laid out in rows for family and guests, with the front row for the couple, their witnesses, Bill and his girlfriend, and Rose's Mum and younger brother, John. Nabeel, tall and slim as ever but now with thinning hair, looked distinguished in his single-breasted beige linen suit, while Rose looked stylish in her scooped-neck white satin dress, with a delicate wreath of silk lilies of the valley, Mum's favourite spring flower, in her chignon hair style. Brother Bill, as 'best man' was in charge of the matching 18 karat gold rings which Nabeel had managed to persuade a Jewish jeweller in Hatton Garden, London's East End, to make to size for them in only a couple of days. They were matching wide bands of brushed gold, which Nabeel had selected and purchased. Rose had paid for the food for the wedding lunch and evening party but hadn't had enough money to buy gold wedding rings before her fiance arrived in London. She had joked with him on the phone to Kuwait that they could always use curtain rings, and she'd bought a couple of brass ones, just in case. Luckily, the jeweller had taken one look at Nabeel's large nose and asked which synagogue the wedding ceremony was to be held in! Nabeel hadn't wanted to disabuse him of the assumption that his client was Jewish in case he refused to resize the rings. He'd simply replied, "Pelham". The less said, the better!

The female Registrar called the group to order and began the simple ceremony. There was no music as Rose hadn't had time to organise any and it was cheaper that way but she had made sure that she was not going to say the words 'I obey' in this civil ceremony. They had chosen to marry in a Registry office, with no religious commitments, as a confirmed Anglican woman marrying a confirmed Catholic man. Rose was equally determined she was not going to marry in a church later, though Nabeel expressed the hope that she would. Rose had heard enough of Roman Catholicism in their reminiscences of childhood days. A Catholic marriage would mean their children would be brought up in the Catholic faith, with its threat of hell fire and its definitions of sin, which Nabeel admitted had been a source of fear to him as a child. Rose saw no place for religion in the secular lives they both now lived.

As a little boy Nabeel had invented penances which he could relate to the priest at confession. "I heard an aeroplane in the sky, but I didn't look up." "I wore a bean in my shoe all day." He hadn't admitted that it was a soft, cooked bean, not a hard, dried one, however! The end result had been a penance for his sister, Asma, who had to wash the crushed bean out of the penitent child's sock. To Rose these notions of mortal sin, or venal sin, seemed like mumbo-jumbo. Although she'd been brought up as a child to believe in God and to go to church three times on Sundays, her faith had weakened in adulthood, and now she maintained her Anglican religion only as a cherished tradition. Nevertheless Rose took her marriage promises seriously: for better or worse, for richer or poorer, in sickness and in health. She had taken three months to decide to marry Nabeel, now she would go through with it and promise faithfully to be his wife, though she had refused to include the promise of obedience which was being avoided by feminist brides. She made sure to keep a copy of the text of the ceremony in her wedding photo album. The vow to love, honour and obey her husband might still be heard at other weddings, but not hers.

The ceremony was almost over and the rings were on their fingers. The Registrar spoke the usual words: "You may kiss your bride." As Nabeel turned to kiss her he whispered, "You had it, mate." The error in his choice of English verb tense was not what turned Rose's stomach. Rather it was the thought that the ceremony she took so seriously he was mocking, while apparently issuing some kind of threat, even if humorously veiled. Rose hoped she had misunderstood the intent of his words. She hoped too that she wouldn't live to regret this day. Her employer had warned her that by marrying and leaving her job and home country she was making a mistake in her career progress which she would regret. Now she saw this as another portent of an ill wind blowing. Was her marriage built on shaky ground?

That very morning Rose had been awakened by the phone ringing. It was Nabeel's family. She had only heard Nabeel's side of the conversation which had lasted several minutes. Afterwards he told her that Adel had rolled his car in Kuwait, but was not seriously hurt, though they wanted Nabeel to return home. It suddenly occurred to Rose that perhaps his family had no idea he was getting married that day. There was nothing Rose could do about it. The die was cast. Too many people would be involved if the plans were abandoned, not least of all the couple who were to take over their flat, a week after the wedding.

Her best friend and maid of honour, Marie, looking stunning in a bright green maxidress, the colour contrasting vividly with her red hair, noticed Rose's serious face. "Cheer up," she said, "It might never happen." "Touch wood," replied Rose. "Come on, I'll race you to the bubbly." Marie set off to walk back through the market with the other younger guests, while Bill drove back to the flat a couple of times, first with the family, for Rose to set out the chilled champagne and the buffet lunch, then a second time to collect the older guests. With family members there were around two dozen people for lunch. That evening there would be about 50 people for the BBQ, including teachers and students from Rose's circle of friends and business people from Nabeel's world of forged steel sales.

August 1976 had been a very hot month, breaking all UK climate records for 350 years. In June friends had laughed when Rose invited them to the evening BBQ party as it was well known that in the UK BBQs were often held under umbrellas. Not this time. There had even been reports of deaths among the city's older population from hyperthermia. Luckily the small back garden was shady. Lunch was a selection of salads, cold meats, pates, quiches and cheeses, for guests to help themselves. The *piece de resistance* was the three tier rich fruit wedding cake made and iced elaborately by Aunt Marie, Mum's sister in law. The top tier had as the centrepiece a small silver vase filled with tiny silk flowers, while the sides were decorated with silvered paper bells and horseshoes for good luck. Sadly, Aunt Marie and Uncle Alec, Mum's brother, had not been able to make the long journey from Berry Vale to the wedding in London. With glasses raised to them in their absence, the bottom layer of the three tier cake was cut in the traditional manner in front of the guests in the garden, the whole cake balanced somewhat insecurely on a kitchen stool held firm by Bill lying on the lawn. Everyone agreed it was a triumph, and later Rose wrapped up the top, smallest layer in aluminium foil, to take with her to her new life, hoping that it would be used perhaps as a baby's christening cake, or at least, as an anniversary cake. She tucked the silver vase into a box, ready for the packers to handle the following week.

The lunch guests departed over the course of the afternoon, leaving family and the closest friends, who stayed on for the evening party. The BBQ, which Nabeel had built from bricks the previous year, was to be used to cook steaks, sausages and garlic chicken (*shish taouk*). The butcher who supplied the pates and meats had done a marvellous job, with one serious exception: He had mistaken the order for ten kilos of chicken quarters as only one kilo of chicken quarters. Younger brother John saved the day by setting off alone on the London Underground to nearby Earls Court to buy ten frozen chickens. These were thrown into the bath in their plastic bags and covered with cold water. After an hour defrosting in this way, BA steward and chef friend Rob rolled up his sleeves and dismembered the icy birds. They were then marinated with garlic and lemon for a while in a huge plastic bowl before Nabeel's former boss, a French count, did the honours on the BBQ for the greater part of the evening, turning out perfectly grilled portions of succulent steak, chicken and sausage. Everyone agreed the food was terrific.

The night was warm and guests lingered, sipping cold drinks and smoking, a common habit at the time, until the small hours. After everyone had departed it was with some relief that the happy couple got into their guest sofa bed in the sitting room. Mum and John were sharing the sole bedroom and had gone to bed a little earlier. The garden was littered with rubbish, and annoyingly for Rose, a non-smoker, a multitude of cigarette ends, but clearing up could be dealt with the next day. The two of them could do no more that night.

"I wish I knew what your family thought about today," Rose whispered to her new husband.

"Oh they're happy about it, you can be sure of that," he responded confidently.

"So why did they ask you to go home this morning?" she murmured anxiously.

"Oh, they forgot, in the panic over my kid brother. He's OK. Nothing to worry about. Go to sleep now."

"OK. Good night."

Rose kissed him and rolled over on her side. Whatever had really been said, she guessed she would find out sooner or later, and she hoped it wouldn't be bad news. For now, oblivion was all she wanted. It had been a long day, which had inevitably changed her life. The implications were huge and still to come. If there was a fault line beneath them, it would reveal itself sooner or later with greater or lesser impact on their marriage. It was out of her control now.

Dear Diary,

The deed is done for better or worse. Too tired for more now but there were a couple of strange incidents: an early morning phone call from Kuwait and Nabeel's strange comment during the ceremony. What did he mean, I wonder? Time will tell. Perhaps I'm worrying about nothing, as usual. Thank goodness I have a new job to look forward to with the British Council.

Thursday, 26 August, 1976, London

The next morning they all slept late. Mum took her morning painkillers in her room with water and a plain biscuit and tried to rest while their effect kicked in. John went out into the garden and began picking up cigarette ends from the night before. It was another fine morning. Over cups of tea, Rose opened the wedding presents brought by guests. Nabeel's boss had brought a pair of beautiful silver fighting cocks, such as might grace a sideboard in a stately home. A student from Colombia had given her a unique bone-handled carving set. Nabeel's Irish colleague brought a large steel pressure cooker. Mum's friend Katie had given the couple a classically styled, solid silver photo frame. Dad had given hard-earned and difficult to spare cash when they had visited before the wedding. Best friend Marie had presented her with a pink tea towel with the logo *Love means never having to say you are sorry!* Rose wondered how realistic that slogan was.

After enjoying toast and eggs for breakfast Rose and Nabeel joined John in the garden with trash bags, while Mum put her feet up on the bed. It took a couple of hours to tidy up the garden. The elderly neighbour looked out from upstairs and waved her encouragement.

"It was a lovely day, and congratulations again!" she called from her window.

"Glad you enjoyed it," replied Rose, waving to her.

This lady had been a good neighbour over the past three years. When Nabeel and Rose had taken over the flat from their friend Rob, they had wondered about the amount of noise that might be generated in the flat above their heads. This kindly retiree, with an amazing history of her own as a dancer in wartime shows in London's Piccadilly, was as quiet as a mouse. Rose used to pop upstairs for a cup of tea once a month to keep her company. As she was planning to move into a retirement home soon, she had her own lifestyle changes to look forward to.

For lunch there were plenty of leftovers, so there was no need to do more than eat and rest for a while. The evening was spent packing as Mum and John were leaving the following day for their home in the Midlands. The next day Rose went with them to the coach station at Victoria. They only had small bags, but would get a taxi from the Mossfield bus station to their apartment. The farewell was tearful as Rose and Nabeel were leaving in a week for a honeymoon in Egypt and thence to Kuwait to start their married lives. They did not know when they would next see each other. Mum only had Nabeel's business address to link her to her daughter in future but she had never expressed any doubts about her Arab son-in-law.

Rose didn't have much time to think about the distance that would separate her from her family as the packers were due two days before their departure and she still had cases to fill, and pictures to take down from the walls. Most of the furniture was staying, as they had come to an agreement with Bill's friends who were taking over the rented flat. However, the gold Dralon-upholstered rocking chair from Heal's, and two beautiful leather pouffes from Lebanon which were unique in their design and luxurious in appearance, were worth keeping and were labelled for the packers to handle. A picture of dark red roses painted on glass given to Rose by her university friend Marie, as well as a framed Utrillo print of a street scene given by Dad, were two other precious possessions travelling to the Middle East.

The upright piano standing in the hall had not been included in the handover deal, but Rose didn't know when or where it would ever be returned to her. It had belonged to one of Mum's older sisters, and Rose had learned to play on it, and had enjoyed the old sheet music that went with it. Old songs with lyrics such as "I'm my own grandpa" had baffled her as a young child, but others, such as "Smoke gets in your eyes" had entranced her. As a six-year-old she had loved learning to play, and had tried to teach Bill, aged 4, to follow her lead. Although she'd given up piano lessons when she was in secondary school, and had never been able to take exams as they cost too much, she still used her ability to sight read in choral singing, and also enjoyed playing the old 'joanna' at Xmas for carol-singing sessions.

She hoped that one day in Kuwait she would have her own piano again. After all, she'd finally decided to marry Nabeel because of his strong work ethic, which equalled hers. He had had a deprived childhood as a refugee and was as motivated to achieve as she was. Between the two of them, they would surely make a success of their married life. Nabeel had assured her he had won big contracts and was expecting commission on them, while she had interviewed successfully in London for a position in the English Teaching Centre of the British Council in Kuwait. She would start work almost as soon as she arrived in Kuwait.

A picture postcard of Buckingham Palace:

Dear Dad,

Sorry you couldn't be here on my big day. Thank you for understanding the difficulty. At least we had some good times when you were here in London. I hope Janet is enjoying her Beach Boys record? She didn't miss out on being a bridesmaid as I didn't have one. Thank you so much for your wedding gift. Bill will let you have some photos of the occasion. So, till next time I write from Kuwait, sending lots of love, Rose.

Friday, 3 September, 1976, London, Cairo

The packers took two days to finish the job, arriving late and leaving early, causing a lot of stress, but finally they had finished. In the hall were two suitcases, Rose's small carry-on 'vanity' bag, and Nabeel's Samsonite briefcase. Rose remembered how almost a year before, on the night Nabeel returned to London after being in Kuwait for a couple of months, he'd left the briefcase outside the front door of their basement flat in his excitement to be back with her. He'd proposed that night, to Rose's astonishment.

"Have you forgotten who I am?" she'd asked him in surprise. "Don't you remember all the fights we've had over the past six years?"

"I remember everything, but I missed you so much and I want to be with you forever," he replied steadily.

"So it's a case of absence makes the heart grow fonder," she laughed.

"Perhaps, but I love you and I want to marry you," he told her sincerely.

"OK. Well, ask me again just before you leave for Kuwait. I'll give you my answer then when I know you are serious," she smiled, touched by his apparent devotion.

He had asked her again, several times, but she'd been unable to reply for three months. She hadn't wanted to give up her job, which she'd held for only three years. She'd become a fulltime Lecturer in Adult Education and Head of Department of a staff of 60 part-time ESOL teachers after serving as a part-time teacher herself in a North London AEI. She'd quickly been promoted to Lecturer II, and her boss had warned her that she was giving up the chance to become a Vice Principal, if not a Principal, within ten years.

Faced with this dilemma, Rose had asked Mum for her opinion. Mum, superstitious as ever, had resorted to reading the Tarot cards, something she'd done previously for Rose. On that earlier occasion the cards had indicated Career Success (the World card). This time the winning card indicated Domestic Bliss (the Sun card)! Whether this truly revealed Rose's fate and future, or simply reflected Mum's preference for her daughter, Rose now couldn't be sure. It seemed Freudian to suspect that Mum's own choice had influenced the Tarot outcome, but anything seemed possible to Rose at the time in her state of indecision.

Rose had eventually got used to the idea of getting married, after weighing up the future possibilities in what she thought was a logical process of measuring the pros and cons. In the final analysis, the two of them wanted a family, they both loved children, and they both were prepared to work hard to make a good life for them. After three months, she had given Nabeel a positive answer. Then she had resigned, and begun working towards this move. As well as leaving her job, Rose had made another big change. She had applied for a passport in her new, married name. Following tradition for girls of her and her mother's generation, she had added her husband's surname to her own first name, moving her family name to a middle name position. She was to become Rose

Clayworth Fardan on her wedding day. Leaving day was here at last, when she would use her passport and assume her new identity.

A friend from work had offered to drive them to the airport to take their Egypt Air flights. Rose noticed little of the journey as she was tired after the wedding preparations and the packing, not to mention her doubts about Nabeel's family's reaction to their wedding. There had been no contact from them that Rose knew of since the wedding day phone call. If there had been negative reactions, Nabeel would not have passed them on, Rose felt sure of that. He wouldn't want to worry her. She closed her eyes and drifted into sleep, her head on Nabeel's shoulder for a few minutes before he retired to the back of the plane to smoke one of his regular 80 cigarettes per day. They were seated in non-smoking at least; he had agreed to that concession. Rose's thoughts turned again to his family. She knew them all. Were they reluctant for Nabeel to marry her because she was a 'used' woman, a girlfriend of six years? Or was it because she was a British woman? The British had conceded Palestine to the Israelis, and it must be hard for the Fardan family to accept the enemy into their ranks, Rose thought. Nabeel must have considered that possibility and surely decided it was irrelevant.

The meeting with the family would not happen for a while anyway. The couple planned to enjoy their holiday in Egypt. Rose had always been interested in Egyptology and she looked forward to learning so much more in the company of her new husband who spoke Arabic. She would enjoy learning some of the language too. After she'd visited Beirut with Nabeel three years earlier she'd bought a BBC introductory text to the language, with English transliteration and a small vinyl disk. She'd tried a few words out with some Libyan students in the London language school, with hilarious effect. She expected Nabeel would help her with the language in future so that she could fit in with the family more easily. Of course, her new in-laws all spoke French and English as she did, but she wanted them to see that she was prepared to be flexible in her language use, and adapt to her new situation. She dozed as the plane continued on its five hour journey, waking only as the stewards prepared the passengers for landing.

After disembarking and going through customs in Cairo Airport Rose had an unpleasant surprise. They had no reservation for a hotel. They hadn't discussed the budget for this holiday, but Rose had assumed that Nabeel had booked a hotel for them. September was high season for Cairo accommodation and therefore expensive for foreign tourists like Rose. She expected that Nabeel, a native Arabic speaker, would be given priority as a local at the airport accommodation desk. The conversation he had at the desk seemed to take a long time, however. Rose was very relieved when eventually it concluded, and they got into a taxi for a downtown destination.

"Where are we going?" she asked as the rather dilapidated yellow car left the airport rank.

"Don't worry! We've got a great hotel. You'll love it," he responded, with a grin.

It was indeed a good hotel. The Cairo Carlton doorman greeted them with a smile and loaded their bags onto a trolley. A porter took them up to their room and waited expectantly by the door.

"Thanks," shouted Nabeel in English as he rushed into the bathroom. The porter grimaced. Rose blushed. There was going to be no *baksheesh*.

"Sorry, we haven't got any Egyptian money," offered Rose in embarrassed explanation.

"*Malesh,*" said the porter and slipped away.

"What does *malesh* mean?" she asked Nabeel when he came out of the bathroom.

"Oh, 'never mind'," he told her with a grin.

"Seems like a useful word," she said noting it mentally.

"Well, are we going to change some money?" she ventured reproachfully.

"Of course, but right now let's take a nap, then we'll go out for dinner and a show. You'll enjoy Egyptian belly dancing tonight."

"Sounds good. I am tired. I'm not hungry at all after the food on the plane."

They had travelled east for five hours, but the time difference was only one hour in advance.

Nabeel got on the phone while Rose had a shower. When she came out, he was smiling.

"Great news - some of my friends are joining us tonight. You'll love them."

"Fine. Let's get some sleep then, so that I'll be fresh. Do they speak English?"

"Of course. All my friends are well educated."

The evening was novel for Rose. Dinner in the nightclub was composed of a wide selection of *mezze*, which she had first tried in Baalbek in 1973, when

21

Nabeel had taken her to Lebanon for a holiday. These small, infinitely varied dishes suited vegetarians as well as meat-eaters. The table was laden with bottles of *arak,* whisky, beer and wine. There was a small band playing Arabic music and around midnight a singer performed, accompanied later by a belly dancer. It all seemed exotic and festive. Nabeel's friends were charming, though a lot of the conversation was about people she didn't know. She couldn't answer questions, such as 'What are you going to do here?' or 'Do you like Egypt?' as they had made no firm plans prior to arriving. It was all impromptu and for now, Rose was content to leave it like that. Tomorrow they would plan the rest of their short stay. There was no need to worry.

Meanwhile, Rose enjoyed sipping her chosen drink, *arak.* She had first tasted it in Beirut. Nabeel's friend, Jean, had given her some of his own special vintage, which she had enjoyed without becoming intoxicated to everyone's amazement. She took it slowly on this evening, aware of her exhaustion, and was able to keep going on the dance floor until 3 am. At that point everyone made their farewells and the honeymoon couple retired to their room.

"Wow, I'm SO tired again," Rose sighed. "I suppose it's the lifting of stress at last."

"But you enjoyed it, *habibti*?" Nabeel enquired anxiously.

"Of course. It was fun. Good night darling," she murmured before closing her eyes, heavy with sleep, her mind uncluttered with doubts for once. This was going to be a wonderful, if short, honeymoon.

A picture postcard of the Pyramids at Giza:

Dear Mum,

Just a quick word to say we've arrived here in Egypt and are having a lovely time. You can see from this postcard that the Pyramids are amazing. Lots of love from us both. Rose and Nabeel

Saturday, 4 September, 1976, Cairo

The next day dawned with the sun shining through the curtains. Rose looked around the room. It was elegant and spacious. She smiled in happy anticipation of the day to come. But where was Nabeel? In the bathroom? No sound emanated from there. She got up and had a look. His pyjamas were hanging on the back of the door, so he'd obviously dressed and gone out. She went to the window to look out. The view towards the Nile was hazy at 8am. But where had Nabeel gone? To get something to surprise her perhaps? Rose decided to take a bath and wait for him to come back.

She was relaxing in warm bubbles when Nabeel returned.

"Well, I did it!" he called out excitedly as he came into the bathroom.

"Did what, darling?"

"I got us another hotel."

"Another hotel? Why? What's wrong with this one?"

"Well, I didn't want to tell you yesterday, but I had to bribe the man on reception to get this room. I gave him one of our bottles of whisky."

"Really? I didn't notice. So when do we have to leave?" Rose was surprised by this turn of events. She was looking forward to a leisurely brunch.

"Check out is 11.00 am."

"Right. And where are we going?" she asked with some suspicion.

24

"To the best hotel you could ask for. The Mina House at Giza."

"Where is that? You know I didn't bring a guide book."

"Just near the Pyramids. You'll love it."

There was no time for more discussion. Rose hurriedly finished her bath, dressed and began packing. They had opened their heavy cases to find something smart for dinner last night, so everything was in a mess. She just managed to get everything together by the check out deadline. Yesterday's bell boy arrived at the door to take the luggage down. He didn't look too happy at the prospect, but Nabeel was feeling munificent today. He gave him a tip as he loaded the cases into the taxi.

"Mina House, Giza," he told the driver and off they went.

"How long will be staying there?" Rose dared to ask now they were on their way.

"Well, it depends on what you want to do."

"I'd like to relax after the rush of the last few months."

"We'll have a real holiday. We are definitely staying for more than one night at the Pyramids."

"How did you manage to get a booking here with such short notice?"

"I asked them if they got my fax. They apologised and gave us a good room to make up for it."

"When did you send a fax?"

"I didn't. I didn't know where we'd stay - we've been hectic, haven't we, since the wedding?

"Yes, and I rather relied on you to use your contacts."

"Well, now I have. So relax."

The taxi had already crossed the Nile and the desert was visible. There was ribbon settlement along the road, but as they neared the hotel, the Pyramids came into view, dwarfing everything around them. Rose caught her breath.

"Amazing. How truly huge they are."

"Yep. One of the seven wonders of the world."

"Indeed. And this is the hotel?"

The taxi had pulled into a beautiful tropical garden in front of a resort-style, single storey building, with an exotic facade of carved hard wood. The doorman was wearing what Rose recognised as Indian clothing, with a turban on his head, and a feather jauntily stuck into it. The porters too were wearing white loose clothing, long shirts and pantaloons resembling *salwar khamees*.

"Isn't the hotel run by Egyptians?" Rose asked in surprise. It seemed strange to see these Indian sub-continent costumes, which she guessed might be a throwback from the old colonial days in Egypt. On the other hand, this could be the result of a modern business venture.

"I believe so. It's got a great reputation this place."

"It's fabulous," she agreed readily.

Rose noted from the signage the Hotel was part of the Oberoi chain. She hadn't heard of it before, and she was a little anxious as Nabeel checked in that this booking would be rejected at the last minute. But all went well, their passports were copied, Nabeel signed the registration form and they were led to a wood-panelled room, with a balcony overlooking a large, blue pool.

"This is lovely," Rose exclaimed when they were alone. "Well done, darling. You've pulled this one off."

Secretly, she felt concerned that Nabeel had used his wiles to achieve what he wanted. She wondered a little about this trait which she'd seen emerge in Lebanon with a Baalbek souvenir pedlar. However, she felt slightly machiavellian herself today. How could she let such issues ruin her honeymoon? It was petty and irrelevant to their happiness.

"Shall we go and have some brunch beside the pool? We haven't eaten today. We could take a swim and cool down too," she suggested.

"Great idea. Quick as you can!"

Within a very short time they were seated by the pool, ordering food and drinks before they jumped into the water - Rose in the shallow end as she wasn't a strong swimmer and Nabeel in the deep end. He wasn't a stylish swimmer, but he was confident. It wasn't until Rose climbed out again and wrapped herself in a thick white towel that she looked up above the waving palms and flowered hibiscus and bougainvillea. She exclaimed in surprise: "We've got a view of the Pyramids! How wonderful!"

Indeed, at that time the Mina House Hotel stood as an oasis in the desert, affording a magnificent view of the three major Pyramids at Giza. It was the icing on the cake for Rose, pushing into the background her ethical concerns.

"I'll never forget this, sweetheart," she told him, excitedly.

"I told you you'd love it," he laughed. In fact, it was better than he'd expected himself. He mentally thanked the receptionist at the Cairo Carlton he'd bribed with the whisky. He was the one who'd recommended this and given him the idea for getting a room.

"You have to play the game to get what you want," he told her smugly.

"If you don't have millions, you do, I suppose," she agreed.

"Well, till then we do. Now, do you want to go to the Pyramids this afternoon?"

"Perhaps tomorrow would be better? Half the day is gone already and I want to take it all in slowly."

"OK. Let's make a plan then, for the whole of the stay."

"Good idea."

They spent the rest of the afternoon alternately snoozing in the warm air, wafted by gentle breezes and poring over the guidebook they found in the lounge. They would spend the remaining nights of their stay here. On Thursday they would take the flight to Kuwait. The honeymoon would be over and the family loomed large in Rose's mind again. Nabeel's voice interrupted her slight melancholy:

"Let's go out tonight. I saw a Bedouin tent on the roadside. They advertised a cabaret. It will be touristy but still worth a look, don't you think?"

"Sounds good. Do you think we need to book?"

"I shouldn't think so. We'll go around 10pm - nothing starts before then in this part of the world."

The huge tent they entered that night was decorated with brightly coloured camel hangings and lit by candles.

They were seated on huge cushions at low brass tables. Dinner resembled the one they'd had at the Cairo Hotel - a huge selection of *mezze* dishes, accompanied by their choice of beverage.

"Whisky is ridiculously expensive," Nabeel warned Rose. "Let's have *arak* again, or beer?"

"Beer's fine by me. It suits the under canvas experience!"

They enjoyed their chilled drinks, and Nabeel got a hubbly bubbly (*nargile*) going, to Rose's amusement. It actually smelled better than his endless cigarettes.

"It's better for me too, you know," he assured her. "The water filters the tobacco."

"Oh, so you think cigarettes might be bad for you, do you, at last?"

"Never. They kill germs. You know that."

Rose didn't know that, but she knew that Nabeel liked to believe it. Despite the research that was beginning to be done in the mid-1970s into the potentially harmful effects of smoking tobacco, Nabeel resolutely stuck to his guns: smoking kills germs.

The cabaret began, distracting them from what was to become a more serious topic of conversation over the years. First came a belly dancer, then an acrobat, balancing an elaborate chandelier with lit candles on his head, a sword swallower followed, and the grand finale was a singer, with another belly dancer accompanying him. The songs were endless, mournful and loud to Rose's ears. She was pleased when around 1am Nabeel turned to her.

"Had enough?"

"Yes, it was great, but I'm tired."

"Off we go then."

He paid the bill and they went outside into the cool night air.

"We could walk, but it might be dangerous."

"Really? Why?"

"There are a lot of poor people who would like to rob tourists if they get the chance."

"But you're not a tourist, you're an Arab."

"Not in their eyes. I'm not an Egyptian."

It was an interesting viewpoint that Rose hadn't considered: Nabeel felt himself in a foreign country as much as she did, although he spoke the local language. She mulled it over as they drove back to the hotel in a little yellow cab. There was so much to learn, and so much NOT to assume. She reminded herself not to over-react. They were both away from home.

"*Shukran jazilan,*" Nabeel said as he paid the bill. Rose added the Arabic for thanks to her own repertoire of vocabulary.

"Goodnight, darling," she said, as they climbed into bed, exhausted again. "Sweet dreams."

Dear Diary,

No energy for much tonight – we had a very interesting day. Nabeel is as much out of his comfort zone as I am, it seems. But we had a good time and avoided any potential dangers. This hotel is fabulous.

Sunday, 5 September, 1976, Cairo

Even in the early morning hours the three major Pyramids at Giza and the majestic, though noseless Sphynx, were thronged with tourists, most investigating these amazing feats of engineering from their exteriors, clambering onto the huge stones at the base and taking photos. (Selfies were not common then!) Others queued to investigate the steep, dark, interior staircases which had been sealed by the pyramid builders after completion. Some, even more daring, took the opportunity to ride a camel or a horse, although Rose had heard tales of tourists who paid for such a ride, then were taken far away from the Pyramids, having to pay an exorbitant price to return on the animal since they had only bought a 'single' ticket!

Neither Rose nor Nabeel wished to ride around or enter a Pyramid but they had to use a lot of energy to resist the continuous calls of the horse and camel keepers, and to turn down multiple offers by self-styled guides, so as to wander on their own around the three monoliths. By mid-afternoon thanks to steely resistance and focussed inattention to both kinds of *entrepreneurs*, they were exhausted but satisfied with their close up of the sights at Giza. Back at the hotel for a cool, leisurely swim and a late lunch by the pool, they checked their guidebook for 'must see' tourist sites. They would need to visit Egypt another time to see some of the lesser known Pyramids on the way to Thebes, as well as Luxor and Abu Simbel.

"Perhaps we can come back on our wedding anniversary," Rose suggested.

"Good idea. It's a deal," Nabeel promised with a smile.

As they swam, they discussed the *Son et Lumiere* program which promised a historical review of the Pyramids they had just seen close up.

"How do you feel about going to the Sound and Light Show at the Pyramids tonight?" asked Rose.

"Are you up to it after our visit to the desert?" Nabeel countered.

"Well, it's only up the road."

"OK. Let's go. It starts at 10pm I think. I didn't want you to get tired."

They took a nap and set the radio alarm to get up for an early dinner. After eating in the coffee shop, with Rose clutching a warm wrap, they took a taxi up to the Pyramids. The site was completely different at night. Floodlights illuminated the Sphynx and the Pyramids. There was a raised seating area, and a ticket booth in front of it. After a morning spent avoiding people who wanted to 'help' them for a probably hefty *baksheesh*, Rose and Nabeel's hearts sank as they were approached by a smartly dressed, middle-aged man, who spoke good English.

"Can I help you? I am an official guide," he told them.

The two of them backed away, declining his services with muttered 'no thank yous', but he followed them. It was the same kind of persistence they had resisted all morning.

"I can show you the best seats," he offered.

"No, thanks," they both said in unison and turned in the opposite direction.

Having found their own seats as far as possible away from the 'guide', the couple sat back and enjoyed the splendour of the light show, with the English language commentary. In the interval, it was with some chagrin they later noticed the same man helping some Americans, and declining the tip they offered! A case of mistaken motivation, they noted, feeling ashamed of their prejudice.

A picture postcard of the Sphynx at Giza:

Dear Mum and John,

We're having a great time here. We've been to the Pyramids and the Sphynx. It's amazingly huge as you can see on this postcard. I hope you are both OK? I will write more from Kuwait. Thinking of you and sending lots of love, Rose.

Monday, 6 September, 1976, Cairo

After the busy previous day, they decided to laze by the pool in the sun and eat in the Hotel that night. Nabeel was not exactly a fussy eater, he simply didn't care for food, preferring to smoke cigarettes. As he smoked so many each day, he hardly ever felt hungry. He often said he wished he could take a pill so that he didn't have to bother with food. His preferred dish when he did eat was steak, well grilled, and doused with a liberal squeeze of lemon juice. So eating out wasn't usually much fun, but that night they tried out the Indian dishes on offer in the Moghul restaurant. The delicious curries and dhals were served in beautiful copper pots but as usual Nabeel wasn't particularly interested in the food.

"Do you remember the first curry I cooked you in London?" Rose asked.

"Not really. Why?"

"That was when you cried out 'Cocorico' and upset me. I took it as an insult."

"Well, you know now that we had nothing to eat but rice and tomato soup in the refugee camp, but our special meal once a week was always chicken."

"Yes, I'm sorry. Is anything on your mind?" Rose asked. "You're smoking a lot."

"No, what should be?"

"I wondered what's going to happen when we arrive in Kuwait, that's all."

"Well, we'll go to the family house."

"But are they expecting us? Can they put us up?"

"Of course. It's a big house."

"Oh, that's a surprise. As we didn't hear from them, I thought we would stay in a hotel."

"Don't worry about it. Everything's under control."

Rose decided to close the subject. She didn't want to spoil the mood of their leisurely day. After all, she would find out soon enough what was in store for her arrival in Kuwait.

Dear Diary,

The honeymoon so far has been quite surprising. I was expecting Nabeel to be comfortable in this environment as an Arabic speaker. What do they say about 'assume': It makes an ass of you and me? I suppose I have to be patient and take things step by step. But I've had time to think today and I'm still worried about what is to come in Kuwait. Fingers crossed.

Tuesday, 7 September, 1976, Cairo

They woke refreshed after an early night, ready to go into Cairo to visit the famous Museum in Tahrir Square, the main mosques and the Khan al Khalili Bazaar. Their fearful anticipation of meeting guides who were really 'rip-off agents' had been subdued by their experience at the Sound and Light show. So when Nabeel tried to pay their taxi driver with a 10 guinea note for a one guinea fare, they were amazed to hear the driver say "no change". It was quite apparent that he expected them, as tourists, to acquiesce and hand over ten guineas for the fare, a 90% mark up.

"In that case, wait a moment," said Nabeel, getting out of the cab and leaving Rose hostage.

"Where are you going?" she asked desperately.

"To get some change, of course. Stay there."

He stopped a passerby and asked in Arabic whether the man could change a 10 guinea note.

"I'll give you nine for it," was the response in Arabic.

Nabeel looked amazed, while Rose looked on in bewilderment, unsure of what had happened.

"Hang on," Nabeel told her, "I'm going into the Museum."

After a good few minutes he reappeared with several coins in his hand.

He thrust one at the taxi driver and held the passenger door for Rose to get out.

"*Baksheesh*?" asked the driver.

"Not on your Nellie," said Nabeel in old-fashioned English, disgusted.

"What happened?" asked Rose, bewildered.

"I'd never have believed it if it hadn't happened to me," said Nabeel as he recounted the details. "It seems I really am a foreigner here. What happened to Arab solidarity, I wonder?"

"I suppose they must be really poor to treat tourists like this," Rose suggested.

"It's a terrible attitude though. You can't really trust anyone here."

Putting the events behind them they looked for a map of the Cairo Museum. There didn't seem to be any informative documentation, so after paying their entry fee they wandered into the huge, dusty, disorganised rooms which contained the exhibits. In every corner there seemed to be a middle-aged man with a feather duster, who claimed to be an official guide. They studiously avoided them, determined not to succumb to any more wiles. They were really keen to see the treasures which had recently been put on display after the boy king Tutankhamun's tomb had been discovered and opened in the Valley of the Kings in Luxor in 1922. On enquiring, they were told the exhibit had gone on a world tour, and was at that moment in London.

"Another example of Murphy's Law," murmured Rose, "What can go wrong, will!"

As for all the other intriguing artefacts, it seemed to the couple that they were visiting a jumble sale of antiquities. There was no signage in English that Rose could read and it became obvious that Nabeel was not a good translator.

Rose had expected insider information from a native-speaker of Arabic, but instead, she discovered she was travelling with a tourist who was less knowledgeable than she was. After an hour or so, they had had enough. It was very impressive in a haphazard way. They almost felt like tomb robbers themselves, so higgledy piggledy was the state of each room.

"Let's get out of here," suggested Nabeel, urgently in need of a cigarette. "We can get a coffee in the Bazaar."

"Sounds great," agreed Rose as they walked out of the Museum. "I hope you've got change for a taxi, though?" she asked laughing.

After a short ride they found themselves on the edge of the huge market, or *souk,* known as the Khan al Khalili Bazaar. It seemed like a ramshackle shopping mall to Rose, who had never seen a *souk* before. Some of the stalls were covered with canvas, like a street market in England, while others resembled proper shops, with solid interiors and back rooms. The most striking feature was the noise of people shouting to each other, people moving things on trolleys, carrying things on their heads, or hammering things. It was certainly a lively atmosphere after the relative quiet of the Museum.

"There's a coffee place," Nabeel touched her elbow and guided her down one of the alleys. Taller than Rose he had spotted the brass tables and smelled the coffee and the smoke from the *argile* pipes. There were mostly men sitting at the small, low tables, drinking from small cups or glasses, and several of them puffing away at hubbly bubblies.

As they took their seats at a front table the waiter came over. He had on his head a red fez, which made him seem official, but was wearing a huge white pinafore, which made him seem more like a butcher.

"Drink?" he asked. "*Chai, qahwa?*"

Rose asked for tea, but Nabeel warned her it would come loaded heavily with sugar.

"*Chai biddun suqr,*" he told the waiter, "*wa ahwa saada.*"

The waiter looked at him more closely. He realised he was dealing with someone who knew Arabic. *Ahwa saada* has no sugar, but it is like asking for a virgin bloody Mary, only those familiar with the language can use these terms and understand them.

"*Ya ahlan wa sahlan,*" the waiter cried out, realising he was speaking to a brother Arab.

"*Ahleen,*" replied Nabeel politely in the Lebanese way.

"*Hadratak lubnaani?*"

"*La, falistini.*"

For Rose, the words referring to nationality were understood as clear as bells. She hadn't heard much Arabic in London, but she knew Nabeel referred to himself as *Lubnaani Falistini*, or, *Falistini Lubnaani*. He used the former when he was with Lebanese folk and the latter when with other Palestinians. Of course, Palestine no longer existed as a viable political reality, though emotionally and historically it was there in all Palestinian hearts, even if the person had not been born there. Not having the right of return to Israel as a Palestinian refugee, was not only hurtful, it was downright damaging to the Muslim Palestinians living in camps like the Sabra and Chatila in Beirut. Nabeel's family were fortunate to be Christian. They had been granted full Lebanese nationality back in 1948 when Israel was created on Palestinian land. As such they had been able to travel with proper passports, unlike their Muslim peers, who could only use *laissez passer* refugee papers in limited countries.

"*Beetna beetkum,*" cried the waiter. "Our house is your house!"

"*Shukran, habibi,*" Nabeel replied. "Thank you, my friend."

The tea came in a small glass with its matching little saucer, the coffee in an even smaller porcelain coffee cup, with two glasses of cold water on the side. It was refreshing and interesting to sit and sip their beverages while watching the parade of different shoppers go by. There were European and American tourists in sandals, flip-flops, shorts, T-shirts and sundresses, all with the necessary sunhat and a camera in hand. There were Egyptian ladies in their colourful long dresses and black headscarves. However, the majority were men, wearing cotton *gallabyas*, as the Egyptians call the full length, loose flowing kaftan. These were usually pale in colour, often striped, and on their heads the men wore an untidy turban, with a tail end usually draped over one shoulder. It was novel to Rose, who had never visited Egypt before. She wondered what people would look like in Kuwait.

Every table had a big ashtray and of course, Nabeel smoked a cigarette as they relaxed.

"Don't you want to smoke a hubbly bubbly?" Rose asked him.

"They take time. Best smoked in the evening really," he replied.

"Do you smoke them in Kuwait?"

"People do, but we don't. It's a peasant thing."

"Do all of you smoke?"

"All the brothers do. But it's not usual for Arab ladies to smoke. At least in public."

"Thank goodness," Rose murmured. It was going to be a trial sitting with the family with them all smoking, she could imagine.

After a while they moved on through the market. They saw the spice stalls, vats piled high with ground cumin, turmeric, coriander seeds, ginger roots, vanilla pods, cardamom pods, chillies and garlic cloves. It was picturesque as well as exotic with the spice aroma surrounding the stalls. They had no need for spices or food of any kind, so they wandered on to the clothing stalls. Rose was intrigued by the belly dancing costumes displayed in shop windows. She wondered if she might learn to belly dance in Kuwait.

"Belly dancing is not allowed in public in Kuwait," Nabeel said, reading her mind. "It's a strict Muslim society, not like Egypt."

The costumes were heavily sequinned and cost a lot of money, so she declined a closer look inside the shops. The bric a brac stalls were more attractive, selling cheap items like *zills*, the brass castanets belly dancers used, coffee cups, tea glasses, tiny teaspoons and other small household items.

"I'd like a small souvenir of our honeymoon," Rose remarked.

"Well, we'll have a lot of photos and memories," Nabeel chided. "Our budget is not that strong at the moment."

Rose realised she'd left all the money worries to him

so far on this trip. It wasn't fair to put him under extra pressure by wanting to shop.

"That's OK, *habibi*," she assured him. "You're quite right. One day we'll come back, when we've made our fortunes, won't we?"

"Are you ready for some lunch? I know somewhere we can go that will make a great memory for you."

Nabeel knew how much Rose loved her food. She got cross if she was hungry, and her blood sugar fell promptly every four hours, like a baby's.

"Yes, it's about time for lunch. Where are we going?"

They had reached the edge of the Bazaar where there were several restaurants with large, simply furnished seating areas. The wooden benches and huge tables were shaded with canvas, and waiters rushed around serving food to hungry shoppers.

"What's on the menu?"

"No menu, just three traditional dishes: omelette with parsley (*fines herbes* as the French say), *fuul medames* (large brown butter beans in a garlicky sauce) and *kijaree*, or as we call it, *mejedarra* (brown lentils cooked with rice and noodles, then heavily garnished with browned, fried onions)."

"Let's try one of each, shall we?" Rose suggested. "They all sound delicious. We can share."

The food came quickly. A delicious fresh onion and tomato sauce was served with the *kijaree*, and the omelettes and beans came with soft, warm pockets of freshly made flat bread (or *pita* as the Greeks have it). Rose enjoyed the lunch immensely and for once, Nabeel appeared to be eating with pleasure. It reminded her of the first time she had eaten Arabic cheesecake in Beirut, when Nabeel had taken her there as his girlfriend. She had never tasted *konafa* like that again. She wondered if this would be another inimitable event. They drank water with their meal. It was cool and refreshing on the hot day, with this delicious food.

"Do you want to visit the mosques today?" Nabeel asked.

"Well, after this lovely food, and our big walk in the Museum and Bazaar I can't say that I do, really."

We've got tomorrow, so we can leave it till then, OK?"

"OK. Let's go back for a swim."

After all, they would both be starting work when they got to Kuwait. They should enjoy the break while they could.

Dear Diary,

We did a lot today – the Cairo Museum is huge – but Tutankhamun has gone on tour to Britain! We visited the souk and ate some delicious food – yum! And it was really cheap. We need to work within our budget – even though I don't know what that is exactly. It's in Nabeel's hands. When we get to Kuwait I'll get a better picture of our finances, I'm sure.

Wednesday, 8 September, 1976, Cairo

Because it had become obvious after the Museum visit that Nabeel was not familiar with the 'must see' sites of Cairo, Rose booked a guided cultural tour with a group of tourists to avoid stress. It included a visit to the Citadel, the Sultan Hasan and Muhammad Ali mosques, the Al Azhar University and Mosque and finally, the City of the Dead. It was amazing and fun to be guided and informed without having to use the guide book. The Egyptian guide spoke good English and was friendly and amusing. Back at the hotel although Rose was tired after the city tour, her nerves returned that evening as they packed their bags again for the flight to Kuwait the next day.

"Will the family meet us at the airport?" she asked.

"Of course. They will all be there. They'll probably bring flowers for you."

"Really?"

"It's our custom. So don't be surprised!"

Rose smiled, thinking she had worried unnecessarily. She slept better that night, even though she was about to start a completely new life in a country she had never visited before. She was also about to undertake a new job at the British Council, which she had interviewed for in London. She was glad they had been able to relax and rest up after the busy time they'd had in London, with the wedding and the packing. Now she could look forward to the new challenges with fresh energy.

"Thank you for a lovely honeymoon," she smiled happily.

"Well, you know, it wasn't a honeymoon. That is a whole month in Arabic, *shahr al asl*."

"So we had a honey week then? A short version?"

He laughed. "I guess so. Good night, sleep tight."

"You too."

Dear Diary,

The tour of the city was fascinating. The City of the Dead was spooky. How terrible that people have to live there. I'm not sure how I feel about Cairo – a city of extreme contrasts, with luxurious tourist hotels and poor people living in mausoleums. It leaves me unhappy but glad to have seen one of the wonders of the world.

Thursday, 9 September, 1976, Kuwait

They took a cab the next morning to the airport. The scene was chaotic, but after some deep breaths, they managed to check in, rid themselves of their luggage, and take their flight. It was only two and a half hours, with lunch served on the plane. Because of the one hour time difference, they arrived in Kuwait in the late afternoon. The customs officers were very thorough; they had to open both of their bags. Fortunately they had not purchased any duty free alcohol, which Nabeel had warned her was totally forbidden.

"It's going to be a long dry future, then," she groaned.

"Oh, no. We can get black market booze," he assured her, "though it's expensive."

As they walked out of the restricted areas, into the open arrivals hall, they found a noisy crowd of people, some bearing flowers, but there was no sign of Nabeel's family. Nabeel looked around, puzzled.

"Well, perhaps they didn't get my message," he explained.

"Was it a fax?" Rose asked drily, thinking of the fake hotel booking.

"Don't be like that," he replied. "Come on, let's take a taxi to the house."

They walked outside pushing the luggage trolley into what seemed like an oven. Rose reeled a little with the impact of the heat. She had never felt anything like that before, except when baking a cake. At least the temperature took her mind off the absence of a welcome party. Nabeel got their two heavy cases into the boot of the small sedan car with the taxi sign on top, and they set off.

"How far is the house?"

"Quite a way. The family live near the centre of the city. They will all be at home on Thursday, the first day of the weekend here, probably having a BBQ dinner."

"Remind me who lives here?"

"Well, you met Henri, my oldest brother, then there's my younger brother, Adel, and Edouard, who is a bit older than me. And of course, Asma, our sister, looks after us."

"Wow. That's lucky for you guys," Rose remarked. "Poor Asma. Four boys to cook and clean for."

"She could get a maid if she wanted to. She likes taking care of us. Luckily Joseph is married. Claudine takes care of his needs, but they come over to eat on Fridays."

Rose knew the second eldest brother, Joseph, had married Claudine, a young French woman he'd met when visiting Nabeel in London. She'd been swept away by the handsome, wealthy playboy, and to everyone's surprise, despite the 15 year age difference, they had married within six months of meeting. Rose wasn't sure where they had got married, nor how they had been received by the family. Now wasn't the time to ask, however, with the taxi driver sitting in front of them, not separated by a screen as in London taxis. Rose sat back and looked through the window at the dry, sandy environment alongside the road.

Nabeel explained: "Kuwait has six ring roads around the city centre. My family live on the second ring road near the sea and the city centre. They are lucky. They've got an old villa with a nice garden and a swimming pool."

"It sounds lovely. I can't wait to see it and meet the family again. It's been so long since I met them all in London."

The taxi pulled up outside a low cement-rendered bungalow with luxuriant pink flowering oleander bushes lining the fences. The gate was closed. The afternoon sun was still hot as they got out of the car.

Nabeel paid the driver and placed the suitcases inside the gate. As he did so, the large, cedar double doors to the bungalow opened and Edouard came out. Rose recognised him and called a greeting.

"Hi, Edouard."

"Hello, Rose," he responded, unsmiling. "Come in and sit down, Rose. Nabeel, come in here." He spoke tersely, gesturing to Rose to enter and sit.

Edouard led Nabeel away into a room further inside the house. Rose sat bewildered in a large, rectangular sitting room, with Chinese wooden chairs, upholstered in yellow Chinese figured silk, placed formally around the four walls. In the middle of the room was a large, rectangular, glass-topped coffee table, the glass covering intricate carvings of Chinese figures. Smaller tables were interspersed between the chairs. There were ashtrays on all the tables as well as some of the small cups which Rose recognised as coffee cups. Clearly the family had been drinking coffee when the couple arrived, equally clearly, unexpectedly. There was another, smaller room adjoining the one where Rose was seated. The furniture was also Chinese, but of a different design and the upholstery silk was red. The entrance to that room was framed with two massive ivory tusks, set in a wooden stand. They were both macabre and threatening in appearance to Rose, who knew they represented the killing of a huge, mature elephant as well as a huge amount of money. They were distasteful to her, and she looked away. She could hear raised voices. Things were not going as Nabeel expected. She wondered what would happen next. She wasn't frightened, but she was shocked by the brusque treatment. Another ten minutes passed. Then Nabeel reappeared, with Edouard accompanying him. None of the other members of the family appeared. Rose was stunned. Was this the famous Arabian hospitality she'd read about?

"Come with me, Rose," said Edouard tersely.

She stood up and followed the two men as they went out of the house and down the path to the gate. They picked up one case each and went to a dark blue car parked outside the house.

"Get in. Sit in the back," ordered her new husband without explanation.

Rose did as she was told. She felt like a naughty schoolgirl, but she didn't know what she had done wrong. She clutched her handbag on her lap as the car sped off. She didn't say a word while the brothers spoke to each other in Arabic. The car entered what was evidently the city centre, with shops along the streets, and shoppers walking around. They parked after a little while, in front of a brightly lit sign: Bristol Hotel.

Nabeel got out, signalling to Rose to do the same. Edouard opened the boot without leaving the driver's seat.

Nabeel took out the two bags, closed the boot and the car drove away. Rose looked at him in amazement.

"So that was the great welcome? What went wrong?"

"We'll talk later." Nabeel was stony-faced.

He walked into the Hotel's Reception area, and after a few minutes the pair were in a small, rickety lift, going up to the fourth floor. A porter followed up the stairs with their bags. The room they entered had a view of the city from the small, curtained window. It appeared clean, but was certainly not luxurious.

"Can we afford this?" Rose asked, after the porter had left their bags.

"Not really," Nabeel replied, "but Edouard has given me enough cash for this weekend."

The Kuwaiti weekend was already upon them, being Thursday and Friday rather than the Western Saturday and Sunday. Rose wondered how they would manage for the following week. Nabeel had not expected to pay for a hotel in Kuwait, assuming they would stay with the family in the bedroom he had used. She sat down on the bed and stared at her husband.

"Well, are you going to tell me what happened?"

Nabeel was obviously uncomfortable. He slowly explained the situation.

"Well, they said they hadn't realised I was serious when I said I was getting married."

"What? You asked me to marry you more than six months ago! Didn't you tell them you were hoping to marry me?"

"I didn't know you'd accept me..."

"But I accepted you more than three months ago - I

50

had to give notice for my job, remember. Didn't you share that information with them?"

"Well..." Nabeel mumbled, clearly upset and at a loss how to clarify the events of the past hour.

Rose was furious and raised her voice.

"Have you got me here under false pretences? How are we supposed to live?"

"Well, I still work with them..."

"Yes, and I have a new job, I suppose. But what about our relationship with them?"

"They don't want to see us. We don't have a relationship."

"Oh my God, I can't believe it. Are you such a dreamer, or a brazen liar?"

"Don't talk so loudly, everyone will hear. It's not unusual you know. They didn't talk to Joseph for six months after he got married to Claudine."

"I didn't know that and I can't believe you would do the same then. Are you mad?"

"Please don't be angry. I feel terrible."

"You feel terrible. I feel worse. I have nothing here except you and you have lied to me."

"Not really. I just didn't tell you."

"Lying by omission is as bad as lying to me."

"Come on, you're tired. Let's have a rest. It's Ramadan now..."

"What does that mean?"

"It means we have to go through the day fasting - it won't really affect us as strictly speaking we are travellers, so we don't have to fast."

"Plus we are not Muslims, are we? Or is that something else you forgot to tell me?"

"Of course not, but by law everyone has to follow the rules for fasting. So we won't be able to eat until the sun goes down."

"Nice. I can't even have a whisky to help me calm down."

"No. Sorry. Just have a rest. I can't smoke either."

"Well, don't expect me to feel sorry for you," she muttered. "This is your home, not mine."

Short of bursting into tears, there was nothing else Rose could do. She had no money of her own, no bank account here and very little left behind in the UK. She had to make the best of this bad job. As her Grandma used to say: 'You made your bed, now you have to lie on it.' What a start to her new life this had been. Stifling a sob, she lay on top of the bed in her underwear. "Wake me when it's time to eat," she said angrily. What had she done to merit this treatment? Was her decision to marry based on a structural weakness in their relationship?

Dear Diary! I'm so confused. This is not the welcome I expected. I'm so tired with everything that's happened over the past few weeks, and so sad at being alone. But I've got to get a grip and try not to panic. We'll see what happens next. Touch wood my job works out OK.

Friday, 10 September, 1976, Kuwait

Dinner the night before had been a miserable affair, given the change of circumstances. However, Rose's nap had left her in a more positive frame of mind. This challenge left the two of them very much on their own. Perhaps this would be a better way to start their married lives, facing the problem together? They were both in a position of weakness now. Over dishes of *hummus, baba ghanoush and tabbouleh* in the small hotel restaurant, they had made a plan.

Rose would go to work as expected on Saturday morning, and ask for her salary for the month to be paid in advance, rather than in arrears. Surely the British Council would understand their plight? At the same time, Nabeel would go to work at his brothers' offices and hope that the percentage due on his contracts already won would be paid promptly. He didn't receive a salary, but worked on the basis of commission from his principals. He sold pipeline supplies to Kuwait Oil Company (KOC) and its subsidiary, Kuwait National Petroleum Company (KNPC). He didn't know if his brothers would agree to loan him some money, but it was clear they would not be able to stay in a hotel, even a third rate one like the Bristol, for long. It would be cheaper to find a flat, even though they had no money as yet. Working hours in Ramadan were short so they would spend their afternoons flat-hunting and the cheaper, the better.

After morning coffee in their room, since the coffee shop was closed for fasting, the couple took a walk on the beach nearby in this seaside State. It was warm, but cloudy, so not unbearably hot. They sat on the sand after a while, and as they gazed out to sea, Rose felt herself relax. It would not be so bad, she thought. After all, the world was their oyster!

Nabeel turned to her and she anticipated some romantic words, like, 'I love you. I'm sorry.'

"Don't look now," he said, "but just over there, behind you, is a dead dog."

"Oh, thanks very much," she gasped in disgust. "I hadn't noticed and I probably wouldn't have done, so thanks for pointing it out."

Angry again, she got to her feet and walked away from him. Was he stupid, trying to upset her, she wondered? Or just not romantic? Did she know this man at all?

He caught up with her, and took her hand.

"I'm sorry, I didn't want you to see it. I know you love animals."

"I'm not that observant you know. I spent a whole summer at Guide Camp in the USA, thinking the large column of wood in front of our camp counsellors' tent was a huge redwood tree. I looked up on the last day of camp and discovered it was a telegraph pole."

They both laughed and the good mood returned.

"Sorry. I'll remember in future."

"Come on, it's getting hot. Let's go back to the hotel for a snooze before dinner."

That night the waiter who had served them the evening before started a conversation with them. He was a handsome, rather short, young man, with a pale complexion and thick, straight brown hair rather than black, and he spoke English well with almost no accent.

"I notice you are staying here. Have you no family in Kuwait?"

Rose smiled. "It's a long story."

Nabeel got a little huffy. "No," he finally uttered.

"Well, can I help you in any way? Are you here for a long time?"

Rose took the plunge. "Yes, we are here to work. We need to find somewhere to live."

The waiter introduced himself.

"My name's Fouad, and I could help you if you like. I'm free in the afternoons, before the *iftar* meal. I know my way around. I'm from Lebanon, and I've been here for a couple of years."

Nabeel deigned to look interested. Rose smiled with relief. "It would be so kind of you. We don't have transport, so getting around to see apartments is going to be difficult."

Fouad asked the necessary question: "What kind of place are you looking for?"

Nabeel declared abruptly, "cheap and small."

Rose softened his brusque reply: "We just want somewhere we can start to settle down in. We don't have furniture as yet."

Fouad smiled. He could read between the lines of their story. It was a common one in the Arab world, where the family wishes to control all members, especially in their choice of marriage partners.

"OK. I'll meet you here tomorrow, at 3pm, and we'll go to some new buildings in Salmiyah."

"That would be great," Rose breathed a sigh of relief. Hopefully they would be able to find somewhere, pay the first month's rent and move out of the hotel before their money ran out. They had to keep their heads and stay steady despite this tremor in the ground.

Dear Diary,

We are managing to keep our heads above water despite the family rejection. I daren't write to Mum or Dad though. They would be horrified but they wouldn't know what to do to help. I don't want to seem like an idiot or a baby. I have to try and work this out, though it's hard.

Saturday, 11 September, 1976, Kuwait

Rose and Nabeel had to face the challenges of their new life without any familial support. Neither of them had a Kuwaiti driving licence. Public transport was available but it was 'classist': Buses were used only by labourers or Indian male office staff or female cleaners. It was unheard of for Westerners or locals to take a bus, she discovered, to her amazement. So Nabeel stopped a taxi outside the Bristol and escorted Rose to the British Council (BC) building in Mansouriyah. It was a villa, which housed the BC Representative's office. At the gate, Rose said goodbye to Nabeel and he headed off in the same cab to his own office, shared with his brothers, with some trepidation. He hadn't heard from them since they had been shown out of the family home on Thursday.

"I hope all goes well," she told him, refraining from kissing him in front of the Pakistani taxi driver. PDAs (public displays of affection) were most definitely frowned on here.

"You too, *habibti*," he replied in a subdued manner, his usual exuberance vanished.

It was exactly 9am as Rose went up the wide steps to the two storey glass-fronted building. She was greeted by a *farash*, an office assistant, who was short, slim, greying, with a tidy beard and moustache.

"Good morning, I've come to see the Representative," she said loudly and clearly, uncertain of the language proficiency of this office worker.

"Welcome, welcome," said the middle-aged man with a broad smile. "Me name Ahmed."

"Good morning, Ahmed, pleased to meet you. I am Rose." She did not offer her hand as warned by Nabeel that handshakes between Arab men and women were not usually allowed.

"Welcome, Rose. Come," he told her, leading her up another flight of stairs to the first floor.

He knocked on a door, and they went into a large, airy office, well lit by double windows. At an imposing desk sat a grey-haired man in a suit and tie.

"This Rose," said Ahmed, smiling proudly, as if he'd discovered something wonderful.

"Thank you, Ahmed. Welcome, Rose," said the Representative in formal, Oxbridge-accented English. The *farash* left the room, and the top man gestured to Rose to sit opposite him.

"How are you? How do you find Kuwait?"

Rose had been interviewed in the British Council offices in Central London by Philip Foley. She had not met the Rep. before, but he seemed approachable. Should she tell him her story as planned, she wondered, or was it too shocking at this stage?

"Would you like some coffee?" he asked.

She looked at him doubtfully.

He explained: "I know it's Ramadan, but we are in a little bit of England here. So long as it's behind closed doors. We make it ourselves, we don't ask the *farasheen* to do so."

Obviously the boss was a practical man of the world. Just the sort of person she could confide in, she thought.

They each fixed a cup of coffee from a drinks trolley then sat down together on a sofa suite.

"We've heard a lot of good things about you. But we've got some news for you."

"Oh, really?" Rose was surprised.

"Yes. Foley interviewed you, remember?"

"Yes, of course."

"Well, he's just got a promotion. He's going to Baghdad as the BC Representative in Iraq. Of course, it's a very good thing for him, but it means you will be working with the new English Language Officer, his replacement. He isn't here yet, but he'll be arriving in a couple of weeks, and his family in a month or so. He has four boys so he has lots of arrangements to make for school and so on."

"I see," said Rose, focussing hard on this change to the plan. "So who will I report to for these first two weeks?"

"My Assistant Rep. He has lots of contacts in your language world. At the moment he is responsible for planning for classes, teachers and their timetables right now. However, we have closed our classes down for Ramadan, as this is a new Centre, and we wanted you, as Senior Teacher, to be able to have some input in the pattern of enrolment for the coming year. Our Admin. Officer will be a big help too. His office is downstairs. He's been with us for several years. Have you any questions right now?"

Rose had finished her coffee as she'd been listening, not talking. She wondered if it was diplomatic to start talking about her problems when she was clearly supposed to be focussing on her new job.

"Well, where were you teaching previously? Is there a record of previous curricula, materials, ongoing students and so on?" she asked calmly.

"Most of our work till now has been directly to students in their workplaces, such as Embassies and Consulates. Some classes have been given to Ministry workers. There's a lot of interest, but we haven't had proper premises till now. We will be holding an opening ceremony at the beginning of November, by which time we hope to have this place well organised. There will be a public lending library in the basement. Come on, let me show you the building and introduce you to some of the staff."

The opportunity to ask for her salary in advance had disappeared. Rose stood up, forcing herself to dismiss her personal problems to the back of her mind. She followed the Rep out of the office, clutching her handbag.

After meeting the Administrative Officer, the Financial Officer, the Assistant Librarian, and the Rep's secretary, Rose was introduced to the Assistant Representative, Leslie Keene.

"I'll leave you here, Rose," the Rep said as he went back to his office.

"Are you ready for another coffee?" Leslie asked, smiling at her.

"Not really, thanks," she replied. "I am trying to remember everyone's name. It's a pleasant building. How many classrooms are there?"

"We've got four upstairs, and there are two downstairs. It's not huge, certainly, but it's a step in the right direction."

"Indeed. I've been working in Adult Education prior to this, so we had access to entire day school premises after school hours, but of course the teachers were part-time, except for myself as Head of Department."

"Well, we use mainly part-time teachers too, mostly wives who've come out on contract with their husbands. You are our only local full-timer. Len, the new English Language Officer will be working with you on the school, the English Teaching Centre (ETC), only part of the time. He has other duties with regard to teachers at the University of Kuwait, as well as scholarship students, IELTS testing, and liaison with overseas universities."

Rose noted the word 'local' in her mental notebook to consider its implications later.

"I see. So what should I be doing in these two weeks before his arrival, do you think?"

"Well, you need to set up your office and his. There is furniture in the large open plan space next to the library. Did Reg, the Rep, show you? As you'll be working together on the ETC, you'll be sharing office space with Len."

"OK. And are there any materials or records of curricula I can have a look at?"

"Yes, Samir will show you where these have been stored. There are shelves you can use for unpacking and sorting stuff. We won't work you too hard during Ramadan, but you do need to be ready with a timetable and a curriculum for mid-October. We'll be enrolling students then."

"And teachers?"

"They will be returning to Kuwait with their husbands during this fasting month, or after the *Eid*. This holiday,

Eid al Fitr, which means 'breaking the fast', lasts three days usually. Things return to normal after that."

"OK. I get the picture. Well, I suppose I should go down and see my area."

"Come on, I'll show you. And by the way, you'll have to come for a drink this weekend. Bring your husband. He drinks, doesn't he?"

"Yes, he's a Christian, not a Muslim."

Rose wondered whether to introduce personal topics now, but decided against it. She didn't want to create the wrong impression on this first day. She wanted to look like the professional she was, but the words 'local full-timer' had wormed their way into her mind. She needed to consider that issue carefully too. She followed Leslie downstairs and into the basement office that would be hers for the next year at least, according to the contract she had signed in London. The contract was yearly, renewable, and had no perks such as air tickets or accommodation. Now she realised that this was because she was regarded as 'local' and therefore cheap, available labour, just as the part-time housewives were. This was food for thought in the dire straits of her personal life.

For the moment, however, Rose needed to maintain her professional demeanour. She chose one of the two desks which had been set up in the large, spacious, but windowless office. There were huge fluorescent lights above which lent a Kafkaesque effect to the space. There was plenty to look at inside the office: Packing boxes were piled up in each corner, and there were empty metal shelves and two metal cabinets against the walls.

"Well, here you are," said Leslie. "What do you think?"

"It looks as if there's unpacking to do. So, I'll get on with it shall I? But first, could you tell me the office hours during Ramadan, please? I need to call my husband at his office to arrange for him to pick me up."

"We start at 9am to give the local staff time to sleep a little after their dawn breakfast, but we close at 1pm. Some of us stay on to complete our work, but there's no need for you to do more than the regular hours."

"Thanks. Can I use the phone for local calls?"

"Yes, they're free. The phones on the desk should be working. You can give your husband the number and your extension. The Rep's secretary answers the phone and transfers calls."

"That's great. Thanks, Leslie."

"Well, if you get thirsty before one o'clock, just pop upstairs for a tea or coffee with me."

"That's marvellous. I'll check in with you before I go at least."

"Bye for now then."

Left alone Rose stared at the boxes. The shelves were dusty, so she went in search of the *farash*, Ahmed, to get a duster.

"*Ya* Rose, how you?" he called as she approached his chair at the front door.

"Ahmed, have you got a duster I can use?" she asked.

Ahmed stared at her uncomprehendingly. Rose mimed dusting with a cloth duster, but there was no spark of understanding in Ahmed's face. Fortunately Samir's office was close by, so Rose opened the door after tapping.

63

"Samir?"

He smiled at her. "Yes?"

"What's 'duster' in Arabic?"

"Duster? I've no idea. Men don't do housework here you know! Have a look in the kitchen where the supplies are kept. See what there is."

"Good idea."

Rose asked Ahmed's permission, as the kitchen, normally his territory, was locked up for Ramadan. When she got inside, she saw a couple of brightly coloured feather dusters. She picked one up, and Ahmed cried out, "*Riyash! Riyash!*" She found out later that this was the word for 'feathers'. Dusting with this long stick required a different mime than the one she had demonstrated! They both laughed and Rose repeated this new, useful word, *Riyash!*

While she was in the kitchen she picked up a sharp knife to help her open the boxes.

"I help you," Ahmed offered.

"It's OK," Rose told him. "I'm fine."

She preferred to empty the boxes herself so that she could categorise their contents and store them appropriately. This was going to be interesting. But first, she needed to let Nabeel know when she would be free.

His number was a direct line and he answered the phone immediately.

"Hi. How are things? Are the brothers talking to you today?"

"Well, I'm on my own, so no need to talk really."

"OK. Listen, I haven't been able to talk about getting my salary yet. I feel embarrassed about it."

"Don't worry about that now. When do you finish?"

"One o'clock. Does that suit you?"

"Yes, we finish then too. So I'll be in front of the Council at 1.10pm."

Rose looked at her watch. It was 11 o'clock already. On with the boxes.

The time flew by as she opened up course books, textbooks, dictionaries, grammar books, files and folders, as well as audio and video cassettes. She stacked them neatly, and taking a break from standing and bending she sat at her desk and made an inventory of what she had found. She had something to show for her work today, if anyone was interested. As she clipped the papers together, Leslie came into the room.

"How has it gone? You've been busy I see. Great work." He admired the shelves she'd filled. "You can leave the empty boxes outside the door for Ahmed to fold up. It's time for you to go now."

"Everything OK?" he asked, prompted by her subdued expression.

Rose hesitated then took the chance he'd offered to speak of her personal issue.

"Leslie, I'm sorry to raise a difficult subject, but I'm having a financial crisis. The family are not very happy about our marriage and they've put us in a hotel. But we can't afford it. We hadn't expected to pay a hotel bill."

The Assistant Rep looked concerned.

Rose continued: "I wonder if you could ask Reg if he'd be able to pay my salary in advance this month? It won't be a permanent arrangement. Just until my husband receives some commission he is due from Europe. He doesn't get a salary as he works with his brothers in the family company. They aren't speaking to us, but at least he can do his business alongside them."

Leslie's face showed his relief. "Wow, I was worried for a while. I thought you were going to leave us. Don't worry about Reg. I'll arrange for your salary to be paid in advance. Do you want cash?"

"Yes, please. I don't know anything about Nabeel's bank accounts and of course I haven't got one yet."

"Well, it will be ready for you tomorrow, or the next day, Monday. Na'aman will need to go to the bank. Is that OK?"

Rose breathed a huge sigh of relief. "That's marvellous. Thank you so much."

When Nabeel drove up in a taxi, she got in, smiling.

"How did it go?" he asked.

"Fine. I got a lot done, and I asked for my salary in advance. It's not a problem."

"Thanks. That's a big relief. I'm expecting a large sum in commission, but you can never guarantee when money comes through. It all depends on equipment delivery dates."

"Well, we can cope for a month at least."

Back at the hotel they ordered lunch in their room then took a nap in anticipation of meeting Fouad. At 3pm he was in reception as promised. His small, four-door Mitsubishi sedan was outside. *"Ahlan,"* he greeted them in the Lebanese way. *"Keefkum?* How are you?"

"Fine! Thanks so much for doing this," Nabeel replied. "I've looked in today's paper and there are three new buildings in Salmiyah we could look at."

Fouad looked at the newspaper cuttings. "Right, let's go. I live in Hawalli myself. It's cheap and close to the city, but Salmiyah has a lot of foreigners, so it would suit you better. Not too far from the BC for you, Mrs Rose."

They drove for about 15 minutes on almost empty roads. People were indoors preparing the *iftar* meal with which they broke the fast at sunset. The area they parked in was obviously a new housing area. There were streets and paved sidewalks, with tall, 10 or 12 storey buildings constructed of pale cement blocks, not bricks. Some had balconies, but the apartments the trio visited were all on the ground floor. They also had bars at every window. They were the cheapest, as well as the most easily broken into, it appeared. The search procedure was to knock on the door of the building caretaker, usually indoors snoozing before breaking his fast. After looking at three buildings, all very similar, they decided on a flat which had its front entrance facing that of the ground floor flat opposite. It also had central airconditioning (AC), so they wouldn't have to buy AC units, a great saving.

As they went inside, Rose had seen a blonde-haired young woman coming out of the opposite flat. They had greeted each other politely. The other tenant spoke English with a slight accent, so Rose felt it would be good to have a neighbour she could talk to. The rent was within their means, so Nabeel was to go and sign the contract the next day with the building proprietor. If he agreed, they could move in immediately, paying only half of a month in advance. It was a lucky reprieve from their money worries. Their new friend drove them back to the hotel. As they drove they heard the cannon fire from the Emir's palace. This daily ritual marked the moment at which the requisite fasting ended.

"Fouad, thank you so much for your help. Would you like to have *iftar* with us?" Rose asked.

"Not today, thanks. I have to serve in the restaurant today. I'll come and visit you at the British Council. I might take a class there when you start up."

Dear Diary,

How amazingly kind our new friend from the Hotel has been. He has helped us find a flat just in time. I hope we can thank him one day. He is an angel. As for my job, it is the only place where I feel safe and secure. Leslie was so understanding about our finances. The BC is my solid ground from now on. A little bit of England, as Reg said.

Sunday, 12 September, 1976, Kuwait

Arrangements with the landlord went well. It was agreed that they could move in straight away, that very afternoon, if they cleaned the place themselves. They would only pay rent for half the month. This represented a welcome double saving on the hotel bill and the rent. Nabeel borrowed a mop and bucket from the office, as well as a packet of Tide washing powder, the most readily available cleaning aid and detergent in Kuwait at that time. They took their suitcases in a cab, and Rose moved them from room to room as she washed the floors. There were two bedrooms, a small kitchen, and a large lounge. As they had no furniture, not even beds, Nabeel went to the *souk* in Hawalli and bought two single sponge mattresses. They had no bedding in their suitcases, but he bought four towels, two for bathing, two to spread on the mattresses for them to sleep on.

That first night in their own flat was exciting if primitive. But as darkness fell they realised they could not sleep in any of the rooms as they had no curtains. With the light on, their every movement was visible to passersby. So they put the mattresses in the tiny, square, hall space which connected the four rooms. It was also cold because they couldn't work out how to turn down the central AC. So they took out large items of clothing from their cases, including dressing gowns and socks which they put on, but still shivered under the icy blast of AC. Somehow they managed to get some sleep under the pile of clothes. Rose made an urgent shopping list for sheets and a blanket, plus some kind of window covering.

The next day, finding a cab to take them to work was more challenging in these residential suburbs than it had been from the hotel in the city centre. Nabeel discussed the issue with the driver they finally found. He made an arrangement for the two of them to be picked up each morning, with another two regular commuters, to go into the city, first to the British Council, then to Nabeel's office block. The lunchtime and hometime journeys would not pose a problem, starting from the city where cabs were numerous.

Rose had obtained her month's salary in advance as cash, but the pair needed to be frugal with it. They used old newspapers and sellotape 'borrowed' from Nabeel's office to cover the bedroom windows to establish a dressing room where they placed their suitcases, and a bedroom with the two mattresses on the floor. Rose put up on the wall the *Love is never having to say you're sorry* cartoon teatowel which Marie had given her. The slogan was highly ironic now, given their circumstances. They wouldn't be able to afford curtains or proper furniture until Nabeel's commission came in. Until then Rose's salary had to pay the rent, daily transport costs and food bills. In a month or so their shipping would arrive and they would have the rocking chair and the beautiful leather pouffes. Meanwhile they bought two plastic garden chairs and a small plastic table for the sitting room, where they could eat. They were camping and despite all the odds, it seemed they had been able to establish a routine for their married life. At least they could laugh about it. So they did.

Dear Diary, Events so far have been weird, but we are coping.

Thursday, 16 September, 1976, Kuwait

The first weekend in the new flat began quietly for Rose as Nabeel had only one day off, the Muslim holy day, Friday, while she had Thursday and Friday free. She had kept the mop and bucket they had borrowed so that she could clean the flat in the morning. With no washing machine, she used the Tide powder to complete some hand washing in the bath. She then strung it out to dry in the tiny enclosed space which the kitchen window looked out on. Since leaving the hotel meals had been sandwiches and bottled water or juice from the snack bar near Nabeel's office block. Food had been the least of their problems.

When Nabeel came home at lunchtime they used the taxi to go to the nearest Cooperative supermarket to stock up with an electric kettle, a single electric hotplate, a can opener, some cans of tuna, and tinned, ready cooked *fuul medames* (brown beans) which Rose had first eaten in Cairo, some butter, salt, eggs and a frying pan, plastic bags of Arabic flat bread, a tub of *hummus*, a tub of *labna* (very thick yoghurt) which she had enjoyed in Beirut, together with some succulent black olives, some large ripe beefsteak tomatoes and a few red onions, plus tea, coffee, juice and milk. Two plates, two glasses and two cups, two forks, two knives and two spoons completed their purchases. They had no fridge but the AC in the kitchen was cold enough to keep a small amount of food fresh. After eating lunch Nabeel went back to the office as usual while Rose took the chance to relax and read one of the library books she'd borrowed from the BC library. At work Leslie had not repeated his invitation to his home for drinks, but Rose was grateful for the chance to rest and not be stressed by anything other than settling into a routine in her new home.

When Nabeel returned that evening he had bought a spitroasted chicken, a plastic container of *aioli*, garlic mayonnaise, another of brightly coloured turnip and carrot pickles, and two folded pieces of Iranian bread, each very thin and as huge as a serving plate. They ate their celebration meal with glasses of juice, toasting their success at reaching the end of their first week in Kuwait with a home, against all the odds.

"What shall we do tomorrow?" asked Rose. "It's our first day off together."

Nabeel was thoughtful. "We could take a walk along the beach around the Towers. You haven't seen them yet, have you?"

"Of course not. I've only seen my office and our humble abode."

"And we should have an '*iftar*' meal at one of the restaurants near here. Ramadan ends on 25th September, so next weekend will be the celebration of the end of Ramadan."

"Really? What kind of celebration is it?"

"People have a holiday from work, the banks close and everyone enjoys being able to drink, eat, smoke and have sex in daylight hours!"

"Oh my word. I didn't realise 'afternoon delight' was banned too! Really? Having a drink at work will be a relief. No more hiding away at coffee time in the Council!"

"Yes, but at least you could have coffee there behind closed doors. In our office we have to be careful in case we have a Muslim business visitor. No one can drink coffee because you know our Arabic *qahwa* smells so delicious, it's a sin to tempt a Muslim! It's the same with cigarettes!"

"Gosh, I hadn't thought of that. Have you cut down then?"

"Not at all. I don't want to get sick, you know. Smoking kills germs!"

Rose laughed. She'd had more than a few worried moments during the past week, wondering if she'd made the right decision in getting married and certainly, in coming here. She'd left her comfortable flat and her enjoyable job, as well as all her friends and family, to come to this weird scenario. Living in a camp site, with newspaper on the windows, wasn't what she'd expected when she'd accepted Nabeel's proposal. She realised he had not been completely honest with her about his family's reaction but then, who would have been? He probably hoped they would give in when the deed was done. His gamble hadn't paid off though.

On the other hand, the job was proving interesting, and they'd survived so far financially. She tried to accept what each day brought. In fact, she'd taken up the challenge to learn Arabic now that she had the motivation to speak it. She set herself a target of one new word a day. They'd mostly been words connected with food so far. *Dajaj meshwi* (grilled chicken) sounded as delicious as it tasted, but so far her favourite words were *mumkin* (possible) and its negative, *mish mumkin* (impossible). They sounded like two Disney characters and made her smile. They were also remarkably frequent in everyday conversation!

"Well, only one more week to go. At least I've learned a lot about Ramadan. And the working hours have been easy. Now there's a holiday to look forward to! When will it be exactly?"

"The moon-sighting committee decides that."

"What?"

"There's a group of religious men in Saudi Arabia who watch for the new moon to appear. It indicates that the holy month of Ramadan is over. Then there are usually three days of holiday."

"Wow. So how do we know when Ramadan ends?"

"The news is broadcast on the radio."

"And I thought I knew everything about Ramadan. Live and learn, hey?"

Dear Diary, They say endurance through hardship is a test of true love. Or as the teatowel says, Love is never having to say sorry!

Friday, 17 September, 1976, Kuwait

The next day they lingered in 'bed', uncomfortable as their thin sponge mattresses on the floor were. It was a pleasure not to have to get washed, dressed and take the taxi to work.

"I haven't seen the neighbour yet. I suppose she's busy with her children," Rose mused.

"Yes, we'll have some soon, won't we?" Nabeel giggled like a schoolboy discussing a taboo subject.

"Well, now that you mention it, I'm still taking the pill, you know," she reminded him.

"Why don't you stop it then?"

"I'm sorry, but given our precarious financial situation, plus the emotional stand off, I think it's not the right time to start a family. Don't you?"

"I suppose you are right."

"How is it in the office? Do they talk to you?"

"Not much, but we are all busy. Edouard represents different companies, and Adel has his construction projects."

"What about Henri?" Rose hated the oldest brother, who thought himself better than the others. He had made a pass at her when he came to London, and she had tried to forget it, but the memory still rankled.

"I don't see him, though you can hear him all across the offices. He's got a big mouth."

"I bet. He's certainly got a big head. But let's forget about nasty things. It's our lovely free day today."

76

They chatted about their plan for the day as they had a cup of tea in the sitting room. They would take a look at the newly built Kuwait Towers, return home for lunch, then go out for an *iftar* meal at dusk. The Towers were a short taxi ride up the Corniche, the road which skirted the Arabian Gulf. The Iranians referred to it as the Persian Gulf, as Rose had learned long ago in school geography class. They left the apartment at 9am to avoid the worst of the day's heat. Even though it was Ramadan, taxis were ferrying poorer Muslims who had no car of their own to the mosques for Friday prayers, the most important prayer meeting of the week. Drivers who already had male passengers in them would not stop for a couple in Western clothes, so they walked for a while until an empty cab stopped. As usual the driver began a conversation in broken English. The questions were always the same.

"You children?"

"No."

"Why not?"

"We new couple."

"But you not young! Quick quick!"

Sometimes Rose thought it would be easier to say they had 10 children and had left them at home with their granny. The assumption that they were old, she thought, was based on the fact that Nabeel, in his late thirties, had thinning hair with some grey. She thought she still looked good in her late twenties, but of course, the cab drivers were judging on their own standards. Girls should be married in their early teens, and boys in their late teens or early twenties, to keep both out of trouble. To Rose, that philosophy was as difficult to accept as theirs was for these people. They represented a rare phenomenon in this part of the world: a 'middle-aged couple' with no kids in tow.

Once out of the cab, the sea air was fresh and inviting at this hour of the morning.

"We can take a walk around the Towers, then head towards the city for a look round," Nabeel suggested. "The Towers will have a revolving restaurant and viewing platform, but they are not open to the public yet."

"They are beautiful! A symbol of modern Kuwait, I suppose."

As they walked they met very few people on foot. Rose felt exhilarated to be free, even though they had concerns. For once, she could simply enjoy being in a new country, feeling like a tourist. After half an hour's brisk walk they came to the Fish Souq.

"The Fish Market opens twice a day on weekends," Nabeel told her. "They are cleaning up before the midday heat. They'll open again at around 4pm."

"It's a pity we can't see it, but it's pointless as we can't cook any fish without a stove."

"Yes, but wait till we can. Kuwait has the best and biggest shrimps you've ever seen."

"Do you mean prawns? Shrimps are usually small in the UK."

"Same thing - just huge and delicious."

"I look forward to them. Yum!"

Rose had been a vegetarian since her twenties, but from time to time she enjoyed a little seafood. They stood for a few minutes watching the men in white T-shirts and what appeared to be checked tablecloths wrapped around their waists, swilling away the entrails, spines, scales and waste from cleaning the fish they sold.

"They are wearing a type of sarong," Nabeel explained. "It's what fishermen and the pearl fishers used to wear when they went on their long sea journeys in the wooden boats we call *dhows*."

Several dhows were anchored at the wharves close by. They wandered over to take a closer look.

"There's a dhow building yard to the north of the city," Nabeel told her. "I've never been there, but it could be worth a look."

"That would be great. I feel doing anything is so difficult though, don't you, with no car, and no money?"

"Yes, I'm sorry, it's not the life I thought we'd have. Thank you for accepting it. Things will be better soon."

"Do you think you'll get that commission shortly?"

"I'm waiting now - I've asked them to pay me urgently. Perhaps our luck will change after *Eid*!"

Slightly comforted by Nabeel's optimistic words, Rose mentally wiped away the creeping feeling of depression that threatened to mar the day. A loud *muezzin* call to prayer began, and she noticed the mosque on the opposite side of the road, with crowds of men washing in the courtyard outside before prayers began.

"It's going to be hard to get a taxi now. Let's walk back along the beach to the Towers, shall we? We can do it before it gets too hot. This is about the only thing we can do that's free, after all!"

They set off southwards briskly, inhaling the ozone, feeling again that sense of freedom which helped to lift their spirits. Once back at the Towers a few taxis were prowling looking for sightseers. They climbed in and gave their address. The driver looked at them in surprise. He obviously expected them to be staying in a hotel. This time he spoke Arabic.

"*Eesh el mushkila? What's the problem?*" the driver asked Nabeel directly.

"*Wallashi, yalla,*" replied Nabeel, in a tone which suggested there would be no more discussion.

Rose looked at the two men. She guessed there was an issue, but sat silently as became her status as a woman.

Once out of the car, she questioned her husband. "So?"

"He was nosey, as taxi drivers always are."

"So what did you tell him?"

"To mind his own business."

"So what does *Wallashi, yalla* mean then?"

"Oh, I see you've got a tape recorder with you," Nabeel said sarcastically. "It means 'Nothing, just go.' Happy?"

"Thank you," she said, muttering the new words to herself. "That's lesson one from you. It's like getting blood out of a stone, as we say."

"Yes, well, I can't be expected to remember every word I say, you know," he said, reaching for a cigarette.

"OK. Calm down, I'm going to take a shower and have a rest."

"Good. We'll go out for dinner at dusk exactly - wait for the gun and we'll go!"

"I think I might need a gun if you keep getting bad-tempered every time we take a cab."

"Right. Let me smoke now."

Nabeel settled onto a plastic chair in the 'lounge', putting his bright blue pack of *Gitanes* cigarettes and his expensive blue enamel Dunhill lighter, his pride and joy, on the table while Rose freshened up after their walk. There was no point pursuing the matter. Nabeel was obviously stressed by the situation they were in, and feeling touchy about it. She had learned some new words at least. A nap was very welcome after their walk and would reduce the pressure.

As the sun went down, the cannon roared and they left the apartment again to find a 'family' (i.e. no single male customers allowed) restaurant where they could have 'breakfast'. Most Muslims took *iftar* at home then went out for a later dinner with friends or in restaurants. As a rule, only bachelors needed to break their fast in a restaurant. They walked over to Salmiyah's main shopping centre, where the shops were still closed during *iftar*. Most people ate lightly after the long fasting day. A traditional drink, *amardine*, made from dried apricots, was a popular choice to refresh the palate and quench the thirst. In the 'family' seating area of the cafe they found, the waiter also offered tamarind '*sharbaat*' and fruit juice cocktails. This drink was followed by a small cup of light chicken soup, flavoured with nutmeg and cinnamon, with chopped flat leaf parsley sprinkled on top. *Hummus* and aubergine dip (*baba ghanoush*) served with strips of lightly toasted flat bread for dipping with, and *tabbouleh* (finely chopped flat leaf parsley and mint leaves mixed with steamed cracked wheat and lots of lemon juice) salad with cos lettuce leaves on the side for dipping. After that there was a choice of mains, including lamb *kofta* (minced lamb, onions and parsley mixed together then shaped into sausages) or *meshwi* (pieces of marinaded prime lamb) both cooked on long skewers on the grill, which even to Rose's vegetarian nose smelled delicious. Rose chose the *shish taouk*, the garlic chicken skewers, which she knew from her visit to Beirut and had also prepared for her wedding party BBQ menu.

A colourful platter of whole salad vegetables accompanied the grilled meat. It amused Rose to see that the diners were expected to make up their own side salad from the small, dark green, Lebanese cucumbers, large, bright red tomatoes and crisp, green hearts of cos lettuce. She noticed a ready-mixed salad, chopped as in the West, served to another table. Nabeel explained that this was *fattoush*, a salad with fried bread croutons in it.

"Another time I'd like to try that," she suggested.

"We should be eating at home. My sister Asma is a great cook."

"Ah well. Maybe one day!"

"Bukhra bil mishmish," Nabeel muttered.

"What's that? Those words sounded cute."

"It means 'tomorrow in the apricots', which means it might never happen."

"So it's a metaphor! I like the sound of *mishmish* ... and hey I guess that's what the *amardine* drink is made of *mishmish*!"

Nabeel concurred absentmindedly, paying slight attention to her Eureka moment. But Rose felt pleased: She'd tried an *iftar* meal, eaten in a family restaurant, which even with no wine, beer or other alcoholic beverage on the side, had been an interesting experience, and she'd picked up another Arabic expression. She realised Nabeel was no teacher. She would have to practise all her independent learning skills so as to improve her Arabic. They walked home in the dark, feeling pleasantly full. Week one was almost over.

"Can you believe so much has happened in such a short time?" she asked Nabeel.

"Wait and see. There'll be a lot more happening when I get my money," he replied.

Rose could see that the delay in receiving his commission was preying on his mind. She reassured him as best she could.

"Well, we're OK for another week, aren't we? Fingers crossed your money will come in after *Eid*."

When they got home, Rose stripped off her sweaty clothes before going into the kitchen to make a cup of tea in her underwear. As she filled the kettle she sensed someone watching her. Her spine tingled. She whirled round to the window and there, staring into the brightly lit kitchen was a man in a *galabiyya*, with a turban on his head. She screamed out loud involuntarily. The man turned and ran. Nabeel rushed into the kitchen. "What is it, a cockroach?" Even in brand new buildings, the insect that had endured longest through the world's lifespan could appear when least expected.

She pointed frantically at the window. "There was a man, staring in at me."

Nabeel rushed outside to the small enclosed area where Rose hung her washing. He came back shaking his head.

"There's no one there now."

"Of course not. Peeping Toms don't hang around to be caught. Why on earth didn't you warn me this might happen? We could have put newspaper on this window too!"

"Well, I didn't know it would happen in a Muslim country like this. I suppose it's easy to peep into ground floor flats."

"Thanks for being wise after the event." Rose was shaking with fright and anger. "So now we have to put newspaper in here too. Right now. Have we got any left?"

Still upset, Rose rushed to put on her dressing gown. Her own naivete angered her as much as his ignorance. How could she have put herself in this position?

"You do realise that I hate this flat now? I really hate it. It was bad enough at first, but now I don't feel safe. I thought the bars on the windows were ghastly. It's like a prison, but now it's even worse."

Nabeel was at a loss to say anything reassuring. He was as much of an innocent abroad as she was. The only thing that could improve their position was to move, but they couldn't afford it. Rose managed to put a brake on her temper and not take the next reactive step, saying "I want to go home." Instead, she made tea while he covered the window.

"Come on, sit down and drink this. I suppose it's good that I had my underwear on. I wonder if he's been around before? I shudder to think of it."

Nabeel's shock had abated a little, but he was embarrassed. He hadn't expected this. Living ten years in the UK had changed his expectations of people's behaviour. They were both out of their depth in this new environment, where bachelors were segregated from families because of their threat to domestic security. They needed to be more aware of potential dangers. He finally expressed his own feelings.

"Me too, *habibti*. I'm really sorry about this. Be sure, as soon as we can, we'll move to somewhere better. I only signed a contract for three months."

"That takes us up to Christmas. Perhaps the New Year will be better."

"Inshallah."

"What?"

"God willing."

"I can put that down in my notebook. It sounds very useful."

She had no idea just how useful, even necessary, that phrase would be.

Dear Diary, I hate this place. In taxis we have to put up with personal questions, and tonight, a Peeping Tom. I can't believe N set me up for this. Didn't he have any knowledge of what happens here? Just as in Cairo, he's like a fish out of water. I feel so angry I don't know how I'll cope till we get out of here, but I suppose I have to.

Saturday, 18 September, 1976, Kuwait

Samir greeted her as she went past his office into work the next morning.

"Good morning, Rose. Leslie would like to see you," he called out.

Samir was Pakistani, not Arab, and although he spoke fluent Arabic Rose preferred to speak to him in English to show respect for his fluency in her native language.

"Good morning! Thanks, Samir," she responded as she climbed the staircase to the Assistant Rep's office on the first floor.

"Good morning, Leslie," she called as she tapped and opened the door.

He smiled a hello. "How was your first weekend?"

She was too embarrassed to mention the frightening incident of the evening before, but simply said,

"Interesting!"

He continued, "Well, this weekend is the end of Ramadan. It should be Eid from next Saturday, 25th to 28th. So I'm giving an informal party on Saturday evening. Can you come?"

Rose smiled: "We'd love to. What time and where exactly?"

"I'll give you a map. We live out in the desert suburbs, in a new villa. You have to follow some improvised signposts to get there. Kuwait City is expanding fast and new roads are not yet mapped. Perhaps I can get someone to give you a lift. I'll let you know. Where do you live?"

"Salmiyah, not far from the main street. Informal dress, you said?"

"Yes, smart casual."

"Fine. Thanks very much for the invitation."

"Len should arrive on Friday, so I might get the BC driver to pick him and you two up. That would be best. You'll be sure to get a lift back home with someone."

"That's very kind."

Rose went down the backstairs smiling. The Eid holiday wouldn't be an empty shell for them now. With no furniture, radio or TV, life without work at the weekend was going to be a challenge. As she passed the kitchen on the ground floor, Ahmed greeted her.

"*Ahlan*, Rose!"

"Ahmed, please tell me how to say 'Good morning' in Arabic."

"Of coures," he said, putting an extra vowel between the /r/ and /s/. "*Sabah al kher.*"

"*Sabah al kher,*" she repeated, breathing the /h/ sound at the end of *sabah* softly as she knew she should. Foreigners unaware of the difference, often turned the /h/ ending into a /ch/, as in the Scottish 'loch'. However, Rose heard Ahmed's "*la*," "no" response with consternation:

"*Sabah innur*, Rose, not *Sabah alkher.*"

"Sorry, Ahmed, what did you say?" Rose was understandably confused.

"*Sabah al kher* then *Sabah innur,*" he repeated.

Rose frowned in concentration, trying to grasp his meaning. Just then Samir came by on his way to see Na'maan, the BC accountant.

"Rose, Arabic is a very polite language. There are fixed responses to many greetings. This is one of them. If someone greets you with *Sabah al kher,* you reply *Sabah innur,*" he explained.

"Oh, thanks so much. I get it. *Shukran.*"

"Afwan," he replied, laughing. "There's another couplet for you!"

"Great. I want to be able to speak to our beginner students, to make them feel at home, when registration for classes starts."

Repeating the two couplets to herself, she continued down the backstairs to the basement.

Seated at her desk alone, with her work diary in front of her, she thought back over the past week. She had been too troubled to write much in her personal diary, a daily routine she usually enjoyed, noting down what she had achieved each day. She made a promise to herself to get back into it. She didn't think of herself as a Type A personality, a high achiever. Normality is what she aspired to, even though each New Year she always set herself certain tasks to complete. So far in her life she'd ticked off her BA Honours French degree after spending three years at Uni and a year as a teaching assistant in France, then her Translation and Secretarial Diploma, followed by her secondary school teaching qualification, the PGCE in French and English from London University, and most recently, her TESOL Diploma, issued by the Royal Society of Arts (RSA), and achieved part-time over one whole year, while working at a London Adult Education Institute.

So far in life she hadn't obtained a driving licence, as it wasn't a useful qualification in busy, public transport rich London, but now that would have to be placed at the top of her task list. She had seen plenty of women drivers on the roads as she made her taxi journey to and from work. She thanked heaven Kuwait allowed women to drive, given the unacceptability of using public transport. Nabeel was emasculated in her eyes by having to take taxis, which were embarrassing because the drivers were inquisitive, as they had found. She wondered why Nabeel had not bothered to obtain a driving licence for himself. It was extremely annoying and hard to understand.

She turned her eyes back to her job list. Unpacking was still to be done with categorising, storing and inventorying to finish. It would be good to be able to present a well-organised office to her new line manager when he arrived at post. There were just five days of morning hours this week, then a three day holiday, with normal hours resuming after the *Eid*. She needed to find out what those hours would be. It had been interesting, starting work in Ramadan. Instead of dreading the fasting month in future, it was something she could look forward to next year, as a break from schedule.

When Nabeel came to collect her at 1pm, she asked him about his driving licence.

"I'll tell you at home," he said, not in front of the driver.

Over their tuna salad sandwiches he explained that he had learned to drive in Lebanon as a teenager, but he hadn't had a car, with three older brothers around, and a bus service to take him to school in Beirut. So he hadn't taken a licensing test. As Rose already knew, after secondary school he'd been sent to the UK to learn

English and to study for a business diploma. He had already spent four years there before meeting Rose. They had a platonic relationship for three months before Nabeel travelled to Beirut to attend a family wedding. Rose was still sceptical about the next part of their story. After attending the wedding Nabeel had disappeared off the radar. Rose had managed to keep his London bedsitter for him but she had almost hooked up with a Frenchman she had met in Paris. She believed Nabeel's explanation that his brothers had 'kidnapped' him in Beirut and forced him to go with them to Kuwait to work. He hadn't been allowed to drive because the brothers suspected he might run away. In fact, he had done exactly that when Rose had written to him about her new French boyfriend. But after his six-month absence she discovered that he had come back to London via Germany, meeting up with his former girlfriend, Heidi, in her hometown.

"OK. I see. I hadn't woven the details together before. But why didn't you take your test when you went back to Kuwait to work with them? You know, before you asked me to marry you?"

"Well, I was very busy trying to set up some deals so that we could get married. I didn't have time to think about driving. We have a driver at the office."

"So what are you going to do now?"

"Well, I'm going to take my test as soon as I can, but I don't have a car to practise in, so it's back to the money situation again. But, as soon as that money comes, not only will we get curtains and furniture, we'll get a car and I'll get my licence!"

"Promises, promises," Rose muttered, but with a smile. His life hadn't been easy.

Dear Diary, I haven't written to my family from here yet. I know my negative attitude will show if I write a letter. Perhaps I should find a couple of postcards and send them instead. I can hide my feelings in a short note. Good idea for tomorrow.

Saturday, 25 September, 1976, Kuwait

The weekend had passed without major incidents. The couple were looking forward to the break from what had become a rather dull routine with the party on Saturday evening. Leslie had arranged for Na'maan to pick them up. As an Iraqi Christian he was invited to the party because he could be with people who drank alcohol. When they got in the car they found a dark-haired, bearded man in the front passenger seat. He leaned over to shake hands with them.

"Good evening. I'm Len O'Reilly."

"Pleased to meet you," Rose said, introducing Nabeel to Na'maan as well as Len. It was still light at 6pm, but dusk was falling.

"I'll bring you all back if you don't stay too late," Na'maan offered. "My wife doesn't like me drinking and driving."

"What about the police?" asked Rose.

"Well, they don't expect you to be drinking and driving, as officially this country is dry. But in fact most Christians either buy whisky and gin on the black market, or they make their own wine and beer. Some even make *siddiqui*."

"*Siddiqui?*" queried Rose.

"It means, literally, 'my friend'! It's illicit booze, hooch, moonshine, whatever you like to call it."

"That sounds interesting," she said, intrigued. "I'll have to find out more on that subject!"

"Me too," said Len. "I can't imagine living without some booze for very long."

"And you're only just off the boat, my friend," Na'maan joked. "But you will get an official allowance as a British Council 'officer', so don't worry about it!"

"Where are you staying?" Rose asked Len, noting mentally the booze allowance comment.

"In the Sheraton for the moment. I have to get my house furnished ready for my wife and the boys to come out in a couple of weeks."

Na'maan rejoindered, "We'll be going shopping straight after Eid, so make a list!"

Len replied at once, "Beds, a fridge, a lounge suite and a dining set."

"Wow," said Rose, "it's obvious you've lived overseas before."

"Yes, most recently in Africa! The boys are still young enough to transport around the world."

"I suppose it's complicated when you have to get them into schools."

"There are excellent secondary as well as primary schools here," Na'maan informed them.

"Don't worry, we won't be needing primary schools again," Len commented wryly. "Four is our absolute limit, even as Roman Catholics.'

Nabeel was prompted to join in. "I'm Catholic too, but Greek, *Roumi*, which means, we follow Rome."

Na'maan chimed in, "Me too. Iraqi Catholic."

Len was intrigued. "That's very interesting. Are there many Christians in Kuwait?"

"Quite a few of the guys who work as coolies in the supermarkets are Egyptian Copts," Na'maan told them.

Len asked Nabeel, "Have you got a Church building here in Kuwait?"

"Our brother Muslims haven't allowed us *kaffir*, unbelievers, to build another church, as there is already the Roman Catholic building near the Sheraton in the city centre. We meet in a converted villa in Salmiyah. It suits our purposes."

Na'maan added, "But even the Roman Catholics are forbidden to ring church bells."

Rose sat silently absorbing the information. As a lapsed Anglican she had been warned to state her religion on any official forms as Christian rather than atheist or agnostic. She spoke up. "If you don't mind my asking, why are Christians regarded as unbelievers? Don't we believe in one God and have a holy book and a prophet, like Muslims?"

Na'maan replied, "Actually, *kaffir* refers to an unbeliever who is negative towards Muslims, so the term *kaffir* is mostly used by fundamentalist Muslims ... but if you compare the monotheist religions, Christianity is much more easygoing than either Judaism or Islam. For instance, both Judaism and Islam have strict food rules. In fact Islam has five 'pillars' which the faithful must observe: confessing faith in God, praying five times a day, fasting in Ramadan, charity (*Zakat*), and completing the Haj (pilgrimage to Mecca). On top of that there are major differences between Islamic sects, such as Saudi Wahhabis, Syrian Alawis and Iraqi Baathists. I could go on for a long time."

"Gosh," Rose replied thoughtfully, "so there's a lot to learn."

"OK. Here we are."

They climbed out of the four-wheel-drive onto the sand surrounding a two storey, brightly lit villa, with a high wall, a large gate and broad steps up to the entrance. They could hear people chatting and music playing in several areas of the house as they walked in. Leslie came towards them with a young woman beside him.

"Hi, everyone. This is my wife, Louise."

They all shook hands while Leslie made the introductions. They then turned to face a waiter whom Rose recognised as the younger of the two *farrasheen* from the office.

"Juice, beer or wine?" asked Jamal as he proffered a loaded tray. Rose selected a glass of white wine, while Nabeel took a beer.

They looked around the room. There was no one they knew among the group of around 24 mainly Western-dressed men and women. Len had been commandeered by Leslie and Na'maan had joined a group of people. There was a difficult hiatus while they sipped their drinks. Suddenly they were joined by a short, pleasant-faced Indian man, who greeted them warmly.

"Welcome to Kuwait," he said, shaking their hands. "My name is Raj. I'm the Vice-Consul at the British Embassy."

"Pleased to meet you!" Rose introduced herself and her husband.

Nabeel immediately seized the golden opportunity which had presented itself and began talking to Raj about business opportunities. As a middleman for UK, European and USA suppliers of hardware and software to the petrochemical industries, he needed to have his fingers in many pies. The chance to get access to the British Consulate's services for British businessmen was a potential source of future contracts to him. Rose stood patiently by, listening as Nabeel explained his specialist suppliers. Raj was obviously interested but not willing to spend too long going into details. He called over a younger, British man, and introduced him.

"This is Barry, our Commercial Affairs Attache. He will be helpful, I'm sure."

Barry was pleasant, but equally unwilling to commit too much of the evening to discussing business. "How about I put you on our list of local companies willing to do business? That means you will be invited to various meetings and get-togethers when we have trade visits. We will also contact you when we have individual enquiries we think might be of interest to you."

The two men exchanged cards and Rose and Nabeel were left on their own again, this time with empty glasses. Fortunately at that moment the host and hostess opened up the buffet for dinner, so they could mingle with the rest of the guests as they approached the table in the centre of the spacious dining room. The buffet was beautifully presented, with hotel-style, stainless steel, chafing dishes keeping the hot food warm. There was a wide array of salads, and a large sideboard spread with half a dozen different desserts. After people filled their plates they found seats to eat their meal. There were *diwan* type couches along the walls of one room, as well as Western lounge seats in another and dining chairs around the walls of the room the food was served in. Some stayed in close proximity to the buffet, tempted by the savoury smells, succulent sights, and delicious dessert delights.

Nabeel and Rose wandered out onto the wide balcony overlooking the compound and the desert beyond. The balcony had some comfortable garden furniture where they sat to eat. There was hardly any other light to be seen out in the vast darkness, other than the stars twinkling brightly above. After eating, Nabeel stood up to return their plates. While he was away a lady in Indian sari approached, smiling shyly at Rose.

"I'm Raj's wife. You met him earlier I believe?"

Rose smiled in return at this charming lady, so beautiful in her traditional dress, with a warm smile and a soft voice. "Yes, I work at the British Council. My name's Rose."

"I'm Manjula. I don't often go out in the evening, but *Eid* is very special. How are you enjoying Kuwait?"

"Well, it's certainly interesting, but to be honest, if I didn't have my job, I would be feeling quite lost."

"It is difficult for new wives here, but we have a Ladies Club which meets each month. We get together and discuss events here and we do some charity work. Would you like to join us?"

"I'm afraid it's going to be difficult for me to do anything other than work and keep house," Rose said regretfully. "I'll be working two shifts most days after Eid. So far it's been an easy life. Now I have to get serious, with Len here."

"Well, keep in touch," she said as she stood up.

Nabeel returned with Len in tow.

"They are serving coffee and dessert, ladies. After you!"

"Shall we?" Rose asked Manjula. They joined other female guests who were helping themselves, while the male guests dutifully obeyed protocol and waited their turn.

As Rose went back to the balcony, she noted Nabeel had lit a cigarette.

"Do you smoke, Len?"

"Not at all," he replied. "That's one vice I don't have."

"Oops," said Nabeel. "It's not a vice, you know. Smoking kills germs."

Rose sighed almost inaudibly. Here we go again, she thought. I hope Len doesn't take the bait. Luckily, Len listened to his inner man, and went off in search of dessert, leaving them alone.

"Why do you have to try to persuade everyone that your smoking is a positive trait? Don't you see how stupid it is?"

"Oh, leave me alone, Rose. I've smoked all the time I've known you. Why don't you give up nagging me?"

"You're right. I suppose you can't teach an old dog new tricks," she muttered angrily.

Rose ate her dessert in silence, turning her focus on the food. She'd sampled the Bombe Alaska, lemon meringue, apple pie and trifle - made with sherry! What an unexpected spread of delights, here, in the Kuwaiti desert. There had also been a platter of fruit, with a centrepiece of fat, juicy fresh dates. She'd taken just one, and the succulence of the fruit was amazing. The taste of this date bore no resemblance to the rather dry, sticky, sweet treats rigidly aligned beside the plastic serving prong down the middle of a long cardboard box, which she'd been accustomed to enjoying only at Xmas in England.

As soon as everyone had had coffee, people began to leave and Na'maan came looking for them to take them home. They said their farewells and thanked the hosts. In the car, they discussed how normal the evening had been, how Western, and how incongruous in the middle of the desert.

"That's how the Brits do things here," said Na'maan. "They serve lavish food and don't stint on the drink. Then they count up how much salt and pepper has been used, and they put in an expenses claim for it."

"Are you kidding?" asked Rose incredulously.

"Believe me, it depends on the host, but it is not unknown."

Laughing at the pettiness of such procedures, the couple got out in Salmiyah, leaving Na'maan to take Len back to the Sheraton.

"See you on Tuesday," Rose called out. "Bye now."

Two more days of holiday to go, thank goodness, before a return to the office. But what on earth was there to do at home on the holiday she wondered as they went inside the empty flat. The last day of this month, the 30th September, would be her 29th birthday. How would they celebrate it, if at all, with no furniture, no booze and no money? She kept her thoughts to herself, however. Raising these issues would seem like nagging again and would ruin the pleasant mood of the special evening.

Dear Diary,

I usually enjoy my birthday, but this year I'm not sure. I can't even talk to Mum as we don't have a phone and that day is a working day so I can't go to the brothers' office. I guess it's a punctuation mark, a full stop, in the saga that my married life has become. I hope the new sentence is NOT a sentence!! ha ha! I can still pun - where there's a pun there's a way, hey?

Sunday, 26 September, 1976, Kuwait

The next day Nabeel surprised her with a cup of tea on awakening at around 10am.

"Guess what we're going to do today?" he asked, excited.

"I've no idea," she said, intrigued.

"Well, some of my friends live and work in Ahmadi, the oil town to the south of the City. They've invited us for a BBQ lunch today. They are Christian, so they celebrate Sunday as their holy day. It should be fun. They have two small kids."

"Great. But how will we get there?"

"All sorted. They've invited some friends who live here in the City, so they'll take us along. They are newly-weds, from Jordan."

"What time do we leave? I need to wash my hair after the smoke last night at the party. You should have told me last night and I'd have got up earlier."

"They're coming round at 11am. It takes about 45 minutes to get to Ahmadi and we're expected by noon."

"OK. What are the names of the people we are travelling with? I'll try to memorise them in the shower."

"Ahmed and Monique."

"Easy peasy! Won't be long."

As she showered Rose marvelled at the inability to share information which Nabeel continued to show. Why couldn't he have told her even last night about this invitation? Once again, she found herself confused and unable to speak about her resentment at being expected to jump when Nabeel said jump. This wasn't how she wanted to live her life. She was a planner, an organiser, and no matter how nice the spontaneous events were, she preferred a life with no surprises, good or bad. So far in Kuwait she seemed to be living life on a knife's edge of surprise. But then, she told herself, she might be exaggerating. Let it go.

Ahmed and Monique arrived promptly, which surprised Rose. Punctuality wasn't something she expected in the Middle East. The couple were charming, fluent in English and a little younger than Nabeel and Rose, though Ahmed was already balding. The drive to Ahmadi passed quickly. Monique sat in the back with Rose and they talked of their families and houses, while Nabeel and Ahmed talked about work. Ahmed worked for one of the Emir's brothers. The couple rented a small villa near the Emir's private palace, just opposite Kuwait Towers. Monique didn't work. She was expected to stay home and produce children now she was married. With the help of a part-time maid she looked after her husband and her own brother who lived with them. Rose noted that she wore the latest designer fashion labels and had some stunning jewellery on her arms and neck, including a large diamond ring on one finger. Rose knew she mustn't compliment Monique on her possessions: to do so might risk attracting the evil eye, or would require Monique to give her the ring/item of clothing. So she tried to avoid looking too closely at this lovely young woman. She didn't feel jealous of her possessions, as she'd never been used to having them herself and had not mixed with others who had them. Rose's work in the UK had meant that she mixed with professional working people like herself, who dressed down, rather than up.

Monique no doubt noticed that Rose's clothes were high street rather than designer quality and noted the absence of any expensive jewellery at all but of course did not comment. She talked about buying furniture, which in her case had been purchased by her parents, as part of the marriage settlement. It was Ahmed's role to provide a place to live, and his parents-in-law were obliged to furnish it. Monique's brother lived with them as he was a bachelor and newly arrived in Kuwait. He was working with his brother-in-law in the Royal Palace Administration Department. Exactly what the two men did was not clear to Rose, and was probably top secret so she declined to enquire too closely.

"You should get a maid," Monique advised Rose. "You'll find it difficult to manage when you start fulltime work."

Rose didn't know how to tell her that there was no need for a maid to clean around their sparsely furnished apartment. Instead, she asked Monique about arrangements for maids. It seemed there were lots of 'live in' ladies who were allowed by their visa providers to find extra work for cash. That way, the sponsors didn't have to give their fulltime maid a salary. They could simply feed and house them, and expect in exchange all the housework to be done, and perhaps some cooking and childminding as well. It seemed rather unfair to Rose, who would not be seeking a maid in the near future.

Monique talked about missing her family and being homesick. In Amman she had sisters and her mother. In Kuwait she had only her brother and her new husband, although they had been engaged for more than a year so she knew him well. Rose hoped the two women might become good friends. She could learn a lot from her, which would be helpful.

On arriving in Ahmadi, Rose first observed the oil-producing areas, fenced off for security behind high aluminium-mesh walls. The tall flares, burning away, high above the multitude of shiny steel towers, dazzled in the sunlight. It was like viewing a science fiction film set. No one was to be seen in the midday sunshine, except for the armed guards in the sentry box at the gates. As Ahmed drove into the residential part of the city Rose noted the American layout of the streets, with numerical verticals and alphabetic horizontals. The houses were all one storey bungalows, with gardens full of established trees, shrubs and flowers. It was extremely attractive, shady and inviting. A little part of Rose's heart began to experience a twinge of jealousy now.

Ahmed parked in the driveway of one of these pretty villas and the four got out and walked through the garden to the front door. A tall, grey-haired man with a white moustache opened the door as they approached, and called out *"Ahlan wa sahlan!"*

"That's Butros," Nabeel told Rose. "His wife is called Marguerite."

Rose noted that the first two Arabic women she had met both had French names. She noted that she needed to ask about that in future. She smiled as Marguerite joined her husband on the porch.

"*Ahleen,*" cried Marguerite, walking to meet her guests.

Rose noted the smell of barbecuing meat as they exchanged greetings and introductions were made. They were ushered into a cool, shady lounge room.

"What would you like to drink?" asked Butros. "I'm sure you're thirsty after that long drive. Whisky soda? Gin tonic? Beer?"

Rose accepted a gin and tonic gratefully. It was like manna from heaven! The huge crystal tumbler was loaded with large ice cubes which clinked refreshingly, while the tonic bubbled appetisingly alongside the slice of lemon floating on the top of her drink. Gin and tonic had never seemed so exotically appealing as here in hot, 'dry' Kuwait.

"Cheers," they all cried, "*Sahetkum! Your health!*"

Rose noted another new word for her vocabulary notebook.

"Would you like to sit in here for a while, or outside?" asked Boutros.

They all opted to go outside to the shady garden, where a houseboy in white shirt and trousers was grilling kebabs and steaks. Two small children were playing with a little white dog. Rose noted that white dogs are acceptable to Muslims, and then reminded herself that her hosts were Christian. They might have chosen a white dog so as not to upset the neighbours. Marguerite seemed to read her mind.

"Yes, we chose a white one, in case it gets out. Our neighbours would return it to us if they found it, we hope. Help yourself to some nibbles."

Laid out on a central table were traditional earthenware dishes of hummus, *baba ghanoush*, *labna*, and *tabbouleh* salad, with the requisite accompaniments, toasted strips of flat bread and crisp green cos lettuce leaves, as well as sliced raw carrots in lemon juice and small sticks of cucumber and celery.

"This is a feast in itself! Everything looks delicious," Rose told Marguerite.

"Ahlan wa sahlan, habibti, welcome, my dear. *Itfaddali,* help yourself," urged Marguerite. "We love having visitors and it's a pleasure to meet you, Rose. We've known Nabeel for a long time and we know his family so we understand what you must be going through."

At this, Rose felt tears well, unexpectedly, to the back of her eyes. She looked down at her napkin, finding it hard to control her tears. She could only whisper, "Thank you." She looked over at Nabeel who was standing, smoking and speaking Arabic with the other two men. He looked relaxed and happy. Once again she could only push any negative thoughts out of her mind and do her best to enjoy this happy and unexpected occasion.

Over lunch, the three women were able to chat about their own interests while the men continued to speak Arabic, presumably discussing business, but occasionally Rose heard a name which suggested they were also talking about politics. All three men were Palestinian in origin, but only Ahmed was Muslim. Like Nabeel, Butros had obtained Lebanese nationality after the creation of Israel. He was a good ten years older than Nabeel, now in his late 40s, while his wife was about Rose's age, in her late 20s. A twenty year age gap was not unusual in the Middle East, where women expected to be cared for by their husbands rather than join the work force as in Europe. The two children were aged nine and seven, both moving between alternately eating bites of lunch and playing quietly with their white dog and on the garden swing.

"They are very well-behaved children," commented Rose.

"Not always," laughed Marguerite. "They go to the private English school in Fahaheel. It's a very good school and they are doing well, but they don't like doing homework."

"Do they have homework in primary school?" asked Rose in amazement. As a teacher of adults, she had no experience with the school system in Kuwait.

"Yes, they have to study both their languages, and you know how difficult reading and writing are. They really should do more at home, but they love playing in the garden after school," explained Marguerite.

"Yes, I realise it's a challenge to become truly bilingual," said Rose. "They need some fun though, while they are still young."

"We had to work hard when we were young," joined in Butros, "so now it's their turn. They have had far more than we ever had, a much more comfortable life, so they must work hard, study well, get good jobs, and then look after us when we are old."

It was a philosophy that Rose would hear on many occasions from many different people. She had never thought like that herself. Children were a blessing, indeed, but not an investment in her view. But she knew that some parents thought like that. Her own mother said that one of the reasons she had left Rose's father was that he expected his daughter to work in a factory, rather than pursue higher education. According to Mum, Rose would not have been able to go to university if they had stayed with Dad. Rose realised how lucky she had been, not only in having one parent who supported her in staying on in school, but also, in being born in a system where the Labour Government of the time provided children from working class families with scholarships and grants to study at university. Her brother Bill had benefited from the same system, but her younger sister and brother would not be able to, after the Conservatives ousted Labour in the General Election of 1976.

The three women helped the maid and the house boy to clear away the dishes, then sat down again for coffee. Marguerite asked how each guest preferred Turkish coffee: *saada*, no sugar, *mutawasit,* medium, or *helu,* sweet. For each taste the coffee was made in a one handled '*brik*', a tiny, long-handled saucepan, and served in tiny cups. Rose had hers made with a little sugar, though Nabeel preferred it *saada*. It seemed that adding sugar in the cup did not make good Turkish coffee. The sugar must be added while the coffee is being brought to the boil. After Rose had finished drinking the delicious, slightly thick liquid, Marguerite took her cup and turned it upside down in the saucer, so that the liquid would drain from the bottom. Rose looked at her hostess in surprise. What was this?

"I'm going to read your fortune," Marguerite declared.

"Oh! That's interesting. Are you a fortune teller?" Rose asked, recalling Mum's reading of the Tarot cards in Mossfield when she was undecided about marrying Nabeel.

"No, we just do it for fun. Let's see how many children you and Nabeel are going to have," Marguerite told her, picking up the cup and holding it the right way up in her hand. She stared into the dregs for a moment or two, while the rest looked at her with amusement. Putting down the cup she declared, "There'll be lots of kids, but not yet. You have to make a happy home first for them."

"That sounds sensible," said Rose. "We aren't ready yet, that's for sure," she said, thinking of the newspapered windows and mattresses on the floor, as well as the birth control pill she was taking each day without fail.

The others laughed, and conversation broadened to the state of the nation for a little while, which Rose listened to with interest. It seemed the Emir of Kuwait, Sheikh Sabah Al Salim Al Sabah, was elderly and there were issues of the succession when he died. Kuwait was growing very quickly, after the discovery of oil in 1938 and its development since then. The British had made the discovery, but the leaders had nationalised the oil industry in 1975, so that the wealth which came with selling oil internationally benefited Kuwait and its population directly and maximally. Mrs Violet Dickson, the elderly widow of Lt. Colonel Dickson, who had been the British Political Agent in those early years and had later worked for Kuwait Oil Company, was still in residence in Kuwait.

"You can visit her for tea on Sundays, just ask at the British Consulate for an invitation," said Monique. "She lives in a lovely old house on the Corniche, just opposite the Museum. I don't suppose you've been there yet as it's closed during Ramadan."

"That would be very interesting to visit," replied Rose. "I'll have to look into meeting Mrs Dickson too, when I get chance. I'm not sure what my timetable will be like, but I know I'll be busy from now on at work."

"Wait till you get pregnant like me," Monique giggled. "You can give up work then!"

Rose smiled, unwilling to share just how uncertain both those propositions were at that moment in time. For now, she was happy to have had a lovely day out, quite different from the restricted if not boring one she had anticipated. As they drove home, Ahmed pointed out the English school at Fahaheel which Butros and Marguerite's children attended. There were new blocks of flats springing up around what were obviously the original, single storey houses. Clearly Kuwait was in the springtime of development, with undreamed of oil wealth guaranteeing a successful economy. Perhaps this move to a new life would work out well, despite the current hardships they had to keep secret for now, to avoid embarrassing explanations.

Dear Diary,

An interesting day, meeting some lovely people with a lovely family and home. I haven't written home yet, though I said I would find some picture postcards. No shops open that I could see. Need to do this fast as Mum will be worried about me. I wonder if she knows that the address we gave her is a postal address? It might be the first time she's written to a P.O. Box. I must stop being so lazy and get these things done.

Monday, 27 September, 1976, Kuwait

As it was a weekday in Europe, but still a holiday in Kuwait, Nabeel went into the office to check on incoming mail on the fax machine. Having already had a holiday on the Muslim holy day, Friday, there could be enquiries waiting for him that he didn't want to miss. Rose was most surprised when he suddenly arrived back at the flat only two hours later.

"Guess what?" he called out as he burst in.

"The money?" she hazarded a guess.

"Yes, the money! I've had a notification that it's in the bank."

"But the banks aren't open today."

"But some shops will be open, so we can go window-shopping. We can select some curtains and get them made up. I've been so worried since that Peeping Tom incident."

"Wow, that will be marvellous. I didn't realise shops were open today."

"Well, after the traditional visits to family and friends a lot of people go shopping and some use their holiday to refurbish their wardrobes and their apartments."

"So, here we go - the boat has at last come in!"

"I'm so sorry, *habibti*. It's been awful for you, but now we can get some furniture and make a real home."

"Just in time for my birthday, too!"

"Yes, that's wonderful. We can go out for dinner on Wednesday night and feel normal again."

"Or nearly normal," Rose reminded him. "One of us has to get a driving licence, so that we don't have to rely on taxis."

"You're right. But meanwhile, I'm going to fix up a driver and a hire-car for myself. That will make us more flexible. How about that?"

"Terrific. I've had enough of nosey taxi-drivers. How soon can you arrange that?"

"As soon as the office opens tomorrow. It'll be done by the end of the day."

Excitedly, Rose got ready to go shopping. She'd only had a cursory glance at what was available as it seemed pointless to start looking before they had the chance to buy.

"We need to measure the windows before we go, don't we?"

"They do that. They send someone with us to do the measurements. Then they make the curtains and bring them back when they are ready. It's a complete service here, not like in London."

"That's terrific. I've made curtains before, you know, but it will be great not to have to do it myself. Plus I haven't got my sewing machine yet - it's with the packing."

"We have to chase up the packing company as well. They said it would take a month, so I suppose it's still early days."

"Yes. We can't do anything about that. Are you ready to roll?"

They left the flat and walked to the road to hail a taxi. The little, yellow, four-door sedans were in plentiful supply, so they soon reached the cheap shopping area in Hawalli. Curtain and furniture shops lined the main street. They strolled along, popping into one store after another, forming an idea of what they would like. This was the '70s, and orange was a top colour for interior design. They both liked the idea of beige and brown as basics with orange highlights. After combing the area and making notes they decided on a dark brown velvet lounge suite, a teak dining set with eight chairs, a matching teak sideboard and side tables for the lounge, a white five door wardrobe, with matching emperor size bed, a mirrored dressing table with a fluffy-topped stool and two bedside cabinets. As the furniture was all in the same store they were able to discuss the total price and obtain a discount.

When Nabeel explained they could not even place a deposit that day, but would be able to do so the next day, the shop owner laughed. "I can guess your story," he told them. "You didn't marry the one they wanted you to marry, did you?"

Nabeel looked at his feet, unable to answer.

"Don't worry *ya khayyi* (my brother)," the salesman laughed out loud. "This is a story as old as time. Did they beat you?"

Nabeel shook his head, still looking at his shoes.

"Well then you are lucky. They might have killed you, even. So cheer up, and don't worry about the money. I can tell from your accent we are brothers, *falisteeni, mish heki*?"

"*Wallahi* (Yes, by God)."

"Then *fursa saeeda*, well met, my friend. I will keep all these items for you, pack them up, and have them ready to deliver the moment you say. Free delivery of course. *Mabruuk!* Congratulations on your purchases!"

"Allah yibarak fik," replied Nabeel, looking up now with relief. His story was not unique.

Rose looked on bemused: The Arabic was too fast for her, though she could pick out the magic word, *falisteeni.*

Nabeel turned to her and said, *"Mabruuk! Congratulations* - we have furniture!"

He didn't bother teaching her how to reply, as that wasn't his way. At least he passed on a new word for her. *"Mabruuk,"* she repeated with a smile.

"Shall we go and get curtains now, and take the fitter home with us?"

"If we have time before lunch? Isn't it a bit late now? It's almost 1pm. Won't the shops be closing for lunch?"

"Right - why don't we make a day of it? Let's have lunch around here, then go into the shops again at 4pm."

"Well, there's no real point in going home, but it's a long lunch break."

"We can relax over lunch and drink some *qahwa.* Or we can go to the cinema. How about that?"

"That sounds nice. With no TV at home, it would be nice to have some food for our eyes, as it were!"

"OK. I'll check the paper while we have lunch."

They found a family cafe with a rotisserie chicken oven outside, emitting wonderful savoury smells. While enjoying roast chicken with *tabbouleh* and *aioli* on the side, Nabeel had a look in the newspaper at the films on offer in the nearest cinema.

"There's a new American film you might like, called <u>Lipstick</u>, with Margaux and Mariel Hemingway, and Anne Bancroft."

"It should be good. They are Ernest Hemingway's grand-daughters, you know, the writer?"

"Mm. OK. It starts at 3pm. We'll have to take a taxi over to Salmiyah, but it will make a change for you."

After lunch and a Turkish coffee they hailed a taxi to take them to the cinema in Salmiyah. There were family and bachelor seats, just as in the restaurants, but the most surprising thing was that as they walked inside, Rose could feel something underfoot, and she could hear a crunching noise.

"What's that on the floor?" she asked Nabeel in a whisper as the film was just starting.

"*Bizr,* seeds. People don't eat popcorn, they eat pumpkin and other types of seeds. They throw the shells on the floor."

"No! It's like walking into a parrot's cage," Rose exclaimed in disgust.

The velvet-upholstered seats appeared clean enough in the half light, so they sat down and stared at the screen. There were Arabic subtitles, and the dialogue was in English. Events unfolded before their eyes, but they seemed weirdly disconnected. One moment a girl was talking to a man, the next moment he approached her, then suddenly sprang backwards. One sentence often didn't have a follow up from another person, just as one scene didn't always lead to another. Rose stared at the screen uncomprehendingly for about 45 minutes, then she turned to Nabeel.

"Can you make out what's going on?" she whispered.

"The censor has been in with his scissors," he told her. "The review in the paper said it's a violent film, with two rapes."

"Oh no," Rose whispered. "Did you really think I would enjoy a film like that?"

"Don't worry, you won't see them."

"That's a blessing, but the problem is I can't follow the story with big and small bits cut out of it."

"Do you want to leave?"

"Yes. Come on."

As they left, she asked Nabeel about the apparent sudden springing back of the males and females when they appeared about to touch each other.

"It's forbidden (*haraam*) to show men and women touching or kissing."

"Even if they are father and mother? ...or brother and sister?" Rose asked incredulously.

"Oh yes, it's all *haraam*. Men and women who are not related by blood or marriage or milk must be segregated according to Islam."

"Well, I think that's the last time we bother to watch a film here then, thanks very much. We went to the cinema in Beirut and there was no censorship that I noticed."

"Yes, but Lebanon is completely different from the Gulf. Islam is much more fundamental here. Kuwait is virtually controlled by its neighbour Saudi Arabia in terms of culture and religion."

"Why is that?"

"Because Saudi Arabia is the Keeper of the Holy Shrines - Mecca and Medina. All Moslems must perform the *Haj*, the pilgrimage, to the Shrines at least once during their lives."

"I see. So they have religious power, and that's why they call the shots on the Moonsighting Committee.

Have they got a symbolic figure, like the Pope for Roman Catholics?"

"Well, remember I'm not Muslim, so I'm no expert, but the reigning Sheikh, the Emir of Saudi Arabia, is the one responsible for the upkeep of the Shrines. It's a big job looking after the pilgrims who come to perform *Haj*. Quite often there's an accident of some kind. We read about it in the paper."

"I've just remembered from watching the film about Lawrence of Arabia, that Christians are not allowed to enter those two holy cities."

"That's right. You got it. Two completely different civilizations. But in Lebanon, the balance between the two is exquisitely maintained. To date at least. You probably know nothing about it, but a civil war started the year I went back for Joseph's wedding."

"Really? What happened?"

"It's complicated, but there was an attack by the Lebanese Christian Phalangists on a bus carrying Palestinian refugees to a camp called Tell al Zatar. There were PLO activists in the camp, but this attack was unwarranted. It was a massacre and it has thrown the balance of power in Lebanon into chaos."

"I'm not surprised. Violence gets you nowhere. I'd like to know more, but it's awful."

As they waited to hail a taxi to return to the Hawalli shops, Rose mused to herself on the strangeness of the society she was now living in. What else would life here reveal in due time she wondered? Only a few minutes later she noticed something else: On some waste ground she noticed a group of boys playing football in bare feet. She smiled as she watched them, then wondered at the strange shape of the ball.

"What's that they're kicking?" she asked Nabeel who glanced over at the boys.

"Oh, it's a dead rat. They are bigger than the cats here, you know," he told her in a matter of fact voice.

"But the kids have got no shoes on."

"They don't care. It's a free ball for them."

Rose grimaced with distaste and tried to block the image from her mind.

As they dismounted from the cab near the curtain stores, they saw the shops had opened and business was fairly brisk on this last day of the *Eid al Fitr* holiday. Now they had chosen their furniture they could select curtains more easily. They quickly identified a full length, quality linen-look, heavy viscose dark beige material with large sunflowers outlined on it, with the sunflower heads coloured a strong, but not too vivid, orange. The overall effect was classy, and on enquiring the price, the material was reasonable. They discussed the quantities they would need to cover the lounge and bedroom windows. They would leave the kitchen window covered in newspaper for now.

Taking an assistant with them they returned home, had their windows measured, then relaxed with a cup of tea while taking stock of the day.

"We've come a long way, baby," Nabeel said gleefully.

"Yes, furniture and curtains! All in the same day. It will be lovely when they are installed. But we need a fridge freezer too. Can you get one tomorrow?"

"Yes, of course. If I go over to Hawalli and put the deposit down tomorrow, we can get everything installed on Wednesday just in time for your birthday on Thursday."

"Great. Some good luck for a change! Maybe your brothers will relent and come and see us when they can sit down!"

"I don't think so - just forget about them. It's their loss."

"Now, I'd better get ready for bed. Tomorrow I have a new schedule. I'm meeting Len first thing."

The *Eid* holiday over and the rest of their married lives in Kuwait spread out endlessly in front of them, but Rose was still uneasy about the strange differences in culture she was encountering on a daily basis. In the back of her mind the question niggled: Have I made the right decision in getting married and coming here, leaving my career, family and friends behind?

A picture postcard:

Dear Mum and John,

Sorry I haven't written before now. We had so much to do. I'm sending this picture of the Hotel Sheraton Roundabout. It's in the centre of town, with an old city gate on it, called the Jahra Gate. Nabeel's office is in the picture too! Don't worry about talking to me on my birthday or sending me a card. We have no phone at home and the only mailing address is Nabeel's office, which you have already. For now, sending lots of love, Rose.

Tuesday, 28 September, 1976, Kuwait

At the British Council office in Mansouriyah there seemed to be a new, more purposeful atmosphere now that Ramadan and the *Eid* celebrations were over. Samir was bustling around in his office, while the *farasheen* were dusting the furniture in the foyer. The school year was to begin in a month's time and the two new ETC staff members were required to get on with the program.

The Rep, Reg, held a welcome meeting with Leslie for Len and Rose. The agenda was brief: the timetable for the opening of the Centre to students at the end of October, with an official gala celebration on the first evening, Saturday 30th October. The Minister of Education had been invited to cut the ribbon on the new Centre premises. There was a lot to do in preparation for the opening. Working hours for ETC fulltime staff would be five mornings, 8 to 1pm and 2 or 3 evenings on alternate weeks, from 4 to 9pm each evening. The two fulltime staff, Len and Rose, would cover supervision for the whole working week. As teachers would be mainly part-time, the attendance of one of them as the duty officer would be necessary each night.

Len and Rose went down to their basement office to make their plans. Len looked around the tidily stacked shelving with approval.

"I can see you've been hard at work!"

"Well, it's the only thing I could do really," Rose replied. "I didn't want to go ahead with any planning without you."

"Well, look, I think we need to discuss our roles a bit more. I've been appointed here as English Language Officer. That means I have to deal with people outside of the ETC, so I won't be fulltime here. What's your title?"

"I'm Senior Teacher."

"Well, it seems to me you should be the Director of Studies. There's an obvious gap between your title and mine."

"Actually, now you mention it, I was a bit cross to realise that I'd been appointed as a local teacher because I'm married to an Arab. After all, I was appointed in London, and I have good qualifications and experience. I feel they are getting me on the cheap."

"I see. Well, why don't we do a bit more thinking, and after we have something to show for our efforts, let's talk to Reg about a salary increase for you and a new title. That should make up for the lack of overseas contract conditions."

"Yes. Accommodation and annual airtickets are expensive items!"

"Indeed. I'm expecting Ngaire and the boys to come out at the weekend. I have to finalise the school arrangements for them, and get our accommodation properly furnished. I've got a lot on my mind."

"Well, do you think we should work on a potential range of levels for the Centre, with a syllabus, textbooks and a corresponding placement test?"

"That sounds sensible. If we sketch something out straight away, then we can divide up the jobs and you can get on with things even if I have to go out to meet people."

"OK. And let's decide our evening schedule for the coming month, shall we? How about we do Sat, Mon, Wed, or Sunday, Tuesday evenings?"

"Yes, that sounds good. Shall we toss for tonight, Tuesday or tomorrow, Wednesday? Whoever does tonight will have three nights next week though!"

Rose laughed. "OK. Have you got a Kuwaiti coin? I don't carry money."

Len smiled. "Why? Are you worried about getting mugged?"

"No. I just don't have any money. Nabeel looks after all that."

"What? No bank account?"

"Well, my salary goes into Nabeel's account. It's a joint account I think, because I had to give him some papers with signatures on them. But I don't have a cheque book. I trust him."

"Ngaire usually looks after our financial affairs but I'm going to have to step up here. It's a man's world but as an expat it's complicated going to banks and sorting out accounts. I can understand you not wanting to bother with them."

"Yes, I'm a Kuwaiti princess. But not really. A Palestinian princess."

"OK princess - let's toss for tonight's shift. Heads or tails?"

"Tails," shouted Rose.

The 10 *fils* coin flew into the air and came down with the Kuwaiti boat, the dhow, showing.

"So, it's my choice or my shift?"

"Your choice, my dear princess."

"OK. I'll do Tuesday, tonight, and give you a lighter schedule next week because Ngaire and the boys will be here. You do two nights then and I'll do three."

"That's very kind of you. Are you sure?"

"Yes, don't worry, and by the way it's my birthday on Thursday and we are going out for dinner. Would you like to join us if you've nothing else on?"

"That would be great. I won't ask your age!"

"Cheeky! Ladies are over 21 and then that's it! The clock stands still."

Len and Rose worked on the basic principles of the ETC teaching schedule for an hour or so, before Len left to go the University for a meeting. The British Council was responsible for the contracts of overseas teachers of English as a Second or Foreign Language (ES/FL), and Len's role was to ensure all the details of meeting, greeting and settling the teachers into their apartments at the start of this new academic year were taken care of by the University Administration. Around 25 teachers had been hired on overseas contract conditions, so Len would be busy during the coming week. He was also required over the rest of the academic year to liaise with the University's senior academics in the ES/FL world, with a view to organising conferences, helping with accredited publications and other professional issues.

Rose rang Nabeel and checked that he was picking her up for lunch as usual at 1pm. She told him briefly the details of her new schedule, as she would be working that evening. It wasn't unusual for Rose to work evenings. In the Adult Education Institute in London it was normal to teach evenings. Rose had been used to arriving at work for the first class at 9.30am and not leaving at night until the last class of the day had finished at 9.30pm. Her 16 teaching hours had been with the morning and afternoon classes, from 9.30am to 11.30am and 2pm to 4pm. Morning students were mainly sub-continental housewives from India, Pakistan and Bangladesh. Afternoon students tended to be European *au pairs*, while evening students were mostly workers from local cafes, such as Hong Kong nationals, and Indian and Pakistani men and single women. She had had to work four afternoons and evenings a week, from Monday to Thursday, supervising schedules, interviewing students and observing classes. Only Friday had been a half day, with no afternoon or evening classes. She could see that the teaching schedule she had devised for London would be easily transferrable to the new teaching context, with some adaptation. She had no worries about her professional life at all. If anything, it would compensate greatly for the lack in her personal life so far.

When Nabeel arrived to collect her at lunchtime she had already completed an embryonic timetable and was working on a placement test for new students. Textbooks would have to be ordered and she needed Len's permission and assistance with those decisions. She wrote a note about what she had done and what was to be done and left it on Len's desk in case he came back after his meeting, although they had decided that officially he wasn't at work. At 4pm she would be back, working on the placement test and tomorrow morning they would decide on the timetable and textbooks together.

A picture postcard of Kuwait City:

Dear Dad,

I hope you are all well? I've been too busy to write before now, but everything is OK. I like my job very much. From this card you can see how modern Kuwait is. More later, with lots of love, Rose.

Thursday, 30 September, 1976, Kuwait

It was wonderful good luck to have her birthday on a weekend, thought Rose, as she stretched lazily in her own real bed. In the UK she would have been at work! The new furniture had been delivered on Wednesday afternoon and the flat now not only looked, but also sounded completely different. There was no echo when they spoke, and their footfalls no longer sounded so loud. They had no carpet or rugs, but it was amazing to be able to sit comfortably in the lounge. They were still using the small plastic table for meals as they needed table cloths and place settings to protect the beautiful teak table. Rose had worried a little about the size of the bill with the furniture store and the curtain shop.

"Are we going to be able to pay the bills with your commission as well as the rent for October? My salary won't come in until the end of the month," she had reminded Nabeel the previous night.

"Yes, of course. Don't worry," he'd told her. "Women are better without brains. They shouldn't think."

The statement had astounded her, rather like the comment he had made at their wedding ceremony. Once again she had ignored it, hoping he was being humorous, rather than a manifesto of his real sentiments. After all, he'd married her presumably because she had a brain. Or was it despite her brain? That way of thinking led only to stress and unhappiness, so Rose turned her thoughts elsewhere. She started a list of essentials to complete their home comforts when the time or budget was right. She had lists galore, made on the back of envelopes usually, from what she needed to do, to read, to remember, and to buy. She even listed what she'd eaten on days when she felt her calorie intake was running away with her.

When Rose met Nabeel in London she had been very slim, as a result of a carefully controlled intake of food. At university she'd been in danger of serious anorexia nervosa, running off any excess calories she'd eaten by pounding the streets late at night, or, if it was raining, by walking 1,000 times around her bedroom. She'd been in danger of wearing out the carpet in that room! She had then ricocheted into bulimia, stuffing her face with the contents of a whole packet of chocolate wheaten biscuits while in the bath, then getting out, sticking her finger down her throat and regurgitating the unwanted calorific value. It had been a painful, ugly routine, which no one else had known about even though it went on for years.

After uni, while working as a summer camp counsellor in New York State she'd been able to limit her diet to protein and veggies only. Then, when she'd started her postgraduate secretarial course there had been a financial reason to keep up the control. On her student grant she could only afford to eat either two pounds of carrots or two pounds of apples for one shilling. That had been her daily diet until she met Nabeel while on the way to interview for a barmaid's job. The job had provided her with more substantial food as well as an increased income. The bar staff were allowed to take home any rolls or snacks not sold during the evening. When she started staying over at Nabeel's he had thought she was praying before falling asleep at night, whereas she was counting under her breath the calories she'd eaten that day. She had not been grateful for a meal he had cooked for her to eat when she returned from work at 10.00pm one evening. He didn't realise that it was too late for her to consume more food when she'd already eaten what she allowed herself each day. He had been hurt and upset, not understanding where she was coming from. He had no idea of the seriousness of her obsession with food control. She had come out of the bulimic stage, however, which was a blessing.

For her birthday they were going to the Sheraton for dinner, so Rose, still calorie conscious, would not be eating anything for breakfast, and very little for lunch. Len would be joining them, as would Leslie and his wife. No alcohol was served in public in Kuwait, nor available for purchase, so it would not be a champagne occasion, but there would be good food on the menu, Nabeel had promised. There was also a small dance floor and a live dance band, which seemed rather un-Islamic in contrast to the liquor ban. Rose and Nabeel loved dancing, and dressed smartly for a happy night out. They set off to the hotel to meet their guests at 8pm. People in Kuwait did not eat as late as those in Cairo, which suited Rose better. She knew that food eaten late at night was not easily digested, and would lead almost inevitably to thickening of the waistline and hips. So she'd saved up her calories to allow for tonight's meal and would look forward to using up some of the energy immediately on the dance floor.

After meeting the others in the foyer, they all went up in the lift to the top floor of the Hotel where there were views from the wide windows over the city, the sea and the winding Corniche road illuminated with street lights. The restaurant was elegantly decorated with dim lighting and candles on the tables. When they sat down, Rose was surprised to see that Nabeel handed a brown paper package to the waiter, and asked for tea to be served.

"What's happening?" she whispered.

"Something special for your birthday," he replied, equally *sotto voce.*

The waiter returned with a silver tray on which were two silver teapots, an ice bucket with tongs, and some small bottles of soda water and cola. He also poured mineral water from a litre bottle into clear wine glasses for each person. Rose noted that there were brown glass goblets next to the water glasses. Into these, once the waiter had gone, Nabeel asked Louise, Leslie's wife, if she would like a scotch and soda or scotch and cola, or simply soda or cola. Louise accepted a scotch and soda, as did Rose, blinking at the surprise of it. Scotch was her favourite spirit but where had this 'cold tea' come from, she wondered.

Len, Leslie and Nabeel sat back with their drinks and beaming, Len proposed a toast.

"To Rose, Happy Birthday!"

"Happy Birthday!" they all echoed.

Rose thanked them. "I don't know how this miraculous libation arrived," she said, "but it's marvellous! A new year of life at the start of my new life!"

A typical starter *mezze* was brought to the table as they sipped their drinks. Rose was now familiar with the basic dishes, *hummus, mutabbel, tabbouleh,* but on this occasion there was also a dish of tasty *labna* and a small platter of egg-shaped balls of *kibbe* - 'Syrian torpedoes' joked Nabeel, explaining they were made with minced lamb mixed with cracked wheat, stuffed with more savoury mince and pine nuts, then deep fried. While nibbling these they ordered their main meals. Rose selected the grilled Gulf shrimps as a main, which were as delicious as Nabeel had promised when they visited the fish souk. The large pink shellfish were served on skewers with a delicate, savoury rice dish and mixed salad on the side. In between courses of their meal they danced to Western hits played by the small band which performed only at weekends when the expatriate community tended to go out to dine.

As there were only two ladies, one of the men was obliged to sit out some of the dancing, but the ladies were kept busy on the floor. After a while, Rose and Louise called a halt to the activity and they simply sat and enjoyed their food listening to the musical entertainment. The band played Arabic songs which a few people danced to. Rose was not familiar with them, but the popular song of the day, *diggi diggi diggi, ya rababa*, by the Lebanese musician Samir Yazbek, took her fancy with its rhythm and onomatopeic words. She found herself quietly singing along with the male vocalist. Neither Len nor Leslie spoke any Arabic as far as she knew, but she asked if anyone knew the translation of the words to the song that had pleased her. Nabeel translated the first line: 'play, play, play o rebab player'. He also explained that the *rebab* was a traditional stringed instrument, with a limited musical range, but a strong percussion effect, accentuating the rhythms of Arabian music carried by the *tabla* or drum.

Rose had heard some songs by the Egyptian singer, Umm Kulthum, in Cairo and she suddenly recalled that in London, Nabeel had had a 78rpm vinyl record, with a black and white photo of the singer on the sleeve. Rose wondered why Nabeel had never played it on his red and white Dansette in their bedsitter days. He loved dancing, and appreciated music, but it wasn't a passion for him as it was for her. She'd learned to play the piano at age six, and could still read music even though she'd given up playing when she went to secondary school. Her parents hadn't been able to afford to let her take examinations, so it seemed pointless to continue. She knew she didn't have the self-confidence to become a solo instrumentalist. However, she did enjoy singing, and even as young as six she'd been a soloist at a nativity concert, dressed as the Virgin Mary, and nursing her baby doll, she'd sung the Rocking Carol, 'Little Jesus, sweetly sleep...we will rock you, rock you, rock you..' Another song with a repetitive chorus line she mused, before coming back to earth with a start as Nabeel asked if she wanted coffee.

"No, thanks, it might keep me awake."

"On the contrary, it makes me sleep," cried Nabeel, as he always did.

Rose noted to herself, that quite likely it was because his system was used to it. All day and every day he drank endless cups of black coffee accompanied with cigarettes. He had no difficulty keeping his slim figure with that daily diet, and his lack of interest in food. The others, however, declined to have coffee, so they said their farewells as Leslie and Louise generously dropped Len at his home.

"Thank you for a lovely evening, darling," Rose said, as they got ready for bed. "How did you manage to get that whisky? It tasted so good!"

"Well, it was good old Johnny Walker Red Label. That's about the only one you can find here. I used one of my contacts."

"Did it cost a lot?"

"25 dinars a bottle is the going rate."

"That's 50 English pounds! It's like drinking liquid gold."

"Exactly. But it was worth it, wasn't it?"

"Yes, it made a big difference to the meal. Drinking tomato juice would have been the only option for me, or of course, plain water. Cola is a kids' drink!"

"Well, come on, you can pay me back now. Jump into bed."

Usually their lovemaking was efficient and sufficient but with protracted foreplay which Rose sometimes felt impatient with but Nabeel could not forego. She was sleepy after the unexpected and liberal alcohol, so was surprised to find that Nabeel had a new trick to try that night. As he cuddled her he tried to penetrate her from behind. When she protested, he held her wrists forcefully. She screamed in fear and anger, as well as pain. Kicking and struggling against him she leaped out of bed.

"What the hell are you trying to do? Is this what you think marriage is about? You think you can do what you want to me now we're married? This is a criminal act, you know!"

She was yelling at him, and didn't give a thought to who might hear in the quiet of the night, when windows might be open. In her anger and fear she had hit the nail right on the head, as her husband replied, in a disappointed, hurt voice:

"Well, you said you would obey me when we got married, didn't you?"

"You must be joking!"

All tiredness forgotten, Rose stormed into the second bedroom where she stored those few things they had brought with them. Amongst their sparse possessions she quickly found the text of their marriage ceremony with the exact wording of their vows and marched back into the bedroom with it.

"Look at this! I wondered what you were getting at when you said "you had it mate". There was no 'obey' in our ceremony. I made sure of that. Not for sex, nor anything. So," she continued, "if you want to forget our marriage and break up now, that's fine by me. I'm ready to leave on the next plane."

Nabeel was obviously shocked. Whether he'd drunk too much and gone too far, or he'd thought she would agree to what he wanted, Rose could not tell, but he immediately backed down.

"I'm sorry, *habibti*, please forgive me. I was just joking."

"Well, you've hurt my wrist, and I don't find that funny at all. I'm serious. Let's discuss this in the morning."

As she got back into bed, threatening to retreat to the couch if he touched her again, Rose looked up at the pink and white teatowel Maggie had given her, which she'd pinned on the bedroom wall. *Love means never having to say you are sorry.* How ironic that was now, given the state of her marriage. Had this been the underlying intention beneath those words in the registry office, "You had it mate?" Not a joke, but a threat of something she found vile.

Her grandmother's words rang in her ears: 'You've made your bed, now you lie on it.' That was the Victorian philosophy of life. Did she really have to stay in this marriage? Was she brave enough and hurt enough to get out of it though? During the six years they had lived together they had had rows about silly things she couldn't even remember now. But she had tried to leave him at least once, packing a bag and going to Victoria Coach Station to catch a bus home to Mossfield. But she had gone back, not trusting her own emotions, and not wanting to upset Mum by turning up unexpectedly, believing she was being hysterical as Nabeel always suggested when she got angry with him. Had she wrongly suppressed that original instinct for self-preservation? She had found herself doubting her own reactions, wondering if she over-exaggerated her feelings. Was this just a bad dream now, or something real she had to face up to and handle?

Dear Diary,

I hate this man I've married. Shall I leave him? How can I buy a ticket out of here? I need to work out a plan of some kind. But I don't even have a bank account, so I have no money for a great escape. And how would

I face people back home? What would I tell them? I can't explain this sudden revulsion, after knowing him for six years. How a leopard can hide his spots, hey?

Friday, 1st October, 1976, Kuwait

The next day Rose woke up with that sinking feeling which lets you know something is wrong. Nabeel was not beside her, for which she was glad. She got up and went into the bathroom, then into the kitchen to make a cup of tea. The kettle was hot already. Nabeel was in the lounge, smoking as usual. She called out to ask if he wanted some tea. There was no reply.

Taking her own tea into the lounge, Rose realised that she hated the smoke pervading the room. She opened two windows to create a through draft, making a noise to let him know that he should have opened them. He still said nothing.

"Well?" She opened up the conversation despite the stonewalling. "How are you today?"

"I'm OK," he said slowly. "I'm sorry about last night. I thought we could try something new. Just for fun."

"Well, I'm afraid that won't work, not now or in the future. So if it's something you really want, now is your chance to decide. I can leave, or I can stay, but only on condition that you never try anything like that again."

"OK," he said hurriedly, obviously glad of the chance to keep her with him.

"My wrist hurts a lot, where you held me. I feel you stepped way over the line, trying to use force. I'm serious, Nabeel. If you try anything like this again, I'm out of here."

"OK, OK. I understand and I'm sorry. I've said I'm sorry you know."

"I know, but meaning it is more important than saying it. If you mean it, then I'll try to forget it."

"OK. I mean it. I'm sorry I hurt your wrist."

"Well, I'll have to go and get a pressure bandage to support it. Let's get ready and get the food shopping. We can go to a pharmacy on the way. By the way, what's happening about a driver?"

"Oh, I forgot to tell you. He starts tomorrow. I had to rent a car for him. He's Indian, called Raji."

"So he's Muslim?"

"No, Hindu. My secretary, Johnny, is Hindu too. He hired him for me."

"I didn't realise you had a secretary! Wow! Life at the office must be interesting."

"Would you like to go and have a look round?"

"Will anyone be in the office today?"

"Well, if they are, what does it matter? They may not talk to us, but it doesn't matter to us."

"OK. I'm interested in your office set up."

They set off in a taxi to the central roundabout near the Sheraton Hotel where they'd had dinner the previous night. The offices of the family company were in a semi-circular building facing the lush lawn of the roundabout which had an original antique City gate in the centre. Even though it was late morning the streets were quiet, with the local population heading to morning prayers rather than shopping. The taxi dropped them in front of the building, and Rose noticed a newsagent and tobacconist as well as a barber's shop on the ground floor. Some men in national dress, white *dishdashi,* with white headdress and black *agal,* were sitting in the picture windows, waiting their turn in the two chairs. A white-haired man in a crisp white overall waved a pair of scissors in greeting at Nabeel as they passed.

"Who's that?" asked Rose.

"It's Bader, the Lebanese Christian barber. He's a great guy."

"So he's open on Fridays to prepare the Muslim men for the mosque?"

"Yes, that's it. Friday is the day to clean up ready for the most important day of prayer."

The pair took the stairs up to the fourth floor. Nabeel explained that there might be a powercut, so it was better not to use the lift. However, he opened the door to the lift and showed the sign revealing the builder, Otis, and the date of the last maintenance overhaul, saying proudly, "This was the first lift to be installed in Kuwait." Rose willingly accepted climbing the stairs instead of using this antiquity, carefully maintained though it may have been. Thinking of Otis Redding as she climbed the dark, narrow stairway, she realised that Kuwait was indeed a young country.

Arriving at the fourth floor they came to a landing with the family company signs. This was the first time she had seen the reality of Nabeel's working world. The offices were dimly lit from the wide windows covered with plastic Venetian blinds. There was a faintly dusty atmosphere pervading the suite of four private offices, with a central reception and secretarial area. Each single office had a huge desk, and each desk had a large ashtray on it. There was a telex machine and several large typewriters on the desks in the central area. Rose could discern a few plaques from client companies fixed to the wood panelled walls and paper calendars with Oriental script on them hanging randomly on walls, but the overall impression was forgettable. She could see that work was really work here. There was a water cooler near the front door and a tiny kitchen area, more like a cupboard, with clean Turkish coffee cups and a single burner visible, but no one was inside. Nabeel checked the telex machine and took her to the windows over the parking area to observe the view, which was splendid.

"It's a pity you can't see this lovely view of the Jahra Gate clearly on account of these wretched plastic blinds," she commented.

"We don't come here to look through the windows, you know. It's serious stuff here."

"I realise that. Now I know where you are. That's great. Let's go."

As they passed Bader's barber shop, he called out to them to come for a coffee. His shop was empty now so they sat and chatted with him. Rose told him about the new ETC, as he might be able to generate some customers with his contacts. Bader was from Jounieh, a Christian town in Lebanon. He'd come to work in Kuwait hoping to make enough money to pay for his house in Lebanon. His wife, two sons and two daughters were still there, he explained.

"It's no life for a Christian woman here," he told Rose. "My brothers help my wife when I'm not there and I go home as often as I can. The kids love their school and my wife is free to move around."

She smiled, wondering what would be her best response. Should she agree with him? Or would that show

141

a lack of trust in Nabeel? A trust she had so recently doubted. Luckily Nabeel jumped in, pointing out that Rose had a job, which would make all the difference to her settling in.

"*Sahih, sahih,* true enough," said Bader. Rose smiled in agreement and they said their farewells. As they walked through the parking area Nabeel pointed out the car he had rented. It was a small, four-door sedan, a Toyota, in a non-descript colour. The driver would pick it up in the morning and drive it all week, leaving it parked at the office over the weekend. As they waited for a taxi to take them grocery shopping, Rose asked about learning to drive. She felt life would improve for her if she had that freedom.

"You can certainly learn to drive here. In fact, if you already had a British licence you could just change it."

"Is that what you are going to do?"

"No, the Government doesn't accept Lebanese driving licences. You can bribe someone for a licence over there. We have to take the test again."

"So, when are you going to do that?"

"Well, now we've got the car and driver, I can get some practice in, and apply for the test. Give me a month and I should be driving myself. Then I'll buy a car."

"Great. That's something to look forward to. After you get a car, will you teach me to drive?"

"I don't think that's a very good idea, do you? You know I'm not a teacher."

"And I don't know what kind of driver you are," laughed Rose. "I've never seen you drive, have I?"

"Indeed. So let's take it one step at a time. First my licence, then our car, then I will find a driving instructor for you."

"Great. I like to have a new challenge each year. That will be my challenge for 1977."

"What's your challenge this year, then?"

"Staying married, learning Arabic, and settling into my new job."

Nabeel smiled, but stayed silent, her words reminding him of the events of last night. Luckily at that moment a taxi came by and conversation was closed. The taxi dropped them at their local Cooperative Society supermarket, where they picked up their week's food. There was a small display stand of sports injury supports, so Rose picked out a wrist bandage, which she put on at once, a little ostentatiously.

"You don't have to rub it in, you know," remonstrated Nabeel.

"Rub it in? I think I do. What's that we say about old dogs? And new tricks?"

"OK, I get it. I've learned my lesson."

"I hope so. If that happens ever again, I'm gone. Be sure."

Although her words were strong with the shock of the previous night still vivid in her mind, Rose's heart was feeble. How could she possibly go back, after giving up her home and her job? She would look such a fool. She had to stick it out, and make a go of it. Weighing up the pros and cons, there were advantages in working overseas, although at the moment those advantages were not financial. The chance to set up a new school, to learn a new language, and to extend her own teaching skills with adults were things she loved about her work. Meeting new people, both teachers and students, was at the heart of ESOL and Rose enjoyed that aspect of her work very much. In her heart she set herself the challenge of increasing her financial rewards for her job, so that the little worm of jealousy of other women's lives did not creep in and spoil things for her.

Having filled their shopping trolley they waited in the cashier's line, and paid their bill. A greying, facially wrinkled man packed their shopping into plastic bags with the supermarket logo on them, then placed the bags into a trolley and followed them out of the store.

"Lahza shwoya," Nabeel told the man as he walked over to the taxi stand. Having engaged a cab, the shopping was placed in the boot, and the couple got in. Nabeel gave the porter a tip. The man smiled and showed them the inside of his left wrist, where a dark blue tattoo was visible. Nabeel nodded and said:

"El hamdu lillah."

Rose looked at him in surprise. She knew his words meant 'Praise God'.

"Do you want to go anywhere else?" Nabeel asked as the taxi pulled out of the supermarket parking lot.

"No, just home. I've had enough for one day. But what happened with the porter?"

"Nothing. I tipped him. That's expected."

"No, I mean his tattoo. He showed you his arm."

"Ah yes, it was a Coptic cross. He wanted me to know he was a Christian, like me."

"How did he know you are a Christian?"

"Habibti, don't you get it yet? I'm wearing Western clothes, walking with a Western woman who is not veiled. Am I likely to be a Muslim?"

"OK. But was he Kuwaiti?"

Nabeel laughed out loud. "Of course not! All Kuwaitis are Muslim. He was Egyptian."

"I see. Are there lots of Egyptians here?"

"Yes, and lots of Palestinians, Jordanians, Iraqis, Syrians, and so on and so forth. Kuwaitis are in the minority in their own country. But they treat us well. We don't pay tax and we have free health services. So, *elhamdu lillah*. Praise God."

"For sure, e*lhamdu lillah*."

The taxi driver smiled, as Rose practised her Arabic. She'd learned a lot in her second week in Kuwait. *Elhamdu lillah*.

Dear Diary,

Things are not so bad. We've talked the issue over but I'm still concerned about what he said at the Registry Office. You had it mate. Did he really think I was under his thumb after he'd married me? I don't know if his sexual preferences are normal. Perhaps I should have done more research. I wonder if he's homosexual? Why does he need all that foreplay? And then last night. I daren't even think about that, but it has crossed my mind. Better hide this in case he reads it.

Saturday, 2 October, 1976, Kuwait

The fourth week of their married life in Kuwait had an uplifting start. Raji, the new Indian driver, arrived early in the rental car and knocked on the door to signal his presence. He waited outside while the couple finished getting ready, then drove Rose to the Council. He would return with Nabeel at 1pm to collect her and take her home. Then he would make the trip in the afternoon, depending on Rose's afternoon schedule. The contract with the taxi driver had been terminated.

The Council offices seemed pleasantly familiar this Saturday as Rose climbed the stairs, greeted Samir and the *farasheen*, then made her way to her basement desk. She was settling in, and despite the ups and downs of the past three weeks, she felt secure in this environment. Her six years' teaching and management experience on top of her degree and two teaching qualifications were enough to make her feel confident. Len hadn't arrived but that was to be expected. His family would be settling in to their first week in Kuwait.

Rose started to tackle the tasks she had left on her desk the previous Wednesday. She enjoyed designing placement tests but she wished she had some of the materials she had packed from her previous job in London. Together with the Technical Advisor at the Adult Education Institute she had planned and he had drawn a set of three A4 visuals to elicit written and spoken language from prospective students. Culturally the pictures might be inappropriate, but they would not be offensive. Copyright was a major issue when using visuals in test design. For a few moments she mused over the idea. As far as she could recall, the basic level was a classroom scene with students and female teacher. The elementary level was a street scene typical of London traffic and pedestrians. For the intermediate level there was a set of six pictures illustrating a story. Having spent so much time on this work, it would be a blessing if the packing arrived on time and she could use her own work. Surely, after one month on the high seas it was about to arrive in port? She made a note to herself to ask Nabeel about it at lunchtime.

After a couple of hours Ahmed popped his head in and said "*qahwa?*" in a questioning tone.

Rose didn't really fancy strong Turkish coffee at this time of day. She ventured to say Nescafe and was met with a smile.

"*Naam,*" replied Ahmed, testing her language progress. "*Maa halib wa sukr?*"

"*Maa halib, biddun sukr, min fadlak.*" Rose was able to produce her first Arabic sentence, thanks to some homework with her BBC book over the weekend.

Ahmed smiled happily and went off to get her coffee with milk, no sugar. While he was away Len breezed in, followed by a fair-haired woman.

"Hi Rose, this is Ngaire," Len called happily. "We've just dropped the boys at school."

"Hello, Ngaire, welcome to Kuwait. That's a quick start for the boys, isn't it?"

"Yes," said Ngaire, "they need to keep busy. They've already had an extended holiday, so they have to get back into a routine now."

147

"Which school are they going to?"

"The New English, on Airport Road. Have you got children?" she asked.

"No, not yet, I've only just got married," laughed Rose.

"OK. Enjoy the peace while you can," Ngaire replied drily.

"Yes, yes," cried Len. "They drive you insane, but they keep you young too. By the way, thanks very much for Thursday night's dinner. It was a great treat."

"For me, too," said Rose. "I'm sorry you missed it Ngaire. It was quite a highlight for me after three weeks here."

"Once we are settled you'll have to come over and meet the boys," said Ngaire. "I don't know when that will be though. We have to sort out some furniture shopping today."

At this point Ahmed brought in Rose's coffee.

"Are you going to join me?" she invited.

"Not this morning, we need to get going, or else we won't be able to cook a meal for ourselves, never mind for guests. All we have is a dual electric hotplate so we have to splurge on a proper cooker, or else I'll never be able to feed five men!"

Laughing, the pair went out of the office, leaving Rose to her Nescafe and placement test design. At lunchtime Rose remembered to ask Nabeel about the packing.

"Have you heard anything from the transport company yet?"

"No, but you're right to remind me. It's been exactly a month since they picked our stuff up. I'll contact them this afternoon. Are you working this afternoon?"

"Gosh. I forgot to check with Len. That's so annoying. We don't have a phone at home and I guess neither does he. But I did say that I would do the three night shift this week to make his week lighter with his family. So yes, I'm working tonight, Monday and Wednesday."

"OK. When I pick you up I should have an idea of where the packing has got to."

That afternoon Rose pushed on with her course design, and spent some time reading catalogues so as to choose a textbook series that would suit Kuwait culturally. So many ESOL books used topics and themes relating to the Western way of life, such as dating, going to the pub, and wearing the latest fashions, such as mini-skirts and bikinis. It would not be appropriate to open the new Centre with texts which offended the students. Although there would be a mix of nationalities attending classes, the majority were likely to be Muslim, so their preferences were of the utmost importance, even in this little corner of England.

By the end of the day Rose had some suggestions to put to Len the next day. The book order would have to be placed urgently this week so as to receive the texts by air in time for classes beginning. She and Len would also have to find teachers for the proposed classes. She made a list of jobs for the next day, then went out onto the steps to wait for Nabeel's car to pull up. When he arrived, she could see he had some bad news.

"Is everything OK?" she asked. "Trouble at work? ...with the family?"

"No. It's the packing. The local office hasn't received it yet."

"Really? Is it still on the boat?"

"Yes, but it's coming up the Gulf right now. So with any luck it should be in port next week. Then everything has to go through Customs. That could be a problem. Sometimes they want to check all the books and videos for illicit content."

"Never! How long could that take?"

"You never know. They do what they want to do."

"And will they censor anything they find?"

"Pictures in books get the black marker pen treatment, like the women's magazines you see in the shops here. Tapes would not be delivered, they'd be confiscated."

"Nice. Well, it doesn't matter now, about the placement test, I mean. I've decided to use some visuals I've found in the files. So I'm not worried about getting anything else, except it would be nice to have all my clothes and my household goods. Then there's an opening ceremony for the ETC and I'd like to wear my yellow silk evening dress, with the cape, which Mum made me for me."

"Touch wood we'll get our things by then. I've told them I'm not very happy about it. But at this early date I can't make too much fuss."

"You're right. Let's wait and see what next."

The rest of the week passed by in a flurry of work, with Rose making 'to do' lists even on evenings when she was officially off duty. She talked to Leslie about previous teachers and he gave her a list of names, including wives newly arrived who might be qualified and prepared to do a few hours of part-time teaching each week. She called each one and made appointments for those interested for the following week, when she and Len would interview them together.

Classroom carpets and furniture had to be chosen too. She and Len decided on the classic study chair, with a small writing fold out, which could be raised and lowered, arranged in a horseshoe of 20 students with a teacher's desk and chair in front of a white board. All these things had to be found, ordered and delivered by the end of the month. Rose called the chairs they eventually chose 'Rolls Royce' chairs, not simply because they were well designed, with glistening chrome, light wood writing tables and burgundy mock leather seats, but they were available at the Rolls Royce Automobile agency in town. They were expensive, but they set the tone for a smart learning area. The majority were for right-handed writers, but a few were also ordered for left-handers, or 'south paws'.

The carpet they selected was a cosy and calming mid-blue. Its pile would drastically reduce the echo which had been noticeable throughout the building. Echoes in a language classroom would not be beneficial for listening comprehension tasks or speaking. The carpet fitters came in as soon as the carpet was paid for and did a good job. Only after a month's wear did the outline of a pair of scissors begin to appear in the centre of the semi-circle of seats. It lent humorous reality to the beginner's class teacher's question and answer technique: "Where are the scissors? Under the carpet!"

The white boards and coloured felt tip pens and soft erasers were modern and much better than the old blackboards and chalk which Rose had been used to in the AEIs based in secondary schools in London. Things were looking up in the professional area, she felt. This was where she felt truly at home and could be confident, capable and relaxed. Surprises here did occur, but were not so earth-shattering as those she had experienced at home with her husband.

Dear Diary,

Our new classrooms are looking good. I'm quite excited about the opening of the ETC and the start of teacher and student recruitment and classes. I must write to Mum and Dad with more information about my new life. There are ups and downs every moment, but basically I feel I can survive here with my job and work colleagues.

Friday, 8 October, 1976, Kuwait

By the end of the week Rose felt she had broken the back of the workload, and she was ready to relax. Len had by now purchased his own 'people mover' and proposed that they should all go and find a beach where they could bathe. Beaches on the Corniche, in town, were not suitable for Western ladies to swim from, though lots of Arab men jumped at will into the water all along the sea front. In Salmiyah, there was a large, relatively inexpensive beach club (compared to the Hilton or Sheraton Beach Clubs) called the Messilah Beach, where expatriates and locals could pay an annual fee, or a daily subscription, to use the swimming pools and beach facilities. Some expats headed out of town towards Fahaheel, to beaches where only Westernised Arabs, such as Egyptians, Lebanese, Jordanians, bothered to go with their children. Neither Rose nor Len wished to spend money on a beach club, but they were keen to get into the sea. Nabeel as usual worked on Thursday morning, so the two families opted for a Friday mid-morning rendezvous, when most Muslims would be occupied with their families and the prayer meeting. Len would drive them, so Nabeel's driver could have his day off. They took along soft drinks and water, as well as easy picnic food, in newly purchased cool boxes. It was exciting to be doing something new. Even if Ngaire and Rose could not swim in their swimming costumes because of male observers, they would enjoy paddling in the beautiful blue sea.

The day was warm and dry as usual. Len picked them up punctually and the children all introduced themselves. They were a good-looking, well-behaved crew, aged from 12 to 8 years old. After driving through the quiet suburbs, about half an hour out of town, just before the outskirts of Fahaheel they found the beach Leslie had advised them of. They pulled the car alongside a high wall where a few others were parked, then carried their towels, beach umbrellas and cool boxes over to the beach. The sea breeze was delightfully refreshing, despite the growing heat of the noonday sun. Both women wore sunhats and liberally applied suntan lotion as they installed themselves on towels on the sloping beach. The boys ran madly into the sea, splashing and shouting with glee. There were a handful of adults and a slightly larger group of children spread along the 50 metre stretch of sand. From where they sat they could not be seen from, nor could they see, the road. Len and Nabeel followed the boys into the water, keeping an eye on them.

"It's lovely here, isn't it?" said Rose, running her fingers through the golden sand.

"Yes, it's a real treat to get away from the house," responded Ngaire. "I'm so tired of all the work involved in settling in. It's impossible to do anything on my own as a woman. I have to have my husband with me, or my husband's permission in writing, to do anything. We're trying to get a phone installed. You'd think it was a Herculean task, the bureaucracy involved!"

"We haven't got a phone yet either," Rose told her. "But I can use the phone at work, so I'm not going to bother about a home phone yet. Can all the boys swim?"

"Yes, they were all born on overseas postings. Our last one was born in Fiji. So they are like fish in the water. I don't think this ocean has rip tides, either, so it's quite safe."

"Fiji - that's interesting - quite different from here I would think?"

"The complete opposite. Poor rather than rich, but the people are very open and women are free to do whatever they like. I loved it there."

"So is this a promotion for Len?"

"Yes, it's a good step up for him and we need a good salary with four kids. I can't go back to work just yet, but I hope to."

"Do you teach?"

"Yes, but I'm a music teacher. I'm hoping to find something in a school here."

"More and more English schools are opening up here as the population expands. You might be lucky!"

As the sun got hotter the group took shelter under a couple of huge beach umbrellas while they ate their picnic lunch. Then they all snoozed for a while, as the breeze played over their bodies, warmed by the sun. By 3pm it was time to make a move back to the city.

"Come on boys, T-shirts on, then help us carry the stuff back to the car," cried Len.

Everyone pitched in to help, as tired, sandy and sweating a little they got back into the SUV.

"Oh no," cried Ngaire, as she spotted one of the boys' feet as they scrambled into their seats. "There's oil on your feet!"

Sure enough, the reminder of Kuwait's oil bounty was there on the soles of everyone's feet. Not visible to the eye in the sea or on the beach, it had been lying hidden in the sand. No doubt a tanker loading in Fahaheel had spilled a little in the process. It was strictly forbidden to wash out ships' tanks in the sea, but it could happen without anyone noticing.

"Kerosene will take it off," said Nabeel helpfully.

"But we haven't got any here," Len groaned. "Detergent will do it at home. Just don't rub your feet on the car seats or floor mats, please. I want it to last at least one contract!"

They all laughed, but a small note of rancour resounded in Rose's heart. How long a contract did Len have, she wondered? She was on a yearly renewable one, on local conditions. She began to feel a hardening of resentment towards her lowly position as local wife, married to an Arab. There was obvious discrimination there and she needed to think about how to remedy this position which did not suit her. Although she wasn't ambitious, she didn't appreciate going backwards in the hierarchy of the ESOL career path. After all, she'd been head of department in her last job, as well as Lecturer 2 on the Further Education scale. Plus, she had been interviewed in London for this job in Kuwait. She would have to speak up about it before long, she told herself determinedly.

On returning home, there was the tiring job of washing towels and swimsuits as well as feet cleaning to take care of. An early night seemed just the thing to refresh their happy but tired bodies.

> Dear Diary,
>   I must pluck up the courage
> to talk to Reg about my contract

conditions. I'm beginning to get seriously pissed off about not having an overseas contract. But we had a great day by the sea today and I do like my work. Swings and roundabouts, hey, diary?

Saturday, 9 October, 1976, Kuwait

As she sat down and looked at her desk diary, Rose realised she'd been in Kuwait for a whole calendar month, and at work for four weeks, minus three days holiday for *Eid al Fitr*. Things had improved at home, with the furniture and the driver, and at work plans were moving along nicely for opening the ETC. This week she and Len had several interviews with teachers. The timetable for classes had to be segregated by student gender according to the laws of the land, but the teachers could be male or female. It seemed strange, but it was helpful, particularly when they had no idea which classes would be popular, nor how many teachers or students they might get. Rose made a note to herself to ask Len to advertise the opportunity for extra teaching with the University contract teachers.

Meanwhile, she still needed to complete the placement test, get it proofed and printed, and match the cut off scores to the levels of the syllabus the textbooks embodied. There was a lot to do as the test was important in the eyes of the student, as well as in its function, but the fun would be meeting the students for the essential interview after they had taken the written test. She would need teachers to assist with the student placement test marking and interview process. The textbooks had been promised for the end of the month, with special consideration given to the British Council order. Rose realised that sometimes the words Council and Consul were confused by the listener at the other end of the phone, but while it worked in the ETC's favour, she was not at pains to point out the error!

When Len came in to prepare for the first interview of the day they worked out a schedule of performance questions to elicit as much information as possible from the interviewees. Nevertheless they did not wish to put off anyone, so they planned an informal setting and provided coffee, tea or cold drinks to relax the candidate. In the late '70s there were very few teacher education courses for ESOL, or ES/FL teachers, as they were called then. So most teachers would be primary or secondary trained. What Len and Rose were looking for was a personable character who could bring the English language to life in the classroom, relating it to the needs of the students and getting them to use the language themselves. Lecturers were not wanted in the language classroom.

The first to be interviewed was a primary school teacher from Fahaheel. Fiona had a broad Scottish accent, and appeared to be at ease in her new job and in the desert environment. With her bright red hair, her pale blue eyes, simple cotton maxidress and her sturdy Birkenstock sandals she resembled a missionary in her educational zeal.

"I want to pass on the language to the adults here as well as the children," she asserted firmly. "I'll enjoy meeting some older people after spending all day with the younger ones."

Her expressed teaching techniques and strategies were borrowed largely from the day school classroom, with an emphasis on communication and the use of visuals and songs. Appropriate material for adults was a concern, but Fiona was not dismayed by the question.

"I'll bring in a shopping bag each lesson with items for everyday use."

"Don't you think that will give you a lot of work? How about visuals rather than realia? Have you got any sets of photographs or magazines which you could use?"

"Och aye, the staffroom at school has piles of magazines. I can make some picture sets, cutting and pasting on card."

"That would be great. Would you be happy teaching lower level ladies? We can't be sure right now of the exact levels of students we will recruit. We may have to mix together elementary and lower intermediate for example. We won't know until we start classes, I'm afraid," explained Rose.

"That's all the same to me. I'll be talking to them and giving them little conversations to make amongst themselves. There's no need to fuss about levels."

Fiona had the character traits and teaching ideas which would equip her for the ladies lower level classes. She was also able to come and do some placement testing in the week before teaching started. Her husband was a teacher too, but as Head of Department in his day school he wasn't looking for more work. However, Fiona was a gem. She promised to put the word out in her staffroom about opportunities at the ETC.

"I hope there'll be lots more like her," said Rose. "We need independent, pioneering types. We won't have to worry too much about recruitment then."

Over the rest of the week they met with Elaine, from Basingstoke, on 'housewife' visa status, as she had come out with her engineer husband. She had a degree, a secondary teaching qualification and had worked in a school for a couple of years, so was looking for as much work as possible to keep her busy. She was not impressed with Kuwait at all, so was keen to be amongst the expats at the ETC to retain her sense of self. As a blonde-haired, blue-eyed, attractive young woman she already had her Kuwait driving licence, but had experienced harassment on the roads from the young Kuwaiti men whose only pastime was driving around in their expensive, fast cars. She had plenty to say about her experiences.

"Would you prefer to teach men or women, Elaine?" asked Len.

"Women, please. Not men," she stated firmly. "I get enough stares from the locals. The men go crazy when they see blonde hair. I've thought about wearing the *abbaya* to keep my hair under cover."

"That's fine. We will make sure you have female classes only. You won't need to resort to the *abbaya*."

"Thanks. I'd like the support of a textbook. Will you be getting one?"

"Oh yes, and there'll be tapes for listening skills practice. We haven't received them yet, but as soon as we know which class you'll be teaching you can have the teacher's book, student's book, and class cassette."

"Great. Have you got any grammar books I could borrow? Our baggage allowance wasn't huge, so I didn't carry any books."

"We have a small teachers' library in our office here, and the BC Library has an ES/FL section too."

"Right. I'll go and get a subscription straight after this. If there's morning work available, I'd prefer that so that I can be home when my husband finishes in the afternoons."

"We'll have to see how recruitment goes for the moment. We just don't know. But you can choose to have three evenings, or two evenings a week, from 4.30 to 6.30 or 7-9, or both slots. We've designed the timetable to attract students who have fulltime jobs."

Elaine was the kind of young woman who would cope well with the evolving framework at the ETC so it would be worth facilitating her preferred choice if possible. Other married women like her, and perhaps those with children, would most likely be free only during the day time, but Rose needed to do her teaching hours then too, so that she could be free to substitute for sick teachers in the evenings when she was supervising classes.

Also interviewed that first week, Diana and Steven were an ideal teaching couple who worked fulltime in Fahaheel. They could make the long drive together and would enjoy visiting the big city as well as making some money to stash for their holidays, or for that house purchase back home in Scotland. With her long, dark hair, and his bright orange mop, they were both striking looking and had the character and independence to provide lively lessons which their students would enjoy. It was almost like staging a play, selecting teachers for different classroom levels and genders, thought Rose. Diana was strong enough to manage a class of men, and Steven would be a good role model for his male students.

Although there was not a huge range of qualified, experienced personnel from whom to choose here in Kuwait, by the end of the week Len and Rose had handpicked a dozen teachers they could rely on. Some of the University teachers, like Sara and Daphne from the UK, had come in and offered their services, so there were both men and women available who could take a class. The Uni teachers had the advantage of Master's degrees in TESOL, so they would easily cope with any available classes. As many of them were on single status, they were keen to work at the BC in the evenings to enjoy the different teaching environment. In Kuwait University English was a compulsory requirement in the Faculties of Engineering, Science and Medicine, but not in Arts, Social Sciences and Shariah Law. Uni students varied in their motivation to learn English, and lessons could be quite challenging. At the BC, the part-time salary rate was good, and of course, tax-free as in the rest of Kuwait, so was extremely motivating to those who had come out on contracts with the aim of returning home with a pot of gold in their savings banks.

With the stress of interviewing gone, Rose's attention wandered to her own financial situation. When there was a quiet moment in the office she asked Len about her dilemma.

"Would you support me if I went to Reg and asked him to reconsider the terms of my contract? I'm feeling quite resentful about my status and my pay. I know I don't have a master's degree, but I do have two teaching qualifications and six years' teaching and management experience. I'm getting a basic salary and that's it. Now I've heard what the school teachers are getting I feel worse than before."

"Yes, it's not good enough, Rose. Why don't you go and see him and ask him to consider your status. I think you are in a strong position. We've met no one else like you in our recruitment drive."

Without losing any time, Rose made an appointment to see Reg on Wednesday. If he was upset, he had the weekend to get over it, and hopefully would not be cross with Rose the following week. Even though their paths rarely crossed, Rose didn't want to have to stress about meeting him if this meeting didn't go well. She put her case briefly and succinctly, making her points calmly. She had prepared them in a short supporting memo, which Len had signed. Reg listened, thanked her for coming to him and asked her to wait for him to consider the issue over the weekend. Breathing a sigh of relief, Rose went downstairs and told Len how it had gone.

"So. The die is cast. Let's see what next!" he commented. "Who's on tonight? Is it me? Well, see you Saturday. Have a good weekend!"

As Rose left the building, she wondered if she'd gone too far, asking for a rise after only a month in the job. But if she accepted her status and salary now, it would be harder to complain later. Better to get it over with. Nabeel was outside the gate with the driver. Another week gone, and a weekend lay ahead. What would this bring, she wondered? They had no social engagements, but she had food to cook and books to read, as well as Arabic to study.

She'd be fine. She could write to Mum and Dad and her friend Marie. It would be a weekend for getting settled into a routine of making meals for the week ahead and freezing them. Lasagne was something Nabeel would eat, despite his general lack of interest in food. She'd make a cottage pie too, and spaghetti bolognese sauce. She loved cooking and was gradually building up her spice cupboard contents. Yes, it would be a good weekend.

Dear Diary, I've had a busy week, and now a quiet weekend in front of me. I should be grateful. But I'm a bit worried about Reg's reaction to my request. Nothing ventured, nothing gained I suppose!

Saturday, 16 October, 1976, Kuwait

Back at the office after the weekend, with her new freezer stacked with freshly cooked meals in plastic containers saved from previous takeaway meals, Rose felt a sense of satisfaction. It was good to balance being a careful housewife with her job. She couldn't have coped in this new life without work. Once at her desk she got on with her task list, only to be interrupted by the phone. It was Reg, asking to meet her. They exchanged cordial greetings before Reg launched into his topic, while Rose quaked silently in her shoes. Was she about to be given the sack?

"Now, Rose, about your contract... It's highly unusual to discuss promotion so soon after starting but I take your point about being interviewed in London. Since you are appointed from this office, rather than from Spring Gardens, it does lie within my remit to make any changes I think necessary."

There was a pause, and Rose smiled enquiringly.

"So, having given the matter a good deal of thought over the weekend I have decided to increase your salary by 50 dinars a month and to retitle your job description as Director of Studies rather than Senior Teacher. What do you think of that?"

Rose was ecstatic. She was happy with both suggestions. She had known it was a risk, asking for a change, and she hadn't really any idea what Reg could offer, but this would mean 600 dinars more per year, and more importantly, acknowledgement of her status in the

ETC. She hid her elation but with a smile accepted the proposals.

"That sounds acceptable and much more appropriate. I'm very grateful to you for spending time on this."

"No problem. I don't like hard work to go unrewarded. You've made a good start here. Both Leslie and Len speak highly of you and you get on well with the office staff. So, well done. We will backdate your title and salary as of the first of October."

Rose left the Rep's office floating on Cloud Nine. This was more like it. She had lost her status as Lecturer II, Further Education, and Head of Department for Director of Studies, British Council. The Council had a worldwide career structure, so even if she was still on local status, it was a better fit than before. She broke the good news to Len when he came in.

"That's great. I didn't like to see you unhappy. You deserve the new title and the money. Good job!"

The rest of the morning flew by. When Nabeel came he looked pleased but he didn't know Rose's news yet.

"What has happened? You look like the cat that got the cream."

"Not exactly the cream, but the packing! I heard this morning it's in Customs and I can pick it up this afternoon."

"That's terrific. Wow! Unbelievable. It never rains but it pours!"

"What on earth do you mean? There's no rain expected here for a while - not till winter at least."

"No, it's a saying, an idiom. It means lots of things happen at the same time - good or bad. In this case good."

"OK. So what else has happened?"

On the way home Rose told Nabeel about her 'promotion' to Director of Studies (DOS). Nabeel wasn't as ecstatic about it as she was, since he viewed the change as a minimal increase in salary only.

"The work's the same, isn't it?"

"Yes, but I have the position now. It's better."

"If you say so. More money for more work is what I see."

"OK. Let's beg to differ. Hungry?"

"Not really. Work tonight?"

"Yes, it's my three evening week. Will you go straight to Customs?"

"Yes, I'll clear it this afternoon, and if I can I'll get some coolies and a lorry to transport the cases home."

"That's so exciting. I can't wait to see what they've censored! Not too many things I hope."

After her usual nap Rose returned to work. The afternoon shift flew by and before she knew it, Nabeel was at the door to collect her. By now he knew Samir and Na'maan, as well as Ahmad and the other *farasheen*. He came into the office, beaming for once.

"Well, we got it! I haven't unpacked, but only one or two cases were opened, so touch wood we haven't lost anything."

"Great. Let's go and open the boxes."

The wooden packing crates were in the kitchen and hall and had been opened, but not unpacked. It took some time for both of them to extract the Heal's rocking chair from its packing material, then Rose searched for the uniquely crafted Lebanese leather pouffes, the only other items of furniture they had brought with them, while Nabeel pulled books, tapes and clothes out of the other boxes.

"They're not here. The pouffes. And where are the pictures? The Utrillo reproduction from Dad and the roses painted on glass from Marie? I can't find them."

"Really? We've opened everything now. Perhaps there's a box missing."

"Isn't there an invoice? Or a packing list? I don't recall having one myself. I left it to you in all the rush. Isn't there a record of what they packed?"

"I can't remember either. So much was going on."

"But what about insurance? Did you get any cover for our stuff?"

"No. I don't believe in insurance as you know. It's just a ploy to get money out of people by creating fear. I trust Panmarina. I'll speak to their office tomorrow and see what the story is."

"OK. Perhaps it's just an oversight."

"At least we've got our things. And I've got my clothes. But I can't face organising things any more tonight. Let's call it a day."

With a sense of relief they climbed into bed that night. Things were settling, even though sometimes it felt like one step forward, one step back. What was it Einstein said? Life is like riding a bicycle: You have to keep moving forward to stay on! Or something like that.

Dear Diary
   Our packing is here! Some important items missing, and yet

again, Nabeel found wanting on the admin side, but I'm to blame too. I should have paid more attention. Let's hope tomorrow the mystery is solved.

Sunday, 17 October, 1976, Kuwait

While Rose went to work, Nabeel went to the shipping company's offices to discuss the non-arrival of some items. As he reported to Rose that afternoon he did not meet with any success. No one could explain where the leather pouffes or the pictures had gone. It was uncertain whether the items had left London, so they might have been stolen by the packers, or from the warehouse where they were crated. Nabeel was extremely angry, but there was nothing to be done. However, to recompense him for the loss and to retrieve their reputation which was now tarnished, Panmarina did not charge him for the shipping. Rose was extremely disappointed by the news despite the financial saving. The pouffes from Lebanon were unique designer items, while the pictures had sentimental value. Nevertheless, she had her clothes to look after. She spent the afternoon hanging them up in the wardrobe and organising her chest of drawers. She was especially pleased to have her yellow gold silk evening dress in time for the ETC opening ceremony in two weeks' time.

That week at work was hectic, finishing off test materials, syllabus documents, and checking on the books which were delivered. Students would pay a fee for this term which included their student textbook. A local bookshop arranged to stock the text in future, to reduce the workload on the ETC. Rose made sure the master cassettes were copied, and the originals stored in the library. Recruitment and placement of students was advertised in the local press and on the TV and radio. Refreshments would not be provided for students, but teachers were allocated a staffroom with a kettle with which to make their own drinks. A small fridge was also brought in for cold drink storage. Everything seemed ready to roll for recruitment week when Rose left the office on Wednesday night.

Once again her weekend was quiet, with cooking, cleaning and language to study. Rose was hoping to be confident enough to use her Arabic with the students who had no English at all. She asked Nabeel for help with pronunciation practice and made sure she knew the words for 'test', 'level' and 'class'. She practised the sentence "You must take a test." *Laazim fih fass* is what Nabeel advised her was the correct Arabic translation.

At that point in her life in Kuwait Rose did not know that for any word in English there is a range of translations in Arabic, either classical or colloquial, and in addition there are regional variations for many words. The language of the Muslim holy book, the *Qu'ran* (*el karim*) is in Arabic which cannot be changed. Muslims memorise this language for their prayers. Modern Standard Arabic (MSA) is the educated form of Arabic, which is spoken by TV announcers and schoolteachers. Students have to learn to read and write MSA, which has a complex grammatical structure, as well as diacritical marks to indicate the short vowels in words. These marks are not printed in newspapers, which makes it challenging for students of Arabic to decipher newsprint. Texts which teach Arabic to foreigners do include these marks to assist in transliteration and reading.

On top of these two formal versions of Arabic, there are four major spoken variants of Arabic. They correspond with the following geographic areas: Egypt (*umm iddunya*, or mother of the world, because of its ancient civilization) and Sudan, the Arabian Gulf countries, including Saudi Arabia and Iraq, North Africa (Algeria, Morocco, Tunisia and Libya) and the Levant (Lebanon, Palestine, Syria and Jordan). An example of the differences in pronunciation in the four areas is the word for coffee, *qahwa*, pronounced with a guttural /g/ in the Gulf, a solid, but less guttural /g/ in Egypt, and /k/ or no sound at all in the Levant and North Africa. Whichever variant a learner chooses to study there are also variations in vocabulary. For example, an Egyptian calls a towel *fouta* whereas a Palestinian refers to a towel as *manshafi*. They each recognise what the other is talking about, but produce their own preferred word. So much to learn, as yet unknown to Rose.

Dear Diary,
A big week ahead, with student recruitment for the Centre. I hope it goes well. I need to show that I deserve my promotion. I'm going to dress up for the opening ceremony. It's a special occasion.

Saturday, 23 October, 1976, Kuwait

Rose dressed carefully for work, aware that she would be meeting students for the first time today. The morning hours for placement testing were 10-12am, with only Rose on duty for testing as there would more likely be only a few students who could study in the morning hours. Other teachers were coming in from 5 to 7pm to test the students who would wish to study from 4.30 to 6.30 or from 7 to 9pm. She went down to the office to bring up papers, pencils, marking keys and registration documents for the morning testing hours. She checked with Samir that he was ready with his assistant to take fees and help her with the administration of the tests. The classroom on the ground floor close to Samir's office was selected so that he could be on call at any moment to help her.

By 10am she was seated in Room 1, ready to welcome students. About half a dozen ladies appeared sporadically over the next hour. Rose seated them and handed each the objective test sheets and a pencil. A glance at the paper with its example item informed most of the women what they must do. However, one of them, a middle-aged, heavily made up lady, looking very nervous, wrote her name in barely legible English then stood up and came over to Rose, who smiled at her. Now was the time to use her rehearsed Arabic sentence. *"Laazim fih fass,"* she announced clearly, pointing to the example test question.

At that, the lady looked at her in amazement, while one or two of the others raised their heads from their work.

Again, Rose repeated her mantra. *"Laazim fih fass."* At this, all the ladies began to giggle.

Rose was surprised - something was funny, but she didn't know what. She called Samir, and told him what she'd said. He laughed out loud.

"Do you know what *fass* means Rose?" he asked.

"Isn't it 'test'? That's what my husband said."

"It's close but not close enough - it means 'fart'. So 'you have to fart' is what you are telling these ladies! You need to say *fahss*. The h sound changes the meaning!"

Rose collapsed into giggles too. Now the whole room was rocking with laughter.

"Well, that was a good lesson in Arabic pronunciation. Thanks very much! I won't forget it."

Rose's *faux pas* with Arabic not only broke the ice with the 'beginner' ladies, but it also made her a role model for them. If the teacher was learning Arabic, then they should try hard to learn English. Rose was to be their teacher in the morning, and she was delighted to find she had a class of 10 ladies from 10 to 12am on Sundays and Tuesdays. On Saturday, Monday and Wednesday, she had a parallel class of male beginner students. Although they had more face to face class hours, their learning was slower than the ladies, which matched the research findings that the average male learns languages with more effort than the average female. Class preparation was simpler for Rose with two classes at the same level, so she was relieved by the registration of 12 men. Some of them had to get permission to attend class during work time, but most of the students were either looking for work, in which speaking English would help them, or were running their own businesses with a need for English language.

Over the whole week registration was successful. There were sufficient students to create lower intermediate, intermediate and upper intermediate classes for males in the afternoons over the week, and lower and intermediate classes for females. Rose rang teachers as the classes became viable, and teachers began coming in to collect books and tapes and to check their student rolls. Work was going to be busy from now on, it was clear. With a teaching load of 10 morning hours, and the usual evening duties, time would fly. Rose felt her life was now really beginning in Kuwait, after the previous weeks of preparation. First of all, though, there was to be the opening ceremony, with the Minister of Education coming to the villa in Mansouriyah to do the honours at 4pm on the first evening of teaching.

Dear Diary,

So much to do this weekend. I need to buy a set of little coffee cups and saucers and a set of tea glasses as well as those tiny teaspoons used to stir sugar in the doll-sized vessels. I'm going to use them in my first lessons on Saturday and Sunday, at least.

Saturday, 30 October, 1976, Kuwait

The first morning of teaching arrived after Rose had spent a busy weekend preparing her first class. She was planning to teach *some* and *any* with countable and uncountable nouns, using tiny coffee cups, tea glasses, teaspoons and saucers, as well as tea, coffee, sugar and milk in containers, so as to extend her teaching to 'there isn't much coffee'/'there aren't many cups' if some and *any* were already familiar to the students. One of the problems with starting a new class, even after a placement test, is the fact that each student is an individual with different individual knowledge of grammar and vocabulary. On top of that, each student's needs and motivation for learning were different, so planning a lesson with interesting content was always a challenge. Given the importance of drinking tea and coffee in Arab culture, Rose hoped both the men's and women's classes would enjoy the lesson. The men's class went well, but Rose only achieved the first aim with them, whereas the next day with the women she achieved both her aims, the ladies enjoying talking about the realia introduced into the lesson. After teaching the class, Rose had to tidy up, write lesson notes ready for the next lesson, then go home for lunch and prepare for the afternoon classes and the official opening of the Centre.

As the weather was mild in the afternoon, the short ceremony was to be held at the top of the external flight of steps leading up to the villa entrance. Reg would make a speech about the role of the ETC and the British Council in Kuwait and other countries. Then the Minister would make a speech, followed by his cutting of the red satin ribbon which would be tied across the glass doors of the building. A pair of scissors was to be handed to him, and to make it more ceremonial the scissors were to be placed on a small cushion resting on a tray. The problem was no one had a suitable cushion, or at least, no one remembered to bring one. So at the last minute, Rose, who had come back to work wearing her gold silk evening gown with its gold and ivory silk-lined cape, to add some glamour to the occasion, had to fold up her cape and use it as the cushion. Her shoulders were showing as a result, but the gown was not low cut, so there was no comment or outcry, though Rose noted that her photograph did not appear in the next day's newspaper report on the occasion!

Non-alcoholic cold drinks were offered after the ribbon was cut, but guests quickly disappeared to go about their normal weekday business. Rose went to change into her work clothes, putting away her dress carefully and not forgetting her cape *aka* cushion! All had gone to plan. Afternoon students and teachers had observed the ceremony if they were early, if not, they carried on planning for teaching their first class of the term. This term would be eight weeks long, terminating just before Christmas on Wednesday 22 December. There was no national holiday for Christmas, but New Year's Day was an official holiday, so the timing was just right for teachers to enjoy the festive season. There would be a two-week break between terms, with the second term starting in early January.

Dear Diary, Well, the new Centre
has been launched and classes
have started. All good at work.
Now to improve home life.

Thursday, 25 November, 1976, Kuwait

The weeks began to take on both a steady sense of routine while at the same time they began to fly by. Nabeel was able to get his driving licence at last so he could drive the rental car and dismiss his driver. As before Nabeel dropped and collected Rose on a daily basis. From time to time, however, he called on a Jordanian friend of his, Salem, to do these duties if he had early appointments in Ahmadi, the oil town south of the city. Salem was a short, gentle, softly spoken man of about 35. He had no wife, and probably very little prospect of finding one it seemed as he earned very little as a driver. Nabeel introduced him to Rose by inviting him for coffee one Friday. Rose was able to practise her Arab hospitality skills: First, offer a cold drink, next, offer fruit or sweets, cakes or biscuits, lastly, offer coffee. Offering coffee first was tantamount to asking someone to leave, although Nabeel explained that Palestinians also had the concept of 'welcome' coffee - *ahla wa sahla* - as in the West, but it had to be explained as such to the guest. Rose was delighted to learn a new expression from Nabeel as she set the food in front of their guest: *Mid idak*, Nabeel said. *Mid idak,* copied Rose, and Salem laughed. She thought it was because speaking Arabic was a novelty. She found out much later it was another mistaught lesson.

During that first term of teaching one student in particular became close to Rose. Her name was Amira (princess) because she was indeed a Princess from a noble

Kuwaiti family. As in so many cases which Rose would read about, and occasionally meet, later in her life in Kuwait, fathers were very proud of their status and were reluctant to allow their daughters to marry a man who was not of the same rank, or who did not have a similarly sized bank account. In Amira's case she had been compelled to wait until her forties to marry. Only after her father's death had her mother been able to find a suitable partner for her daughter. He was not from the royal family, but he was a kind, still handsome and wealthy businessman. He and Amira lived in a splendid palace but maintained a simple, loving life of companionship together. There would be no children from this union, but there was certainly happiness, as Rose witnessed when Amira invited her home for lunch with their husbands.

This was a very special occasion for Rose and also for Nabeel. Kuwaiti families kept themselves very much to themselves. Kuwaitis were a minority group within their own country: In 1976 there was a total population of just under a million, of whom roughly two thirds were expatriates from Arab, Sub-Continental and Western countries, as well as *bidooun jinsiyah*, mostly nomadic people with no passport, i.e. stateless. Amira, a wealthy Kuwait lady of middle age, had been learning English with Rose as her teacher for five weeks by the end of November. She had struggled with grammar and accuracy, but like so many wealthy housewives, was reasonably fluent on account of her daily practice with her English-speaking housemaids and houseboys from the sub-continent.

Rose's Arabic had not progressed very far, but with Nabeel in attendance at the luncheon, there would be no problem with communication, she guessed. In fact, Amira's husband, like so many Kuwaiti businessmen, spoke good English. As a result, the lunch party was a great success. At first Rose and even Nabeel had been overawed by the opulence of the palace and extravagance of the interior decor. There was enough gilt and sparkle to equal Louis XIV's style. In contrast, Amira's warm welcome and bright smile, together with a friendly simplicity in her manner, made them feel at home.

After a chilled juice in a huge sitting room, the four went into an equally large dining room, where the table was set for four people, but was loaded with serving dishes and chafing dishes with enough food to satisfy a party of 25. As is the custom with Arabic hospitality, Amira personally served Rose, while her husband served Nabeel. Both hosts urged more and more food upon their guests, until there was absolutely no room for another morsel to pass their lips. The dishes were meticulously presented and tasted delicious. There were fresh vegetable and salad platters, long green beans in tomato sauce, lasagne with aubergine instead of meat, as well as lasagne with meat sauce, since Amira had remembered Rose's food lesson, when she had taught the word 'vegetarian'. There was roast lamb with *biriani* rice, stuffed courgettes in warm, creamy yoghurt sauce, and ladies' fingers (*okra*) in sweet chilli sauce, spicy but not too hot.

It was impossible for Rose to recall all the dishes, since so many could not be tasted. It seemed rude to stare at the incredible array of food in front of them. After the savoury food came half a dozen sweet dishes, including trays of *baklava*, but most memorable was a silver tureen, filled with a creamy, pistachio nut-laden bread and butter pudding called *Umm Ali*, Ali's Mum. This simple English dessert was interpreted in a new way for the Arabic menu. It tasted delicious, even if Rose could only manage to taste a small dessertspoonful.

The meal took two hours as the women had chatted and lingered over the food, enjoying and discussing the different dishes and their recipes. The two men had discussed business, but they were in different fields of operation. Amira's husband was in retail, specialising in luxury cars, while Nabeel was in supply to the petrochemical industry. Turkish coffee was served in the sitting room and then farewells were said. Rose could not express her thanks adequately. They had brought with them a splendid bouquet of flowers for the hosts but it was small thanks in comparison with the feast they had been treated to.

"Wasn't that amazing?" asked Rose as they passed the guard on the palace gate.

"It was very special, Rose. Not many people get to see Kuwaitis inside their homes. You are very lucky to be treated so well."

"I feel overwhelmed by the personal attention she gave to our enjoyment. I thought she would be formal and stand-offish. I don't think we'll ever be able to thank them."

"Don't worry, Rose. In the Arab world, teachers are prized and respected. It is an honour to have a teacher as a friend, and especially a British one."

"I see. Well, that's very nice! What a wonderful experience."

Dear Diary, We had lunch in a royal palace and ate with a real Princess. It was a luxurious but also an enchanting and intriguing experience. A rare insight into how the other half lives!

Friday, 3 December, 1976, Kuwait

In the Islamic Calendar of religious festivals, two months after *Eid al Fitr* comes *Eid al Adha*, the Festival of Sacrifice otherwise known as *Eid al Kabir*, the Big Festival. It celebrates the occasion when Abraham offered to sacrifice his son Ishmael to God, an event which is recorded in the Holy Bible too. Some liken it to Christmas, as it is a time when people prepare their houses for visits by spring cleaning, they buy new clothes and give each other gifts. It is a four-day holiday which that year fell on the weekend, giving only one additional day of vacation to the ETC fulltime staff. Part-time staff were not paid for holidays, and their classes were simply lost, they were not made up.

Rose made no special plans for the weekend as Nabeel would be going to the office on at least one day and she had exams to prepare for the end of the month. Students and teachers expected to have achievement tests to assess their levels for the following term, and she was the only one who had the time to make them. She took all her books and tapes home to prepare a reading and listening test for each level, together with a short objective test of grammar and vocabulary. There was no time to train students or teachers for writing or speaking assessment. The thrust of most classes was the acquisition of reading and listening skills through speaking, so testing could be kept to a minimum but needed to have face validity. Rose knew she was in for a long weekend of work, rather than a holiday.

As Rose had been too busy to go food shopping with the driver on Thursday, just before midday on Friday Nabeel went out to get a rotisserie chicken for a quick and easy lunch. While he was out there was a knock at the door. Rose was surprised. She had no idea who it could be. Perhaps it was the female neighbour from the flat opposite? Cautiously, remembering the Peeping Tom, she opened the door a little to see who was there. She was stunned to find that it was Edouard, Nabeel's older brother, holding a large bouquet of flowers. Rose didn't know what to say. What could have brought him here? Rose was at a loss to know what to do. She was aware that a woman alone could not invite a male into the house, but this was her brother-in-law. Did the same rule apply, she wondered? In addition, the lounge was a complete shambles. She had her books and papers spread out all over the chairs and coffee tables. There was hardly room for a visitor to sit down. She had to appear calm and polite, nevertheless.

"Hello, Edouard. How are you?"

"Fine, thanks, Rose. Is Nabeel here?"

"No, he's just gone out to get our lunch. He'll be back in a few minutes. He's only gone up the street."

"OK. I'll wait in the car till he gets back. These are for you."

"Thanks so much. You'll see him come home I'm sure. If not, I'll tell him to come and find you."

Rose breathed a sigh of relief as Edouard turned and went to his car parked outside the building. At least she could create a space for their visitor to sit down. She rushed into the kitchen to put the flowers into water.

They didn't have any vases. This was the first time flowers had entered the flat. So she cut an empty plastic water bottle in half to make an impromptu container and then tried to tidy up the lounge. After several minutes of hectic activity Rose was relieved to see Nabeel come back, followed by Edouard. Nabeel had recognised his brother's car. Neither man was smiling. What on earth was going on she wondered. The two men went into the lounge and sat down opposite each other.

"Would you like a cold drink, some coffee or some tea, Edouard?" Rose asked, following them.

"No, thanks, Rose. Asma is expecting me for lunch in a few moments. I came to invite you both for lunch with us on the holiday tomorrow."

Rose almost fell over with shock. She sat down next to Nabeel. An invitation to go home was not what she expected, nor did Nabeel from the look on his face. He spoke Arabic to his brother, none of which Rose understood, but she sensed his mood. He was not accepting the invitation, it was clear.

Edouard spoke in English again to Rose.

"Asma sends her best wishes to you Rose. She's sorry not to have seen you yet."

Rose replied calmly, "Thank you. Please give her my best wishes. I'm sorry not to have seen her too."

Nabeel closed the polite conversation down as his brother stood up.

"Well, see you in the office, Edouard."

"Thank you for the beautiful flowers. Goodbye," said Rose.

"Bye, Rose. Happy Eid."

"Happy Eid to you too!" she replied.

When Edouard had left, Rose asked for full details of what had transpired between the brothers. It seemed that Rose's work at the British Council was known to the wider family in Kuwait and relatives had been asking when they would get to meet her. The family were embarrassed to say that they were not on speaking terms, so they wanted to bring the couple back into the fold to avoid any unpleasant revelations. Of course, Edouard had not said that overtly, he had simply asked Nabeel to forget the past and come back to the family. Nabeel had refused. He was not going to let them get away with treating his bride so rudely, nor himself. He had suffered a loss of face in being shown the door so peremptorily in September. It would take more than a bunch of flowers to redeem the situation in his eyes. As they ate lunch, Rose reminded Nabeel that despite everything the family were his only close relatives. Nabeel agreed and told her of an Arabic saying, brothers may fight against brothers, but brothers united must fight against cousins, and cousins united must fight against the rest of the world.

"In that case, are you thinking of softening some time in the future?" she asked.

"Let's see how it goes. I've had to do everything on my own to make our life here, and now they want to be friends?"

"Well, perhaps they were testing us. Think about it. Not for tomorrow, but perhaps for Xmas?"

"Perhaps."

Dear Diary,

This holiday has been mostly work, but there was a surprise: Edouard came to see us. Nabeel surprised me even more with his rejection of the overture, again showing me that I still have a lot to learn about this man.

Wednesday, 15 December, 1976, Kuwait

The first term of the newly opened ETC in Mansouriyah had progressed successfully and was now ended. Sometimes in the afternoon and evening, as Rose made a tour of the corridors outside the classrooms she would smile to herself. The students in Diana's and Steven's rooms were evidently studying at the Scottish Council as their repetition drills proved. Number drills practised with the pictures in L.J. Alexander's *First Things First* were pronounced with a strong, rolled 'rhotic' /r/. The students chorused thirrrty one, thirrrty two, thirrrty thrrreee, after their teacher's model. The end of term exams went off quite well, though most teachers reported cheating incidents in their classrooms. It seemed that 'helping each other' was the reigning motif so students found it almost impossible to stay silent for an hour at a time. They were constantly whispering to each other instead of raising a hand to ask the teacher a question. Rose circulated amongst the classrooms, encouraging teachers to take a relaxed approach to the 'testing' event. Most students had no problems with their achievement tests, but borderline cases were carefully considered, and to use Len's terminology, a little fudging was sometimes applied. Negative reactions to the test results could seriously affect next term's registration!

Christmas Day 1976 was to fall on Saturday, a working day, so the weekend beforehand Rose went to some effort to make festive snacks for the staff room. She found, to her amazement, fruit mincemeat on the supermarket shelves, and was reminded of a student's funny story in London of making spaghetti Bolognese sauce with a jar of sweet mincemeat, thinking it was 'minced meat'. She bought a couple of tart pans and made mince pies. She didn't bother with making a Christmas cake but decided they would eat the top layer of their wedding cake instead. It had arrived safely in the packing and thoughts of saving it for their first child's Christening were no longer in Rose's mind. The past three months had rather dashed her hopes of a happy married life with children as the inevitable outcome. Even now it seemed a struggle to keep going, given the relative compartmentalisation of their lives. They were both hardworking and their different jobs kept them apart from each other for long days.

Work was the only thing that kept her going. She had no leisure activities at all, and no close female friends, although she got on well with everyone at work. Talking to the University teachers had shown her how much more advantageous their situations were. Daphne and Sara, two young British women who had travelled extensively with their work previously were now enjoying their lives in Kuwait. Their master's degrees had given them not only professional status but worthwhile material benefits. As a result Rose was considering how she would be able to get a master's degree. The only option for attaining a postgraduate distance degree at that date was through London University, but candidates had to be graduates of the University. As a Postgraduate London University Teaching Diploma holder, Rose might have had a chance to bypass that requirement, but she wasn't one to push at the boundaries. She needed a second Bachelor's Degree, in English this time.

The Christmas season was celebrated by the expatriate Kuwait University teachers with parties in their furnished apartments. Uni teachers only had to provide soft furnishings. Rose and Nabeel went to two parties given by Sara and Daphne. Rose was impressed with the exotic décor in their homes, with souvenirs of their earlier posts overseas. Len had become very cross about the level of mundane administrative support he had to offer to some of the teachers, referring to himself not as ELO (English Language Officer), rather as English Loo Officer! It seemed plumbing was the major weakness in the free accommodation. Older apartments did not have adequate sewage pipes, resulting in blocked loos on several occasions, which the bachelor status female teachers expected him to sort out. It was common to see a notice posted inside the toilets: 'Please dispose of toilet paper in the bin provided, NOT in the toilet.' This could be disconcerting, if not disgusting. Some of the high rise apartments, however, were delightful, with sea or city views, and Rose sensed a little worm of jealousy creeping into her heart. Their own ground floor apartment was far from delightful, and after the Peeping Tom incident, Rose had never felt safe. She decided on another project for the new year: a new apartment.

On the Wednesday before Christmas Reg gave a drinks party for all the staff, including the part-time teachers, and it was a pleasure to meet his wife. They were a charming, elderly couple, with a faint tinge of the British Raj about their home and their attitudes. Sherry was served, as well as glasses of beer, gin and tonic and scotch and soda water. There were trays of finger food: prawn vol au vents, sausage rolls, pinwheel sandwiches and cheese cubes on cocktail sticks, circulated by the younger *farasheen* dressed in waiter's uniforms. It was a pleasant occasion, mingling amongst colleagues, and surrounded by lovely artefacts all around the house: brass trays, copper coffee pots, silk Persian carpets hanging on the walls, Nain blue and cream wool carpets on the floors in different sizes and shapes. There was a low divan sitting room where the younger teachers gathered to chat, as well as a more formal sitting room furnished with sofas covered in bright orange and pink woven Iraqi carpets. These were quite garish but in a completely white room, with marble floors, white walls, and ceilings, they provided a vivid splash of colour.

This time not only the setting but also the alcohol provided a spur to Rose's aspirations for the New Year. She had to learn to make her own wine and beer as the Uni teachers did. There were plenty of recipes in circulation. She just needed to begin brewing. But if they were going to move apartment this would be a dangerous liability. Transporting alcohol as well as making it was punishable by deportation after flogging. So that would have to be put on hold.

While planning for Christmas festivities Rose needed to send cards to Mum and John, Dad and his wife and daughter, as well as Bill and his girlfriend. Mail took at least a week, so Rose wrote her cards, apologising for the lack of gifts this year. She expected to be able to make up for this in the coming year, but made no promises.

Things might be improving but they were by no means perfect yet.

> Dear Diary,
>   Christmas is different this year – first, it's not an official holiday, second, there's no Christmas spirit at our house!

Thursday, 23 December, 1976, Kuwait

On the weekend before Christmas Rose felt more than a little glum. There was no point in making a special meal for Saturday, the big day itself, and the mince pies and small top layer of her wedding cake were small compensation for missing what Rose considered the best meal of the year. She loved Brussels sprouts, a traditional British winter vegetable, and despite her vegetarian tendencies, she enjoyed them with a slice of turkey breast, sage and onion stuffing and gravy with roast potatoes, mashed swede and carrot, and creamed potatoes. Rather wistfully she wondered what they would eat: another rotisserie chicken dinner for the two of them? They still had no oven, just a hotplate for warming soup or making Turkish coffee. She would go to the Co-op as usual and see if there was anything different they could buy. There would be no ham or bacon or sausages, as all pork products were *haraam,* forbidden in Islam. *Basturma,* a cured, heavily garlic-flavoured beef salami looked inedible to vegetarian Rose but she had noticed some small glass jars filled with tiny black eggs - surely they couldn't be caviar? The low price suggested not - but perhaps they were worth a try.

As she was making her grocery shopping list for Friday, a knock came at the door. Nabeel wasn't due home for a while. Who could it be? She wondered if it was Edouard again, and opening the door, she saw she had guessed right. Once again he carried flowers, but this time also a large basket of sweets wrapped in cellophane paper and tied with a red bow.

"Hi, Edouard. How are you?" she asked politely with a smile.

"I'm fine, Rose. Is Nabeel still at the office?"

"I'm not sure. He's due back soon for lunch. Come in."

"Look, I won't come in, but I just want to ask you to try to help us. We want you to come for lunch on Christmas Day."

"But it's Saturday, a working day, isn't it? No break for Christmas in Kuwait, I thought?"

"Yes, but we will eat quite late. What time can you be free?"

"We're doing minimal hours on Saturday, with no evening duties, so I'm free from 1pm."

"Well, just do your best with Nabeel, please. We would really like to see you for lunch."

"OK. I'll try, but I can't promise anything."

"These are for you," he said, proffering the flowers and sweets.

"Thanks. That's very kind of you."

"See you on Saturday, *inshallah (God willing).*"

"*Inshallah,*" she replied as she had learned to do.

As soon as Nabeel came home Rose told him about the invitation to his brothers' home. Nabeel was astounded.

"How dare he come here! Why didn't they ask me at the office?"

"Perhaps they thought it would be easier to talk here. He brought some lovely flowers. Look! And sweets too!"

"Flowers and sweets don't speak so loudly as actions. They treated us badly. I'm not going to forget that easily."

Rose realised that hunger might be stressing Nabeel. She resolved to raise the matter the following day, when perhaps emotions would be less high. At least he hadn't thrown the gifts out!

Dear Diary,

I need to get a vase because I've received my second bouquet from the in-laws! We've also had an invitation to Christmas lunch. I'm happy to go, but Nabeel's pride is still wounded. So let's see what next! I'm ready to forgive but perhaps I won't forget.

Friday, 24 December, 1976, Kuwait

The next day, Friday, Christmas Eve, Nabeel was home, reading the *'mulhaq'* (illustrated newspaper supplement) so Rose went into battle with her two new objectives: finding a new home for them and more pressing, visiting the family for Christmas lunch. She raised the topics after a late breakfast of *mana'eesh,* a delicious flat bread, soaked in rich olive oil and spices, including thyme (*zaatar),* oregano and sumac, topped with a sprinkling of crunchy sesame seeds. She had first eaten it in Beirut but now it became their traditional Friday breakfast, which Nabeel could collect while going out for his newspaper.

The *mulhaq* episode had been a learning event for Rose. Daily newspapers were sold at road junctions by paperboys. Drivers would call out the name of the newspaper they wanted while waiting at the lights. Nabeel always shouted *'mulhaq'*, which she assumed was the name of his preferred newspaper. But she noticed that each day the Arabic header on the newspaper he was given was different. Was there a paper called *'mulhaq'*? On questioning him she found to her amusement that instead of being committed to reading one particular newspaper, Nabeel preferred to buy the paper which offered a pictorial news supplement. Was it his level of Arabic literacy that guided his choice she wondered? She daren't question him on that! But Rose realised that she would not learn much Arabic if she relied on Nabeel to teach her. She needed to get into the family to be able to soak up more information. She broached the lunch invitation first.

"Nabeel, why don't we accept the invitation from your brothers? It is Christmas, the season of brotherly love after all. Does it really matter that we had to wait a while to be accepted? They needed time to think about it."

"Yes, but they are only doing it so that they don't lose face with their friends. Other people have made them feel ashamed. And your being at the British Council is a key card in the game."

"Game? Is this really a game? Surely it's about being with your family at this important time of the year. I love Christmas and I am missing my family, so why not be with yours?"

"Well, I suppose I should be thinking of you. If you would really like to go to their house, I suppose I should try to forget the past."

"Exactly, that would be a wonderful Christmas present. If I can forget the way they treated us, then surely you can?"

"OK. I'll go to the office and call them later on so that they can prepare for us."

"What will we take for them? Do you buy presents for each person at Christmas as we do?"

"No, not really. We don't bother. But I'll get some Samadi pastries as a special treat - everyone loves those. In fact, you should come and see the Samadi shop. You haven't been there yet, and it's like an Aladdin's cave of sweet treats."

"That would be lovely. Thanks for thinking of something new for me to do."

Rose was surprised by Nabeel's attitude. He seemed to have completely reversed his position, from resistance to acceptance in one brief moment. Never mind, it was the result which counted. She looked forward to the trip to the pastry shop later that afternoon.

The Samadi pastry chain of shops was an institution in Lebanon which had spread to Kuwait. Everyone bought their *baklava*, in endless varieties, and their cheesecake, as well as their handmade chocolates, and nut-encrusted Turkish Delight and nougat. The shop in Salmiyah was a wonderland for Rose. It would take a lifetime to sample all the sweetmeats on offer. They bought a selection of pastries, carefully packed in an elegant box, as well as a large box of chocolates. Everything looked so delicious and smelled so sweet, it was a mouth-watering experience to be in the shop.

"I can't wait to try what we've bought tomorrow!" said Rose.

"But you must be careful, Rose, they may not open these boxes in front of us. It is not polite to open gifts in front of the giver."

Rose was amazed! How could that be? However, considering the issue and recalling how sometimes at birthday parties and Christmas tree present opening sessions, people had to pretend to like what they received, she decided it was probably a sensible cultural practice. There was no need to pretend to like what you had been given! You could open your gift in private and complain about it if you didn't like it! She would have to hope that since these gifts were obviously food, they would be opened and shared by everyone, otherwise she wouldn't get to taste the goodies they'd bought. It was going to be a magical mystery ride on Christmas Day, quite different from any other she'd experienced. She hoped it would be happy and peaceful with goodwill to all men - and women!

Dear Diary,

It's Xmas Eve but the strangest one I've ever had in my life. Some of the shops have stuck cotton wool snow on the windows, and strung tinsel around too, but there are no Xmas carols playing in public. We are going to the family house tomorrow, so I'm excited but nervous too. The weather is cool, so I'm going to wear something Christmassy, but I can't think what at the moment. Must check my wardrobe. I have to work in the morning, so not too dressy I guess.

Saturday, 25 December, 1976, Kuwait

Christmas Day was a short working day with cooler winter weather, so Rose dressed in a green corduroy skirt, with a red velour top and red leather flats. She put a red ribbon in her hair and her gold-framed antique cameo brooch on the front of her top, adding some red plastic clip on earrings, a trend of the late 1970s. The morning at work was pleasant, with everyone thinking about the afternoon festivities in their own homes. Len in particular was busy with family plans. As a Roman Catholic he had already been to Midnight Mass at the big church near the Sheraton Hotel. All four boys had attended Mass with their mother and father, and obviously, presents were on their agenda. Both families were on tight budgets so no cards or gifts were exchanged, nor with office staff members, most of whom were Muslim.

Rose drew some holly leaves and berries on the whiteboard in their office in an attempt to mark the day as different. She no longer believed in the Holy Trinity, although accepted that historically there was evidence of a Jewish activist who had tried to revise the Judaic religious tradition. When applying for her visa before coming to Kuwait she had been advised to state Religion: Christian, Sect: Anglican, since the Kuwaitis preferred 'people of the book' rather than atheists or agnostics. However, she knew she fell firmly into the latter group, and was moving steadily into the former as she matured. As Karl Marx had said, *Religion is the opium of the people*. Having studied

Sartre and Existentialism during her French Honours degree program, she was aware that most people had a dread of the nothingness that existence without religion presents. Rose could frighten herself on occasion if she let her mind wander over the spinning blue ball hanging in space which human beings live on. But most days the business of daily existence didn't give her time to dwell on matters of 'being'. While some adopted Buddhism as their philosophy, Rose had already worked out a theory of goodness. I believe in Good, was her creed. She wondered about Nabeel's family's religious practices. Would they say 'grace' before the meal? Had they been to church last night? How much would she find out about them today? Perhaps it would be a polite but superficial occasion. Perhaps there would be a big row. She hoped not.

At 1pm sharp Nabeel arrived to collect her. So that they could go straight to the family house for Xmas lunch he had taken their gifts to work with him and kept them fresh in the work fridge. Rose began to feel a little nervous as they drove towards the villa she had entered once before just three months earlier. The memory of that unexpected rejection was still vivid, but she pushed it away, and focussed on what was to come.

"So who will be there for lunch?" she asked.

"Well, there should be the whole family: my brothers Henri, Edouard and Adel, and of course, Asma my sister. Hakima, our Egyptian secretary might be there too. She and Edouard had a bit of a fling a few years ago, but she is Muslim and a marriage with a Christian is not acceptable to her parents. But they are still good friends."

"Right. So she's the only one I haven't already met."

As they pulled in and parked beside the garden wall, Rose began to feel really nervous. Nabeel was not relaxed either. They both obviously had total recall of the events of September. They held hands as they walked up to the double wooden doors. This time when they walked inside, there was a cry of welcome from the three men who were sitting in the lounge. Asma was in the kitchen, but she came out to meet them when she heard the others greeting them. "Merry Christmas," "*ahlan wa sahlan*," were the greetings exchanged as the men and women exchanged the traditional 'French' three kisses on the cheeks. How natural it now seemed to be with these people, compared with the frozen atmosphere of only three months ago.

Rose had been worried that Nabeel might be standoffish and cause a row. Instead, he dropped into what had previously been his normal stance as 'baby' brother with his siblings. Although Adel was the youngest, Nabeel had been the spoilt child. Anecdotes were told during the afternoon about his weak health as a child. He had grown very quickly as a young boy, and there was a threat of him 'outgrowing his strength' in those World War 2 years. In the early '40s, the war years, there had been food shortages in the Levant, and by 1948, when Israel was created officially, the family were refugees in Lebanon. They had had very little food to eat some days, so Nabeel had been given vitamin supplement injections by the Red Crescent. He recalled the ignominy of being held up to a window as a small boy, his pants pulled down, and a needle inserted in his buttocks.

Rose recalled the small bottles of cod liver oil and concentrated orange juice which families with children were given in the post-war years in the UK. In their six years of getting to know each other in London Nabeel and Rose had often found they had experiences like this in common, despite their different cultural and geographic backgrounds. Their shared knowledge of French language, culture and literature had created a bond between them, especially in their enjoyment of French films and literature.

After sipping a little of the drink Edouard had poured her, a surprising and delicious, scotch, ice and soda water, Rose went to join Asma in the kitchen. Without a servant and the only woman in the family it was obvious Asma needed a helping hand. Rose had met her in London when she came on a one month visit, so there was some familiarity between them.

"What can I do, Asma?" asked Rose.

"Please clean the parsley for me," Asma replied in her well-modulated, low voice.

"Right. I'll take off all the big stalks. Is that right? Like this?" Rose checked her instructions by demonstrating.

"Yes, that's perfect. I'm going to put it into the soup."

"OK. What kind of soup is it?"

"Meatballs in chicken broth. They all like it."

Rose was a little dismayed. Meatball soup for a vegetarian didn't sound appetising. She didn't like to mention that she never ate red meat and she didn't know if the family remembered her food preferences. Their visits to London had been few and far between. Christmas turkey was one of the meals Rose relaxed her vegetarian principles about. At home Mum made a delicious stuffed bird, with loads of vegetables, including Rose's favourite

Brussels sprouts. She wondered what else was on the menu, but didn't like to ask. Luckily Asma was forthcoming.

"We're having soup, then roasted chicken with roasted potatoes, and *tabbouleh* salad, and *beitinjan* and *zahra mittleh.*"

"*Beitinjan* and *zahra mittleh*? What's that?" asked Rose.

"Fried eggplant I think you call it in English, and fried flowers."

"Oh, I see, that's aubergine and cauliflower. That sounds delicious." Rose had not tried those vegetables fried before. It was going to be an interesting meal.

"For dessert I have made an English trifle. Specially for you."

"That's very kind of you, Asma. Thank you. I'm looking forward to lunch."

In fact Rose was already hungry and she could see from the state of the kitchen that lunch was not going to be ready for at least another hour. Rose had left her drink in the lounge and it seemed there wouldn't be a chance to enjoy it, there was so much to do in the kitchen. She popped back to see what Nabeel was doing: The brothers were playing cards and speaking Arabic. Nabeel didn't even look up, he was so engrossed in their poker game. Rose returned to the kitchen and carried on with the vegetable preparation. After Asma declared the meal ready, she swept and mopped the kitchen floor. Rose had been amazed to see that vegetable peel and other food waste was just dropped on the floor instead of being placed in a bin. So that was the routine. It was a habit from a time long past, perhaps. Eventually, lunch was served at 3pm, by which time Rose was ravenous. She was even prepared to eat meatballs to satisfy her hunger.

The dining room was narrow but long enough for a table which seated 10 people. They were a group of six, but Rose noticed that two extra places were set. Following her gaze, Edouard told her that Joseph and Claudine were expected for lunch. Rose had completely forgotten about Nabeel's other brother, who had married a French girl they had introduced him to in London He hadn't been mentioned at all, so Rose had simply thought they were no longer in Kuwait. In fact, they had returned for Christmas, and were expected at any moment. No sooner were their names mentioned than they appeared!

"Talk of the devil," cried Nabeel. "Where have you been till now?"

"Is this a hotel?" asked Edouard drily. "You must have smelled the soup."

"*Bonjour,*" said Claudine gaily, paying no attention to the intended criticism as she greeted the men but came to kiss Asma first, then Rose on the cheeks, three times, in the French way.

Joseph too embraced the women in French style. Charming and handsome as ever, he was wearing tan Bermuda shorts and a white Crocodile knitted cotton golf top, with white leather boating shoes. Claudine was in a fashionable flowered cotton dress. They both smelled of smoke: They'd probably put out their cigarettes in the garden just before they came in. Asma was radiant now, smiling, her happiness complete to see her obviously favourite brother. Rose wondered why no one had mentioned that they were coming? Probably Nabeel had not known.

Rose knew Claudine from her stay years earlier in the same London bed-sitter house as Nabeel. A typo on his business cards had erroneously but humorously stated: Blackburn Palace. The building had 14 separate bedsitting rooms, each with washbasins and cooking facilities, but shared toilets and bathroom. It was typical of London student accommodation at the time. Claudine had come over from France to learn English. She had worked in a shop near Gloucester Road Tube Station until she met Joseph, fell in love, married and moved to Kuwait where the family had treated them as they treated Nabeel and Rose: They ignored them for a few months, then gave in and forgave them.

"How are you, Rose?" asked Claudine as she sat down at the table.

"Fine, thanks. And you?" responded Rose politely. "Are you staying here for long?"

"Ah yes, about a month, we are enjoying some sunshine, and we are sending our boat to Cannes. It's pointless leaving it here now we have a marina berth over there."

Rose could see that Joseph and his wife lived a completely different life from her own. In light of that, she found it difficult to keep the conversation going. Luckily there was no need to talk, as the food was served. Two large, covered, porcelain tureens were brought to the table. The dinner service was an elegant matching set, with a large dinner plate, a side plate and a soup bowl for each place setting. The family served themselves from the tureens, and Rose realised Nabeel was watching her take some soup with a couple of meatballs. She smiled at him pointedly raising her eyebrows, silently warning him to say nothing. The broth in which the small balls were floating was clear and light, flecked with parsley which gave a tasty vegetable flavour to the meatballs. There was another flavour which she couldn't quite distinguish which made the soup seem oriental. Biting into one of the meaty morsels Rose realised they were made of very finely minced lamb mixed with *snobar*, pine nuts and cinnamon. The dish was delicate and delicious. It was also satisfying, so her ravenous hunger was assuaged to some extent.

The brothers had brought their whisky glasses to the table, and Nabeel had also brought Rose's. Joseph had served himself and Claudine while the soup was being brought to the table. As one, before dipping their spoons into their bowls they raised their glasses in a toast to Asma, their sister, housekeeper and cook, who did not drink at all. Asma smiled demurely. She spoke little at the table, while the men ate silently. They too were very hungry it appeared and served themselves second helpings until the tureens were drained. Rose breathed a mental sigh of relief. She'd put in a couple of hours' work in the kitchen and she was ready now to relax and enjoy the rest of the meal. The men picked up the soup dishes and took them back to the kitchen, while Asma prepared the main course for the table. Joseph and Claudine went out into the garden for a cigarette. Rose had a quiet word with Nabeel while the others were away from the table.

"Don't mention my being vegetarian," she warned. "I

don't want to upset them. There's plenty for me to eat, and you know I like chicken occasionally."

Nabeel was relieved. He seemed quite different in this family setting. He even looked physically smaller with his three tall brothers, Henri, Joseph and Adel, beside him. Edouard was smaller in stature. Both Asma and Edouard were petite, shorter than Rose. Rose had met their other sister in Beirut three years earlier when they had gone there for a two-week holiday. Marie was tall like her brothers. So five of the seven siblings were tall, while two were short. However, Nabeel's usually cocky attitude had changed. He seemed quieter and less sure of himself. There had no doubt been some words exchanged while Rose was in the kitchen with Asma.

After a few minutes Adel appeared with a large serving dish laden with pieces of roast chicken. They were sprinkled with cinnamon, pine nuts and minced meat, the stuffing which had been cooked in the birds' cavities. Clearly the soup meatballs were the same recipe, which explained its intriguingly exotic flavour. A clever idea, Rose thought, to make a stuffing and use the excess to make a soup. The fried vegetables had been warming in the oven and draining off excess oil on cooking paper with the cooked whole chickens, and were now brought to the table on plates decorated with parsley and sprinkled with cracked pepper. Rose enjoyed the meal as did everyone else. Water was drunk when the whisky glasses were emptied. The drinks had been generous, and Rose knew that each had cost a lot of money, so she did not miss the glass of wine she would normally have enjoyed with a Christmas meal.

After the dishes for the main course were cleared Asma suggested they might have a break for digestion before eating dessert. Rose took the hint that this might be an appropriate time for the ladies to do the washing up. There was no dishwasher in the kitchen, and in fact, at that time, very few people in England had one, so Rose had not expected it. When she had been in the USA for Camp America after finishing her first degree studies, she had noted that everyone had a dishwasher, and the material standard of living in the USA was so much more advanced than in the UK. Claudine made no move to go into the kitchen. Instead, she waved a freshly manicured hand, with an ostentatiously large diamond ring on it as an excuse to stay in the lounge. While washing up together Rose thanked Asma for the delicious meal.

"You know, Rose, I was very sorry we didn't welcome you before."

"It's alright, Asma. It's forgotten now."

"I just want to tell you that we didn't know Nabeel was marrying you. He didn't tell us. So we weren't prepared when you arrived here."

Rose almost took a step back, she was so shocked. Nabeel had told her a completely different story. This was a most surprising turn of events. Who should she believe? Her husband, or her sister-in-law? She realised that she shouldn't allow this to become an argument, so said nothing. She simply murmured, "Oh, dear." Asma didn't pursue the topic, and Rose didn't wish to question her further, though later in the car going home she would raise the subject with Nabeel. Having put the dishes away, the women joined the men in the lounge. This time only Nabeel and Adel were there. The others had gone for a rest. Rose looked at her watch. It was almost 6pm.

"Would you like to take a rest on my bed, Rose?" Asma suggested.

"No thanks, Asma. I have to work tomorrow, so I need to go home soon."

"But not before dessert, surely?" insisted Asma. "We'll serve it now, with some Turkish coffee. How do you like your coffee?"

"Saada," replied Rose, making both Asma and Adel laugh. Rose was bemused. What was funny?

"So you've started learning Arabic, Rose," Adel commented.

"Of course, I need it for work, as well as for my new life here."

"You'll find most people speak English here," Adel warned her. "You won't get much chance to practise."

"Don't worry, I've already had practice at the Council. Can I come and watch you make Turkish coffee, please, Asma?"

Asma was surprised but pleased, while Rose was thrilled to watch the two *briks* being filled with finely ground coffee, flavoured lightly with ground cardamom or *heil*, one teaspoon for each cup, then one had a spoon of sugar for each cup added, while the other had no sugar for those who preferred *saada*. The *briks* had to be boiled and then the coffee was brought back to the boil at least three times, Asma informed her, though five times is best, she advised her.

Back in the lounge with dessert and the coffee cups on the tables beside them, the family resumed the discussion of the need for Arabic. Rose felt she needed to remind them that she had a job and she didn't need to depend on them to learn Arabic. Claudine, however, supported the opposite argument.

"Oh, you know, I never bother with Arabic, it's just not *necessaire*." She mingled her good English with the occasional French word as it pleased her.

"Even if it's not necessary, I want to learn. I love learning a new language," exclaimed Rose.

"Well," said Adel, "at least we won't have to have the UN translation service here when we watch Arabic TV together!"

Rose smiled. So there was an expectation that they would be back at the house. The job was done for today then. They made their excuses about work and said their farewells.

"What about New Year?" asked Edouard as they were leaving. At this, Joseph came into the conversation.

"You have to all come to us on New Year's Eve. We'll have a typical French *Reveillon*!"

"Yes, that's right! It will be superb! We'll see you next Saturday then. *Au revoir*!" added Claudine.

Dear Diary,
What a surprising Christmas Day! We had some good food and drink, and met Joseph and Claudine again. I haven't seen them since before they were married.

And we're going there for New Year. Things are looking up on the family side. Touch wood. And I learned how to make Turkish coffee!

Saturday, 31 December, 1976, Kuwait

The week had been a quiet one at work, the lull before the storm of the new year and the planned four ten-week terms for 1977 which would start in mid-January. There had been a planning meeting to discuss whether the Centre could manage five ten-week terms, or four 12-week terms over the year. Both these options gave little wiggle room around national, school and university holidays. The part-time teachers would be taking statutory holidays in summer, i.e. July and August, so it seemed safer to opt for 40 weeks of teaching. Start and end dates could be adjusted as the year went along to suit the religious holidays.

Of course, Rose also had a party on her mind, and what to wear was her top priority. She had two evening dresses which she had brought from the UK. She was considering whether to wear her silver lame dress, bought for only ten pounds sterling in a little shop in North London when she was doing her Postgraduate Diploma, or her gold satin dress, made by Mum, with the cape that had played a role in the ETC opening ceremony. She had silver as well as gold sandals to match each dress. As it was a home-based party, she opted for the silver lame dress, which didn't have a jacket. It was flattering, as she was slim and tall at 5' 8". She hoped it would give her the confidence she needed to visit Joseph and Claudine's home, which she felt sure would overwhelm her with its opulence, judging by the size of Claudine's diamond ring.

Rose had only her gold wedding band and a gold dress ring which Nabeel had given her after his return from the 'kidnapping'.

Saturday was a working day, but as there were no classes and the next day was a holiday, the Council closed at lunch time. So Rose went home for lunch and a nap, before dressing for the party. Nabeel had picked up a lovely bouquet of flowers and a box of chocolates from Samadi. They set off as advised to arrive at 9pm. It was going to be a late dinner and a long night. Joseph and Claudine rented a penthouse apartment (only Kuwaitis could own property in Kuwait) in an ultra modern building, the Marzouk Pearl, right on the Corniche, with its own boat marina. This made the building especially suitable for 'boaties'. It was the first of its kind in Kuwait, and was regarded as one of the best places to live for expats. Even some Kuwaiti bachelors had apartments in the building so that they could lead their bachelor-style lives well away from their family home lives.

Joseph had been a successful businessman in Kuwait both before and independently from his brothers' firm. With his wealth and contacts he had set up the trading and contracting company to help his brothers, and he still held a share in the company, though he kept his business affairs completely separate. Henri was the oldest brother but he had none of the physical attractiveness nor the charm of his younger brother Joseph. However, Henri had not had an easy life, and he had done his best to make his own way. He had been obliged to fake his age at 14 to go as a manual labourer to the newly discovered oil fields in Saudi Arabia. Sadly, the money he had earned he had spent mainly on himself, only giving his housekeeper sister, Asma, some of his earnings when he was back at the family home in Beirut. Nabeel hadn't told Rose much of the detail, but Henri was a gambler, and a selfish, greedy person. Joseph was the complete opposite: generous and kind to his brothers and sisters.

Nabeel and Rose parked in the visitors' parking zone and walked along the spacious walkways to the building entrance. It was elegant, with a duty porter who greeted them and the lift was modern, unlike the one in the brothers' office building. They took the lift to the top floor and found themselves in another spacious lobby with a wide corridor leading to the apartment. The double doors were exquisitely carved hardwood, with a splendid brass Hand of Fatima decorative door knocker, as well as a doorbell which Nabeel pushed. Joseph came to open it, expansive, smiling and beautifully dressed in a smart white shirt with a bowtie. Rose had paid no attention to what Nabeel had put on, but he liked to dress well, so he had chosen a grey double-breasted suit and lavender silk tie. They both looked at their reflections in the ceiling to floor wall mirror as they entered the apartment. They had done well: They looked smart. Rose didn't have any expensive jewellery, but the silver lame dress didn't need any. Her silhouette was slender, her hair glossy, dark and long. She felt pretty and happy. Things were looking up in her new life.

Asma, Adel, Edouard and Henri were all in the lounge. The apartment was designed like an American movie set. There were steps down into the sunken lounge seating area. The decor was orange and beige, following the 1970s trend. The ceilings were high, and there was a staircase up to the second level where the bedrooms were. Claudine was not in the kitchen. She was seated, smoking, wearing a gold-coloured gown, similar in style to Rose's, tight and clinging to her figure. She was petite and not very well endowed in the bust, but the dress flattered her small frame. Her bleached blonde hair was long, and she had a close-fitting skull cap made of gold mesh. The effect was striking, *a l'Egyptienne*, she called it when Rose complimented her on her look.

Obviously Claudine was able to enjoy the exotic nature of her life in Kuwait. She didn't work, so pleasure seeking was her daily objective. Joseph gave her everything she wanted, and at weekends together they spent time on their boat. They were studying to get captain's licences, as they were planning to move permanently to Cannes in the coming year. They had purchased two apartments and two boat berths in Cannes Marina, and planned to rent one out for income. Rose thought to herself that if French law was the same as British, they would also need to pay the taxes they would incur on Joseph's savings when their domicile was no longer Kuwait. Clearly they had spent some time working out their future plans.

Rose felt a tinge of jealousy that they were looking forward to a life of leisure in France while she and Nabeel were at the start of their working lives in Kuwait. However, Joseph had worked long and hard for this early retirement. He was a lot older than Claudine, and around ten years older than Nabeel but he had put in the hard yards much earlier when he was only a teenager. Really, Nabeel was the spoilt baby of the family. He had been sent to the UK for his English education, and had only just started working with the family in his thirties. So, she couldn't complain. She had made a choice and she needed to make it work.

Rose's musings were interrupted by the cry in French, *'A table'*. While they had been having drinks - icy, bubbling, scotch and soda - the family had discussed the language issue. Claudine and Rose spoke both French and English. All the family spoke French because they had been educated in French in Beirut. As Christians, Greek Catholicism was their sect and as Lebanese, a former French colony, French was their second language.

Asma had 'kitchen' English, picked up through having an Indian maid. Adel had studied for a Civil Engineering degree at the American University of Beirut (AUB) so his English was impeccable. Neither Joseph, Henri nor Edouard had a tertiary qualification, but had acquired their English language skills through their business dealings, and conversations with many acquaintances and friends, but Nabeel had spent six years in England, first improving his English at a language school and with a work placement in a factory, then pursuing studies for a Higher Diploma in Marketing at the College in Westminster where he met Rose.

It was a family joke, Rose found out that evening, that Nabeel had had trouble even achieving his Baccalaureate from the *Freres Maristes* secondary school. The brothers joked that Nabeel refused to kiss the Bishop's ring, and never accepted the doctrine the priests taught, so they wouldn't give him a pass in his subjects to allow him to graduate from high school. Privately Rose wondered whether his atrocious handwriting, which she had seen when he wrote to her before their marriage, had had anything to do with his failures in school. His writing was almost illegible, as he mixed upper and lower case alphabet letters at random!

As they sat down at the long, elegantly decorated table, Rose realised it was now 10.30pm. She was hungry, even though she'd been nibbling the pistachios and cashew nuts which were set out on the side tables in the lounge. Claudine had placed goblets filled with silver balls and candles along the length of the table. The centrepiece was a large goldfish bowl filled with silver balls and tied with silver ribbons. They had crystal wine glasses, and with great pride, Joseph served everyone with a French white wine, a delicious *Pinot Gris*, chilled to perfection.

"Smuggled in especially for you guys," he stressed.

Rose knew that there were rare opportunities to obtain French wine on the black market. However, the foreign embassies and expatriate staff appointees were allowed to bring in wine, and sometimes it found its way out to friends and clients. The wine was delicious, and the family toasted their host and hostess with it.

"Salaamtak, ya Joseph! *Salaamtik, ya* Claudine!"

The first course was presented to them on square white china platters: a trio of sliced smoked salmon with lemon wedges, a Turkish coffee cup of caviar with crisp crackers surrounding it, and three of the biggest peeled prawns Rose had ever seen, piled onto a small mound of mayonnaise. It was a feast for the eyes and mouth. The preparation meant that finger bowls were not needed.

It was a real treat and the wine complemented the food perfectly.

"How on earth did you manage to get real caviar?" Rose asked. "It's such a rarity, even in England. Did you import it?"

"Well, kind of," replied Joseph. "But not from France. It's from Iran. They produce some of the best caviar, and the Iranian car-cleaners bring it in on boats across the Persian Gulf, and sell it cheap. So enjoy!"

Rose felt embarrassed that the cost of the caviar had come up. Of course it was terribly expensive, but politeness did not allow the issue of money to be discussed! She hoped she hadn't upset her hosts.

"I've seen some black fish eggs in little pots in the supermarket; what are they?" she asked.

"I'm afraid if you try them you'll find they are very salty, and the artificial colour runs. They are coloured cod's roe, not sturgeon eggs. Iran is as famous as Russia for caviar: They produce Beluga, Sevruga and Ossetra. We just take whatever we can get. This is Sevruga."

"It's so delicious. The prawns must be from here, is that right? We haven't bought any yet," Rose admitted.

"You are missing something fabulous. You must go and get some as soon as possible. They are plentiful and not expensive," Joseph explained.

Rose noted that Asma was picking at her food, while the men were eating greedily, enjoying the meal. Claudine, too, didn't seem to have an appetite. Rose took her time, trying to match her consumption to the other two women. She didn't want to look unladylike. After everyone had put down their forks, Claudine began to clear the plates. Asma and Rose got up to help her. The three of them went into the large kitchen and helped stack the dishwasher and get the plates for the next course ready.

"We are having *Coquilles Saint Jacques* next," Claudine informed them. "I have to grill the top of the dish, that's all. They are ready in the oven."

"Are the scallops from the Gulf?" asked Rose.

"Of course, and I have prepared them in the French way, with a white sauce and gratinee with cheese and breadcrumbs. I hope you like it."

"It sounds fantastic. Do you like cooking?" Rose asked Claudine.

"Not at all. I never cook. But this is *Reveillon*. I 'ave to do it for you all."

Asma smiled and thanked her. "*C'est tres gentil, cherie,*" she told her sister-in-law.

Rose could see that the ice which their marriage had created had been broken between the two women. She wondered if she would be able to say the same in a year's time.

"*Voila!*" Claudine opened the oven door wide and pulled out a baking tray with eight scallop shells on it, brimming with savoury sauce, and trimmed around the edge with piped *duchesse* potatoes, lightly browned. The effect was stunning, and the smell was extremely appetising. The scallops were served with garlic bread and a green salad *a la vinaigrette* with olives and sliced radishes as a garnish. A cheese platter followed, with a wide selection of soft and hard French cheeses and fresh baguette slices. The meal was light, but satisfying, and the various courses took time to eat, so that there was no pause in conversation, either about the food, or about Claudine and Joseph's future plans. The women took charge of moving used dishes to the dishwasher and bringing out fresh plates. Rose realised the kitchen was extremely well stocked, compared with her limited range of crockery. All the men and Claudine too, had cigarettes between the courses. Rose wondered how they could spoil the taste of the food. Perhaps that is why Claudine didn't eat much, her appetite was suppressed by smoking. It didn't bother Rose. She enjoyed the meal immensely. After the last savoury dish, Rose noted it was almost midnight.

"*A minuit*," Claudine announced, "we will have the *Buche de Noel*, with champagne!"

"*Magnifique*," cried everyone. "Champagne and cake too!" As they spoke, they saw their watches move to twelve so everyone stood up and kissed each other on the cheeks. "*Joyeux nouvel an!*" they all cried as they embraced each other. It was a happy and festive moment.

"*Maintenant*, our cake and drinks." Joseph opened the champagne with a loud bang, the cork nearly hitting the huge mirror at the entrance. "*Attention!*" cried Claudine. "We don't want to break anything when we are renting the flat furnished!"

Rose realised that although her new brother- and sister-in-law were leaving, they were keeping the flat in their name and subletting it. So they would gain an income there too. Clever ideas, she mused to herself. She could learn a lot from their plans.

As they ate the delicious chocolate sponge cake, covered with white icing and silver *dragees*, to match the table setting, and sipped the slender flutes of champagne, Rose realised they looked like any other European group of people who had the best of everything to hand. There was no suggestion of any kind that they were celebrating the start of 1977 in a Muslim country, in the Arabian Gulf. How surprising was that? If this was a taste of how life could be, then she was happy. It suited her very well. She and Nabeel needed to work hard to achieve the same sort of life style as Joseph and Claudine. And she would begin by changing their apartment. She'd had enough of living in fear of a Peeping Tom. That was at the top of her list of New Year's Resolutions, for sure. As they drove home at around 2am, Rose raised the subject with Nabeel.

"You know, it would be so much nicer to live in a better place, don't you think?"

"What do you mean by better place?" Nabeel asked, apparently amazed at the thought of the flat not being acceptable.

"Somewhere safe, where I don't feel scared of going into the kitchen, wondering who may be peeping through the curtains when I open them."

"I guess you are right. Let's talk about it in the morning. We should rest now."

> Dear Diary, I've opened up the subject of a new home, but I don't know if Nabeel realises how much I hate this flat.

New Year's Day, 1977, Kuwait

Rose and Nabeel woke late on New Year's Day, a national holiday, unlike Christmas Day. For once, Rose felt a little excitement cause a flutter in her stomach. She had enjoyed the previous evening and had a glimpse now of the future she might be able to enjoy with Nabeel. It was quite different from the depressing beginning to her married life in Kuwait. Now she needed to make some resolutions and get her plans into action. She had always made New Year's resolutions, and prided herself on achieving at least one goal each year. 1976 had been a strange one: a new life, a new job, a new culture and language to learn. She needed to work on her new goals: to move to a new apartment where she didn't feel scared and in the realm of her personal professional development, to find out how to obtain the master's degree qualification which she needed so as to either obtain an overseas contract position at the Council, or at the University of Kuwait.

Nabeel went out to get *mana'eesh,* and as they had breakfast, drinking the Nescafe which the TV ad proclaimed was the drink of the *rajul najih* - the successful MAN, not woman - Rose raised the topic of a new apartment again.

"You know, I still feel scared here. The neighbour opposite obviously doesn't have time to be friendly as she's busy with her two young kids and I haven't even seen the other people in the building. Every time I go into the kitchen I relive that spooky moment when I saw the

Peeping Tom. And, to be quite honest, I hate the memory of that awful row we had in the bedroom. Plus, this is the apartment we had to get with the help of a waiter, with my advance salary, and no happiness in our hearts. I'd like to leave it all behind and start again, now that we are back in the 'bosom of the family' as it were."

Nabeel listened while smoking, a sign that he was thinking hard.

"OK," he said, "You're right. It's not a good place to live. I can't bring any business visitors back here, it's not good enough. So I'll have a look round for somewhere else. I have had to sign another contract so we may not be able to move until April."

"Well, better late than never." Rose was glad Nabeel had worked out his own rationale for moving. The end justified the means!

He continued: "And you know what? I think it's time I got my own car. I've had enough of that awful little rental."

"That's great," agreed Rose. "What have you got in mind?"

"Why don't we go and have a look at cars in the showrooms today?" Nabeel suggested.

"That's a great idea. It will mean we both have achieved something. Can I tell you what else I am considering?"

She explained her goal of achieving her master's degree.

"You know how upset I was to be treated as a local at the Council. I was lucky to get the salary increase and new title, but if I have a master's I could probably get an overseas contract, either with the Council or the Uni. I finished my bachelor's in 1970, and by now I expected I would have been studying for my MA. But here it's not so easy. I need to find out which universities offer distance learning courses. Distance courses are just starting up, and they would suit me. What do you think about it?"

Rose knew Nabeel would have to agree if she was to begin studying at home after work. But he worked long hours, and so it shouldn't bother him, she thought.

"Well, I'd be happy if you were thinking of studying instead of working but I don't think you should work at the same time. It would be too much. I also have a small worry that you might become too big for your boots, *les bottines de Caroline*," he told her. This phrase from an old French children's book often cropped up in Nabeel's conversation.

Rose was amazed at this notional opposition to her desire to improve her qualifications.

"What on earth do you mean?" she asked him.

"You know, you might think I'm not good enough for you," he told her reluctantly.

"I can't believe you think that. When have I ever talked about my qualifications compared to yours? Has that ever entered my head, do you think? The only problem we had on that score was when you were looking for a job, and you were overqualified! Remember your application to be a dishwasher?"

They both laughed as they recalled that difficult time when Nabeel was doing nothing but go for job interviews in London. With no income from his family, and living on Rose's salary at the AEI, Rose had suggested he just get a part-time evening job in a restaurant to make him feel independent. He'd been turned down as over-qualified! Their mood lightened, Rose returned to her idea. "So, can I go ahead and find out about degrees?"

"Of course, do what you want to do. I suppose you will anyway," he said, rather begrudgingly. "Now let's go and look at cars."

They went out to the Al Ghanem Motors showrooms, which surprisingly, were open on this holiday. Obviously other folk were interested in buying new cars, so there were quite a few people around. American cars were much cheaper in Kuwait than in the UK, and the range available was huge. There were stocks in abundance, and each new season brought a huge advertising campaign for new models. Cars were a symbol of the family's living standards and Kuwaitis prided themselves on having the latest models. Some of the customers in the showroom were upgrading their cars. There was no lack of choice: from GMC utility vehicles to Toyota (pronounced 'toota') sedans, with a fair sprinkling of luxury sports cars, especially Corvettes for the younger men who liked speed. Taking advantage of the opportunity to try different models Nabeel and Rose climbed in and out of cars for a good hour or so. In the event, they chose a Chevrolet Impala four-door sedan, in two-tone blue, Rose's favourite colour. It was going to be available in 24 hours, after being brought in from the stock kept in the desert, and getting registration and licence plates from the Ministry of Transport.

"Let's go and have a coffee to celebrate," Rose suggested. "It's been a great day, and I can see we'll have a good year. Happy New Year, darling!"

"Happy New Year, *habibti*! Sheraton Coffee Shop, OK? We can have some lunch."

"Do you want to tell the brothers about your new purchase?"

"No, I'll leave it till I have the car. I'll have to buy sweets to ward off the 'evil eye' then."

"Really? That's the superstition? How amazing."

"At least I won't be cutting a chicken or rabbit's neck, putting my hands in the blood, and marking the car body with the hand, the symbol of Fatima."

"Oh no. I hope I never see that."

"*Hatt n Shuuf.*"

"Sorry?"

"Wait and see! It's a common practice here."

Rose shuddered and closed the subject as they found seats in the Coffee Shop and ordered lunch. As she sat down Rose suddenly remembered something important.

"You know, it's Mum's birthday today. She's 49, not old at all but in such pain. I hope she got my card in time as well as our Christmas card."

"When we get a better flat, she will come and visit us."

"I hope so. That would be lovely, but the flight might be too much for her. Anyway, I hope she's doing OK."

"We missed our Mum when she died. I was only little but I knew she had gone. It was so sad. She was 28. Life can be hell on earth, so let's do our best to be happy while we can."

"Yes, my poor little refugee orphan. I'll look after you now. Keep your *bottines de Caroline* clean, please."

Nabeel laughed. "*Touche.* You've seen me wipe my shoes on my trousers, haven't you!"

"I've got a writing teacher's eagle eye, remember. So be good." They both laughed.

Dear Diary

Well, we are moving along in the material world! A new car — it's lovely. Life will surely start to improve now.

Sunday, 2 January, 1977, Kuwait

The first month of the new year passed quickly at work, with students returning to register in a higher level class and new students coming for placement tests. There was a steady rather than phenomenal growth in numbers, so enough teachers were available to cope with the increase. The development of the curriculum and creation of new achievement tests fell entirely to Rose because Len became more and more busy with his outside work. He was involved not only in the University and several committees there, but he was also invited to join the Ministry of Education English Department curriculum development group.

In the office, Len's stress showed in the explosion of his use of the F word, a swear word which Rose had never used. She never swore because her childhood home life was free of expletives. At university she had been amazed at her flatmate's use of curse words. 'Jesus, Mary and Joseph!' or 'Jesus wept!' were the most blasphemous, which had been uttered once in a lift with two shocked nuns present. Ngaire obviously disapproved of Len's habit, which probably was not new, but had been controlled till that point. Len realised he had to find a way to break it, so he began to tally his usage on the metal cupboard doors with chalk. Rose found it amusing, but the tallies were tricky to explain to the casual enquirer. Also, hearing the F word up to 20 times a day familiarised and normalised it, so that she became aware that under pressure she might use it. Nabeel's worst curse words were 'bloody' and 'bugger', but combined in a novel way: 'bloody bugger'. Rose found those amusing too, but she hadn't committed them to her own usage as yet.

At work Len and Rose were determined to improve their Arabic. Both were independent learners, picking up phrases on the daily circuit, picking out appealing sounds, and getting Arabic speakers to help them translate their usage. One day Len came back to the office with an amusing anecdote from his Ministry curriculum meeting. He had sat through most of the two-hour session, which was conducted mainly in Arabic, without comprehending more than a couple of words. His face must have shown his boredom, so his new colleagues asked whether he agreed with the issue they were debating and recommending so as to give him a chance for input. The question was in English, but Len decided to impress the committee with his use of Arabic. He banged on the table to show his enthusiasm and commitment, shouting *Taabaan!* which he intended to mean, *of course.* On hearing this word, everyone stood up and rushed over to him, a glass of water was brought and he was asked if he needed a doctor, all this to Len's complete amazement. He assured everyone he was well, so they asked why he had cried out that he was ill? *Taabaan,* with two long a vowels, means ill, whereas *Tabaan,* with one short /a/ vowel and one long /a/ vowel, means 'of course'. Len never muddled those two syllable words again!

Rose began her own list of malapropisms too. The weather in January was decidedly wintry, with the famous *shmaal,* cold north wind blowing from the snowy

Iranian mountains. One morning, therefore, she greeted the *farasheen* with, "*Inshallah intu mish baraadi?*" They assured her they were not curtains, neither were they cold, *bardaaneen*!

Shopping for food at the supermarket could be done without using Arabic as all the produce was clearly on display and could be pointed to. But requesting something she couldn't see was a linguistic challenge. She tried to ask for lettuce with the word Nabeel had told her, *khus*, and found she was asking for a private part, or female genitalia, *kuss*. She learned later that a common curse, or insult, among men, was *kuss immak*, referring to a person's mother. She decided to ask for salad, *salata*, as it was easier to say, instead of the specific green vegetable. Mostly, however, as the family had told her, the shopkeepers spoke English, at least well enough to serve their foreign customers.

Nabeel had asked around for advice on where to find a better place to live than their ground floor flat. The inner city areas were mainly occupied by Kuwaiti families while expatriates usually lived in the outer suburbs, like Salmiyah. Surprisingly, Nabeel chose to rent in the inner suburbs, close to the British Council. They would be occupying a first floor flat in a private house, owned by a Kuwaiti, Abu Ali, with his Egyptian wife and his four school-age children, two boys and two girls. The house had five apartments on three floors, with the Kuwaiti owners living on the first floor. Their front door was directly opposite Nabeel and Rose's front door so there would obviously be plenty of contact between the two families.

There were two young Kuwaiti couples in the two apartments on the ground floor and a young Iraqi couple on the top floor. Parking was available outside, uncovered, but safe in this Kuwaiti area. There would be no Peeping Toms to fear here. Surprisingly, some families kept their own goat or even several goats, for milk, and a goatherd would collect them each morning and take them off to graze on the nearest common land. Rose would comment: 'The kids are off to school!' and laugh at this unusual pastoral scene in suburbia!

The new low-rise building was completely different from the high-rise apartment block which they were leaving, although the living space was comparable in size. The layout was rather old-fashioned. The front door opened directly into what would have to be a dining area with a small lounge on the right hand side, two bedrooms opening directly from the dining area and entrance, and a short corridor on the left led to the bathroom and then the kitchen. In their newlywed state, with no intention of starting a family till they had settled in, they decided to turn the second bedroom into a formal lounge big enough for their eight-seater suite. Nabeel planned to furnish the smaller lounge with custom-made cupboards and divans, as Kuwaiti families did for their *diwaniya*s.

They moved into the new apartment at the end of January without penalty for breaking the rental contract. Nabeel called in the help of a driver and labourers from the contracting company for the move. The landlord and landlady came out to greet them when the moving was done and invited them in for coffee. They seemed very friendly and both spoke some English. With Nabeel's

Arabic translation it was fun for Rose to meet the four children who had come in from school. They were immaculately dressed in smart school uniforms, and were not only attractive children but polite and friendly. It was clear their new flat would bring with it an entirely new life style and an extension of cultural learning for Rose.

Dear Diary, The new flat is like a new beginning. I feel very happy.

Friday, 4 February, 1977, Kuwait

Work at the ETC was settling down a little now that the first course of the year was underway. Rose was always busy, but Len provided some distraction. His family were settling in and getting to know Kuwait rather more quickly and thoroughly than Rose, given their contacts with other families with children. They were making friends and getting out and about, including to the public, family beach clubs. They also belonged to the Catholic Church, so were involved in events organised by the priest. Ngaire was intent on finding a music group and getting some choral singing going. It was interesting to hear about their leisure activities from Len, whose attempts at reducing his swearing were not succeeding. The filing cabinet tally for January was counted, setting a new target NOT to reach and a new set of tallies began for February.

Rose still could not drive, so she was restricted in her free time, with family visits on Friday becoming a ritual. They would go over mid-morning, Rose would help Asma in the kitchen, learning the recipes slowly by practice and observation, while Nabeel played cards with his brothers, then they would eat around 2pm. Joseph and Claudine came over to eat with the family too, as they were still working on their *demenagement* (move) to France, but Claudine was careful to avoid arriving too early, so she didn't have to put in any time in the kitchen. She usually had a perfect manicure and wouldn't want to spoil it. The first Friday after New Year Rose had given in and accepted the invitation to stay after the meal and take a siesta in the family home. She was shown into absentee Henri's room and was horrified to see that he not only smoked, but he dropped his cigarette ash onto the floor rather than into the ashtray. She was too upset to snooze in the room and after that refused the offers of siesta. She had to make the same excuses Friday after Friday, that she needed to go home to prepare for work the next day. It was getting a little annoying, but it was hard to get out of the standing, virtually compulsory, invitation.

At home they still had no telephone but Nabeel worked on the application which involved paying a fee, being given a number and then waiting for an indefinite number of weeks. As elsewhere in the mystic East bureaucracy worked slowly in Kuwait. There was no such thing as a minimal wait time. Finally and relatively speedily, the '*harara*' was provided at the end of the month, when their phone line became active. It was going to be wonderful to call Mum in the UK, if expensive, and useful for Nabeel to ring Rose and tell her if he was going to be late in the evenings, as he often was. Also, she was home alone on Thursdays because he became busier at work, and often needed to stay at the office to meet contacts. Of course, Asma could also now ring up and make sure they were coming to lunch on Fridays. In other words, the phone became a blessing and a curse: There was no escape from the day at the family villa.

Nabeel's time commitment to work did not worry Rose at all. She had her own lessons to prepare, and she was also considering how to improve her qualifications. She found out that on Thursdays and Fridays Samir did extra work as an academic administrator, running various examination sessions for Chartered Accountants, Surveyors, and University Scholarship and UK examination board papers. She did some research on the new distance learning degrees in TESOL which were being established in the UK and discovered that London University had a distance master's degree program, one of the first at the time. However, it was open only to graduates of London Uni. So Rose decided she would pursue a second undergraduate degree in what was obviously now her chosen career focus, the English language. As she was teaching English fulltime now, her French Honours degree was not directly relevant to her career, so she thought English would be both interesting and useful.

She discovered a correspondence college, Wolsey Hall, which offered London University distance bachelor's degree courses, so she enrolled in an English Honours degree program. She chose language courses as well as literature, and had enough to keep her busy outside of work for the coming three years, the recommended time commitment for the course of study. For the next three years this would be a work in progress as she had only her off duty hours to study in but at least she would be on the path to her target, a master's degree.

Wishing to make sure she was on the right track she contacted the distance learning college, as advised by Samir, and registered herself for the BA English Honours program. Distance education was new and it would be challenging but Rose was eager to have a goal. She could easily pay for her fees with her salary, although she actually had no direct access to her own earnings, which went straight into Nabeel's bank account. In the Middle East, a man's world, Nabeel took care of all the payments for the flat and the services, so he also arranged the transfer of fees for Rose's first year of study with Wolsey Hall. She had to complete a total of eight papers over a minimum of three years.

There wouldn't be much time to study while she was working but perhaps in future Rose might reduce her hours. The topic of starting a family was edging onto the agenda with their neighbours at least. Abu and Imm Ali, occupied the flat directly opposite, sharing a small landing with Rose and Nabeel. They had already been to their landlord's home for coffee and a return invitation was expected very soon. The older children, Ali and Nadia, spoke English with some hesitation, while the younger pair, Hassan and Iman, seemed to understand but were unwilling to speak as yet. Obviously there was some benefit to them all to have an English neighbour, both in terms of kudos and practice in conversational English for the children. Rose half expected to be asked to tutor the children, but the subject was not raised.

Rose was intrigued to think that the married couple, four children and an Egyptian maidservant occupied the same number of rooms that they had. This must have crossed their landlord's mind too: Abu Ali made no bones about it, patting his own stomach and asking, "*Fih* baby?" Rose was rather taken aback by the forthrightness of the question as well as the implication that she was getting thick around the middle. Nabeel assured her that it was normal for married couples to be chivvied about their production of children. In Arab families it was expected that the first child would appear around a year after the marriage. Abu and Imm Ali had been very welcoming of Rose as a foreigner to Kuwait, perhaps because Imm Ali herself was from Egypt. She wore 'Western' clothes, as did her children. It never became clear how they had met, but Abu Ali, who wore the dishdasha (long white robe) and gutra and agal (white headscarf and black cord 'tie') and his mother, who wore the abbaya (black cloak) and face veil, were more open and flexible than their outward appearance suggested. The flat was immaculate, and the maid was cheerful. The whole family gave an impression of happy co-existence. It was interesting to experience, but Rose didn't want them to become too close. She valued her privacy and independence too much.

A new girl in administration at the Council, a pretty, tall, blonde, from Scotland, was married to a Kuwaiti she had met while he was studying in the UK. Marianne's life in the family house had been totally taken over by the family, but as she was pregnant, she appreciated not having to cook or clean, or even wash clothes. She was only responsible for keeping their own bedroom clean and tidy. The idea of such closeness to other people and dependence on them made Rose shudder. She would have to be careful if she became pregnant herself, to be able to cope with normal life, rather than being cocooned and restricted.

Having made a formal sitting room from the second bedroom in the apartment, the 'official' smaller lounge room was now dubbed the family room, and furnished with a custom-made, Nabeel-designed wall unit, made by a local carpenter of solid, heavy teak, which could house the library which Rose's study program would entail, as well as the new television. Rose also needed a desk, so Nabeel designed a lift-up one which fitted into the shelves and cupboards but which could be put away if not in use. So as to accommodate any visitors who might stay with them, a double sponge mattress was designed, similar to the sofa bed they had left behind in London. They also had a single fold-out bed made into an easy chair. These custom-made options provided comfortable seating while they watched TV. As a final touch Nabeel had a wardrobe fitted into the right hand side of the massive wall unit, which gave ample storage for heavy coats and jackets, and provided space for future visitors' clothes too. The effect was total '70s, teak, solid and appropriately functional.

The time was ripe to start making wine and beer too. Winemaking involved minimal equipment. Rose bought two white rubbish bins with lids, each holding 25 litres, one for red and one for white wine, but decided to attempt only white at first. She bought 10kg of sugar, and 10 bottles of white grape juice. She poured these into the bin, then added the equivalent amount of water, some of it boiled, so as to raise the temperature enough to dissolve the sugar. Once the liquid was cooled to blood heat she added her secret ingredient, a packet of Sauternes yeast she had been given as a Christmas present by one of the part-time teachers, an expert brewer. This gave far better results than bread yeast but had to be smuggled in. Rose put the lid on and waited for fermentation to start, wrapping the bin in a blanket. She kept it out of sight behind a large kitchen cupboard. Within 24 hours there was a strong smell of yeast in the kitchen and Rose knew she had started her brew successfully. Now she had to keep the bin at a steady temperature so that the yeast 'ate up' the sugar and turned it into alcohol, without dying prematurely from getting too cold! Rose smiled to herself. It was her new baby!

Dear Diary, I've finally started my brewing career. It's an interesting process!

Friday, 25 February, 1977, Kuwait

Dear Diary,
Today is Kuwait's National
Day, but it's a Friday, so not
an extra holiday!

As usual Rose and Nabeel were summoned to lunch at the family home, a meal always eaten between 2 and 3pm, but they were required to be at the house early so that Rose could help Asma with the food preparation. She didn't mind this, as Asma was such a good cook and Rose was interested in learning new recipes. Her favourite dish, *tabbouleh*, took a long time to prepare as it involved picking the stems from a huge pile of parsley and mint before washing and chopping it for the salad. Adding the pre-soaked *burghul* and lemon juice were relatively easy tasks. Since it was a special day Asma had decided to make *kibbe bi saniyah*, kibbe cooked in an oven tray, something which Rose would be able to cook at home as an easier version of the *kibbe* balls, or 'Syrian torpedoes'. Although this was a lamb dish, the quantity of *burghul* in the outer layers made it less meaty and therefore appetising for Rose. The inner layer was minced lamb with pine nuts, *snobar*, heavily flavoured with cloves and cinnamon, equally tasty, even for a vegetarian.

After experiencing total separation from Nabeel's family for her first three months in Kuwait, Rose's sole day off with Nabeel, Friday, had become a traditional family get-together, but Rose balked at having to spend the whole day at the family house. She wanted to go to the beach sometimes to get some sea air, to swim and sunbathe, so she resented the constant commitment the family insisted on. Independence and individuality were not appreciated in the Arab family, whether Muslim or Christian it seemed. When she raised the issue with Nabeel he didn't take it seriously.

"You are learning some good skills," he told her with a laugh. "Arabic cooking and language."

"Yes, I agree, but you men do nothing except sit and drink and play cards while we work. That's not fair. AND," she said, raising her voice, "I would like to go to the beach sometimes. What's the point of living next to the sea and having all this sunshine if we can't get out and enjoy it. Why don't your brothers fill their swimming pool? That would be nice, if I could sunbathe and swim at their house."

"They will fill it when the weather gets hotter. They emptied it because the water got very dirty with the leaves of the oleander bushes. They are poisonous, you know."

"Gosh. I didn't know that. Why do they have them round the pool then?"

"They are tough so they can resist the drought conditions here. They hardly need watering. We have to pay for water, you know."

"OK - but we're going off topic - it wouldn't be so bad if you had Thursday off, but you work at least half the day and then we have to do the shopping together."

"I know, and I really want you to get your licence too."

"Oh, that would be great. How can we do that?"

"Well, I've heard of a Tunisian driving instructor who

speaks French. He could teach you in the afternoons when you are free."

Rose had taken a few driving lessons in South London after work, but she had never managed to control the manual gear system, which her instructor insisted she grasp theoretically. As a teacher, she felt she needed a different approach. "That would be wonderful. Wow. I really appreciate you thinking of that. But let's not get off topic: I want you to say NO to Asma sometimes when she rings and asks if we are going to lunch, OK?"

Nabeel nodded agreement and Rose relaxed a little, thinking of the free time ahead. She hadn't expected their lives to veer to the polar opposite from banishment to being joined at the hip. She was a Libran according to the Western Zodiac and she recognised some of the stereotypical traits of that personality in herself: She liked balance, not extremes, in all things. Nabeel had another slant on the topic of visits, however. "You know, we have to invite them round one day. We have to attempt to return the hospitality."

"Oh, my word. Don't say you expect me to cook for everyone while I'm working!"

"No, of course, not, but they should come round for coffee at least."

"Not yet, though. I really couldn't face having to entertain just yet."

"No, but be ready, one day we will have to."

"OK. I understand. But we'll need to buy more crockery and glassware, so you have to be ready too! We have to go shopping! But perhaps they'll like my wine!"

Rose had taped the lid on the wine bin to keep it

closed and clean for a month, and now had to acquire enough bottles to hold the fermented liquid syphoned off with a simple plastic tube. To vary her repertoire, Rose next tried a red wine recipe with frozen blackberries and red grape juice, mixed with sugar, water and yeast as before, but this time she had to use bread yeast. Once again she was rewarded with a successful 'must' and a yield of young wine after about a month. She labelled the bottles carefully and put them away in one of her capacious kitchen cupboards. The third trial recipe was rose wine with strawberries and white grape juice, with sugar, water and baker's yeast. The extra step as with the blackberries was straining the must to remove the fruit pulp before bottling, but the product was very satisfying. Beer was her next project. Beer-making was more complex than wine as the bottles had to be super strong to retain a secondary fermentation. Using Reubenkraut malt extract sold as a health food, Rose achieved creditable results. She felt pleased with her efforts and was ready to entertain friends and family at home.

Dear Diary, I can call myself a brewer now. It's fun! A new skill.

Thursday, 3 March, 1977, Kuwait

Dear Diary, Today is the Prophet Mohammed's birthday (Peace be upon him). It's a holiday so I start my driving lessons today. They say you need one lesson for every year of your life. So that would mean I need around 30 lessons. One a week for 30 weeks would mean I get my licence by the end of the year.

Mohammed the Tunisian driving teacher was a short, moustachioed, amiable chap who spoke French well. He was also, as a Tunisian, no threat to Rose, according to Nabeel. Tunisia, though Islamic, had had a secular constitution since the 1950s, and Tunisian women were emancipated, unlike the women of the Arab Gulf in general. There was no need for a chaperone during the lessons conducted in his manual gear car. At first Rose was anxious recalling the earlier attempt she had made when teaching English in Crystal Palace. She needn't have worried. Mohammed kept his lessons practical and did not bother her with the workings of the gears under the bonnet. Rose much preferred it this way. After all, she wasn't going to be repairing her own car. In the Middle East women didn't even put petrol in their own cars:

Attendants on the petrol station forecourt did all the dirty work.

Rose realised she was fortunate to be in Kuwait and not Saudi, where women were not allowed to drive, according to the tenets of the strict version of Islam practised there, Wahhabism. Kuwait 'followed' Saudi to some extent, but women in Kuwait were stronger and more assured of their worth. Driving was their right and their pleasure, but those who preferred not to drive employed Bangladeshi or Pakistani drivers.

Rose noted that Imm Ali did not drive. She didn't feel she should ask her about it, but it seemed to be the norm though it wasn't the law. Likewise, the downstairs neighbour, a young Kuwaiti woman, relied on her husband to drive her around. The young couple had a beautiful blue two-seater Cadillac coupe. Rose was quite envious of it, even though they now had their Chevvie Impala. She looked forward to the day when she would have her own car parked outside the building.

Abu and Imm Ali seemed to accept that she was learning to drive. In fact, Abu Ali was a little derogatory, assuming she could already drive. "Learning late, ya Rose," he chided. Rose laughed appropriately as she served the Turkish coffee which she had learned to make. Deep down inside she felt a little bitter, because it did seem rather late to be acquiring what for many women was a basic skill. Her best friend in secondary school had learned to drive while they were in the sixth form, and had even had a small car to pop around in. Rose's parents being both poor and divorced had not been able to provide such opportunities. She pushed such thoughts out of her mind and concentrated on her duties as a hostess in the Arab world. First, she was required to serve soft drinks, such as fresh orange juice, or fizzy drinks like Pepsi Cola, Fanta Orange or Seven Up, not in bottles, but in glasses, and preferably in the best glassware she had. Stemmed crystal wine glasses were regarded as suitable receptacles for soft drinks in alcohol-free Muslim Kuwait.

There was a soft drinks factory in Kuwait which made Pepsi, or *bibsi* as the Arab pronunciation had it, and other soft drinks, including soda and tonic water, which was very useful for those who could afford black market alcohol. Another popular and delicious drink was bottled mango juice. It was very convenient to have these soft drinks in the house ready to entertain unexpected guests. Every household bought crates of these drinks in small, returnable, glass bottles. The Pepsi man came each week on a regular day, visiting his customers to retrieve crates of empty bottles and deliver full ones as required. These crates were heavy, especially when the bottles were full, so the delivery man would carry them through the flat to the kitchen balcony for a small tip.

Rose had learned from Imm Ali that she should not shut the front door when receiving the Pepsi man. That would signal to him that she was inviting him to have a relationship with her. The press had stories about similar misunderstandings, and Rose was glad she had been warned about the danger of closing the door. She stored her crates on the kitchen balcony which was at the furthermost end of the flat, so it seemed normal to close the door to keep the cooled air inside the flat. But it was '*mamnua*' - forbidden - one of the most important words Rose learned in that first year in Kuwait.

As a hostess, after the cold drinks had been served, a tasty snack was to be offered. This could be fruit, such as grapes, slices of watermelon, or tangerines, or biscuits and small cakes. Savoury crackers, chips and/or nuts should have been on the table while the soft drinks were being served, but if the main snack was to be savoury, such as the triangular pastries filled with vegetables, meat or cheese, called *samosa,* small round pizzas, or *fatayer,* little pastries filled with minced meat and pine nuts, or cheese and spinach, then there was no need to serve salty nibbles too. The etiquette was complex, but by dint of observing and making mistakes, Rose had learned a lot. She now knew the right language to use too, *Itfaddalu* - 'help yourself', rather than *Mid idak* - 'stretch your hand', which Nabeel had used with his driver friend in those early days. Imm and Abu Ali had been shocked when Rose invited them in this casual way to help themselves. They had quickly taught her the correct expression. After the snack had been eaten and cleared away then coffee could be served, with glasses of cold water. The serving and drinking of coffee indicated that the visit was over. The hostess could relax and wait for the visitors to politely take their leave.

Rose didn't mind returning visits to their host/hostess occasionally, but there was a constant pressure to visit more frequently. She therefore tried to stretch out the return 'match' so that the visits were bi-weekly. As she worked either two or three evenings per week, she had a reasonable excuse. However, the neighbours often reminisced about their previous tenants, who had kept their front door open all day so that their children could run in and out and play with each other. Nothing was further from Rose's mind. She had enough contact as it was. After all, the children were now teenagers and more interested in their own concerns than their neighbours. A close watch had to be kept, nevertheless, that visits were restricted to once a month one way or the other.

April, 1977, Kuwait

Dear Diary,

I'm taking my driving test at the end of this month. Mohammed thinks I'm ready. Fingers crossed that I get my licence. On the down side, Abu Ali and his wife are getting a bit possessive. I have to work out how to control the visits somehow.

The driving lessons went well and before the 30 lessons were up, Mohammed suggested she should try for her driving test. Rose had mastered the three point turn, parallel parking against the kerb, and reversing round corners without stalling the car, which had been her bugbear to start with. Although there were no hills in Kuwait, she also was able to handle the hill start which was included on the practical test. People made jokes saying there would be flyovers soon on the roads, which would mean the hill starts would come in handy. As she had no British licence, before going for the practical test she took a written test to demonstrate her knowledge of the road signs and the highway code. Signage was virtually the same as in the UK except for the warning sign for camels on the road, which she found amusing. They could be found wandering in the desert, so drivers there needed to beware of killing one and perhaps themselves too, in a night crash. At this point in time roads out of Kuwait were basic but sufficient, towards Iraq in the north and Saudi Arabia to the south and west.

With the written test under her belt she attended the practical test in Mohammed's car, with Nabeel in attendance too. To Rose's surprise, the parallel parking manoeuvre was the first step in the road test. As it happened, she didn't get past that stage. Parallel parking was to be completed between four empty oil barrels, rather than between two parked cars. There were three spaces for test-takers: large, for American cars, medium, for Mohammed's type of car, a Toyota, and small, for minis. To her horror, Rose was directed to park in the smallest space, and there was no way she could object, being alone and not having the language skills. She did as she was told and attempted to reverse into the too small space. If she had been very skilled she might have done it, but being nervous she stalled the car, then on restarting the engine, she nudged a barrel. The driving inspector came over and shook his head, indicating that she should drive away from the test area. That was it. She'd failed the test. Red faced, embarrassed and angry, back at the office she said goodbye to Mohammed, fixing another date for another lesson, and went home with Nabeel.

"They didn't give me any leeway. They put me in the smallest space," she told him angrily as they drove away.

"Never mind. They'd probably decided to show you who's boss. You're obviously a foreigner and as a woman they want you to know that they are in charge. Plus, their administration likes getting the money for the entrance fee. You'll probably pass next time. Don't worry about it. Give it another month or so."

"OK. I need to build up my confidence again. I feel so stupid. I didn't really expect to have to park between oil barrels."

"At least they weren't full!"

They laughed at the thought. Causing an explosion or an oilspill would have been unthinkable.

Rose was now busy with her study program from Wolsey Hall, so time was flying by. They were invited out occasionally, and what with the family lunch, the neighbours' social calls, the driving lessons and the studies on top of a fulltime job, Rose was beginning to feel fully occupied. There was, however, one area of her life that still needed attention to make it seem normal: the acquisition of real alcohol. As it was forbidden to transport alcohol the few occasions when Nabeel had access to the black market presented two major problems. The first was transportation. The discovery of alcohol at the frequent police checkpoints when police searched boots/trunks and interiors of cars, would mean deportation for Nabeel as a Palestinian holding a Lebanese passport. The second was the cost of the illicit booze. A box of 12 bottles of Johnny Walker Red Label whisky cost about 300 dinars, or 600 sterling pounds, that is 50 pounds a bottle.

Rose had heard from Adel, the engineer brother who was sometimes invited to *diwaniyas,* that whisky was drunk by some Kuwaitis by the bottle, like wine, with the outcome often being a brawl or a fatal car accident. Gin was very occasionally found but was mostly replaced by *siddiqi* – 'my friend', or medical alcohol, ethanol.

Westerners who had access to medical ethanol flavoured it with juniper berries to get a close approximation to the taste of gin. Rose was afraid of home-made *siddiqi* as there was a danger of methanol being produced, which could cause blindness or death. The press had stories about such mishaps, often in Indian bachelor houses. Winemaking was not so risky, and she'd tasted some successes and some failures. The key to the solution was time, allowing the 'must' to finish fermenting and the yeast to die before attempting to drink the new 'vintage'. Some people didn't even get round to bottling the liquid: They simply put a jug in the bin and served it 'raw'! Rose had more patience, and enjoyed labelling and dating her bottled products.

Nabel and Rose's social life had heated up this year, with several visits to Kuwait from overseas business contacts. Rose's wine was a great attraction, with most visitors happy to eat takeaway pizza at home, accompanied by Rose's home-brewed beer, or white, red or rose wine. Spirits were not necessary, she had to admit.

Dear Diary, The taste of my beer would be improved with some real hop paste, I've been told by the experts. I'm going to try smuggling some in as a hair treatment. I hope I won't get flogged or deported if it's discovered!

May, 1977, Kuwait

Rose and Nabeel had been invited to some functions at the Embassy where real beer and wine were offered by waiters. They had also been to several parties given by the expatriate University staff. Their parties were lively affairs, with music, dancing, a pot luck dinner and home brewed wine. Several recipes were in circulation for Jeddah Gin, made from citrus fruits, but Rose was satisfied with her wine fermentation using local ingredients and baker's yeast without importing any forbidden (*haraam*) substances. Her beer was prized by guests and so social life had become quite busy, returning the hospitality they had enjoyed now her drink cupboards were well stocked. It was sometimes difficult to get business visitors to leave, so happy were they with the unexpected treat of beer and wine at home. On occasion Rose had to remonstrate with Nabeel about having to stay up till the small hours as hostess when she had to go to work in the morning as usual. He rejected her complaints. "You could just go to bed, you know. We don't need a woman's presence in our business talk."

"OK, point made, but can you promise to talk quietly?" she rejoindered. "And don't let me hear about your little 'gifts' to ease business along. I don't agree with that."

Another complaint Nabeel couldn't counter was the heavy smoking that accompanied the home hospitality. Rose found it hard to breathe and the sitting room curtains were absorbing the smoke too. "I'm afraid you guys will burn down the house, waving your cigarettes around as you drink. My beer is potent, you know."

Occasionally business guests had to be put up in the 'diwaniya' room, when there was 'no room at the inn' in downtown Kuwait, which at that time only had a couple of five star hotels, the Sheraton and the Hilton. Rose didn't mind the extra laundry that entailed as there really was no other choice. Business visitors were on expenses, so they usually preferred to stay in hotels, but Nabeel had to drive them after he'd been drinking, so there was a risk involved.

"What if the police stopped you? How would I know where you were if you didn't come home?" she remonstrated.

"It will never happen. The police are probably fast asleep in the small hours," he replied.

However, Rose now had some social life of her own. Ngaire had found friends who wished to sing so a choral group was established, with singing practice once a week. There were also Thursday morning belly dancing classes with university teacher friends. It was very enjoyable to break the daily round of work, study, cooking, brewing and cleaning with singing and dancing. The family long lunches on Friday were still compulsory so Rose was always grateful when friends invited her to join them for a couple of hours of sun, sand and sea. There were also visits to the theatre and to concerts put on by talented ex-pats, so with her work, her studies and her expanding social life, Rose was busy and satisfied with her lot.

Dear Diary, I'm getting a better work-life balance now! Happy!

June, 1977, Kuwait

Dear Diary,
    I've had lots more lessons to
get my driving confidence back
and Mohammed thinks I'm ready
to try again. Touch wood.

Rose had been having driving lessons for long enough to try the oil barrel parking test again. She was extremely nervous. This time, to her surprise, she was pointed to the correct, medium-size space for her instructor's car. Having successfully negotiated the barrels and parallel parked her car, she was then joined by an inspector in the passenger seat who directed her to drive to a special road area where she was not required to reverse round a corner, nor to do an emergency stop but to drive around a little. There was some confusion since the inspector only spoke Arabic, and his dialect was Kuwaiti, or Gulf Arabic. Rose was more familiar with Lebanese/Palestinian, so when the officer told her to drive *seeda*, by a process of logical deduction she worked out not left, not right, but straight on, which till that moment in time, she had known as *dughri* in Arabic. The next stressful element in the test was the hill start. Rose had practiced the hill start a little. By some fluke she remembered how to balance the pedals though she had no idea how she managed to handle the gears without stalling the car. After a few moments of extreme stress, she was delighted to be directed back to the starting point of the test, where the officer got out. She still didn't know if she had passed or failed, but Mohammed and Nabeel were smiling broadly while talking to the inspector, so she had high hopes. Indeed, this time she got her licence. Celebrations were in order, though Rose simply felt relief.

From then on driving became a reality. Rose drove to work each morning with Nabeel in his car and from work to home each lunchtime. Driving in Kuwait was so notoriously bad that an expat journalist working at Kuwait Times newspaper published a series of cartoons about a dangerous, but endearing character called Wizr. Just reading the cartoon strip made Rose nervous, but as Fiona told her, "Just drive on your own little rat tracks and build up your confidence. You'll get used to the traffic soon." Indeed, that's what happened, with only one hairy moment when coming out of a side street onto the main road. Rose misjudged the speed of the oncoming car from the left. As not too many women drove in Kuwait in the '70s, the other driver, who approached too fast and had to swerve to avoid hitting her, went ballistic when he saw a woman behind the wheel. No harm was done, however, and Rose took even greater care from then on. She did not yet have her own car but she was quite satisfied with the progress she'd made on the driving front.

Nabeel's birthday was at the end of the month and now that Rose had excellent wine and beer to offer she felt ready to give her first dinner party. Nabeel invited two British Consulate officers whom Rose did not know well and whose wives Nabeel did not know either. Rose invited a British Council couple whom she knew slightly better. They would be eight around the table, which was perfect.

For her first menu Rose prepared the trendy food of the day: caramelised oranges for dessert, beef wellington with *dauphinoise* potatoes and green beans for the main course, and as a starter, fake black caviar surrounded by concentric rings of finely chopped white onion and the chopped but separated white and yolk of hardboiled eggs. It was an attractive presentation, served with toast fingers.

After spending the whole of Thursday morning shopping and the afternoon cooking Rose was feeling tired when her guests began to arrive. The first couple to arrive were John and Lesley, followed soon after by Marina and Peter. Introductions were made and the couples sat in the lounge sipping black market whisky on ice. When the third couple arrived Rose was completely amazed to realise she could not remember the name of the woman as she stood to introduce them to the four others. Her flustered state was obvious and the third husband, David, offered help by saying, "Marina, like the sea," at which point Rose realised that she had a psychological issue she had experienced on more than one occasion. There was already ONE Marina in the lounge, so having another, which she hadn't fully internalised, had caused a psychological blockage.

Rose realised years later that this was a persistent problem for her: if someone already owned the name in her mental filing cabinet, no one else could have it. Fortunately, the group found it amusing. Marina is an unusual name, and for two women out of four to be called by that name was indeed unusual. The evening went well, the food was good, but there was no return Consulate invitation. Whether this was because of the *faux pas*, or the lack of commercially bottled wine, or the food, or the lower status of the 'mixed race' host and hostess, Rose never knew.

Other dinner parties with teacher friends were given over the months to come. The trendy starter in the '70s was home-made chicken liver pate, which looked more attractive once made and chilled than in the making. Fondue parties were also popular in those days, with home-made white wine providing the perfect base for the melted Swiss cheese, which was surprisingly readily available in supermarkets. Trifle was a popular dessert in those days, with Rose's strawberry wine soaking the sponge base and making a delicious Black Forest treat if cherries were added to the base instead. Strawberries were grown by means of hydroponics in Kuwait, and though they didn't have much taste in comparison to the ones Rose had eaten as a child, soaked in wine they made an attractive and tasty addition to trifle.

Of course, for Nabeel's birthday, the family had to be invited to dinner. It was no longer scary for Rose as she had practised her menu with her friends first. Joseph and Claudine had gone to France, and Henri refused the invitation so the guests were only Asma and Adel and Edouard. Rose made sure to prepare all the food well in advance so that Asma was not allowed into the tiny kitchen at all. The brothers arrived bearing a bottle of black market Johnny Walker (aka liquid gold) and a huge bunch of flowers, as well as Samadi *baklava*, nut pastries. Nabeel had made sure there was enough ice, and the evening went well, for which Rose breathed a sigh of relief.

For Nabeel's birthday present, Rose and Nabeel had gone together to the gold souk, an Aladdin's cave of exotic, intricately crafted 22 karat gold jewellery, to buy him a heavy gold chain and a crucifix for his neck. Although he had not been a believer since his childhood days, he did not profess himself an atheist either. At some point in their marriage one of his regular back-handed jokes, or 'putdowns' for Rose, was based on the fact that they hadn't married in the Catholic Church. "I'll marry you one day," he used to crow gleefully when she made something nice to eat, or served him a drink, pretending it was a way of praising her, saying she was good enough to marry. It made some people's ears prick up though and suspect foul play. How could they live together in Kuwait, a strictly Muslim country, if they weren't married? It fell to Rose to explain that they had married in a civil ceremony in London, but not in the Catholic Church. This simple explanation revealed the immaturity of the joker but Rose chose to ignore the comment, putting it down to childishness.

There were other examples of Nabeel's 'putdowns', singing "She's a heavy hippy Momma, she's got big fat legs" (from an old jazz song) knowing she was concerned about putting on weight; also comparing her legs to the renowned Roman columns in Baalbek, which they had visited in 1973, and her mouth to the Caves at Jaita, another Lebanese tourist spot. Ironically, Nabeel had a prominent nose, and had also had cosmetic surgery free on the National Health Service while he was in the UK, complaining that his protruding ears caught the cold wind which gave him severe earache! His family were shocked by his casual verbal abuse of his wife, chastising him whenever they heard him say such things. It was like water off a duck's back. "It's just a joke," he would retort. But a joke intended to hurt, to harm self-esteem and put down the wife, who perhaps was getting too big for her boots, in his opinion.

The omission of a marriage in the Church became a topic of concern for Rose's future. According to Nabeel, the laws of inheritance in Lebanon were such that if a married couple had no children and the husband passed away, his property would be divided in half between his family and his widow. They agreed that savings in the UK would be Rose's in case of Nabeel's early death. As for children, they both agreed she would stop taking the pill when they were settled. There was another thing, though. If they decided to visit or even reside in Lebanon in the future, then Rose would need visas. To facilitate the process of getting visas if Rose was in England visiting her Mum, Nabeel asked her to sign her name at the bottom of half a dozen blank pieces of A4 paper to be kept in case of need. Trusting, naive Rose had played into the hands of a master puppeteer, whose dread was 'to be taken to the cleaners' in terms of his finances. He had picked up this term in his business dealings, Rose guessed.

Dear Diary
    The gold souk is amazing. I've never seen anything like it. So many windows stuffed with gold chains, ornate necklaces, and fantastic bangles, bracelets and rings. A Kuwaiti bride has to be

covered with gold so there were lots of ladies in black abbayas and hijab shopping. It was like being in another world: Aladdin's Cave!

July, 1977, Kuwait

Dear Diary,
We have new neighbours upstairs: an English couple. The Iraqi couple have disappeared without saying goodbye.

One evening on returning from work Nabeel was greeted on the landing by Abu Ali with broad smiles. His gold front tooth glinted as he broke his exciting news. He had installed new tenants in the upstairs apartment. An English couple! They were all invited for coffee with the landlord to break the ice. It was surprising to learn that their previous neighbours had gone without a word, but they hadn't known the Iraqi couple well. It was of course pleasing for Rose to have English neighbours with whom she would be able to chat and share stories of their strange new lives. Andrew was a civil engineer on a two year contract with the Ministry of Electricity and Water (MEW). He was short in stature, jovial, with a ruddy complexion, reminiscent of a happy garden dwarf in his physical appearance, and stoic and cheerful in his approach to life as they found out on closer acquaintance. Miranda, his wife, was contrastingly tall and elegant, with a pale complexion and fine features. She was a qualified English teacher, though she hadn't had much experience to date she told Rose.

The new couple appeared to be at least five years younger than Rose and Nabeel, and as an expatriate couple their expectations of life were slightly different. They had already spent three years on an overseas contract in Africa where Andrew had worked on water conservation projects, especially dams. Their stories of life in Africa were amazing, such as the number of dead bodies to be found on the side of roads, which were totally ignored by drivers and passersby. In contrast to this experience they found Kuwait much more civilised and slightly boring. Their future life would be driven by the need for Andrew to obtain steady contract work, so Miranda's career would be a sideline for her, while her dearest wish was to become a mother. The two women would be able to share their progress towards this common goal over the coming year and Rose felt it was perhaps time to stop taking the contraceptive pill.

Meanwhile, Rose was keen to engage Miranda's services as an English language teacher at the British Council ETC as enrolment for classes was going well. Even Asma had now registered for morning classes this term, so the ETC needed more regular teachers. Miranda lacked confidence, however, and insisted on simply being a 'supply' teacher, taking classes when regular teachers needed cover for absences. Rose was happy to be a mentor for her and they began to have regular Thursday morning catch up sessions when both their husbands were working.

Miranda's greatest leisure interest was music. Searching the thriving blackmarket in illegally copied tape cassettes for musical gems was her favourite occupation. Kuwait's souk, or covered market, had several shops which specialised in Western and Middle Eastern music. Miranda's greatest delight was to find copies of albums she didn't already own. Making an inventory of the numerous cassettes kept her busy most days. She persuaded Andrew to indulge her passion by telling him how much she had saved by buying these illegal copies instead of paying the full price. She was a dream consumer in this regard. Every weekend she asked her husband to take her to another shop to search out something she needed to have. Andrew never complained. He knew that he had to keep his wife happy in this new country if he was to enjoy his own life, following the old adage: Happy wife, happy life. Rose enjoyed listening to the new music and keeping up to date with the Western music world. She hadn't had time to do so previously, so it was fun to have this younger neighbour to entertain her.

Miranda also quickly began to make use of another good buy in Kuwait: the custom-made clothes from tailors working in every residential area. Ladies either took a dress they already owned to the tailor to be copied, or they looked in his pattern book and chose a design to be made in her size. Rose had not indulged in buying clothes of any kind as yet, though she could see that it would be a good idea to extend her summer wardrobe, given the heat they were experiencing in these months. This was her first experience of the hottest time of year, but to date she had no need of more clothes. As the ETC classrooms were air-conditioned, her London *demi-saison* separates were satisfactory. All Rose's salary was going straight into her husband's bank account, and they were buying only food and household furnishings and other goods. Over the past year setting up house from scratch had been very expensive, but Rose was not required to keep household accounts: Nabeel was in complete charge of their income and outgoings.

Meanwhile at work discussions were taking place to solve the problem of recruitment of teachers. Both Len and Rose were tired of standing in for classes when teachers fell ill or had other engagements. They were the support for the teaching staff and they needed help they felt. So a recruitment drive began for overseas teachers, who, Rose noted wryly, would be given accommodation and return air tickets to their homes. She had not been given a rise or a bonus, no matter how well the classes were going. Perhaps this was the time to get pregnant.

That night as they drove home, she told her husband.

"Nabeel, I've decided something important. I want you to tell me if you think I am doing the right thing. I've decided to stop taking the pill."

"That's wonderful, *habibti*. I'm so glad. We might have a baby by this time next year!"

"Let's hope so. But I've been taking the pill for seven years now, so there may be problems. Don't get your hopes up too soon."

"OK. Just take care of yourself and don't work too hard!"

"Well, you make sure I don't spend all my Friday mornings on my feet in Asma's kitchen!"

"OK. I promise."

August, 1977, London, UK, Spain

Dear Diary, I'm entitled to four weeks' summer holiday from work. We're going back to the UK for a Spanish holiday with Mum and John again! Then I'll get on with my studies during Ramadan.

Rose had started reading for her first paper on the BA Honours English course for London University, supported by Wolsey Hall's distance learning programme. Some papers had to be studied independently so Rose needed expensive texts such as the massive tome by Leech, Quirk, Svartvik and Greenbaum on English Grammar. The British Council had a good library, including some out of print gems, such as the moving account of the Palestinian exodus from Israel in 1948 by Major Glubb Pasha of the British Army, but the core textbooks would be useful to Rose for the rest of her working life so she preferred to own them. A trip to the UK on holiday would allow her to purchase what she needed. Nabeel was pleased to see her involved in her studies and made no complaint at all about her sitting for hours at her desk in the family room, nor about the cost of her books.

Back in the UK Rose spent some time in Dillons, the University Bookshop, and Foyles, her old haunt from teaching in North London, searching for books to use in her BA study program. She left her heavy book purchases

269

with brother Bill while they made their short package holiday trip to Majorca with Mum and John. They enjoyed swimming and relaxing in the warm sunshine. She was thrilled to have her portrait drawn by a local artist and a set of Majorica cultured pearl jewellery gifted to her by Nabeel. They made sightseeing trips around the beautiful island and visited the Dragon Caves (Cuevas del Drach) at Porto Cristo. As always the sunshine was very healing for Mum. Back in London Rose also bought some hop extract and labelled it as hair conditioner before tucking it away in one of her suitcases.

Once back in Kuwait, having got away without paying excess baggage fees for the heavy books during check in at the airline, Rose was feeling more positive about the future. On the evening of their first wedding anniversary they celebrated quietly at home. Then Nabeel confronted her.

"Do you think you should give up work now, Rose?"

She was shocked at the question. "What do you mean?"

"Well, now you have your studies, and we don't need your money, you could give up work and make sure you get pregnant."

"I think it's your job to make sure I get pregnant, don't you? As Abu Ali says, 'Can't you kick football?'"

"I know, but perhaps you need to relax a bit more. Always dashing around...and you are not young."

"Excuse me, I know I'm nearly 30 but that's still young enough to have a baby."

"I know, but I just want you to feel you can give up work if you want to."

"Thanks, but I don't want to right now. After all, these studies cost money. I don't want you to say you are spending too much money on me." (These were prophetic words indeed.)

"Things are going OK at work. I'm getting more agencies. The valve supplier would like me to stock valves, but I've managed to persuade them that that's not a good idea."

"What would it mean if you stocked valves?"

"I'd need to have a warehouse - a 'godown' they call them here. They're not cheap to rent and I can't buy anything as a Lebanese/Palestinian. There's a competitor of mine who has a big site in Ahmadi."

"What's the advantage of the warehouse?"

"Obvious really - no wait time for delivery to the client of the goods they want."

"But is it possible to stock everything the client wants?"

"Not really. It's not exactly like selling shoes because fashion is not involved. But you can't possibly keep everything the client wants in store."

"OK, well, it sounds like a big investment. Is it worrying you?"

"Not really. The supplier has agreed that the current system is working. They know I am doing a good job for them as their agent. I just have to keep my nose to the ground. There'll be more business visitors from now on too. Is that OK with you?"

"Of course. They can enjoy my home-made wine with a takeaway pizza. I'm not going to lay on a three course meal, if that's OK with you?"

"No worries. Well, let's see how next year goes. With any luck we'll be able to go to the UK next August and visit some of my principal suppliers."

"Right. And I'll spend a bit of time with my feet in the air after you've kicked the football, hey?"

"Why?"

"They say it helps the fertility process."

"Right. Strange. Suits me. Ready for a game now?"

They both laughed as they went into the bedroom.

Dear Diary,

Well, we've made it through the first year of marriage. Let's see what year two brings. For better, or worse? A baby, perhaps?

September, 1977, Kuwait

Dear Diary,

Ramadan is going quickly and there's an Eid holiday ahead, then my birthday. A good month! Plus, the new Senior Teachers are arriving. That will make my workload easier for sure.

At home Miranda had been sharing her discoveries about the lighter side of Kuwait while Rose was studying and working fulltime. There were two Kashmiri stores in the outlying towns of Fintas and Fahaheel which she told Rose she should visit. They had lots of handicrafts from around the world as well as Kashmir, including cushion covers and tablecloths and exotic jewellery which was not expensive. As Rose was still improving on the interior design of the apartment, these shops sounded tantalisingly interesting. She could see a window of opportunity for some shopping during the upcoming holiday for *Eid al Fitr* which marked the end of Ramadan. The holiday this year would be a big contrast from last year, when they had been outcasts from the family. This year there were plans for a family meal at home as well as for a picnic in the desert planned before the weather got too cool. But Rose insisted that Nabeel keep some time for them to visit these exciting new shops on their own.

"As well as going shopping one day, what do you think about giving a small party for my birthday? It's the week after *Eid,* but it would be easy to give a small party on the Thursday night after the *Eid* holiday? It would be fun and I'd have plenty of time to do the planning."

"Are you sure you want to spend time on a party? I don't want you to feel too tired."

"Well, I think we should mark the occasion. We'll have been here in Kuwait for a year. Just a few people though, not too many."

"OK. As you like. I'll make sure Asma knows when we are free to go to the desert. Do you want them to come round for the party?"

"What do you think? Will they want to come?"

"I suppose we have to invite them."

"OK. I'll leave it to you to handle it. Just make sure we don't spend more than two days of our break with them, please."

"I'm beginning to think you don't like my family."

"It's not that! You know we hardly get any time together and I'm looking forward to this *Eid* break."

Given the fact that Nabeel's business was private, he was not compelled to take all the days of the *Eid* holiday which began on Thursday, 15 September. So he arranged for them to go for lunch on the first day, and only stay for lunch, rather than spend the morning and whole afternoon together. Asma took the opportunity to make *mulokhia*, a dark green vegetable dish, which was good for a vegetarian, and which Rose had tasted for the first time in Beirut. While they were having lunch they discussed the picnic they would have on Sunday. They would take chickens prepared for grilling on the BBQ, *tabbouleh, hummus* and *fattoush* salad, accompanied by soft drinks only, as they would be eating in public. There'd be water melon, bananas and grapes for dessert. They would buy folded Iranian bread on the way out of town. It sounded like a lot of planning and preparatory work to Rose, but she was intrigued to see the desert. She hadn't been out there at all so she was reconciled to spending a whole day on the project. After all, she would have Friday and Saturday to herself!

As usual, on Friday, a working day in the Western world, Nabeel wanted to check in at the office on orders coming in for his agencies. He had built up several solid relationships with British companies. He was now looking into representing some US companies, so it was important for him to stay in touch with the rest of the world. As a result Rose ended up doing the usual round of chores, washing and ironing, and some study for her courses. She couldn't complain because Nabeel's income was clearly the basis of their hoped for future success in Kuwait. The next day, Saturday, however, she insisted that they venture out to find the Kashmiri handicraft shops in Fintas and Fahaheel.

"I hope you don't want to buy too many things," complained Nabeel as they set off.

"What do you mean? I haven't bought anything for myself since we got here, other than household goods and food. I hope you aren't going to be like my Dad was with my Mum, and give me a new household appliance for my birthday?"

"Well, it would be sensible, but thanks for the warning," he joked, she hoped.

They found the shop in Fintas was closed, but the shop window looked very enticing, so they drove on to the larger town of Fahaheel. The display in the window was similar to that they'd just seen but the shop was open. It was like entering Aladdin's cave: They were surrounded by sights and smells from the Orient as well as tinkling sounds of wind chimes as the few customers moved around the shop. There were richly coloured fabrics in the piles of cushion covers, embroidered bedspreads and tablecloths, as well as some woven carpet runners for the floor. There were accessories for decorating the house, picture frames, containers in brass inlaid with enamel, candlesticks and drawing Rose's eye immediately, lampshades made of capiz shell with intricately formed brass lampstands. An orange shade with a tall twisted brass floor-stand drew her attention immediately.

"That would go perfectly with our curtains and cushion covers," she told Nabeel.

"I agree. It's lovely. You can have it," he said.

"You can have it too," she pointed out. "It's for us, for the house."

"OK." Without more ado he moved to the cash desk and purchased the lamp.

"Happy now? Can we go?"

"OK. I'll come back another day with Miranda, now I know where the shop is."

"Is that a threat or a promise?"

"Just a statement of fact. The shop is lovely and no one bothers you while you look around."

As they drove back they picked up a rotisserie chicken for lunch and resumed their regular routines: study for

Rose, office for Nabeel. At least she would be able to get ahead with her studies, and the lamp was just perfect.

At 10am on Sunday morning Nabel and Rose arrived at the family villa, with ice and soft drinks and several packs of the fresh Iranian bread they had bought on the way. Hakima, the Egyptian secretary was waiting at the villa, helping Asma carry food containers and coolers from the kitchen. Loading the two four-wheel-drive cars belonging to Adel and Edouard with the rest of the food and the BBQ grill took half an hour, so they had Turkish coffee while waiting. As usual Rose was asked to make it and she declined, as usual, not wishing to be told it was *mish tayabi*, the standing joke with regard to her coffee making skills. Once the cars were loaded, the family set off in two cars, Asma and Hakima travelling with Edouard and Nabeel and Rose with Adel. Rose had a much friendlier relationship with Adel than the other two brothers since she had met him when she first knew Nabeel in London. She had also met his 'penfriend' from Norway and realised he was looking for a wife but afraid to make the commitment, given the family's judgemental attitude towards potential partners. He had seen how Joseph and Nabeel had met with difficulties in their choice of wife. If he didn't choose a Palestinian Christian as a bride he would face the same challenges.

As they drove out to Jahra on the new four lane highway in both directions, Rose marvelled at the modern infrastructure.

"Pilgrims have made these roads necessary," Adel told her. "Every year thousands of Kuwaitis and expat Arabs drive to Saudi for the Hajj, the Muslim pilgrimage to the holy cities of Mecca and Medina, which all Muslims should achieve at least once in their lifetimes."

"It must have taken a lot of money to complete such wide roads."

"Yes, but it's funded with unlimited oil," Adel told her. "The Kuwaitis have had the profits from oil sales flowing freely into their national coffers since 1975 so they can easily afford this."

After about 30 minutes of motorway driving they came to a township with very simple, walled compounds surrounding clusters of one storey houses. Even though the houses looked very basic, each one had an air conditioning unit sticking out of a window frame.

Rose commented, "I noticed that in the Kuwaiti areas there are often two or three houses of exactly the same design grouped together in a compound, as here. What's that about?"

Nabeel laughed. "It's the family unit here," he told her. "One Muslim man can marry three wives, but he has to treat them all identically. If he's rich, he has to build up to three villas. If he's poor, he has to have at least three bedrooms, one for each of them, and he alternates his nights between them."

"Wow," said Rose, mouth agape. "That's complicated."

"And that's not all," said Adel. "The husband can have a 'marriage of pleasure' lasting from one night till forever, if he wants to."

"Unbelievable," gasped Rose. "How does that work for the wives, I wonder?"

"Well, if they have children, the man has to support them. He can divorce a wife by saying 'I divorce thee,' three times in succession, not just once, in case he changes his mind while saying it. Each wife brings a dowry gift with her when she marries, and she is entitled to get that back if she is divorced. The fourth 'wife' usually receives gifts to persuade her to accept what is likely to be a temporary relationship. The Emir is believed to have had scores of wives and hundreds of children. It's an accepted way of keeping the different tribes united."

"I see. What about those cases where the wife is foreign and she wants to go back home with her children if she's divorced?"

"Well, she can leave but she can't take any children younger than eight years old with her. They have to stay with the father, unless he agrees to allow them to leave, which is highly unlikely. It's a matter of honour."

"Really? That seems very harsh on the children. Don't they get a say in it?"

"Not at all. If they don't like it they have to lump it as you say in English," he joked, trying to lighten the atmosphere.

"Very sad," said Rose, thinking of her Scottish friend. "I suppose it's an incentive to get on with each other and stay married."

As they came to the outskirts of Jahrah, Rose spied the Red Fort, an old fortified palace made of mud and covered with red plaster, which she had never seen before.

"That's amazing. We have to come and look more closely another day, Nabeel, please."

Then there were the camel farms, with racing camels in enclosures with stables, and mothers and babies in other shelters.

"The Kuwaitis seem to care for their camels well," Rose commented.

"These people are most likely *'gher Kuwaiti'* - or *'biddoun*,'" Adel told her.

"Biddoun? ...not *Beddu?"*

"Bedouin are the nomads, and they need to register with the country they reside in to get nationality, or *jinsiya*. *Biddoun* are nomads who have not been registered, so they are 'without' passports. They have a lot of problems, because they are not given any rights as '*biddoun*'. So they live out here and care for the camels."

After leaving the town behind they headed into the desert proper. This desert was not the sandy, romantic, dune-filled landscape Rose had expected. As far as the horizon there was dry, dusty, scrubland, with occasional pockets of greenery and some scrawny trees. They headed to one of these pockets, avoiding those where other families had already settled, and set up their one-day camp. Rose noticed that some of the other families they had passed had brought goats with them.

"What's that about?" she asked.

"You don't want to know," said Nabeel meaningfully.

Rose realised that this was going to be food on the hoof. There was nothing fresher or more distasteful to Rose than slaughtering an animal, so she averted her eyes.

"Don't worry," laughed Adel, "our chickens are well marinaded."

"Make mine *tabbouleh*," she responded. "Much tastier."

They spread straw mats on the ground and arranged the food on a camping table. Edouard took charge of the BBQ while Asma stood by ready to help. The others decided to play frisbee while the food was cooking. It was warm and slightly windy, which kept the flies away from the BBQ and the food containers and allowed them to play an exciting game of frisbee. Hakima made a team with Adel, while Rose and Nabeel were their opponents.

"I don't know how to score a frisbee game, do you?" asked Rose.

"No idea!" replied Adel. "Let's just count who drops it. First side to drop it 20 times loses that game!"

Nabeel was surprisingly active for a chain smoker and equally matched with his younger brother. Rose in flat sandals had the advantage over Hakima, who was wearing platform-soled shoes, but they were unable to keep score they were laughing so much. Just having fun outdoors was very agreeable. After a quarter of an hour the savoury smell of grilled chicken with thyme and rosemary was emanating from the BBQ.

"I think it's ready, come and see," shouted Edmond, looking rather hot and sweaty in his chef's apron.

The grilled meat met with approval and the party helped themselves to the salads and bread. Everyone was quiet while they tucked into their food.

"We could have brought steak and sausages, you know," grumbled Nabeel. "You know I don't like chicken much."

"Ah, yes," said Asma. "Sorry. After all that time in the refugee camp when we could only afford chicken."

"But at least it was better than rice and tomato soup, our first diet in the camp," Edouard pointed out.

"Indeed," explained Nabeel, then crowed like a cockerel. "At one point I thought I might transform into a chicken myself."

"Is that why you always eat steak when we go to a restaurant?" asked Rose.

"Partly - but also because steak can't be spoiled... and with a squeeze of lemon juice, it tastes the same wherever you go."

At this point Asma expanded on the restaurant theme. "You know, Rose, you have to be careful when you eat in a restaurant. The food can be dirty. I always have grilled shrimp. I know that must be fresh."

Rose was a little taken aback by this prejudice. She wouldn't have thought it such a big deal, but then she hadn't had the misfortune to be hungry in her life, even though she had been poor as a child.

"Do you know," Asma went on, "when Nabeel was little in the camp, he started growing very very fast. At the time there was a... how do you say... problem, not an illness..."

"A syndrome?" suggested Rose.

"Yes, a syndrome... children were growing too tall too fast and dying...so we took him to the clinic and because the clinics were too crowded, we put his bottom through the window and he got vitamin injections."

"Oh dear, that must have been worrying..."

"Very bad," said Asma, "but look at him now...always smoking..."

"Yes, he smokes too much."

"They all do. I don't know why."

"I don't," said Edouard proudly. "I've given up."

Then slyly, he asked Asma, "Would you like one?"

Rose was amazed again. "Do you smoke?"

"Sometimes," admitted her sister-in-law. "When I want to relax."

So there they sat, sipping cold drinks, some smoking, some dozing, until the wind became too cool and they had to pack up ready for the trip home.

"Can we stop at the Red Fort on the way back?" asked Rose.

"I don't think it will be open, but we can try," said Adel. "There's not much to see inside anyway."

"OK. But we could have a closer look and take some photos. It's been a lovely picnic. Thank you very much Asma and Edouard for doing all the work."

"You are welcome, Rose," they chorused. "We'll have to come camping in spring, like the Kuwaitis do."

"Really?" said Rose, dread in her heart at the very idea.

"Yes, they bring huge tents, generators, TVs sound systems, and experience their old Bedouin lives again. It's interesting to see what goes on in the tent cities that spring up."

"OK. I'll bear that in mind," said Rose, climbing into the car with Adel and Nabeel.

As they came to the Red Fort at Jahra they could see people clambering up and down the stairs inside the building, so they stopped and paid the small entrance fee to allow them to do the same. There was no information desk or publication but obviously this had been a fortification at some time in the past.

"It's interesting to see something historic in Kuwait," commented Rose. "Everything seems so new."

"Have you been to the dhow harbour yet?" asked Adel. "You can see men building the wooden boats used for pearl fishing."

"Yes, we must do it one day."

"And, there's a black and white film on life in Kuwait in the old days before oil too. You might catch it on TV one day. It's called *Bass ya Bahr.* You'll enjoy it."

"Right. Thanks for the tip. I love history and finding out more about Kuwait would be wonderful."

As they said their farewells, Rose felt truly grateful for an unusual and happy day. She hoped there'd be more like this in future. *Eid al Fitr* had been fun and she still had her birthday party ahead. Life in Kuwait was getting more interesting at last.

Work should also get less onerous as the new Senior Teachers were due to arrive after the Eid holiday. Na'aman went to collect them at the airport so Rose did not meet them till she went in to work on Saturday morning. Justin was from Scotland, as was his new, younger partner, Lucy. Justin was a tall, stalwart, greying, bearded and moustachioed Scot. Lucy was a pretty, fair-haired petite, slim young woman with apparently boundless energy. They were given accommodation on the top floor of the BC building, which had been converted into a one bedroom flat for them.

They didn't seem to mind living 'on the job' as it were and quickly settled into their new roles. Rose invited them to her birthday party at the end of the month, and took them round to meet Nabeel the first weekend they were at post. They became firm friends immediately and saw each other often for drinks or dinner. Nabeel and Rose were their best man and woman when they got married soon after they arrived, as they had to, to meet Kuwait's laws. It was a simple but fun occasion, with a ceremony at the British Embassy. Rose and Nabeel then took them to lunch at the Sheraton, to celebrate.

Dear Diary,

We have some lovely new friends and I've discovered more about Kuwait. Life is getting better every day.

Thursday, 29 September, 1977, Kuwait

Dear Diary,

I probably shouldn't have asked people round for tonight's party. I feel rushed, even though the menu is simple: chili con carne with rice and salad and caramel oranges for dessert with a cake from Movenpick. I'm sure I'll enjoy it once I get organised.

As so often in her life, Rose experienced ups and downs in her desire to be with people and her need to be alone too. She was always ambitious in her catering plans, but this time she'd set her sights low, preparing a hot dish and dessert in advance, with only rice to cook and salad to prepare on the night. She had purchased dessert from Movenpick, a Swiss patisserie and cafe, selling delicious cakes and ice cream. She had plenty of red and white wine ready, and Miranda had got some cassette tapes set up ready to provide the background music. It would be a pleasant night to mark not only her 30th birthday but one year of life in Kuwait.

Her guests started to arrive around 7.30pm, each bearing a small gift and a card. She put them aside on a table to open later, as she served drinks and made sure everyone knew where the pistachios and other salted nuts were. The evening passed happily, with everyone eating and talking. When the cake came out as the grand finale to the meal, Rose was surprised when Nabeel called everyone to attention, and insisted she blow out a single candle. Everyone clapped as she did so, then her husband gave her a small silver box. She looked at him in amazement. Had he bought jewellery for her? She didn't have an engagement ring. Perhaps he had gone out and splurged on the diamond she hoped for? As she took the parcel she thanked him. Whatever it was, she was grateful. The other guests were all smiling - did they know what the gift was, she wondered?

The small box was easily opened and contained a set of two keys, car keys! Rose stared at them in amazement.

Nabeel could hardly contain himself. "Your car's downstairs," he told her gleefully!

"Really? How on earth did you do that?"

"While you were cooking and cleaning, I brought it round with George from the American Embassy. It's his car, a Chrysler New Yorker, imported from the USA. They are leaving Kuwait and don't want to take it back."

George and his wife Emma were there in the group of guests. She thanked them, knowing they wouldn't have asked a lot for the car. As it was dark she decided to have a look at it the next morning. It was worth the wait. The morning revealed a huge four-door sedan, white body work and white leather upholstery inside: a Chrysler New Yorker. The plush back seat was large enough to give a tea party in, and taking it for a test drive, Rose found it sailed along the road like a stately galleon. It was the most comfortable car she had ever been in, and the automatic transmission was so easy to drive she could hardly believe it. In size it equalled the mass of the Cadillac coupe the Kuwaiti neighbours drove. Abu and Imm Ali were impressed.

"Now you have to kill a chicken," they urged.

"Maybe," prevaricated Rose, while Nabeel grinned widely. "I'll put the hand of Fatima on the rear view mirror though."

These bright blue hands, cast in pottery, or made of wood or plastic, with an eye painted on them, were endemic in Kuwait. They symbolized the protection of Fatima, the sainted wife of the Prophet Mohammed, Peace Be upon Him, or PBUH as the media abbreviated it to save print space. After a time, it became normal to be superstitious here. Whenever they left the family house Asma always sent them on their way with *Allah ma'kum* - God be with you. As for talking about the future, it was almost anathema to make a prediction without qualifying it with I*nsha'allah* - God willing. Whatever her chances on the road, Rose knew she would be feeling much safer with this great big metal box around her. She was both surprised and impressed by Nabeel's initiative. She was now independent and could go to work and go shopping for food alone. Perhaps there lay the rationale for Nabeel's unexpected purchase? He hated going to the Coop and now he needn't go! Rose pushed the thought away - whatever the motivation, the result was marvellous and she was grateful. This was her very first car, and one she would never forget.

Rose was doubly spoiled that birthday. To make up, no doubt, for the frosty start to Rose's first year in Kuwait, the family invited her for dinner on Friday evening, the actual day of her birthday, to the Sheraton with Len and Ngaire as guests too. The photos show the waiters with flaming torches singing Happy Birthday and Rose, in her Marilyn Monroe look-alike white gown, cutting the huge Black Forest cake, specially decorated with her name. This year, however, there was no Johnny Walker served in teapots! Rose was tired after her own small party the evening before, but glad that life was becoming happier at last and the family feud was finally over. The foreign wife was accepted at last, it seemed.

Dear Diary,

What a difference a year makes – now we are happy families at last. The troubles of the first year have disappeared. I have a home I can be proud of, a job I love, and a husband who seems to be improving steadily. Will we have a child next? I hope so.

November, 1977, Kuwait

*Dear Diary, I'm learning some
more about Kuwait now. It's been
a rapid escalation of progress for
the citizens since oil was discovered
and production nationalized and
the city is growing exponentially
around us.*

Eid al Adha fell in the third week of November and this
year Nabeel felt secure enough in his financial situation
for them to leave the country on a short visit to Bahrein.
Rose was thrilled to discover this lovely island, named
after a geological phenomenon: two seas in Arabic. This
was on account of the fresh water springs from the ground
underneath the salt water, which allowed the stalwart
pearl fishers to refill their leather drinking water sacks by
diving down into those currents when out at sea. In this
way they could stay at sea for weeks or months, eating
fish they caught and collecting as many oysters as possible
by the simple but dangerous technique of weighting
themselves with a bag of stones around the waist or ankle,
putting a peg on the nose, and diving to the ocean bed
to find potentially lucrative natural pearl-bearing oysters.

Dilmun was the ancient name for this island on the
trade route from India to Persia. Rose and Nabeel spent
a day on a guided tour around the island, from the oil
producing south to the northern shores where excavations

were being carried out on the ancient sites of habitation. They also visited some villages where basket weaving craftwork was practised, with products for sale. Rose purchased a woven pot with a lid, made from mauve, pink and natural coloured raffia as a souvenir of their happy but short escape from Kuwait.

Although Nabeel had a business associate here they had booked themselves into a hotel for their stay, so as not to spoil the holiday for their English friends. Hotels in Bahrain were small but comfortable in the late '70s and there was no bridge across the narrow sea channel to Saudi Arabia so visitors from that severely restricted Islamic state were not often found there. However, Rose did experience an unpleasant but not overly threatening ladies toilet invasion in a hotel, on Thursday night by three or four obviously drunken Saudi youths in *dishdashis, guttras* and *agals*. The ladies using the toilet were able to repulse them with cries of *haraam*. There were no attractions for the youths other than alcohol and secret brothels. For Westerners, a sole Italian restaurant offered pasta with real, imported wine, a paradise after the home brews most visitors were used to. The food was delicious too, so a meal there was a huge pleasure. Only in the United Arab Emirates (UAE) at that time were alcohol licences given to Christians, Rose learned. Expatriates living in Saudi, Qatar and Kuwait had to risk deportation, prison and/or flogging by making homebrew. So, sitting by and swimming in the hotel pool was a double pleasure, with waiters happily serving cold beers to the residents.

Rose heard from their friends, Brenda and Tom, who were local residents, that the Emir of Bahrain was very friendly towards expatriates and on Friday afternoons held a regular tea party at his beach house. This beach was open to Westerners only, and his guards sometimes selected guests from the beachgoers to attend the tea party and meet the Emir briefly. They decided to go along as a foursome, with Nabeel under strict instructions to play the Westerner and to ensure he did not speak Arabic or even show that he understood the guards, if spoken to. The beach was pristine, with white sand and amazingly azure blue sea gently lapping the shore. Women were wearing bikinis, although no alcohol was available or allowed to be brought onto the beach.

"Wow, this is lovely," commented Rose as they settled onto their beach mats and applied the necessary sun tan lotion. "Do you come here often, Brenda?"

"Not really, it's best to come with a group, or your husband, and Tom is not often free. I go to the Intercontinental pool. You can join as a resident for an annual subscription."

"That sounds good. I don't think we've got the same in Kuwait, have we, Nabeel?"

"We've got ladies beaches, which are low cost, but you wouldn't like them, Rose. The women swim in their *abbayas* I've heard. You would have to wear a one piece swimsuit."

"Well that's OK but I don't like the sound of it really. What about hotels?"

"I think the Intercon near the airport has one, but you've seen the Sheraton - nothing there."

"Well, I might try out the ladies beach one day, perhaps with someone from work. I can investigate now that I have my own car!"

As well as visiting the beach and touring the island there was an opportunity to visit the *souk*. Bahrein's *souk* wasn't as large as Kuwait's but there were some clothing stalls and small shops selling what appeared to be Indian garments. Rose indulged in a couple of 'tie/dye' cotton dresses and some coordinated silk shawls which would be suitable for parties, especially as Christmas and New Year were coming up. With her slim figure she could easily buy and wear off the peg clothes, which were cheap and in this case fun. She loved nothing more than a bargain, though Nabeel had commented on his friend Ahmed's wife's designer labels and how nice she looked.

"If you want me to dress like that," she told him, "you're going to have to give me a dress allowance. Dior is not cheap. You should think yourself lucky that you've got a bargain basement wife from the West!"

Nabeel made no comment, though the point obviously sank in, as he never mentioned it again.

Christmas was to be a happy time this year, their first in the security of Abu Ali's house. As Rose had noticed the year before, shops began to show signs of the festivities to come during the month of December. Cotton wool was stuck onto windows to simulate snow and plastic Christmas trees began to appear with tinsel decorating them. Rose made sure she got hold of an artificial Xmas tree this time and a couple of boxes of glass baubles to hang on it. She remembered with wry humour the apocryphal occasion at Mum's rented house when the artificial tree lit with real candles had suddenly ignited in the front room. In a superhuman feat her teenage brother Bill had grabbed the burning torch by its metal base with one hand and flung open the front door with the other and thrown the flaming mass onto the street. It was very lucky that no one was passing at that time in the evening!

Rose wasn't sure they needed the electrical complication of coloured lights on the tree, but she searched for and found an angel for the top. Ensconced on one of the four small coffee tables in the corner of the lounge, the tree made a lovely focal point. She invited Imm and Abu Ali and their children in for coffee and the other ritual refreshments to enjoy the spectacle. Ali, the oldest son, was now nearing the end of his school life, and there was talk of him going to study in the USA. The Kuwait Government was giving scholarships for male students who were willing to complete a degree program overseas. To ensure there was no brain drain and that society would benefit from this investment in education the prospective students had to sign a contract stipulating that they would return and work for the Government for at least five years after qualifying.

It seemed a good deal. Government workers in Kuwait only worked for 25 years before retiring. Abu Ali was a local government employee, working at the *baladiya* (municipality) as a supervisor in waste management. His title was lofty but his work was less so. He sat in an office and signed out the garbage trucks as they left to make household collections and as they returned to base. Although the trucks left early in the morning, the job was over before midday so Abu Ali had plenty of free time. As his marriage to an Egyptian lady showed, he was open-minded and far-sighted enough to see that his older son's career would benefit from a scholarship.

Over the next few months there were discussions over the locations available for the general education course Ali would need to follow first of all, to get his English language up to scratch. Once brochures started coming in showing unisex bathrooms on American college campuses, there were some uncomfortable conversations. Kuwaiti national dress, of course, with the white thobe resembling a dress, was an issue which would confront Westerners. Kuwaiti students were warned about this. It was not a problem since many students wore jeans and baseball caps for casual occasions at home. National dress with the *guttra* and *agal* was only worn for formal occasions.

However, males in Kuwait were noticeable for their overuse of the strongest smelling and often the most expensive perfumes on the market. Rose felt she had to gently point out that these heavy fragrances might cause some misunderstanding of Ali's sexual proclivities. She tried to explain that male colognes/aftershaves in the USA were much lighter and less noticeable when the wearer entered a room. Rose's warnings were to no avail: When Ali had been in the USA for a month he wrote home that many students wore perfumes. He didn't mention if they were male or female, however!

A few years later Ali returned with an American wife. This became an issue for the Government, as Kuwaiti women were being neglected in favour of foreign brides. Even maids from the Philippines were being preferred to local girls because they didn't need a bride price. A law was eventually passed forbidding the marriages of Kuwaiti men to foreign women.

December, 1977, Kuwait

As usual, Christmas was an official working day but New Year's Day was to be a holiday. Although Rose and Len had arranged the ETC programme timetable so that it avoided teachers coming in for classes on this important family holiday period, office hours still had to be observed. Nabeel and Rose spent the afternoon of Christmas Day, Sunday, as usual at the family villa, with Rose helping in the kitchen and Asma excelling this year with a huge, savoury, stuffed turkey, preceded by her delicious parsley and meatball consomme. This year, Joseph and Claudine were not present as they had made their home in the South of France, leaving their condominium to Henri. He was obviously enjoying being king of the castle in their luxurious condo in one of the best locations in the city.

As ever the issue of whether to take a siesta or not came up around 4pm. The men went on smoking and playing cards, but both Rose and Asma needed some time to put their feet up. As Henri had moved into Joseph and Claudine's condo, the bedroom she was shown into was clean. At least Rose could rest and think about the future, coloured as it was by the past 15 months in Kuwait. They seemed to be a united family now, with holiday traditions to maintain. Letting fate take a hand Rose had decided that she would stop taking the pill five months previously but so far there had only been negative changes. Her menstrual periods had become irregular without the hormones provided by the pill, and her breasts and womb had frequently been painful enough to make her take sick leave.

Meanwhile, in Lebanon, the Palestine Liberation Organisation (PLO) had moved into the south of the country after the Black September uprising of 1970 in Jordan had caused the leadership to be expelled from there. They had taken over the towns of Sidon and Tyre, and were active among the 400,000 Palestinian refugees in the Lebanese camps. They had in effect created a state within a state, which stirred up sectarian dissent. This increased into violence starting in April 1975 in Sidon and resulting in massacres in 1976. Peacekeeping troops were deployed to hold a ceasefire in October as a result of an Arab League summit meeting. The Government began to lose control of the many sects within Lebanese society and the PLO too, developed factions which were more or less aggressive, such as the Popular Front for the Liberation of Palestine (PFLP). The family never discussed what was happening to their sister in Beirut, even when the city became divided into East and West, with a green line and checkpoints between the two sides, Palestinian and Christian Lebanese.

Having a baby was a huge decision, and Rose wondered if she was just trying to make a bad decision about her marriage right. Thinking about the creation of Israel she had often thought that two wrongs don't make a right. Hitler's Holocaust had been a horrific act of genocide but driving the Palestinians out of their homes and pushing them to near extinction was not fair, to say the least. Was she wishful thinking, hoping to make her marriage happier by having a baby? Would it help, or would it be another mistake? As usual, time would tell, Rose thought. Let's see what 1978 brings us.

January, 1978, Kuwait

New Year's Eve, a Saturday, was a working day, so parties were organised around that slight obstacle to planning. Rose got up early as usual to drive to work on Saturday morning, only to find all the cars parked outside the house and a deathly still over the area, with hardly any cars moving along the ring road which could be seen from the street. Rose went back inside to check with the neighbours about the situation. They had been watching TV late the previous evening and learned that the Emir, Sheikh Sabah al Salam al Sabah, who had been suffering from cancer, had passed away in the early hours of New Year's Eve. He had ruled from 1965, and was the political leader during the pivotal Six Days War in which Israel had 'won' Palestinian lands. His long reign merited a period of national mourning, so work was off. Parties that night had to be subdued so as not to attract unwelcome attention. The public fireworks display planned for midnight was cancelled.

During the day the TV played informative videos from the past about the discovery of oil in Kuwait in the 1930s. There was a legend about a dream Lt. Col Dickson, the British Political Agent at the time, had had about the discovery. His widow, Dame Violet Dickson, wrote a book entitled 40 years in Kuwait and still resided in Kuwait, courtesy of the Emir. Rose was reminded that she hadn't had time to consider finding out how to attend one of her weekly tea parties. Rose also discovered from watching daytime television that Muslims were buried without a coffin in a simple shroud, as soon as possible after death in an unmarked grave. There were lines of men in white *dishdashi* robes and light black cloaks, many edged with gold embroidery showing their status, lining up to offer condolences to the Emir's male family members, and to show their allegiance to the new ruler, Sheikh Jaber al Salim al Sabah. The process took hours. Rose wondered how they could physically stand the waiting around in the heat. Luckily it was winter but at noontime the sun was very hot.

For the evening, Rose was torn between staying at the family house till midnight to celebrate the incoming New Year or attending a party given by friends. As the parties would have to be subdued so as not to attract attention, Rose felt it better to stay home with the family and celebrate quietly. However, on New Year's Day there was no choice. Joseph and Claudine were in France, but Nabeel and Rose went round to the family villa on New Year's Day to drink chilled vodka and eat Iranian caviar smuggled into Kuwait duty free by Iranian fishermen and sold by Iranian car washers, who cycled around car parks from early morning looking for clients for their trade and their side lines! The food was delicious, the vodka was a treat, but once again, the ritual activities, Rose working in the kitchen with Asma before and after the meal with no dishwasher meant that the day was dreary. It would have been better if the men did more than simply drink and play roulette or '*tawla*', backgammon. When they did chat, it was in Arabic, so Rose couldn't follow or join in the conversation. This always made her feel like an outsider. On top of that, the usual question put to Rose when they visited was: "What's happening in the UK?"

Her irritated response was "I have no idea. I get the same news as you." As New Year's Day was Mum's birthday, she felt homesick and slightly sad, but was able to call Mum in the evening with their home phone.

Sometimes there was the attraction of TV to pass the long-drawn-out family time. On Friday afternoons the TV program often included musical performances by dead singers such as Umm Koulthum, who was familiar to Rose from Nabeel's record collection in London. The program also included an Egyptian film which lasted around two hours or more. Usually these were in black and white and had no English subtitles as they were old films, but the Arabic accents were clear and easy for Rose to follow, especially given the histrionic overacting. The films were mostly set in Cairo or Alexandria, with the city scenes contrasting with the countryside or the beach. Sometimes the setting involved travel by Middle East Airlines to Lebanon. It was amusing to Rose to see Beirut airport which she had already visited before their marriage, to the astonishment of the family.

Having visited Egypt for her honeymoon, Rose knew the country people or *fellaheen* were peasants who still lived in feudal conditions, with the *Bey*, their landlord, controlling their simple lives. These films were very popular in Kuwait because many Egyptian people had come to this rich oil state to find work as labourers, secretaries and teachers. By dint of watching TV with the brothers, Rose got to know the comedians who made them all laugh, and the singers they most appreciated, although she was forbidden to ask for translation into English: "We don't want to become like the United Nations, with a row of interpreters," Adel had declared, warning her not to disturb their viewing to seek translation.

The Lebanese singer and actress Fayrouz reminded her very much of the French chanteuse famous at the time, Mireille Matthieu, both from her physical appearance and her rigid posture. Some of Fairouz' songs were easy to understand and Rose enjoyed singing to herself *Bint shelebiya, taht irroumiya...* Beautiful girl, under the olive tree. The songs by the older but much more flamboyant singer known simply as Sabah were harder for Rose to grasp. Sabah was famous for not looking her age and for marrying several much younger men. Surprisingly she was not condemned for this, but admired in the Middle East. She travelled extensively with her stage show and her glamorous costumes. Male singers such as Fareed al Atrash, a stocky, middle-aged man, whose name in translation amazingly means Fareed the Deaf, had a lovely tenor voice reminiscent of Mario Lanza. Rose found his songs soothing but repetitive, similar to those rendered by the younger and much more handsome Abdul Haleem Hafez. The latter was as popular in the Middle East as Elvis Presley was in the West.

In the evenings, and in the daytime during Ramadan, there were TV series with weekly episodes. Having watched several episodes of one in particular, in which the phrase *sitt dinaneer* was repeated very often, despite the ban on translation in the family house, Rose was compelled to ask the importance of six dinars in Egypt where she knew the currency was lire, pounds, not dinars as in Kuwait. There was merriment all round as the family realised she did not know that *sitt* means both six and Mrs in Arabic, while *dinaneer* can be the plural of dinar, but also is used as a first name. Mrs Dinars was a key character in the series! Such mistakes are the stuff of learning, so Rose was not discouraged by the laughter.

Dear Diary, Sad and moving scenes today after the passing of the Emir. No work, but lots of TV programs to watch.

Saturday, 25 February, 1978, Kuwait

Dear Diary, My second national day in Kuwait. Perhaps this time I'll get to see some of the traditional celebrations, such as 'hair dancing'.

Kuwait's National Day falling on Saturday this year gave everyone a holiday from work, and national TV ran informative documentaries on the growth and development of Kuwait from a small pearling village to the bustling oil-producing State and member of OPEC since 1960. It was interesting to see the long queues of men in pristine white national dress waiting to personally greet the Emir with the traditional 'nose to nose' greeting. In addition, there were TV programs showing groups of men dancing in circles, solemnly brandishing unsheathed swords and girls in ornate kaftans doing the dramatic long hair swinging dances which were customary in Kuwait.

Also, to Rose's great pleasure, the film she had long wanted to see, *Bass ya Bahar,* was to be shown. The English translation of the Arabic title is <u>Enough o sea</u>, but the English title was given as <u>The Cruel Sea</u>. The film had won an award and although black and white, the portrayal of simple village life under the hot sun, and long dhow voyages diving for pearls to sell on the international market, was gripping. The rituals of sacrifice to the sea made by the women to appease it and bring their men folk home safely was intriguing. For once, Nabeel was home to watch it as he'd never seen it before.

"Why don't we go out to the dhow building village at the weekend?" Rose suggested. "It must be very interesting to see how these boats are made. Who knows how long the craft will persist in today's world?"

The following Friday they drove out to Doha on the spit of the 'old woman's nose', which is what the outline of a map of the State of Kuwait looks like. On the way they passed the huge, concrete, electricity power station, which stood out eerily from the desert and seascape. It was very quiet out here on the morning of the holy day, but it was easy to walk around the boats in the process of being made and see the workmanship. Logs of different types of timber imported from India were soaking in the water, ready to be hewn into planks, and piles of nails were lying around, which almost looked too rusty to work with. As they wandered a voice arrested them. A middle-aged man wearing what looked like a checked tablecloth around his lower limbs, had been sleeping on one of the almost finished boats.

"*Fii shi*?" he asked. (Do you want anything?}

"*La, ya khayi*," replied Nabeel. (No, my brother.)

Despite the response, the man climbed down to them. He obviously wanted to explain to them the process of boat building, but for Rose it was a challenge, trying to follow his words and gestures as he led them around the skeleton of a boat which had just been started.

"I expect you to remember the details and tell me later," she whispered to Nabeel.

The facts were simple. This was one of the last

outposts of dhow building and very few boats were being made now. Large cargo boats brought the wood from India, so it was easier to make the dhows there and then sail the completed boat to Kuwait. Also, pearl fishing was finished now, with the trend for consumers to buy cultured pearls from Japan. Natural Gulf pearls were still prized, but rare and expensive. Fishermen still used the dhows, but most Kuwaitis were turning to the Government for civil service jobs, like Abu Ali. They were steadily losing, if they hadn't already lost, the tradition of going to sea. Young men wanted to wear bright white *dishdashis* with their *gutras* positioned on their heads in the latest style while driving the fastest air-conditioned cars they could afford, rather than sweating and suffering under the hot sun.

Rose felt pleased to have witnessed something traditional and uniquely Kuwaiti. Such experiences were few. A trip to the women's weaving museum was equally informative. Rose enjoyed seeing the women with their looms extended from and stabilised by their feet. The women's *souk* area was also interesting, where the women squatting in their black *abbayas* and *niqab* scarves, sometimes with the face mask made of cloth or leather, sold loofahs from the sea and frankincense fragments together with the small clay burners and charcoal to generate the distinctive fragrance.

Visiting the desert in the spring to witness the mass camping 'villages' that Kuwaitis liked to indulge in to celebrate their past was another interesting experience. The Kuwaiti families took everything from home, including the kitchen sink it seemed. Generators provided electricity for TVs and loud music. Rose would have preferred to visit the Bedouin camps she saw at a distance, with their dark camel hair blanket tents and small flocks of goats around them. Nabeel was too sensitive to politeness norms to approach such a camp uninvited, so Rose only saw these camps from afar. Sometimes, such as in Cairo on their honeymoon, Rose felt that having an Arab husband did not facilitate her getting closer to Arab culture, but distanced her from it, as he was more inhibited than even she was as a foreigner.

Dear Diary,

Sometimes I feel Nabeel is as much a foreigner here as I am. I know there are different language groups within Arabic speakers, and obviously different customs too, having experienced Lebanon, Egypt and now the Arabian Gulf, but Nabeel is obviously more at home in Lebanon where he went to school. I suppose that's normal, but I have to change to fit the social context, so why can't he?

March, 1978, Kuwait

Rose's diary entries revealed that work occupied her time for the most part as 1978 progressed. Although her daily routine was expanded as her confidence and driving skills in her new car grew, she found that shopping for anything other than food was a challenge on her own. When she needed a new pair of shoes she tried to visit a shop in Salmiyah where most expatriates lived. She was horrified when the male assistant - there were no female shop assistants - took the opportunity to stroke her bare lower leg as she was trying on a pair of white leather mules. Unwilling to make trouble for the young man, who was obviously not Kuwaiti, and most likely a Palestinian, Jordanian or Egyptian migrant worker, she paid for the shoes hurriedly and left the shop, determined not to return. She didn't tell Nabeel about this unpleasant incident because he would no doubt feel they had to go back to the shop and complain. Instead, she resolved to buy all her clothing in future back in the UK when the sales were on in the summer. It would be cheaper and easier. The only clothing purchases she felt happy to make in Kuwait were winter- and summer- weight kaftans and wrap around cotton skirts and matching tops imported from India which could be purchased at market stalls. They were cheap and easy to size visually, without the need for trying on.

New friends continued to be found amongst the University English language teacher expatriate population who came to the ETC for part-time work. One of these was Violet, the wife of a University contract teacher in the Faculty of Engineering. Violet was keen to play tennis, and living on the Shuweikh campus she had access to the University tennis courts. Now that Rose could drive she made a point of meeting Violet once a week to play tennis in the afternoon. Rose had been a member of the girls' first tennis six in secondary school so she enjoyed brushing up her skills. It was surprising how she could feel tired after work but become re-energised by being outdoors. Working in the artificial light of the basement office at the ETC was probably draining her energy, as were the long hours, with two or three nights a week on duty or teaching until after 9pm. Rose had worked evenings in London, but she was becoming weary of never seeing the sunset on weekdays, either because she was at work or she was having a long siesta to recuperate from the long hours. Her diary showed that she was getting colds and sore throats almost weekly in the winter weather of Kuwait, which can be cold, with *shmaal,* cold north winds blowing in from the mountains of India and Iran.

Although it was draining, some of the evening work was amusing. It was a good opportunity to eavesdrop on classes by walking around the villa, listening for a few moments outside classroom doors. The soundproofing was not the best in this villa turned school! One night was memorable when Douglas, an attractive, young, male, red-headed teacher rushed into her office to ask her to visit his female class. He reported that the girls had just erupted into loud, raucous laughter and were unwilling or unable to settle down. He didn't know what he'd done to cause the commotion. Rose asked him what he had been doing just before the reaction. He showed her the lesson in the text book. The topic was description of a suitcase or other lost item, so as to claim it at the Lost Property Office in a station. The teacher had wanted to practise oral repetition of the lexical items - "It's made of leather, ... plastic." "It has a handle, ...two handles." "It has a zip." Unfortunately, the letter /p/ is not pronounced in Arabic with aspiration/ air, it is pronounced as /b/. So the girls had heard '*zib*' which is a dialect word for a part of the male anatomy which normally they would never pronounce. This had made them burst out laughing. What had made it worse was that the teacher had thought they didn't understand the word, so he had demonstrated its meaning by pointing to the zip in his trouser front. The girls had thought he was about to show them his private parts, which had made them uncontrollably hysterical. Rose went into the class to clarify and calm them all down. This teacher that evening learnt an Arabic lesson he would never forget.

There was also a local 'pest' who visited the below stairs offices in the late evenings when she was on duty alone. On the first occasion Rose had greeted him politely, assuming he was a potential student, as the ground floor office was closed by Samir at around 5pm. The young man had tried to corner her in her office, but Rose had managed to avoid him by quickly moving to the other side of her large desk, which obstructed him. She had gone straight to the basement public access library which luckily was also open at the same time as evening classes. The male librarian took charge of the intruder and kept him busy with conversation while Rose locked her office from the inside. From then on as soon as Rose saw the familiar *dishdashi* and *gutra* approaching she would lift up the phone and ask for the SM (sex maniac) file. The young Indian librarian was quick to come into Rose's office with a hefty folder and stay with her whenever this young man appeared. Although amusing at first, it was stressful to have these issues to deal with as well as the long working hours.

Both emotionally, physically and intellectually with the unsocial working hours and the pay she felt was not high enough, Rose was feeling ready to give up work, perhaps at the end of the academic year. More urgently, she had experienced symptoms of what she imagined might be miscarriages, with painful breasts and very heavy, irregular menstrual periods. So, eight months after giving up the contraceptive pill Rose felt she needed to get a health check. Magazine articles were full of information about the need for appropriate vitamins and especially folic acid in the diet to prevent birth abnormalities and Rose was keen to avoid any more drama once she had conceived. Miranda upstairs was experiencing similar issues.

In Rose's own case, having a child was not becoming a reality. She had given up taking the contraceptive pill in Ramadan, but there was no sign yet of conception, despite her lying in the recommended position after intercourse. Women's magazines, censored with heavy black marker pen, so not a frequent purchase, were full of hints and tips for conceiving, such as staying in bed for 30 minutes after conjugal relations, and also for ensuring the desired gender of the baby, by altering the ph value of the vaginal secretions. Women were advised to use a vinegar douche, or eat certain foods, so as to create the appropriate acid or alkaline environment for conceiving a boy or girl.

It was also becoming common to consider the state of the man's health in the role of fertility. This was a new trend, but not one that was welcome in the Arab World. A man's fertility was equated with his virility or potency and that should not be challenged in this male-oriented world. In the West, women's magazines were recommending that men should not wear tight-fitting underwear as it increased the heat surrounding the testicles and might reduce the quantity and quality of sperm produced. Boxer shorts were recommended for daily wear, but this American trend was not one which men found comfortable under trousers. Rose drew Nabeel's attention to the information she found, but he simply laughed. "Nature will find a way," he insisted.

Despite his rejection of these suggestions, Rose felt ill enough and worried enough to make an appointment in a private Clinic with an Obstetrics and Gynecology Department which expatriate women recommended to each other. She went along with Nabeel to see Dr Bassem. Kuwaiti, handsome, and despite his youth, he gave the impression of being an expert in his field. He suggested that Rose should keep a temperature chart over the next three months to ascertain the time of ovulation, when her temperature should be markedly raised for two or three days. These were the opportune moments for conception and should be taken advantage of, he suggested politely. Apart from checking her blood pressure and taking a blood and urine sample, no other tests were done. He was reassuring and positive overall, despite Rose's age and the length of time she had taken oral contraception. They went away to get a thermometer from the pharmacy ready to start charting the months ahead.

Dear Diary,

I keep getting sick and I always feel tired. I don't know if it's because I'm no longer taking the pill, but perhaps it is time to stop work to improve my health, ready for the patter of tiny feet.

April, 1978, Kuwait

Dear Diary, I'm taking my temperature and counting the days of my periods, but I feel so tired, I'm just not coping any more.

Over the winter period Rose had caught flu several times and had to take sick leave at least once for a couple of days. There had been no break for Easter, which was in late March, but Rose was experiencing a lot of premenstrual pain in her breasts and womb and her menstruation cycle was irregular. Her menstrual record showed a gap of over 35 days, which had made her think she was pregnant. Her delight had faded when an abnormally heavy and very painful period had followed. Nabeel was concerned, seeing Rose come home in the evenings from work tired out, depressed over failing to conceive and struggling with her studies as well.

"Why don't you stop work for a while?" he urged. "It may be you haven't got the energy to conceive while you are doing work and study. We can afford for you to give up now."

"I really don't like the idea of giving up completely, as it takes my mind off conception," Rose told him. "But part-time would be good. It would allow me to finish this degree and then, if no baby comes, I could start a master's distance program with London, as planned."

"Try to be positive, Rose, about a baby. Negativity might be self-fulfilling," Nabeel urged.

"You are right, but we have to consider that there might be a problem. We have to face facts," she reminded him.

Discussion with Reg and Len about stopping fulltime work and moving to part-time revealed that change was afoot at the Council and the ETC too. Reg was retiring in the summer and Julian Crosby, a linguist famous for his published doctoral dissertation, was coming out to Kuwait as British Council Representative for the next academic year. His wife would be with him, but their children were at university in England. Lydia was an ESOL teacher trainer with the Royal Society of Arts program. She would be able to work with Rose as a part-timer on teacher training programs.

Of course, if Rose resigned from fulltime work, then a new Director of Studies would be recruited from London, with all the perks which Rose had wanted: accommodation and annual return tickets to home base. It was bittersweet to hear that, but it suited Rose, so she made no complaint about her own local contract status. At that moment she was focussing on potential motherhood. But thinking forward, it strengthened her resolve to gain the requisite qualification, a master's degree, to move to the University in the future. There she would not be treated as a 'local wife' but would get overseas contract status with travel tickets and an apartment if she needed to continue working on account of the non-appearance of a baby.

"Well, the die is cast. I'm giving up fulltime work next year. Happy?" she asked Nabeel.

"Thrilled! Well done, *habibti*. Fingers crossed now!" Nabeel was visibly relieved.

May, 1978, Kuwait

Nadia, Abu and Imm Ali's oldest daughter was approaching the end of school and her betrothal to a young Kuwaiti man was imminent. She had been planning or at least talking about going to university to study. Her parents were advanced thinkers in this regard. She would not be entering the job market at a low level, so a university degree was essential. Abu Ali made her studying a condition of the engagement. This was the first time Rose had come close to the social and legal arrangements for marriage in Islamic families in Kuwait. The marriage had been arranged, but Nadia had met her future husband and been given a choice rather than a pre-emptive decision. She seemed happy and was involved in selecting styles and materials for her two dresses: two, because first there would be the Islamic engagement ceremony where the priest or Sheikh came to the house to write the book *'kaatib el kitab'*. This would be a relatively small affair, with family members only invited.

It came out in discussion that there was a problem of location for this ceremony, which should be held at home, but the landlord's apartment was too small. As a result Abu Ali asked if he could possibly hold the ceremony in his tenants' lounge and dining room cum entrance hall and family room. As this was his house, and it would not be a long occasion, Rose and Nabeel were happy to help. They bought flowers to decorate the buffet in the dining room, which looked very fine, reflected against

the long mirror above the sideboard. For this ceremony
Nadia wore a baby pink short dress with matching dyed
taffeta shoes, and a small pink 'fascinator' hat decorated
with a small pinpoint face veil. She looked very pretty,
very young and very demure in her outfit. Abu Ali was
in his smartest traditional dress, a crisp white cotton
dishdashi, with a white linen gutra and black agal, with
Imm Ali looking very attractive and younger than her
years in a new midcalf, long-sleeved, fitted dress. Only
Abu Ali's mother's head and face was covered in her silky
black abbaya and lacy veil. Really, thought Rose, Imm
and Abu Ali were a modern couple who were open to
new traditions. It was fun to live with them and see their
lives close up.

One month later would be the second religious
ceremony, the '*dakhilya*' or entering ceremony. This was
the official wedding ceremony after which the young
couple would set up home together. In Nadia's case, as
for so many young Kuwaiti women, her new home would
be with her mother-in-law. After this, her happiness
would be consequent on the relationship between the
two. Rose reflected that the resulting pregnancy surely
proved she had found happiness in marriage. Nadia was
lucky, mused Rose, that she had experienced as a child
a close and loving relationship between two parents.
Neither she nor Nabeel had had happy childhoods.
Perhaps they were condemned to repeat the past in their
own marriage?

These thoughts were put aside on Thursday, 27 May
when the British Ambassador held a Silver Jubilee Ball at
the Embassy to celebrate Queen Elizabeth's 25th year on

the British throne. They danced till 4am and spent the next day recovering! It was a splendid occasion, with lots of friends attending, and real alcohol on sale at the British Embassy Bar!

Dear Diary,
The UK came to Kuwait tonight. It was a very 'Western' evening at the British Embassy!

June, 1978, Kuwait

As the final course for the academic year came to a close there were two parties for Rose to attend. The first was her own leaving tea party at the Council, where she was presented with a Baccarat cut glass wine decanter - not very appropriate culturally but a wonderful souvenir of her venture into winemaking! Rose was pleased to learn that the new Director of Studies would be one of the two Senior Teachers who had come as a couple the previous year. That would make picking up some part-time teaching easier, once she was ready to resume work. She was already booked for some practical teacher training sessions as some teachers were attempting the RSA Dip. TESOL examinations in summer. So the scary thought of life without any outside work was unwarranted.

Then at the end of the month there was Nabeel's birthday party at home. Although the apartment was small, around 50 people came. Abu Ali must have noticed that guests were drinking alcohol but he was tolerant of his 'pet' Westerners. The next day Rose was able to clear up at leisure from the party now she was no longer working.

It had now been nearly a year since she gave up the pill and three months since she saw Dr Bassem. At her next appointment she gave him the details of her irregular and heavy periods, her painful breasts and extreme mood swings. He was matter of fact as he looked at the temperature data she gave him.

"Well, you seem to be ovulating OK and your blood and urine samples were within normal limits. The next step will have to be checks on your tubes to see if they are patent, that is, open. There is a test called a hysterosalpingogram (HSP), in which dye is injected into your Fallopian tubes to see if they are both open. If there is no blockage then there is a faint possibility that your husband's semen and your vagina's environment are not compatible. After ruling that out we can start you on the fertility drug, Clomid, to increase your fertility and thus the chances of conception. Meanwhile, carry on as you are doing and hope for the best."

"When could I have the HSP test?" Rose asked.

"Well, I'd advise you to go to London to have it done. We don't have the facilities here at the moment."

"OK. Can you recommend someone we should see?" Nabeel asked.

Dr Bassem asked his secretary to pass on the details of a Harley Street gynaecologist he knew had a good reputation. "I'll prepare a report for you to take with you when you are ready to make an appointment."

As they left the Clinic, Rose and Nabeel faced the facts.

"Well, it's obvious that we need to check this out," said Nabeel.

"But it's going to cost quite a bit, I should think. Is that OK?" Rose asked tentatively.

"Yes, of course. It's time to go and see your family again anyway."

"Well, I'll have to get the practical exam preparation

dates organised first. Three teachers are preparing to take the Diploma this summer."

"OK. Sort that out. While we are in the UK I'll visit some companies too. I'll set up a schedule for those, then you sort out the appointment."

"Let me know when you've got your appointments. I'd prefer not to take Clomid - we don't want sextuplets, do we?"

Rose wondered whether Nabeel's eyes lit up with fear or excitement at the thought. Alhough she was concerned about the medical tests ahead she was looking forward to going to the UK to see Mum after another year in Kuwait with only one short break in Bahrein. As August would be Ramadan, Nabeel suggested that they could take a six-week break, starting in mid-July. They would fit in the appointments with the senior gynaecologist in London and also take a proper sunshine break with Mum and John in Spain

Dear Diary,

We spent a lot of money on black market booze for Nabeel's party, but it was also my 'swan song', and everyone seemed to have a good time! And now we are going to the UK - the tests are a bit worrying but it will be good to see Mum and John, and take a holiday!

July, 1978, London

Nabeel having finalised a schedule to visit his major suppliers in Reading and Bath, as well as some other possible business visits for the North of England, Rose scheduled an appointment with Mr Finn of Harley Street. The initial appointment involved a case history and physical examination, followed by an appointment for the HSP. Rose was not looking forward to it. She would be given an anaesthetic but would be able to leave the same day. They were staying at Bill's for the duration of these tests of course. He had now moved into a new apartment in North London with his new partner.

When the day of the operation arrived Rose was stressed but it was relatively painless despite the discomfort. They were both delighted to receive the positive results: her Fallopian tubes were patent, so there was no physical reason why Rose should not conceive. Mr Finn then asked them to have sexual intercourse before their next, early morning appointment, to check the compatibility of sperm and vaginal secretions, as Dr Bassem had warned. This was a challenge, given the 45 minute drive from North London to Harley Street through rush hour traffic. They awaited the results anxiously. Rose had already heard from one of the business friends they had shared their struggle with, how he had split with his wife because of the stress of not conceiving. Each of them had then gone on to conceive a child with their new partners, so this incompatibility could be a real issue. Rose wondered what she and her husband would do should this be their case?

Attending the final appointment with Mr Finn they both felt tense. They had not discussed the possibility of a negative outcome, so they were surprised when Mr Finn looked serious. "Now then," he said, in his serious, senior consultant voice. "Have you had a semen analysis, a sperm count test done, Mr Nabeel?"

Rose and Nabeel looked at each other. The question seemed to require an 'of course' answer, it was so obvious. But Dr Bassem had focussed solely on Rose's health condition and had never queried Nabeel's. Rose wondered if this was prejudice in favour of the male or simply ignorance of the possibility.

"The reason I ask," he went on, "is that there was no sign of life in any of the sperm we found in the vaginal fluids. So, either Rose's vaginal secretions are murdering the sperm, or they are not there in the first place."

Nabeel's face fell, while Rose flushed crimson. This sounded like the script of a murder mystery. Nabeel stuttered his response. "No sperm count test. Never."

Mr Finn looked down at his notes. "OK. Let's start now. Go into the bathroom and give me a semen sample."

Both of them were amazed. Nabeel managed a question. "What? Now?"

"Yes, yes, yes. It's quite normal. You'll find a chair and some literature which might help you."

"Can my wife come in with me?"

"Of course. Just do whatever you need to do and give the sample to my receptionist. Collect a specimen jar from her of course, first. I'll ring you when the results are in and we'll meet again."

He looked up at them dismissively. "Any questions?"

"No. Thanks very much."

They left the room, still in shock. How could they have been so naive? And Dr Bassem so ill-informed, or so reluctant to query a man's fertility in the patriarchal society of the Arabian Gulf?

They collected the plastic container and went into the toilet suite. They were pleased to note there was no one in the waiting room outside to witness their movements. It felt as if they were doing something slightly off colour such as using the airplane loo to join the mile high club. After a while they emerged with the sample in its paper bag, leaving it with the receptionist and then emerging from the building onto sunlit Harley Street.

"I think we need a strong coffee now, don't you?" asked Rose.

Nabeel nodded, reaching for his cigarettes as they walked away from the place of doom. They headed to the coffee shop at the top of the John Lewis Department Store where they could have a coffee and discuss this recent event. Both of them were somewhat lost for words.

"Well, that's a surprise. But aren't we stupid, not to have realised it was a first step in this process?" asked Rose. "We could have saved quite a bit of money if we'd had this done in Kuwait."

"Well," said Nabeel, "we don't know the result yet, so let's not talk about it."

Understandably he was in a state of denial. The thought of his sperm not being viable was a stunning prospect. But a sudden realisation came to them both that they had noted a surprising number of men on Harley Street wearing Gulf Arab dress, the *dishdasha* and *agal*. They had assumed they were escorting ladies, also visible in their *abbayas* and *niqab*, who had gynaecological problems. Perhaps this was an environmental, ecological problem. They had to wait only a couple of days to receive a call from the receptionist who made their next appointment. They went along to Harley Street as soon as possible. Mr Finn was serious as ever.

"Well now, Mr Nabeel," he opened. "I'm afraid it's bad news."

Rose and Nabeel gasped slightly. Rose looked down, while Nabeel stared at Mr Finn in disbelief. "You've got a very low sperm count, and I'm afraid there is also low viability in the sperm that are present. This means, I regret to tell you, that there is no chance of you making your wife pregnant."

Rose and Nabeel looked at each other, Nabeel in dismay, Rose in sorrow. She reached out and took his hand to help him cope with this tragic news. She took charge of the conversation.

"But is there no treatment? Like the fertility drug for women? Can the count be boosted in some way?"

"Well, I believe you smoke, Mr Nabeel?"

"Yes." There was no mention of his standard riposte, 'Smoking kills germs'.

"Well, heavy smoking can destroy sperm. Spermatogenesis takes 90 days, so you could abstain from smoking for three months and then have another test. Also, wearing loose boxer shorts in your hot climate could help, even with some ice application to the testicles when showering, if you care to. Vitamin B might help too. Give these suggestions a good three months, why don't you?"

Rose and Nabeel smiled at each other. Perhaps there was a glimmer of hope.

"I'll prepare a full report for you to take back to Dr Bassem. But between you and me I am rather surprised that a sperm count was not done as soon as you went to see him. It could have saved Mrs Nabeel an operation and you a rather large bill, Mr Nabeel."

The overwhelmed couple thanked Mr Finn.

"My invoice will be available with the report. Goodbye for now and good luck," he told them as he rose to shake their hands.

As they left the building after checking Bill's mailing address was with the receptionist, Nabeel lit a cigarette as they walked to their car.

"You can leave me, you know," he said abruptly.

"What? There's still hope, Nabeel. Don't be so upset. What surprises me is the cause. I wonder if it is smoking? Or the climate? Look at all these Gulf Arab men walking up and down Harley Street."

"I bet the Israelis poisoned our water," Nabeel said, with only a slight smile.

"Do you mean in the refugee camp in Lebanon? Or in the Gulf?" asked Rose.

"I wouldn't be surprised at anything the Israelis do to hurt Palestinians," Nabeel muttered, pulling on his cigarette.

"You know, there is another possibility. Did you and your brothers have mumps when you were in the camp?

That childhood illness can cause infertility in males. I wonder if Asma knows. Joseph and Claudine haven't mentioned a problem, have they?"

"No, but they wouldn't. Infertility isn't spoken of in our culture."

"It's not the same as virility, you know. Impotence is another thing altogether," Rose assured him. "There's no reason to keep it a secret. In fact, it could help you all. Four brothers with no children. It seems unusual."

"OK. Let's forget it now. Let's get back to Bill's and drown our sorrows in that good single malt whisky we bought at Duty Free."

Once back at Bill's they didn't share the news with Rose's brother. He had a busy job and enough troubles of his own. Instead, they all went out to a favourite Greek restaurant for *tzatziki, taramasalata*, feta cheese, black olive and tomato salad, and kebabs for the meat eaters.

"Well, Bill, we will be off to Mum's in the morning. We're flying from Gatwick to Torremolinos, so we won't be able to see you till after the holiday in Spain," Rose explained.

"Mum will really enjoy that, Rose. She feels so much better in the heat. You know, she may have to have one of these new joint replacement operations soon, she's in such great pain all the time."

"Gosh, she hasn't mentioned it to me. I hope I'll be able to come over and help out if she does have to go into hospital," Rose assured him.

"That's good. I'll keep you posted. She comes down to St. Bartholomew's to see orthopedic specialists and stays here with me. But she'd love to have you here to help her if needs be."

"I'm only working part-time now because I am studying to get a better job at the University. I'm enjoying reading English Literature after four years of French!"

Rose and Bill had studied for their first degrees at the same Northern university though Bill was an economist and Rose a linguist.

"Those were the days, weren't they? No jobs to worry about then," Bill reminisced. "But how will another BA help you get a better job?"

"Well, it'll be a long haul, but I'll be able to do a distance learning master's degree with London if I get a BA with them," she explained.

"I see. Well, you certainly are a workhorse, aren't you? Never satisfied with the *status quo.*"

At this point Nabeel nodded his head vigorously. "She never stops wanting to improve. I don't know why she does it."

"You needn't talk, Nabeel," Rose remonstrated. "You're always at work. I never see you. So it's a good thing I like my own company and my books."

Dear Diary, A setback today and a concern about Mum's illness. Life seems rather negative at the moment.

August, 1978, London, Spain

Dear Diary, Yesterday was a shocking day. Really bad news, but maybe stopping smoking might help. It can't be good for him and it's certainly not good for me. And Mum's Rheumatoid Arthritis is getting worse. It must be so hard for her to have to keep working while John is only a teenager. I hope this holiday will do her good.

The trip was memorable because there had been a flight delay at the start of the holiday. The four of them had been driven to a large hotel in Brighton where they managed to get a few hours sleep but in the same room! They had been woken at daybreak to make the long bus journey back to Gatwick airport. They had a lovely couple of weeks in Torremolinos relaxing in the sun, eating paella in beach cafes and drinking long, cold glasses of beer. They had visited the pretty, traditional village of Mijas, high in the mountains with panoramic views of the Mediterranean. They had made a long, hot road trip to visit picturesque and historic Granada, with the beautiful architecture of the Al Hambra palace, and deep in the south they had visited Jerez and Cadiz, with John hanging his feet out of the car window to cool them! They took lots of photos to record the lovely scenery and good times together.

Their hotel was large and modern and the food was good. The hotel management had apologised for not having ground floor rooms and had given them the next best thing, two first floor rooms, but that meant they had to use the lift as Mum could not walk up or down stairs with her disability. On one occasion some other residents, thinking their European language would not be understood by four Brits, voiced loud criticism of the group's use of the lift to go up to the first floor. Rose was not a linguist for nothing. As they left the lift she turned and berated the European tourists in their own language, for their thoughtlessness. "I hope one day you will be as ill as my mother is now." Shock and shame registered in turn on the four sunburned faces. There was no apology, however.

All good things come to an end, and so they headed back to Gatwick to pick up their car. Once again, the flight was delayed and on arrival, they were given another hotel to sleep in for one night, and once again, there was only one room for the three adults and one teenager. They could laugh about it, however, and got on the road next day back to Mum's disabled person's apartment.

"I'm sorry we are leaving again tomorrow, Mum. Nabeel's nephew is in university in Bordeaux and he's having some difficulties so we are going to visit him. Then we'll see some business people in Paris, before flying to Amsterdam to get our return flight to Kuwait," explained Rose. "We'll be back in three months, though, as we have to get another check up in London with Mr Finn." Rose had shared the sad news with her Mum while on holiday.

"It's OK. We had a good holiday. Bill and John will

look after me. Don't worry," Mum reassured her. "It will be lovely to see you again soon. I hope you'll be able to stop smoking, Nabeel."

"For sure, Mum, I promise you. I know you want to see some grandkids, don't you?"

"Yes, that would be wonderful. So be strong, and don't smoke!" she urged him, loving him as her son, knowing he had lost his own mother as a young child.

The next day they set off for London, spending one night with Bill before flying to Bordeaux where Elijah was studying, thanks to Nabeel's intervention with his sister and brother-in-law. Elijah had no difficulty studying in French, and Uncle Nabeel was paying his fees, but he was feeling homesick after his first year of study and was stressed about his upcoming end of year exams. They met his homestay 'Mum' who told them that she thought Elijah was working hard, perhaps too hard for his health. They took the young man out to dinner for a delicious *Entrecote Bordelaise*.

Nabeel tried to reassure him. "Just do your best, Elijah. Don't worry too much. I had problems in England when I first went there and then I ended up staying for 10 years and marrying an English girl!" Rose and Elijah smiled. Indeed the future was open for Nabeel's nephew and he was happy to have this chance. But the responsibility to show his uncle that he deserved this opportunity was obviously weighing on him and causing depression.

After only one night in Bordeaux they flew to Paris to meet up with the French count and other former colleagues at the French forgemaster company. Once again, their time was brief but Rose enjoyed strolling the boulevards while Nabeel was in business meetings. She remembered vividly her happy time with Alex there seven years earlier and how she had told Nabeel about the incipient relationship. Nabeel had wasted no time getting back to her to prevent further developments. Had she made the right choice, she wondered? Should she take up Nabeel's offer to separate on account of the fertility problem? Only two years earlier she had made a vow to stay with him in sickness and in health and had followed him to Kuwait. She had to honour that promise and hope that three months' abstinence from smoking would improve Nabeel's health overall and his fertility in particular.

The following morning they had an early morning flight to Amsterdam. They would be flying onward to Kuwait the next day. Although it was a rush, they took advantage of the stopover to visit the Van Gogh museum and the Anne Frank house. Both visits were tainted with tragedy. Van Gogh's on account of his early death, at 37, by his own hand it was believed. Anne Frank's on account of her diary of her family's hidden life during WW2 and her subsequent arrest and death at the age of 15. The visits reminded Rose to count her blessings instead of lingering on the negatives in her life.

The flight back to Kuwait was different as they had been promised a 'fixer' by one of Nabeel's contacts. The fixer was to meet them at the airport in Kuwait and get them through customs without their baggage being checked. In anticipation of this, Nabeel had bought eight half bottles of whisky and packed four in each of their suitcases, hidden inside clothes. Nabeel assured Rose that the worst case scenario would be the finding and removal of the items by customs. They would not be flogged or imprisoned, he promised. In fact, the fixer worked his magic and they got through customs without their cases being opened. The fixer took his fee in kind - one of the half bottles! Rose breathed easily again once they were in the taxi home.

16 September, 1978, Kuwait

After September's *Eid al Fitr* holiday was over, the new staffing arrangements kicked into place. Justin was promoted to DOS while Lucy continued as Senior Teacher. New arrivals were the Representative and his wife, Dr Julian and Lydia Crosby, replacing the Longs. They were moving into the Longs' villa. Rose went to meet them in Leslie's office. The atmosphere was slightly charged with tension, perhaps on account of Rose's recent departure from fulltime work and concern about her current expectations.

"It's nice to meet you," Dr Crosby smiled and asked at once, "I understand you are interested in working part-time now?"

Rose, a little taken aback at this direct approach, stammered her reply, "Well, yes, it depends on what you've got going. I'm planning to take it a bit easy for a couple of years."

Lydia joined the conversation at this point. "Would you be interested in training teachers with me?"

Rose was surprised, but pleased. "Of course, that would be ideal. I did some introductory teacher preparation courses in London for ILEA before I came here and three refresher sessions for the teachers who took the Dip.TESOL here in June."

Lydia smiled. "That's perfect. I need a practical trainer to work with me so that I can concentrate on the written exams."

Rose nodded in agreement. "I would like that very much."

Lydia smiled even more broadly. "Well, I'll keep you in touch with developments."

Julian joined in now: "And what about English for Specific Purposes (ESP) programs? I'll be introducing more of those, using my Curriculum Design model. I'm bringing out a young man who's experienced in writing materials in this area. We'll need some teachers to put the models into practice."

Rose laughed. "It seems I'm going into overdrive, not coasting along then. I'd be happy to join in any new venture, but I have to keep potential motherhood as my focus, or else my husband will get cross."

Julian laughed. "He's going to regret that - I prefer to have my wife at work, or else she drives me bananas. I've even got a sign for my desk!"

Lydia nudged him, probably concerned that the atmosphere was becoming too relaxed with his new staff. Rose thought it was time to make her excuses and leave. She didn't want to overstay her welcome.

"Don't forget there's a staff meeting on Thursday morning, 10am," Justin reminded her as they said their goodbyes. "I want to get everyone together for our new start. There'll be coffee and nibbles."

Lucy chipped in, "I'll be making some scones!"

Rose smiled at her enthusiasm. "Great. I look forward to that!"

As Rose drove home in her luxurious white Yank Tank, as she had christened her car, she reflected on how things seemed to be moving in the right direction for her career despite the hitch in the plans for her family. Although she still held a tiny grudge about the lack of overseas status during her two years as DOS, she knew the British Council ran as a business, despite its charity status in overseas locations. The ETC was supposed to make a profit, so not giving overseas status to staff when it could be avoided, was an obvious economic strategy. In a similar position to herself as local contract people, the administrators Samir and Na'maan were both hoping that there would be a British Passport perk attached to long service with the Council, but that hope was nebulous and most likely to be ignored, Rose felt, by the British Council hierarchy in London. Rose was as determined to obtain a master's degree as she was to conceive a child at this point in her life.

Meanwhile, back at the flat, she had lunch to prepare for Nabeel when she would report her news from the meeting. She wondered if he'd be pleased at the offers she had had. In the event he took the situation pragmatically.

"It's up to you what you do," he said. "But don't forget, we aren't getting any younger. We need to start our family soon."

"OK. Understood. And I want to finish my degree too, so I'll be happy to stay home even if these ideas don't come to fruition."

A week later she attended the Saturday staff meeting at which she met some new teachers who had recently joined the ETC part-time staff. One of them, a slim, sporty-looking blonde girl with a fair complexion and blue eyes seemed strangely familiar to her, but Rose couldn't recall meeting her before. She certainly hadn't been on staff before Eid al Fitr. At the coffee break she went over to speak to the young woman.

"Have I met you before? You seem familiar to me?"

The young woman was visibly upset at the question. She retorted:

"You always say that! I've met you at least twice before. I'm Ruth!"

Rose was embarrassed and upset, apologising profusely.

"I'm so sorry. I don't have a good memory for names, but that explains why you look familiar. Please forgive me."

That night, Rose had a dream, and in the dream she was back at her secondary school, playing netball on the asphalt terraces, in a short sports gymslip with a red shoulder band. On the opposing team, wearing a blue band, was the very same blonde girl she had met that day. Rose woke up with a start: Now she knew why the young woman was familiar. They had been at school together. She couldn't wait to see her again and pass on the information. Lessons were to start at the beginning of October, so she would probably run into her before then but there was the perfect opportunity to make amends when she invited a few people to a party on Thursday 28th to celebrate her birthday at the end of the month. Ruth's husband Dan was a professor of biology at the University, so Rose passed an invitation on to them through the Uni grapevine.

The grapevine did its job and a large group crammed into the small apartment that evening. It was the first gathering of the new academic year so people were busy catching up with each other, eating snacks and helping themselves to Rose's home-made wine. She had prepared a cold buffet meal of salads, including pasta with tuna and sweetcorn, rice with mixed green, red and yellow peppers, and a huge platter of peeled prawns with a bowl of thousand islands sauce and cocktail sticks to spear them with, as well as platters of cold meats with slices of French bread and a range of cheeses with crackers.

Seeing her guests were settled, she looked around for Ruth. As soon as she had a spare moment Rose asked her:

"Did you go to school in Derbyshire?"

This time it was Ruth's turn to be taken aback. "Yes, I did! How do you know?"

"Because I was at school with you! I remember you on the school netball team!"

Ruth giggled. "That's amazing," she said.

"And do you remember the handsome history teacher?" Rose went on.

"Yes, I do," confessed Ruth. "I went out with him after I'd left school."

"Oh my word! He was the school heart-throb, wasn't he?"

"Yes, that's girls' schools for you."

The two laughed, peace and understanding had arisen between them. The past amnesia was forgiven.

> Dear Diary,
>
> What a coincidence that amongst this small expat population there should be a girl I went to school with before Mum left Dad. It's a small world!

As for work, it seems I'm going to be busier than expected, but that's OK for now. But I seem to have a psychological blockage with names — there was that dinner party with the two Marinas and now the dream about Ruth. What's my problem, I wonder?

October, 1978, Kuwait

The following month found Rose preparing for an ESP language course at the Kuwait Investment Company. Julian's new protege, Sam had only just arrived with his wife and was still finding his feet, so there was no one else available to take the course on. Nabeel was not very happy about it because, having stuck to his no smoking regime, he was keen to get back to Mr Finn to see if there had been an improvement in his fertility as soon as the 90 days were up. Rose spoke to Justin and Julian about her problem.

"We have to go back to the UK for a couple of weeks, I'm afraid. Can we split the course into two units, with a break in the middle?"

"Well, *Eid al Adha* will probably overlap the second and third weeks of November, so if you can arrange to take those weeks that should be fine."

And so it was agreed. There was little research to inform Rose's course preparation. She was simply told to prepare for 10 weeks of lessons delivered twice a week for 90 minutes each, i.e. a total of 30 hours. At this time in ESOL history there were few textbooks available for what is now generically termed Business English. So, working from her knowledge of an older book she had brought from London, Rose prepared her first lesson with an authentic reading text and comprehension and discussion tasks, designed to discover her students' current abilities. She also had to investigate their individual needs, for

341

which she prepared a short questionnaire. Her students were likely to be from different ranks in the company, both male and female.

She was nervous and excited as she headed off down *Istiqlal* (Independence) Street to the centre of town. The offices were in an unprepossessing three storey cement block building. Having parked her car in the Visitor space, she was escorted from Reception to the Boardroom where the class would be held. There was a paper-loaded presentation board for her to use with her own marker pens.

"Can I photocopy these texts and questionnaires, please?" she asked the hijab-wearing receptionist.

"Yes, how many copies?"

"How many staff do you think will be present today?"

"Perhaps 12? I am not sure...."

"OK. Please do 15, that's one for me and a couple extra."

As the young woman left the room another two came in together, whispering. They introduced themselves with their first names and Rose wrote her own on the pad.

"You can call me Rose," she told them, hoping to establish a warm, collegial atmosphere in the group.

"OK, Mrs Rose," they replied, as students were wont to do in the Arab World, using the honorific before the first name in an oddly quaint misuse of English politeness terms.

As the receptionist arrived with the photocopies a stream of people followed her in. Rose was pleased to be able to hand out the needs analysis questionnaires to each person. Once the door was closed she had six men and six women in front of her around the boardroom table, forming a satisfactory U-shaped classroom for communication purposes, allowing direct eye contact. Slightly to her consternation the men and the women had grouped themselves separately, as they tended to do even on social occasions. She introduced herself, pointing to her name on the poster board, and asked the group to complete the questionnaire in front of each person. They were to fill in their full name and give as much detail about their job and their language requirements as possible. As they did this she moved around the group behind them, observing how they were coping with the questions. She relayed any individual question to the group to facilitate their performance.

Once the completed questionnaires were handed back to her, she gave out the comprehension text. She had written it herself, having simplified a report she had seen in a recent business magazine about the Ford Motor Company. It included a brief history and review of current financial performance. She felt it had all the ingredients she needed to test indirectly the simple past tense, the present perfect tense and some common business vocabulary. She allotted ten minutes' reading time and expected silence to ensue, which she would follow with pair/group reading/answering of her written questions. Instead, there was a milder version of the riot which Douglas had experienced with his suitcase description lesson. The students were in quiet uproar.

"What's wrong? Tell me the problem, please," she begged the group.

One of the older men looked at her with some disdain: "It's the company. Ford is on the Arab Boycott list."

Rose was horrified. She hadn't realised Ford was on the Arab Boycott list. What on earth could she do now?

"OK. I apologise for that, I'm still new in Kuwait. I know you have American cars here, so can you tell me the name of a company that is not on the Boycott List?"

"Yes, Jims," the same man replied, still looking down his nose at her.

"Jims?" Rose asked uncomprehendingly. "I haven't heard of Jims, I'm sorry."

She felt completely on the back foot with the group now. "Can you please write it down for me?"

The man took the marker and wrote on the poster board 'GMC'.

Rose laughed out loud as the light went on figuratively: "Oh I see, General Motors Company."

This time it was the man who looked a little taken aback. "OK. That's it. But we say Jims."

"No problem, thank you very much. Now, can you all do me a big favour. Please cross out Ford and write GMC instead."

"Does anyone know who started or in Business English, founded, the GMC company?"

No one did, and neither did Rose. These were the days before Google!

"So let's put a cross through the history paragraph and simply read the information, or data, about GMC instead of Ford, just for practice today."

The group did not want to. A raw nerve had obviously been touched.

"It's not real. It's not good." So numerous were the negative retorts that Rose gave up.

"OK. Let's do introductions. Let's imagine we are all interviewing for a job here. Do as I do."

She demonstrated a two-minute oral presentation of her name, country of origin, qualifications and experience as a teacher, then asked each person to do the same about themselves. Thus the hour remaining was filled, with 12 x 4 minutes of oral presentation each, often expanding into almost ten minutes each. As Rose had discovered in her two years at the ETC, one thing Arab students enjoyed doing was talking, and especially about themselves. So ended her first day of teaching ESP in the Arab World, one she would never forget.

Fortunately from then on the ice was broken between the teacher and the students. They regarded the class as something of a break from work although it was intended to provide them with professional development. The needs analysis had revealed that they rarely used English except for telephone calls and business meetings, so Rose concentrated on pronunciation and dialogues, asking the students to bring in examples of situations in which they were required to use English. The thought of the *Eid al Adha* holiday was an incentive to them, and the study period of five weeks was more attractive.

Dear Diary,

It's been an interesting 5 weeks teaching ESP but now I'm ready for a break. Plus, I'm hoping for some good news from Mr Finn. Nabeel has been good with his decision not to smoke. It must have been so hard for him to stop. So fingers crossed!

2 - 15 November, 1978, England

On the second day of the month, Nabeel and Rose flew out of Kuwait. Their appointment with Mr Finn was on Monday 6 November, so they had time to visit Mum beforehand. Bill had arranged a hire car for them, as after the appointment Nabeel had planned visits to his 'principals' in Leicester, Manchester and Middlesborough. They both had International Driving Licences this time so as to make sure they were able to handle the hectic schedule. Rose had got rather tired of being on duty as navigator even when she was not driving as Nabeel seemed incapable of finding his way anywhere using road signs so this time she was ready to take the wheel. After a two-hour motorway drive they finally reached Mum's apartment and could relax. Mum was still working so they had picked up fish and chips for supper, to eat with the duty free champagne they had bought at the airport.

"Oh, that's nice," said Mum. "Do you think we'll have something to celebrate soon?"

"Fingers crossed, Mum," Rose replied. "We'll have to let you know on Monday. But Nabeel has been very good. No smoking, or at least, none that I've observed."

"Of course I haven't smoked," retorted Nabeel indignantly. "I want a good outcome as much as you do."

"Leave him alone," John spoke up for his brother-in-law. "Don't hit a man when he's down."

"Well said, little brother," Nabeel smiled happily. "I need some support. It's bad enough not smoking, without these two getting at me."

"Come on, subject closed. Truce!" Rose laughed. "The food is getting cold. Let's eat."

The weekend flew by with a visit to Dad and family in Berry Vale, so Monday found them once again in Harley Street. They entered Mr Finn's waiting room with some trepidation. The receptionist gave them the expected sample container and they went into the bathroom together rather sheepishly. After giving the sample, they were asked to wait a few moments while Mr Finn himself did the microscope analysis.

"Can you go into Mr Finn's office now, please," the receptionist invited them.

Mr Finn greeted them warmly, but his face was serious. "I'm sorry to tell you there's been no change at all in sperm number or motility. Although we found nothing noticeable in your blood and urine samples you could try a course of antibiotics as a last chance treatment."

"Is there any evidence that antibiotics would improve the situation?" Rose asked.

"Only if there's a low grade infection that could be interfering with spermatogenesis. Your condition is called oligospermia. It is not rare. The main thing is that you now should consider whether you would be willing to undergo donor insemination, Mrs Fardan?"

Nabeel's face fell and he paled with shock. "No way can I accept that," he shouted.

Rose looked at them both in similar shock. "We

hadn't considered such a thing, Mr Finn, so please forgive my husband's outburst. He's in shock."

"OK, sorry for being blunt. It's a situation I've seen many times, you know. You both have to consider how much you want a child. Donor insemination would mean the child would have one set of genes from you, so it's not such an unthinkable thing, is it?"

Nabeel stood up. "Thank you, that's enough for now. We'll be in touch." He started to walk out and Rose hurried after him.

"Nabeel, hold on. It's not the end of the world, you know. Mr Finn was just doing his job."

"I know. But I can't do my job, which is becoming a father," he said angrily.

"Listen. Being a father does not simply mean having a child with your genes. Caring for a child is another way of being a father," Rose tried to explain, hoping to ease the pain.

"Please stop talking about it. I need a cigarette and I'm going to have one." With that, he strode towards Oxford St in search of tobacco, his familiar friend.

As before, when they got back to Bill's, nothing was said about their fertility problem, but after a fortifying drink Rose made a secret phone call to Mum to let her know the bad news. Mum was sad, maybe even disappointed, but she tried to encourage Rose to look on the bright side. "Maybe antibiotics will help. Don't give up just yet."

"We'll have to forget about it now as we are off to Nabeel's business meetings up North. I've already met some of these business contacts, so it should be pleasant for me. I'll try to go and see Uncle Jeremy and Aunty Dora while we are in Manchester."

"That would be nice. They are so kind. They come over to see me every three months or so. Uncle Alec and Aunty Marie take us out shopping every week as well. Two of my brothers still love me. So, don't worry about me. I'll see you on your way down to London again."

"OK. It's a short trip this time, but hopefully we'll be able to come back next year."

Dear Diary,

Our UK trip was short but not so sweet. The business and family sections were successful, tho it was sad to say goodbye again to Mum. Mr Finn prescribed a course of antibiotics, but he was not very positive about the potential outcome. We have to stay positive and not get too stressed about the situation. Maybe we'll be lucky.

16 November - December, 1978, Kuwait

Back in Kuwait, as the part-time ESP Business course continued towards its tenth week finale Rose met Lydia, the BC Rep's wife, to plan for a Diploma in TESOL program to start in the new year. Lydia had left a training position at a well known UK ESOL institute and was keen to maintain her status as an RSA Dip.TESOL trainer by establishing courses in Kuwait. They determined that she would give the lecture/workshop style input sessions which would culminate in a written examination, while Rose would lead the lesson planning sessions, and demonstrate various practical teaching techniques such as choral/individual drilling of new language patterns, and other behavioural learning strategies, such as Q/A drills, choral dialogues, as well as cognitive techniques such as concept checking, which were essential components for an ESOL teacher to use in the two assessed practical lessons.

Rose was excited to take part in the planning as it would inevitably lead to her endorsement as an RSA Dip.TESOL trainer, after which she would be able to seek Dip.TESOL assessor status. There would be input sessions from January, leading to final exams in June 1979. The professional development aim was to encourage the part-time teachers to improve their performance in class as well as to provide them with international certification in their teaching portfolios. Once again, she felt she was back on the right path, despite her lack of overseas status at the British Council.

Although political life was quiet in Kuwait, across the Persian Gulf in Iran, politics was moving the country from a monarchy, with the Shah at its head, to an Islamic Shiite Republic with Ayatollah Khomeini ruling the people. On 21 August this year a cinema in Abadan was set on fire and more than 350 people died. As a result of the danger, the British Council Teaching Centre in Teheran, which had had an excellent international reputation in those early days of TESOL, had been forced to close. The British and American teachers employed there had to sell up their furniture and other large possessions, pack their bags and either go home or to another destination, such as Kuwait. Personally Rose was disappointed that Iran had erupted into civil war as she had heard much about the beauty of this ancient land, and she had been hoping to take a trip there with Nabeel as soon as their finances had settled down. Now it seemed that trip would not be possible.

Meanwhile at home, Rose was studying as hard as she could, enjoying her distance learning courses and writing essays for the exams which she would start to take in June 1979. The earliest she could complete the course was 1980, and that was her target. This was only the first of a set of objectives: first the distance BA with London University which would allow her to apply for the distance learning MA. Having achieved that, she would apply for an overseas post at Kuwait University. The plan was long term, but firmly focussed.

It was highly unlikely now that a baby would be conceived so her plan stayed fixed, because Rose could not visualize a life at home, given the lack of stimulation there. Nabeel worked long hours at the office as ever, and had returned to smoking his 80 cigarettes a day largely at the office, where he subsisted on endless cups of black sweet Turkish coffee, returning home to have a late lunch with Rose. Then he would go back to work in the afternoon while she had a siesta before sitting at her desk to work at her studies. In the evening they would eat a light meal while watching the 8pm TV news and Nabeel would read the '*mulhaq*', or colour picture supplement, his preferred newspaper. Rose tried to understand Kuwaiti politics.

"Nabeel, what do you think about Iran? Is there any fear of regime change here?"

"Not while the economy is strong. The locals have healthcare, housing and education. Why would they try to change? And they are mostly Sunni, not Shiite. There's no fear here."

As the Kuwait Finance and Investment course came to an end, Rose was looking forward to receiving payment for her work. At 10 dinars per hour she would have 300 dinars cash in hand, a novelty for her. Her fulltime salary from the ETC went straight into the bank account which Nabeel managed. Rose had not been able to touch a single dinar of her salary independently. She had to ask Nabeel for money whenever she needed to go shopping for food, or for the occasional gifts which teachers united to buy for each other on birthdays, giving 10 dinars each to buy gold bracelets for the birthday girl.

"Nabeel, I've decided what I'm going to do with my pay from the Business English class."

"Oh really? What's your plan? A trip to the UK?" he laughed sardonically. He was used to dealing in millions of dinars, so 300 of them were no thrill for him.

"I wish! I have a problem when I want to demonstrate listening comprehension procedures with the teachers, so I'm going to get a 'boombox' audio machine, with built in radio and double cassette player. I'll be able to copy the examples I need from the cassette originals to my own master copy. It will be much quicker and easier in my training sessions. And I can make my own recordings from the radio or TV using the microphone. It'll be great!"

"I see, work first for you, as always."

"I'll be able to make master party cassettes too, for dancing to my favourite tops of the pops!"

"OK. So do I have to take you to the store or can you drive yourself?"

"It would be nicer to go with you, if you don't mind. The assistants are all men and they might give you a discount."

With Xmas festivities on her mind, Rose also found a Christmas carols cassette in the shops. Miranda and Andrew were going home for Xmas. Asma was preparing her special turkey with stuffing, and this year Rose searched for cake tins. She baked two rich fruit cakes at the end of November, following a traditional BeRo recipe. By the 25th December they would be mature and moist, with the addition of red wine instead of brandy. As she looked back on the previous two Xmases, the changes were obvious.

Dear Diary, It's been a busy year, shocking and disappointing on the family side but fine on the career side, to compensate. Of course our fertility problem is a big secret. The family here must not know.

January, 1979, Kuwait

Rose's third Xmas and New Year festival period in Kuwait passed as before, with delicious meals round the family dining table, preceded by long hours for the two women standing in the kitchen preparing the food. Rose brought one of her frosted Xmas cakes for dessert, with a tiny snowman and reindeer on top. The reactions were mixed.

"Rose, what's this cold cake? I thought you English ate plum pudding flamed with brandy after the turkey?" commented Adel.

"You're right, steamed puddings are traditional but they take hours to make and you have to eat them warm. This cake can be eaten at any time, with a cup of tea," explained Rose.

"It's very nice, Rose, thank you for making it. And this year we can celebrate Saint Barbara," Asma informed her. "As you have more free time I will make a special dessert, called '*meghlie*'."

"Really, what is that?" asked Rose politely.

"This dessert is very nutritious. It's made of ground rice with star anise and cinnamon. It's given to mothers after childbirth. But it's always eaten by Christians on Saint Barbara's Day."

Rose wondered how pointed the explanation was, given her failure to produce a child. The admittedly delicious dessert was decorated with pine nuts and coloured chocolate sweets and served on Twelfth Night by Asma. As Google and Wikipedia did not exist at this time, Rose discovered years later that Saint Barbara, known in the Eastern Orthodox Church as the Great Martyr Barbara, was an early Christian Lebanese and Greek saint and martyr. Accounts place her in the 3rd century in Heliopolis Phoenicia, present-day Baalbek, Lebanon. The date of the celebration was irrelevant, because there was obviously a covert connection to be made here between the dessert and Rose's failure to produce an heir after two years of marriage. Of course, their visits to see the gynaecologist in London were top secret, as was the outcome. The family assumption was that Rose was too old to conceive, though these words were never spoken.

Although the ritual meals with the family were always delicious, Rose still resented the long hours beforehand in the kitchen helping Asma prepare the food, and afterwards clearing up and washing dishes, then more long hours sitting around in the ornate, formal lounge watching the brothers play *'tawla'* (backgammon), or watching old Egyptian films on TV.

Rose preferred watching TV as she could follow the simple storyline with her limited but growing Arabic. Sometimes there were English subtitles to assist her. On the other hand, when there was an English program, especially the popular comedy *Mind your Language*, about an English language school in London, there were Arabic subtitles. One day, Rose was thrilled to realise that her Arabic was progressing quite well, when she saw a literal written translation of a figurative spoken expression in the program. The actor said: 'Use your loaf,' the slang expression for brain, but the Arabic subtitle Rose was able to read said: *'Istaamil khubzak,'* literally 'Use your bread!'

instead of '*mokhak!*' (your brain) Interestingly, Rose was picking up more insults and negative expressions from listening to the brothers converse than polite expressions and praise. For example, '*Ma fih mokh.*' Literally, 'there's no brain,' meaning 'you are crazy'.

She persisted in watching Arabic language TV when alone too, especially when ironing, which she liked to do seated in the family room. She especially enjoyed films with the Egyptian comedian Adel Imam - who specialised in farcical elements, using facial expressions to accentuate the emotions generated by his words. She laughed herself silly over "*w ana ayaat...* and I was crying..." and "*min el ird*? who's the monkey?" even though the context was unclear to her. Rose was intrigued to see how the films mirrored the society of the day. Clearly there had been a move in Egypt to discourage men from following their Islamic privilege of marrying three wives, with a rotating fourth marriage of pleasure. The practice was not only expensive, as the husband was obliged to maintain each of his wives in equal conditions, but it caused a lot of friction sometimes, if not between the wives, then between their offspring. Boys being the preferred gender for children, a wife who only produced daughters was looked down on. Some films portrayed the unhappiness polygamy produced in the hope, perhaps, of encouraging families to reject the practice.

In the upstairs flat, Miranda was short of things to do. She too wanted to start a family as she came from a large one herself. To fill in time Rose suggested she should apply for some teaching at the ETC. The classes were growing all the time and teachers were always needed.

In fact, Rose had recently met an American woman teaching at the University who was the cousin of her friend Janet from the ESOL school in Crystal Palace where Rose had worked in the early '70s. Penny was a strong-minded, independent, fun-loving person who informed Rose that Janet was now a widow. Her English RAF pilot husband had passed away from lung cancer, and Penny was urging Janet to make a break from London and come out to Kuwait to be with her. All she needed was some part-time work to keep her going. She had a widow's pension, so she didn't need fulltime work. Without an MA she was in the same position as Rose, she could not work at the University. The ETC would be perfect for her to earn enough to live modestly with her cousin.

> Dear Diary,
>
> I'm making progress to becoming a Diploma trainer now. I'm so pleased. It will be extremely helpful in developing my career. And my old friend from London is coming out here soon. It will be fun to see her, though it's sad she is now a widow.

February, 1979, Kuwait

By the end of January applications for the Dip.TESOL program were full. There would be a small group of eight experienced teachers who wanted to upgrade their TESOL qualifications so as to continue their careers in Kuwait or elsewhere. The only fees charged were those required for the RSA registration and assessment of each candidate because Julian as Rep of the BC had decreed that this would be a professional development project funded by the BC. The Diploma would be much easier and cheaper to achieve than a one year MA course, so it was attractive to candidates. It was also prized by employers on account of its emphasis on both classroom practice and theoretical principles.

Lydia and Rose started their program in mid-February, after the Prophet's Birthday (PBUH) holiday. There would be two sessions per week, one theoretical, one practical on Monday and Wednesday evenings from 6 to 9pm. Rose would be leading a 'review and refresher' series of eight workshops, with practice of techniques among peers, i.e. microteaching, then her sessions would be focussed on observing the teachers in their own classes as they prepared for the formal Practical Assessment. There was an RSA assessor in Kuwait, Neville West, who had come out to lead the Kuwait Airlines Company ESP Project, which Julian Crosby and his ESP team had negotiated. Neville was on a three year contract, so would be available to conduct the teachers' practical assessments as soon as they felt confident and Rose and Lydia agreed they were ready. The written exams were on fixed dates in June while the practical assessments could be tailored to fit each teacher's personal schedule.

Rose used the inputs she had designed for the Drury Lane course in London and expanded the sessions with practical ideas from the RSA Dip.TESOL course she had taken herself from '75 to '76. She particularly enjoyed teaching pronunciation and revealing the important contrasts between written and spoken English. The 1970s were the early days of TESOL so there were not many published texts to draw on and textbooks did not yet include pronunciation practice. George Bernard Shaw's famous riddle 'How do you pronounce *ghoti*?' was a whiteboard starter for Rose's first session. Very few people had heard of it on those days, with its translation as 'fish' using the /gh/ in enough, the /o/ in women, and /ti/ in station. Rose had been fortunate in being at the forefront in the teaching of literacy in ILEA (Inner London Education Authority), so she was confident in her ability to lead the teachers to more effective teaching performance, by underpinning their knowledge with practical techniques. 'Say before you write on the black/whiteboard' was an adage that had not yet been promoted sufficiently, with the result being students who could not use the English they had learned in the classroom outside of it. Rose impressed upon the candidates that only the spoken model should be presented, i.e. modelled and drilled, with choral and individual repetition, before its written form met the students' eyes on account of the mismatch in English between the spoken and written forms of the language.

Rose had suggested to Miranda that she might want to take the course, but procreation was very much on her mind, so she was unwilling to commit to something that might stress her unduly. She and Andrew had been married for three years and they were keen to have children in a child-friendly society such as Kuwait, where home help (part-time cleaners and child-minders) was readily available. Rose needed to bear in mind that she was in danger of putting herself under stress again. The evening part-time course and occasional additional Thursday morning sessions seemed manageable. Many hours of preparation go into an hour's lesson or workshop as Rose knew to her cost from previous experience.

There was a very special occasion on Thursday, 15 February. Queen Elizabeth II and Prince Philip were touring the Gulf States and on this day, they visited Kuwait. All the British Council staff were invited to see them at the Embassy. It was a thrill to stand, even in a crowd, and to be near enough to see the Monarch's beautiful blue eyes, her porcelain complexion and to note how petite she was. There was a little in-house gossip going around the Embassy and Council invitees beforehand. The Embassy had redecorated a bathroom suite with toilet which was intended for the use of the Queen alone. To make sure there was no malfunction on the day the Ambassador's secretary, Tara, had been charged with trialling it. It was a necessary precaution since the lock malfunctioned and Tara was imprisoned in the small room for a short while. The lock was repaired but for some reason this was deemed a wonderful joke and everyone enjoyed passing on the information. Rose suspected that this refurbishment and checking was standard practice before a royal visit.

Kuwait National Day on the 25th saw the usual celebrations take place in public and shown on TV, with long queues of males in the pristine white robes of national dress waiting to exchange the nose to nose greetings with the Emir, Sheikh Jaber al Salem al Sabah. There were the traditional drum and bagpipe music parades and dances of men with swords, young women swinging their long, uncovered hair and special documentary films showing the rapid expansion of Kuwait from the late '70s. It was pleasant to have a day off on Sunday for a change. Rose had almost forgotten that the weekend in the West was not Thursday and Friday.

> Dear Diary,
>
> I'm getting used to the national celebrations and religious holidays now. I can't say I've really experienced culture shock, it's just been cultural adjustment I think. Nothing too outrageous! And I've seen the Queen! She's gorgeous! Prince Philip is very handsome, and much taller than she is.

March - April, 1979, Kuwait

By the time Rose's inputs to the training course group had ended, the Easter holiday was upon them. This year was special because this was the first time Rose was free to celebrate on Easter Sunday, April 15th. The brothers could always arrange their own free time as they owned their own private business, with a 'sleeping partner', a Kuwaiti who had no particular business assets to share with them. By Kuwait law, no expatriate could own a property or a business outright. However, so as not to stifle any opportunities which Kuwaitis might benefit from, the arrangement was that every private company had a Kuwaiti partner who owned at least 51%, i.e. the majority share of the company according to the law. In some cases the Kuwaiti partner was active in the business, or invested funds or provided premises for the business. In practice, each expatriate business owner arranged a private agreement with their 'pet' Kuwaiti on terms and conditions that he was happy with. In the case of the family company the Kuwaiti was a kindly old gentleman who was happy with a monthly allowance. He was kept at a distance so that he would not get greedy if the brothers' profits soared. Of course, Nabeel took every opportunity he could find to joke that he had two 'sleeping partners', his wife and his Kuwaiti business sponsor.

The Fardan family were Eastern Catholics who followed Rome, but were not Roman Catholics. The Roman Catholic Church had a church building near the Sheraton Hotel, but church bells could not be rung. Nor was the family Greek Orthodox. Although there was a large congregation of Eastern Catholics in Kuwait they had not received Government permission to build a church, so they had obtained an old villa and modified it to meet their needs. Their Easter Sunday celebrations were of course preceded by the mourning of Christ's death on Good Friday. This entailed, as Rose found out, going to a Friday morning ceremony, comparable to the Stations of the Cross she was familiar with from the Anglican Church. Then on the evening of Easter Saturday there was another ceremony, which was very strange to Rose, during which the congregation were 'locked' inside the darkened church building, while the priest went outside and knocked on the door with his shepherd's crook. The symbolism was, as far as Rose could follow it, that the priest was knocking on the door of the tomb from which Christ had mysteriously disappeared. It was all very intriguing, and quite a late night.

Despite the late Saturday night, the next morning saw Nabeel and Rose getting up early and carrying their gifts of beautiful chocolate eggs, both large and small, wrapped in thick, colourful foil, as well as a whole tray of 24 hard-boiled eggs which had been soaked in blue, yellow and red food colouring the day before. Rose learned the Palestinian/Lebanese Christian tradition at Easter was to use these hard-boiled eggs in a hand to hand battle to see who could conquer the eggs of the opponent. The tactic was to hold the egg firmly in one hand and attack one end of the opponent's egg, hoping to crack it. If your egg was cracked, you were out. The last standing unbroken egg was the winner. There was also a surprising competition on arrival at the family house to be the first to say '*al Massih kaam*' or 'Christ is risen', with the response 'Indeed he is risen' '*hakkan kaam*'. Although she wished they didn't have to spend the whole day at the family house, it was an interesting first Arabic Easter experience and the family mood was buoyant. As usual lunch was a sumptuous affair with roast lamb for the family and several vegetarian accompaniments for Rose, requiring a good deal of preparation and clean up time, but at least Rose didn't have to go to work the next day.

Over lunch religious fasting rituals were discussed. In the Christian tradition, Rose explained, there was an expectation that Anglicans would give up some favourite food during Lent to symbolise the fasting that Jesus Christ underwent in the desert over 40 days. Traditionally the food was chocolate or another type of sweet. This tradition was gradually being forgotten or neglected in the UK. Asma explained that in their religion no dairy food or flesh was eaten, so she had subsisted on fish, olive oil, nuts, seeds and salads. The menfolk just laughed, so Rose realised that Asma was extremely religious. Rose had already experienced the privations that Muslims imposed on themselves in their fasting month of Ramadan.

"So," she commented "there seem to be similarities between the different faiths."

"Yes, indeed," Asma told her. "Muslims have a prophet, Mohammed, and we have John the Baptist. They have the *Koran al Karim,* and we have the Holy Bible. We must worship together, and we should go on pilgrimage if we can."

At this, the men laughed. "Where would you go, Asma?" Edouard asked.

"To Jerusalem, and Bethlehem, and our home," she retorted with tears in her eyes. "If I could. If the Israelis would let us."

Rose was amazed and saddened. The family had never spoken of politics in front of her. She could understand the longing to revisit their homeland and the need to never mention it, so as to try to forget what had happened to them and their fellow Palestinians with no right to return.

"You know, Rose, I would love to visit the Church in Bethlehem. We were so young when Daddy took us away from the Jewish terrorist group, Irgun, fighting in our city. We hadn't visited many places in Palestine because Mum and Dad were so busy looking after us. I remember Mum more than my brothers and sisters, except perhaps Henri. We try to forget the bad things in our lives and look foward to the future. But we can't forget and we can't help imagining what might have been. You know, many Palestinians still have the key to their front door. They display it on the wall of their homes. But in our case, Daddy gave the key to our Uncle, and he sold our house to the Israelis. It was unforgivable. And he kept the money himself. He's dead now, lucky for him," Asma's face was bleak.

"Come on Asma, let's stop this depressing talk. It's chocolate egg time, to be eaten with a nice cup of coffee. Which of you ladies is going to do the honours?" asked Adel.

"I'll try, if you like? But Asma, will you help me, please?" volunteered Rose. With that the two went into the kitchen, the female domain, to make the coffee.

Rose Clayworth

Dear Diary, I've learned more sad details of the family's past. I understand why they were reluctant to accept me into the family.

May - August (Ramadan), 1979, Kuwait

Having finished the practical input sessions Rose now had a more flexible schedule designed to fit around the candidates' own teaching timetables. Following the Dip. TESOL criteria, Rose evaluated and guided the teachers to meet the standards expected in a student-oriented carefully staged lesson, leading to student performance of the skills described in the teacher's lesson plan at two distinct levels, such as beginners and intermediate, or lower intermediate and advanced. Inevitably there was a range of success, so some teachers needed more support than others. This meant Rose was working two hours on most week days. In this way May flew by, and Rose had to be mindful of her own studies. She needed to devote 15 hours to reading and writing each week. On top of that she had housework and cooking to take care of and social commitments to manage to make sure Nabeel did not feel neglected.

Although she was busy she felt contented. Her papers for the BA English were interesting. She read the whole of Shakespeare for the first time, and especially enjoyed discovering information on topics such as Samuel Johnson's dictionary making. Life with the landlord and the upstairs neighbours continued to have a rhythm of its own, with reciprocal coffee evenings with Imm and Abu Ali or delicious takeaway meals, such as lobster tail and chips, with Miranda and Andrew and home-made wine and beer. The men enjoyed comparing the projects they were dealing with, Nabeel in supply to the petrochemical industry and Andrew in civil engineering for the Ministry of Electricity and Water. The women, of course, discussed Miranda's new music acquisitions, such as Fleetwood Mac, and her visits to the tailor. Rose had some cotton dresses copied for work.

The Diploma assessor's visits were booked for June and July, 16 lessons in all, with only two each week so that the assessor did not suffer from overload on top of his own regular workload. When Ramadan began on 29th July, Rose's work was over so she could focus on her own studies. She was planning to take her eight exams the following summer and had sketched out a timetable which would allow her to complete the essays the course required, so as to be able to revise in time for the examination schedule. Samir would be registering her for the exams, but she would be responsible for paying for registration and also invigilation.

The start of *Eid al Fitr* on 25th August was their third wedding anniversary. Nabeel was doing well so they went out for dinner with the family to celebrate. As Rose's studies were costing a fair amount of money, which of course, she was earning, and they were still adding to their flat's embellishments, with occasional purchases such as capiz shell lamps and brass trays, she did not expect they would exchange gifts. Nabeel surprised her, however, by suggesting they go to the jewellery stores to buy something. The gold souk was an amazing Aladdin's cave. There were many ladies covered from head to toe with black abbayas choosing heavy, richly decorated, 22 karat gold ornaments for daughters to wear for their weddings.

Rose chose a beautiful, Italian-designed, sapphire and diamond 18 karat gold ring and matching pendant. She was thrilled to have such an unexpected treasure, despite the knowledge that this was her consolation prize for not having the son or daughter she had anticipated when she married. "Count your blessings," she murmured to herself.

September - November, 1979, Asia

After *Eid al Fitr* Lydia and Rose got together to plan for a second Dip.TESOL course. Rose was willing to take on another, but she needed to have a break before she started work again so that she could finish her studies. They agreed to let the summer heat subside and begin input sessions in December, since Nabeel once again surprised Rose, this time with a plan for a holiday! He needed a break and had some contacts for manpower supply in Asia. As Kuwait was expanding, the need for manual labourers in construction was growing and Nabeel was keen to investigate the issues involved in manpower hire.

Rose's 32nd birthday coincided with *Eid al Adha*, and saw them flying to Singapore for the first stop on their Asian tour. Rose was excited about the trip and even happier when they discovered the cleanliness of Singapore and the high standard of their hotel on Orchard Road with its exotic hardwood furniture, including a four poster bed. The only challenge was the tropical climate which was very hot and humid with a tropical downpour daily at midday. They enjoyed visiting the Jurong Bird Park and Butterfly Park and exploring the remnants of the old city, the Chinese 'shop houses', then dining at Raffles, and tasting the celebrated Singapore Sling cocktail.

After four days they moved on to Thailand, beginning their stay in Bangkok, where they enjoyed the spectacle of the distinctive Thai temples and visited the floating market. They took a boat trip to the ancient, ruined but beautiful capital of Ayudaya. After three days of city exploring they took a taxi to the beautiful golden sands of Pattaya Beach. Their hotel was excellent, with views over the beach and the sea. On their walks and evening trips to restaurants it was dismaying to note the way in which the local prostitutes tried to seduce the males they saw, even as with Rose and Nabeel, when they were obviously a couple.

"Rose, I'd like to find someone who can give me a back massage. My back pain is killing me," Nabeel complained.

"Let's ask the concierge about therapeutic medical massages," Rose suggested. "I've heard they are given by blind people in temples."

The concierge directed them to what turned out to be an up market brothel in which the ladies could be viewed through a huge glass window in the foyer. They spoke to the manager.

"You tell lady medical message. She do that. They good massage ladies."

Rose looked at him sternly. "Of course, my husband does not want anything else. OK?"

Rose was dubious about the situation but Nabeel was limping from his back pain and desperate to give it a try. He chose a buxom but homely looking girl and promised to make his excuses and leave if he was invited to have sex. Rose, suspicious, but trusting enough to leave the scene of potential adultery in plain sight, walked away and waited in the nearby park. She was joined after a short time by Nabeel, smelling strongly of talcum powder.

"Well, how did it go?" she asked drily.

"You were right to be worried. She didn't speak English and things began to get out of control so I left before anything happened."

Rose did her best to believe his story and put the unusual event behind her, but she never forgot it and maintained a sceptical attitude to the potentially hidden truth.

On the drive back to Bangkok airport a couple of days later in the early hours of the morning they witnessed Buddhist monks dressed in yellow robes, walking past houses to collect their food for the day. Their driver told them that the food they collected would be eaten at midday. That was their entire diet. Every Thai male was expected to spend a period of time as a monk before he became 20 years old. During this time they must avoid female company; even female touch would 'contaminate' them. As Thai kick boxers at the time were known for their ferocity in fighting, this contrast of humility and deprivation as a monk was surprising.

From Thailand they flew to the Philippines, staying in a luxurious hotel in Manila. They enjoyed visiting Fort Santiago in Intramuros, the ancient site of the Spanish conquerors in the sixteenth century. Rose, with her linguistic interests noticed a sign outside a building saying 'sewers wanted'. The ambiguity of the word sewers was not lost on her, but for a moment she wondered why such a huge city as Manila didn't have facilities for sewage! They made a day trip to the Taal Volcano crater lake which at that time was not active, but impressive in its size and beautiful landscape. They took a long river trip in a dug out canoe to the Pagsanjan waterfall where they could swim, and had a delicious lunch in a riverside cafe. It was a very relaxing environment with beautiful scenery and kind, gentle people.

After Manila they flew to Tokyo, where they stayed in the Imperial Hotel within sight of the Imperial Palace gardens and Hibiya Park in the busy Ginza District. They did some shopping in the famous Seibu Department Store, where they indulged in a silk kimono each, with special flip flops and cotton 'socks'. They experienced the Japanese tea ceremony and also made a trip to Mount Fuji. There were lots of coaches in the car park at the snow line. Crowds of people were following guides holding a flag or an umbrella high in the air to keep their group with them. Rose was wearing a red blazer, a navy skirt and a white top. Suddenly, standing alone while Nabeel wandered around taking photos, she was surrounded by tourists asking questions: "Excuse me! How high is Mount Fuji?" "Where are the toilets?" "I'm sorry, I don't know," she replied, amazed. She had been taken for a guide! When she told Nabeel they had a good laugh about it!

Their final stop was Hong Kong where they took advantage of express tailoring. Rose had a white silk dress and jacket made and Nabeel ordered several silk shirts. Their hotel in the Central Business District looked onto the historic colonial buildings, and the couple enjoyed exploring some of the many street markets.

Dear Diary, This was a fascinating holiday. I've really enjoyed it. Such a change from

Rose Clayworth

our daily lives. And we've got
some great souvenirs but I'm
looking forward to getting back to
Kuwait now.

December, 1979, Kuwait

Rose felt happy and envigorated after this exciting Asian vacation but December flew by with the start of the new Dip.TESOL course and Rose's BA English studies to finish. However, as Rose was only working part-time, she could join the family at a Christmas Eve late night church service as well as the usual long family lunch on the 25ᵗʰ. On New Year's Eve they got together for a small celebration, with the four brothers, Henri, Edouard, Adel and Nabeel and the sister and sister-in-law, Asma and Rose. Hakima had gone to her family in Cairo for the New Year holiday. Rose had no expectation of an eventful evening. She had dressed carefully in honour of the night, but there would be no dancing or fun and games without the lighter presence of Joseph and Claudine. Instead, this year the family had decided to clear the air with a discussion about the past. Whether they felt that Nabeel and Rose were now secure within the family, or whether they wanted to test their relationship, Rose was never sure.

The evening began with drinks and nibbles, green pistachios and yellow *turmus*, a kind of chick pea, at around 8pm, followed by a 'help yourself' informal dinner of huge trays of small crabs and large shrimps roasted in the oven, served with a garlic mayonnaise, plus a huge *tabbouleh* salad served with crisp cos lettuce leaves. This kind of food took a long time to eat as it involved shelling each unfortunate sea creature. After everyone had eaten their fill, Asma and Rose cleared up while the men got the roulette spinner set up and began to play. When the ladies brought in coffee, the men took a break and conversation started in Arabic, which surprised Rose. Usually everyone spoke English when she was there so as not to exclude her. She could see from the body language of the group that Nabeel was the subject of the conversation and it was getting heated.

"What's going on, Nabeel?" she asked in a low voice.

"Nothing, don't worry. Just keep quiet," he told her firmly.

Hurt, but not too concerned she watched as the words she did understand began to circulate. The brothers often used a liberal number of swear words and impolite expressions. such as *tuz alek*, *kul khara*, and *uskut*. She noted that she had learned these expressions by hearing them regularly but she had learned no kind words or compliments at all. Listening to Asma she had picked up one term of endearment, *ya ayuni*, my eyes. The conversation was now breaking into English. She heard thief, then coward, then liar. What on earth was going on?

Nabeel seemed to be trying to explain something. When he mentioned the name of a Palestinian office worker who had been with the family for many years, she suddenly realised what was happening. They were quizzing Nabeel on his escape from them in 1971 and 1976. They were angry and they were blaming him for getting his passport and leaving, to come back to her in London. At this realisation Rose felt violently angry. To their amazement, she stood up and said,

"Ya Nabeel, come on, we are going. You are not a coward, a liar or a thief. I will not stay here and listen to this."

To her horror, Nabeel again turned to her and said, "Be quiet. Sit down. I have to finish this."

Rose was conflicted. As a dutiful Arab wife she should obey her husband. But as an independent British woman that was the last thing she wanted to do. The others were staring at her in consternation. They had not expected her to either understand or react. So what to do now?

Asma came to the rescue. She stood up too. "Look at the time, *ya uwlad*. It's nearly midnight. We need to get the toasts ready. Come with me, Rose," and with that the women went into the kitchen again.

Once away from the menfolk, Asma explained. "Ya Rose, sorry about this. We are trying to find out why Nabeel didn't tell us about your marriage, and got his passport from the safe and bought his airline ticket by stealing."

"Oh, dear, Asma. I had no idea about any of this. He simply left London and suddenly came back four or five months later. Really, I was not expecting him to come back and ask me to marry him. But none of this is my fault. He didn't tell me the whole truth about the situation either."

"Well, what's done is done. We just got a bit frustrated with him. He's always been the baby of the family, spoilt, getting what he wants all the time. Let's forget it now."

"OK, it's too late to argue. Let's hope for better in the New Year."

"Indeed. Here's a bottle of champagne which Joseph and Claudine left for us. Come on, bring those flutes and we'll enjoy a peaceful drink."

Back in the sitting room there was a heavy silence. Nabeel looked upset and the other three looked angry. Asma gave Henri the bottle and a glass cloth to hold the bottle as he opened it. With a splendid POP, the cork came out of the chilled champagne and Henri poured six glasses. With aplomb, Adel shouted, "Happy New Year" and they all drank the toast.

Soon afterwards Rose and Nabeel headed home. In the car, Rose asked why the family had suddenly conducted what seemed to be the Spanish Inquisition.

"Who knows," Nabeel told her. "I suppose they have had it on their minds for years. I think they'll close the account now."

"But did you really steal money as well as your passport?" Rose asked.

"Look, how can I steal my own passport? The secretary gave me the safe key and I took my passport and some cash. I was working and they didn't pay me so what could I do?"

The whole thing was so unusual and unexpected, and Rose was so tired, that she gave up. There was no point in discussing it further. "Look to the future," she told herself.

Dear Diary, More revelations of secrets beneath our marriage.

January - June, 1980, Kuwait

As planned previously Rose's workload at the ETC was steady with only one session per week on practical matters such as lesson planning and staging lessons. This went on until Easter at the beginning of April. After that she had to observe the candidates who had registered for the Dip. TESOL exams in their live classes. This increased her workload and she began to panic about the preparation time for her BA examinations. She and the candidates were in a similar whirlwind of regular work and exam preparation so nerves were stretched. Once again Neville obliged as Practical Assessor. By the end of June all was completed and the candidates and Rose could look forward to a more relaxed schedule during the fasting month of Ramadan. Then, out of the blue, Justin asked if she would like to go back to the teaching force fulltime in September as she had completed her studies.

"If my results turn out OK, then that would be great. But if I fail, I want to repeat those courses. I must get the BA so as to do a distance MA with London Uni," she told him.

Over in Beirut there was news of Elijah. There had been no discussion about Nabeel's assistance to Elijah in getting into Bordeaux University to study medicine. Rose did not know whether the brothers approved or disapproved of his unilateral action, in spite of Elijah's father's resistance. After Rose and Nabeel had visited him in France he had, as he expected, failed an exam, but only one, anatomy. He had been given a chance to repeat the course, but with the extra load of second year courses, when summer 1979 came, he had again failed anatomy, a prerequisite for continuing into the third year. As he had not been able to continue his studies he had returned home to Beirut. Neither Nabeel nor the young man had talked about this failure. Elijah had not made a big fuss about his sadness and had volunteered with the Red Crescent to help victims of the Lebanese Civil War which had intensified and in which Syria and Israel had begun to intervene. Volunteers were unpaid, which was putting more stress on the disappointed young man since his father expected his adult son to contribute towards the upkeep of the family.

Rose would not have known about this problem if Elijah had not begun to talk to Nabeel on the phone. Nabeel did not say much, but the war on top of failure and pressure from his father to join him in his workshop was causing Elijah to experience depression. "Why is Elijah ringing you so often, Nabeel?" Rose asked one evening.

"I'm thinking of bringing him over here to work with me," Nabeel told her. "He needs to get away from the war and his father. He speaks fluent French and English so he could work with me and make some money in business."

"That sounds like a great idea. Are you going to send him a ticket?"

"Yes, but not immediately. I'd like to go to Europe during Ramadan. Your exam results won't be in until the end of August will they? So we can go together. How does that sound?" he asked.

"You're right. The results should be in by the end of August. I'd love a trip to Europe!"

July - August (Ramadan), 1980, UK, Italy

At the beginning of Ramadan in mid-July as non-Muslims Rose and Nabeel had a simple routine: Nabeel would go to work in the morning as usual, come home for lunch and return to work in the afternoon till early evening. The only difference for him was that he could not smoke in his car for fear of being reported and penalised for breaking the religious rules. Rose was able for once to file all the English literature papers she had accumulated over the past two years. She had completed the BA Hons English independently but she had her fingers crossed for good results. They planned to leave for Milan at the end of the month to meet Pietro, the overseas market manager for an Italian company specialising in flares to protect the environment from harmful oil burn off in the petrochemical industry. They were flying to the UK to visit Mum briefly, then flying on to Milan. They would not get back to Kuwait until after *Eid al Fitr*, so as to take advantage of the trip and visit Venice, Pisa and Rome while they were away. It would be a first time visit for both of them.

Rose had met Pietro, a short, stocky, jovial Italian on his visits to Kuwait. He spoke fluent English, but when he met them on arrival at Milan's airport he invited them for dinner the next day to meet his wife and family, none of whom spoke English. It was an excellent opportunity for Rose to practise the Italian she had studied at Uni. She amazed herself at her ability to communicate despite lack of practice, with the help of gestures. Nabeel had to spend some time in the office discussing agency terms, but they were both able to enjoy seeing the city sights briefly. The Duomo di Milano cathedral was amazing.After dealing with business in the Milan office, Pietro invited them to go up into the mountains and stay for a couple of nights in their holiday chalet. Here they experienced the delightful scenery and fresh air of the mountains north of Milan. Pietro told them how these very same mountains were the ones that Hannibal had crossed with his elephants back in 218 BCE. The picturesque restaurants they ate in were of the 'trattoria' type, with red and white checked tablecloths and straw-wrapped flasks of Chianti wine.

It was a delightful first stop, but time was pressing so after four days they moved on to Venice. They had not decided how they would move around Italy, but had discussed the possibility of using the excellent train service between the major cities they planned to visit. However, since travelling according to train timetables might not be the best use of their limited time they decided to rent a car in Milan which they could leave in Rome, from where they would return home to Kuwait. This time there was no business meeting planned, but Rose had the address of a student who had studied at the language school in South London a few years previously. She had written from Kuwait to Luciana to advise her of their upcoming visit and to her surprise and pleasure had received a phone call confirming her address and phone number to contact. Rose was looking forward to this opportunity to see Venice from a local's viewpoint.

Luciana had advised them that taking a car into Venice was not a simple thing to do. She suggested they park their car and proceed on foot into this waterbound city. She was living with her mother in Mestre just outside the old city. Nabeel could park the car inside her building while they did their sightseeing. She would prepare dinner for them with her mother in her apartment. Arriving at Luciana's they parked the car and went upstairs for coffee with Luciana and her mother, a white-haired lady of 80. Mamma immediately took a liking to Nabeel, calling him *tesorino,* and reaching up to pat him on the cheek. Luciana laughed and made them a strong cappuccino to fortify them for the sights of Venice. She walked with them to the ferry and waved them goodbye as they set off to see San Marco Basilica, the Doge's Palace and the famous Bridge of Sighs, recalling Shakespeare's Merchant of Venice, so recently a subject of Rose's BA English studies.

As Luciana had warned them, in the height of the tourist season Venice was crowded, so after walking around and taking photos for a couple of hours it was with relief they took a ferry to the island of Murano where glass is made, and indulged in the purchase of two crystal Mary and the Christ Child icons for Asma and for themselves. They purchased a small glass *millefiori* paperweight for Luciana to thank her for her hospitality, then thankfully took the ferry back to Mestre. After a lovely pasta dinner, with delicious, wafer thin parma ham and sweet melon starter, they said their farewells, to cries of a*rrivaderci tesorino* and drove on to find a motel for the night.

The next day, 2 August, they headed for Pisa, to see

the famous leaning tower, before proceeding to Florence where they had pre-booked a hotel. Listening to the car radio as they drove they heard with shock the news of the Bologna railway station bombing. It was horrific, with 85 people killed and around 200 casualties. They blessed the decision they had made to hire a car rather than take a train, given the danger from the terrorist group, the Red Brigade. Arriving in Pisa at lunch time, they had a light lunch and then attempted to climb inside the tower. Rose had to give up on account of vertigo and the pressing number of tourists. She stayed in the Church below, throwing a jacket over her sleeveless T-shirt and a scarf over her hair. It reminded her forcefully of Asma in church covering her own hair with a delicate piece of lace, and offering another scarf to Rose during Xmas and Easter celebrations. The Catholic religion imposed regulations on the apparel of its followers, as did Islam.

Driving on to Florence, they arrived in the afternoon to find their hotel booking was a neat, clean *pensione* with resident parking in the centre of the city. After checking in and depositing their cases, they went out into the warm evening to discover the charming, convivial atmosphere of the *passeggiata*, the evening promenade. The city was much more pedestrian friendly than either Venice or Milan had been, and after viewing the Duomo and the Palazzo Vecchio with the replica statue of Michelangelo's David outside, they soon found a *trattoria* that offered the rustic Italian cuisine they both preferred. After some delicious *tortellini* and a classic *tiramisu* dessert, accompanied by *Lacryma Christi da Vesuvio* and *Vernaccia di San Gemignano* wines which thrilled their taste buds and dulled the pain of their long walk and the memory of the bomb they had narrowly avoided, they walked back to their hotel. It had been a long, but fascinating day. They spared a sad thought for the victims of the bombing as they went to bed. Life may be good but it may be short, so one should take time to smell the roses every day, Rose realised.

Early the next morning to escape the sun and the city, they walked up to the beautiful park with a vantage point above the city called The Boboli Gardens. From there they could see the famous Ponte Vecchio bridge over the River Arno, which figures in the famous song *O mio babbino caro*, from Puccini's opera, *Gianni Schicchi*. The August morning was splendid, quite unlike the heat they would experience when they went home, but with the return home on their minds they needed to move on to their next and final stop, Roma. The drive would take about four hours, so after a late breakfast they set off, reaching Rome in the early evening. They had booked a hotel in the city centre and had arranged to have the car picked up from there, figuring that they would not need it any longer. They had friends who wanted to meet them the next day to take them around the major city sights, such as the Trevi Fountain, the Spanish Steps, the Hippodrome and the Colosseum and finally a relaxing late lunch on the edge of the Villa Borghese gardens. Rome was just as exciting and stupendous as they had expected but they had become tired of the suitcase packing and unpacking so after two nights they were happy to take a cab to the airport and from there back to Kuwait.

Once again Nabeel had been promised a fixer at Customs on his return. In anticipation they had bought expensive brandy and single malt whisky, hiding two bottles in each suitcase. The fixer had done his job well, but sadly, once back at their flat, they found the Remy Martin XO had cracked and one of Nabeel's suits was saturated in cognac! They could only laugh and make a decision to avoid this situation in future. The lightweight polyester grey suit could be hand washed, but it was a lesson well learned. Back at work, Nabeel brought home the mail, with an important envelope from the UK. Rose's exam results were in. She had achieved her aim! The BA Honours English was hers. Exactly ten years after obtaining her BA Honours French she had her second Bachelor of Arts degree.

"Now you can call me BA BA Black Sheep!" she cried! "I'm so happy!"

"*Mabruuk, habibti*! I'm so glad for you. You worked hard for it," Nabeel congratulated her.

"Thanks, sweetheart. I appreciated your support. Now I can move on with the Master's!"

"Take a moment to enjoy this success. *'Ceuillez des aujour'dhui, les fleurs de la vie'* remember," Nabeel reminded her.

"Yes, of course. I mustn't forget to smell the roses! Shall we invite the family for dinner to celebrate?"

"Good idea. We can catch up with their news and tell them about our holiday," Nabeel agreed. "And of course, you can tell them that you are the new Sheikh Esbear."

"Sorry? What? Who is Sheikh Esbear?" Rose asked in bewilderment.

"Why, the one you've been studying, but you didn't realise he was a Sheikh, did you?" Nabeel giggled.

"OK. I get it. Shakespeare. Very funny. 'Nuff said!" Rose replied, shaking her head at the silliness. "I don't even dream of achieving anything like his genius," she remonstrated.

September - December, 1980, Kuwait, Beirut

Having achieved her second Bachelor's degree, Rose agreed to return to work fulltime as there was a new opening for her as an assistant trainer to a new overseas appointee. The Crosbys had left while Nabeel and Rose were in Italy, so they had missed the leaving party. The new BC Rep and the new TESOL trainer had come to post after *Eid al Fitr* and were well settled by the time Rose went back to the same office in the basement where she had been Director of Studies (DOS). This time she did not begrudge the overseas status of the new trainer, Roger, because he had qualifications that she looked forward to attaining for herself: RSA status as trainer for a new TESOL Certificate oriented to novice candidates. She had her objective for the new academic year fixed. In addition she sought references to become an assessor for the Dip.TESOL, as Neville West was the only assessor in the Gulf.

However, there was a major entertainment distraction on the horizon. From the 15-30 September the Asian Football Cup was to be hosted in Kuwait. Nabeel was not a football fan and Rose had no plans to get tickets although as a teenager football matches had been regular dates with her schoolboy boyfriend. To the surprise of those who did not follow 'form', Kuwait won the Cup and the Kuwait anthem for the games 'Our camel is a winner!'

was played over and over on the radio, as Rose noted in her car driving to work. For such a small country it really was a great achievement and everyone was delighted with this result.

Rose's routine was not as demanding as it had been as DOS, but she had new things to learn as she and the new trainer, Roger, developed a program following the new syllabus for the RSA Certificate in TESOL. Meanwhile, Nabeel was busy as ever, and the phone calls with his nephew Elijah resumed two or three evenings per week at home.

"Are you going to send that ticket for Elijah to come here soon?" Rose asked one evening.

"I was thinking after Christmas and New Year would be best. I have to go the USA in November, so it's not the best time to bring him over just yet."

"Where would he stay, do you think? Do you want him to be here with us?"

"I don't think Asma would let him out of her sight. He could have Henri's old room in the villa. Henri's still enjoying occupying Joseph's condo."

"OK but make sure you tell him about the plan so that he doesn't get downhearted."

"He knows I want him here. He's just got to be a bit patient for now."

Rose accepted that all was well so was surprised one Thursday morning to receive a call from Elijah.

"Is Uncle there, please, *Tante* Rose?" the faint voice on the line asked.

"Oh, Elijah, sorry, but Nabeel is at the office. Have you got the number there?" Rose asked.

"I don't want to bother him at work. I thought he might be off work today."

"No, he works Thursday. But can I do anything? Can I take a message?" Rose urged.

"It's OK. I'm OK. Don't worry. Just tell him I called."

With that the phone call ended. Rose rang Nabeel to tell him about the call.

The next day, Friday, came the dreadful news. Elijah had taken his father's gun, gone up to the roof of their downtown apartment building, and shot himself in the head. Death was instantaneous. The family were bereft. So much youthful hope ended in despair. There was no point in trying to attribute blame, though some would definitely fall on Nabeel for raising Elijah's hopes. Yet he had done his best to help his nephew achieve his dreams. Surely that was not wrong? In Elijah's father's eyes it was unreasonable and had caused his son's death.

Nabeel cancelled his plans for the USA while Rose took compassionate leave for a week. Wearing black for deep mourning the brothers, sister and sister-in-law set off for Beirut. Crossing the 'green line' between West and East Beirut was terrifying for both Rose, with her British passport, and Nabeel with a Lebanese pasasport but his place of birth indicating his Palestinian origin. But they made it through, past the young men in camouflage, toting guns.

The religious mourning rituals were complex and involved hours sitting around the open coffin, which was deeply disturbing for Rose. As far as Rose knew there were no arguments at this sad time. They stayed for the requisite four days of mourning, then returned home. The year was ruined. The happy holiday, the exam results, the new job were all as nothing with the loss of this young life. The family would never be the same again. As mourning tradition demanded, after 40 days with heavy hearts they returned again to Lebanon for Christmas, though there were no celebrations, just quiet remembrance ceremonies around Elijah's grave. And yet again, they had to cross the 'green line' check point past teenagers brandishing kalashnikovs. In private Rose asked Nabeel how he felt.

"Don't ask me. I don't want to talk about it. How do you think I feel?" he asked angrily. "I did my best. I couldn't bring him out any earlier. The fault lies with his father, pushing him to leave the voluntary work he loved so as to earn money in the workshop. He hated that."

"You are right, I'm sure. Try not to blame yourself. I won't mention it again."

No one ever mentioned Elijah's name again. It was never forgotten but never discussed. Fate had taken a hand. The moving finger had written, and 'having writ, moved on'.

Dear Diary,

Very sad days. The mourning traditions, sitting around the open coffin, are very difficult to handle. I must admit I can't imagine doing that myself as a widow. The way Nabeel smokes it might happen at any time. Perhaps it's just as well we haven't got those 'hostages to fortune' aka children?

1981, Kuwait, Bahrein, UK

After the New Year festivities Rose's fulltime schedule was mainly daytime rather than evening as there were now plenty of supervisors who could take on the evening duties. This made a relaxing change for her to be able to see the sunset from the small balcony in their apartment at Abu Ali's house. Roger was planning a new Certificate course to be given fulltime over four weeks, which they wanted to schedule for March. It was a completely new venture and new materials had to be written to cater for complete novices in the English language classroom. All kinds of resource texts needed to be ordered for purchase and for the BC library. There would also be a requirement for practice teaching with real students. For the first course the paying students would be used as practice classes with the regular teacher mentoring the Certificate candidate but this was not going to be satisfactory in the long run. It would be important to advertise for free students for future courses.

When the Cert.TESOL course started running, Rose got to know two young British women, Ruby and Susan who became firm friends. The candidates were a small but fun group, excited at the opportunity to take up a new profession while posted out to Kuwait as spouses. Successful graduates could be offered a part-time teaching post, so it was a useful funnel for recruitment of new teachers each year. The courses became a fixture in the ETC schedule with a Diploma course for the experienced teachers and a Certificate course for the novices running alongside the courses for language students. After the successful trial run, with Neville moderating the course and assessing some Diploma candidates, Rose was able to be inducted as a Diploma assessor, which made her very happy. A conference was set up by the RSA in Bahrein for Arabian Gulf trainers on the Cert.TESOL. Roger gave a paper on the new program and Rose was delighted to be able to accompany him. She was excited at this new development and happy to follow Roger's lead.

The sad events in Lebanon were not forgotten but this summer Nabeel and Rose went back to the UK to see Mum, whose health was deteriorating, and John, who was growing up. It was an exciting time in the UK as Prince Charles married his much younger bride, Lady Diana Spencer on 29 July. The family sat glued to the TV to watch the arrival of the bride with her father, Lord Spencer, and the little bridesmaids and pages managing the bride's long train to her huge, crinoline styled bridal dress. It was a very happy occasion and gave Rose some pause for thought as she remembered her own simple wedding ceremony, five years earlier. As usual she put her negative thoughts behind her and concentrated on helping Mum by giving her the comforting hot baths she never got enough of on her own.

There was some concern with regard to John, who was now a rather sullen teenager. It was only to be expected with no male role model or mentor in his life, and a mother who was constantly in pain. Although Mum had held down two jobs in the past - the daytime Singer Sewing Machine job and an evening barmaid position at the Mason's Arms, she could no longer manage the physical impact on her of the evening work. She was, of course, out of the house when John was at school, but now aged 18 he had left school and was training to be a car mechanic in a garage across town.

There had been some 'bad blood' a couple of years earlier between Mum and John and their upstairs neighbours in these council flats. The young couple upstairs ran a rock'n roll band and practised with speakers blaring so that the old lady in the flat immediately above Mum as well as Mum in her ground floor flat, suffered from the constant, excessive noise. Complaints had worsened rather than improved things, and John took it upon himself to enact resistance by whistling the Pink Panther theme tune whenever he saw the couple. This mild irritant had led to the young woman breaking a glass bottle and attacking John when she saw him. Although John was a victim, he, like the attacker, was bound over to keep the peace. This was upsetting to Rose and she hoped she would be able to move them out of the situation as soon as possible. But for now there was nothing she could do.

Back in Kuwait after *Eid al Fitr* at the beginning of August, Rose marshalled her supplies of wine and beer and started planning for her birthday party at the end of September. It would be a rallying of the troops of friends. Her work schedule had begun again after her statutory four weeks break. After Rose's birthday party, Nabeel, however, had to make a business trip to the USA.

"Will you be OK while I'm away? It won't be long, just 10 days," he assured her.

"Of course. I've got your brothers down the road, and my friends and colleagues," she reassured him.

And so it was that Rose attended parties on her own and visited the family on her own. These were two dangerous situations in two different ways. The family at this time had two dogs, a strong, vigorous male and a soft, fluffy female. Unexpectedly during one visit the male jumped up at Rose and tried to bite her face while she was seated. The family found it amusing and laughed out loud but since rabies was present in Kuwait Rose was not amused. She left the house and went straight to the local Clinic to have the graze on her face checked out. Fortunately there was no health risk, but Rose decided to stop going to the family house alone. She was angry about not just what happened but the family reaction to the bite.

The second danger arose at a friend's party when Rose attracted the attention of a young, tall, dark and handsome Lebanese man. Rose was wearing her wedding ring, but her mind was not on her wedding vows. She was feeling lonely and still angry at the family's attitude towards her. She was also wondering if she could cope with the long future of hard work which lay ahead. She wanted some fun, and when she was offered a lift home, she laughed. "I have my own car. I don't need a lift, thanks," she told Lionel. "Oh, but I do. Can you help me?" he asked with a beguiling smile. Rose took the bait and drove the young man home. How crazy had she become, she wondered? She had taken a massive risk, as unmarried couples should not drive together by law, but somehow she just didn't care. She deserved a bit of fun in what had become a life of work and duty with no prospect of children. The flirtation had cheered her up and made her focus on her work with renewed dedication.

Dear Diary, Some cracks are appearing in our marriage. I'm getting tired of the good wife routine. There's obviously no family support for me as an individual here. I want to break free!

1982, Kuwait, UK, USA, Mexico, Bahamas

Rose began the year confidently. She had attained the RSA Certificate trainer status to add to her qualification as an RSA Diploma trainer, and now was looking forward to embarking on her MA studies with the University of London so as to improve her future job prospects. She would have to seek admission, find a tutor and research an option for distance research so it would not be an easy road, but it was the only one open to her at that point in time.

Out of the blue, however, she was informed by a colleague of a new part-distance and part-attendance study program to obtain an MA in English Linguistics with the University of Birmingham. It was a novel program and of course, would enable Rose to be with her Mum for several weeks in the summer of two consecutive years, 1983 and 1984. She applied at once for admission to this new program in September, which would be the beginning of the two terms 'at post' study. The attendance segment was for the summer term and part of the vacation according to the UK academic year. Rose was extremely excited when she was accepted.

The curriculum was sent to her and she could begin her studies as soon as she had her hands on the recommended texts. This early commencement was useful because Nabeel's business was expanding and he had an invitation to one of his principals' international conference in Florida, USA in September. He had other contacts he could meet in other areas over there, so decided to make a clean sweep of the trip, visiting several potential and current principals for whom he worked as a commission agent. As Rose was entitled to four weeks' vacation, she asked for leave from work to go with him.

They began their trip in the UK with a quick visit to Mum, then moved on to meet the other delegates for the Florida convention. It was a wonderful opportunity to visit the new Disney EPCOT Centre, opened the previous year, while Nabeel was in meetings. Rose enjoyed meeting other wives at the social functions. But Nabeel did not waste time. After Florida, they went to Philadelphia to meet with a prospective business client. Rose recalled with pleasure the delicious seafood dinner they had as guests in the refined setting of the Old Original Bookbinder's Restaurant on the Richmond City Canal. On a free day they walked around the splendid city, climbed the 'Rocky Balboa III' steps famous from the 1980 film leading to the Philadelphia Museum of Art and visited the Liberty Bell. They next went to Houston, the Texan oil city, for more business meetings, while Rose took a side trip alone to Galveston Island, where she learned about the dreadful 1900 hurricane and came back singing the 1969 Glenn Campbell song! She enjoyed being in the USA very much.

After that Mexico was beckoning. In Mexico City they were treated royally for dinner by Jorge, Nabeel's business partner. Rose enjoyed *pollo con mole* (chicken with bitter chocolate sauce) for a change from her vegetarian diet. They had time to visit the ancient pyramids 40 kms outside the City where Rose bought silver bangles, while Nabeel climbed the steep steps of the Aztec Moon Pyramid to take photographs.

Mexico was the final stop on the business trip but Nabeel, for once, had prioritised a few days' recuperation. They flew to Paradise Island in the Bahamas. The weather was balmy, the scenery with huge, slender palm trees was tropical, the hotel wonderful and Rose realised again the advantages of being married to a successful business man, as the Nescafe TV ad of the day went, *irrajul najih* - sexist but appropriate in the Middle East of the time. But being a business man's wife was not enough for Rose.

Back in Kuwait, Rose reprised her MA studies. She had to complete and submit her written work for Phase 1 for assessment before the end of March. So with her work timetable life got very busy, but it was the same for Nabeel. He was happy with these developments and spent hours poring over spreadsheets, calculating costs and profit margins. In other words, time flew, with weekends as ever spent with the family and at friends' parties. In fact, business was going so well that Nabeel suggested they should buy a house for Mum and John to move into to get out of the difficult situation they were in with the upstairs neighbours. Rose was delighted. They could search for a property after Rose's summer course, Phase 2, in Birmingham.

1982 had been a good year for Rose and Nabeel but not for Palestinians in the Lebanese refugee camps of Sabra and Shatila. They were attacked by Christian Lebanese forces at the instigation of the Israelis, who had occupied Southern Lebanon. It was a massive tragedy. Once again Rose noticed an absence of discussion in the family of the terrible situation in Lebanon where the PLO had caused trouble for the Lebanese Government, and were finally forced out to Tripoli by this Israeli incursion right into

Beirut. However, Ariel Sharon, War Minister for Israel was blamed for this massacre of civilians, and forced to resign.

Dear Diary

Terrible things are happening in Lebanon but I never hear the family discuss what is happening. Perhaps they don't want to talk in front of me. I wonder if they think I'm a spy? Or perhaps they are so angry about the role of the UK and USA in the Palestinian tragedy that they prefer to keep their discussiions private. I don't blame them. I completely understand. I feel ashamed to be British sometimes.

But then I remind myself, it is not my fault. I have sympathised to the extent of marrying into the problem. The University took one day's pay this year to support the Palestinian people. And I've bought a beautiful Palestinian kaftan, from the Samad charity. What more can I do to show them I am on their side? IS there a fault beneath us caused by the pressure to marry because of Kuwait's laws? Or is it my over-active imagination?

1983, Kuwait, UK

The year flew by, with work commitments to the Certificate and Diploma courses as well as to her MA studies. In March there was a second conference in Bahrein for the new Certificate course leaders, trainers and assessors so it was good to get away to a hotel where liquor could be purchased. However, back at home Rose was steadily producing different varieties of wine and beer, so there was no need to stint on drinking or hospitality. Nabeel's business visitors continued to come out and spend time in their humble home, talking about big contracts and commissions, often nudged along with 'backhanders'. Rose refused to take part in these conversations and chose to ignore them. She submitted her written work for Phase 1 for assessment by the Programme Leader and looked forward to her trip to the UK in May. The BC had not only given her study leave but also a small amount of financial support so she was very happy.

In Birmingham she had booked student hostel accommodation in a five bedroom shared unit but first she went to see Mum and spend a week with her. She had borrowed a car from her brother Bill so could drive around to make the most of available time. Input to the course was over a ten-week period, and she would be able to go home again as soon as she got her schedule sorted out and she had a free weekend. The other course members were from all around the world, so it was interesting to get to know them as well as to discover who the tutors were and what the syllabus for the summer session would be. Of course, the end of course assessments leant a serious nature to the course. There was no time for simply having fun or shopping, though Rose intended to fit a little of the latter in.

Getting to know Birmingham had to be limited to rat tracks between the hostel and the campus, which was interesting and ancient, having received its royal charter in 1900. However, the English Language Research Unit was in a modern tower block with an intriguing 'paternoster' stairlift which absolutely terrified Rose. She never used it as it involved entering an open fronted continually revolving set of wooden stairs. It resembled a Swiss clockwork toy of some kind, or a cuckoo clock with the man and woman coming in and out. The campus clock tower was a notable landmark, visible across the city, and the Masters' students were entitled to eat in the staff dining room, though Rose did not take advantage of that since she preferred to eat her own vegetarian meals in the hostel unit. The other occupants of her unit and the units around were all convivial and quiet, so study was easy to accomplish.

Of course, the brain cannot always be focussed on study as the body needs some respite. There were tennis courts near the hostel which tempted her, reminding her of her enjoyable sessions in Kuwait with Violet. So she was delighted when one of the other candidates invited her to a game of tennis. Over a beer in the Student Union afterwards they discussed their motivation to pursue an MA while working. It was a perfect opportunity for both of them at their similar age and stage in their career. The MA would give them job security and offer new opportunities in future. They became good friends, enjoying tennis and occasional trips to see Shakespeare plays in Stratford on Avon. It was good being back in the UK.

During the final course assessment period, a take-home essay over a long weekend, Rose was stressed but stuck it out and achieved the necessary result to continue on with the course for another year. Nabeel flew over to be with her and Mum and John for a couple of weeks while they searched for a suitable property for Mum and John and themselves in future. They would need to find a single storey house with three bedrooms and a small garden and garage. They drove around Mossfield and to their surprise found a lovely little bungalow with a facade and a chimney exactly like the little houses children draw in primary school. Having viewed the property, and agreed the price, the house sale was quickly concluded.

Mum had some ideas about improvements and additions to make the house perfect for a disabled person. She was given *carte blanche* to make plans and find a builder who could quote for the developments. Once they were completed Mum and John would be able to move in and leave the unhappiness of the neighbours behind. It was with a happy heart that Rose left for Kuwait again in August to resume both work and further studies for the MA. However, she took with her an important purchase: an electric typewriter. It was modern, yellow, self-correcting and would help her with her work for the next phase of the MA.

This time there was a research project to conduct for Phase 3. Rose had already decided on hers: to design, test and validate a new placement test for the ETC. Up to Christmas she was only able to complete the design and piloting of her test with a small group of students from across the performance levels, because she was now the main trainer for the Cert.TESOL. She was able to induct Violet, her tennis partner as a trainer and Neville was the assessor once again. With her Cert.TESOL, Dip.TESOL and MA work completed for the year, Rose was satisfied with her achievements and ready to enjoy the festivities, which took place as they always did with family first, then friends.

Then fate, or rather, death intervened again. On 12 December terrorists drove a truck loaded with LPGas cylinders into the gates of the American Embassy, Kuwait, situated opposite the Hilton Hotel on the Corniche and the First Ring Road. The bomb destroyed the US Consulate but compared with the April US Embassy bombing in Beirut in which 63 people were killed, this was relatively minor. Nevertheless all embassy, consulate and cultural agencies had concrete barriers constructed and checkpoint gates installed to prevent further attacks. Rose told Nabeel grimly each morning: "Don't forget what colour clothes I'm wearing in case you have to dig me out of the basement today."

> Dear Diary,
>   Events have moved fast since I achieved my second BA in 1980. I'm now an RSA Diploma Trainer and Assessor as well as a Certificate Trainer, and I'm

halfway through my MA. But deep down there's a sadness that makes me cry in the shower and pushes me to do, or think about doing, crazy things. It's perhaps the ongoing terrorism and Lebanese civil war, but I feel it's more deep-seated. Is it my dread of the future or am I simply grieving for the past?

January - July, 1984, Kuwait, UK

Back at work after New Year Rose was faced with a mammoth task. These were the days before computers so Rose had to do all her typing on her electric typewriter and data processing by hand, using a calculator. After the piloting of the test she had to collect and process the data. Once certain that she had a valid test she could trial it with a much larger group of students and once again there was the manual data collection and then the data processing. The reliability and validity formulae took many hours over many days to complete but finally the job was done and the writing up process began. The project had taken months and the write up produced two volumes of tables and reports, which were submitted to her tutor and an external examiner, a well published language testing expert at Edinburgh University. It was with some pleasure and a little chagrin that she read the external examiner's evaluation of her project. It was worded as follows:

"Your project is worthy of a Master's degree in its own right. I recommend that you progress to doctoral study in future."

Brimming with happiness she shared the news with Nabeel.

"Look, perhaps I could have got my MA with London Uni by just submitting this project! And I'm recommended to go on to doctoral study."

"Well, don't go getting too far ahead of yourself," he

warned her. "We need a break from all this study, don't you think?"

Rose paid no attention. She had only another summer session to get through and she would have her cherished MA. May and the start of the second summer session in Birmingham couldn't come soon enough for her. She was looking forward to seeing what Mum had achieved in the new house too. Everything seemed to be going well and Mum was happy, though her joints were giving her more and more pain. Rose really wanted to help, but the distance between them was a huge hindrance. She discussed the possibility of Mum coming out to Kuwait for a visit in future.

"The problem is that this flat is too small for long term guests and Mum can't do stairs, so what about looking around for something different?" she asked Nabeel.

"OK, it suits me. I need to live in a better place for my image. But let's get your degree finished first, shall we?"

Back in the UK with Mum they discussed the possibility of coming out to Kuwait for an extended visit in future. The eight hour flight presented a serious challenge for Mum travelling alone.

"I would have to dehydrate myself so that I don't need the loo at all. I just couldn't handle the toilet from what I've seen on our flights to Spain," she reminded Rose.

"You're right. Well, let's put it on the back burner for now. You know we want you out there with us. The warm weather would do you good, I'm sure," Rose told her.

"Well, I'm very happy in this house, so thank you and thank Nabeel very much. It's wonderful to have this lovely garden too, but it seems to be getting a bit much for John to handle now he's getting married," Mum told Rose. "The wedding is in June, so will you be able to come over and be with us?"

"Wow - so soon? He's a bit young, isn't he? Only 21? At his age I didn't even have a boyfriend!" Rose exclaimed.

"What can I do?" Mum replied. "She seems like a nice girl, but she's already got a child, so he's going to have to finish his qualifications as a mechanic or else he'll be in trouble."

"Well, try not to worry too much. I've got to get on with this course, so I'll have to forget it too for now. I'm going to rent a flat this time, so you can come and stay in Birmingham for a change if you like," Rose suggested.

"That would be lovely, but I do like my bath, and I have my bath nurse once a week, so it might not suit me at the moment. I'm going to need some replacement joint operations soon," Mum warned.

"Oh, dear. That's bad news in one way, but good news if it relieves you of pain. Keep me posted on that, won't you?" Rose insisted.

And so, the second summer session began, for Rose's MA. The candidates who had survived the first year were all there again, pleased to see each other. They were more comfortable together than the first summer, of course, and the tutors were more welcoming too. One of the tutors even invited the group to his home for a party one evening. This tutor was a famous name in the published world of ESP, so it was a great honour as well as a pleasure.

Rose had rented a small apartment in an upmarket, leafy area of Birmingham in the hope of getting Mum over for a weekend or two, as John was to marry in June. Rose was able to get over to Mossfield to attend the ceremony and planned to take Mum back with her to Birmingham. However, she had not realised that Mum was not up to the stress and strain of moving across country nor of living without her special aids for living. She needed a chair which could lift her up as her knee joints were not working, and she was in great pain with her hip joints. The rheumatologist she now saw regularly told her that she would have to have her knee joint replaced before a hip could be replaced, so major operations were ahead.

So Mum stayed where she was happy in her new home and new bedroom, looking out onto the long garden, with a bird table for feeding the local flying population, and a visiting squirrel she tempted with shelled nuts. She was not able to handle any gardening or lawn mowing, but although John was no longer living at home and had a family to look after he was kind enough to bring shopping every week and cut the grass for Mum when needed.

At the end of the course, after a tense weekend completing a long, take-home assessment essay, with her final result 'in the bag', Rose picked up Nabeel at London Airport then drove him home to Mossfield after a stopover with Bill and his partner, Katie.

In Mossfield Nabeel was delighted at the remodelled open plan kitchen diner, and the renovated bathroom. He had sent funds for the changes and the addition of a toilet and washbasin at a height suitable for a disabled person. Two bathrooms would be an asset in the case of selling the house, and of course, Rose was earning a salary which went straight into Nabeel's bank account so there was plenty of money to make these changes.

"You've done very well, Mum," Nabeel told her. "You should have been an interior decorator, you know!"

"I'm glad you approve. I will have to have the windows double glazed for the winter, though. It was cold here when the wind blew, so I hope that's OK?" Mum asked.

"No problem. Anything that improves the quality of the house and keeps you warm and cosy is fine by me," he assured her.

"And we are going to find a new place to live in Kuwait, Mum," Rose told her. "We'll make sure it's somewhere you can come to, with no stairs!"

"It's a lovely idea, but don't do anything special for me, because these operations might mean I can't walk at all. They say replacement ops are getting better every year, but I still worry."

"OK, darling. We will take things slowly. No pressure."

The family enjoyed some happy days in the first house Nabeel and Rose had ever purchased. The fruit trees in the small orchard were flourishing and the raspberry canes were already producing fruit. They did a few jobs in the house, such as putting up shelves in their bedroom for Rose's MA books and materials that she wouldn't need in Kuwait and bought new furniture, including an American king size bed for their room.

Sadly they had to fly back to Kuwait before brother Bill and Katie got married in September. Two marriages of two brothers in one year, both at registry offices, just like Nabeel and Rose's! Rose hoped that they would both turn out better than hers had.

Dear Diary,

When I arrived this year my brothers were single, and now they are both married! I have a feeling they will be giving Mum the grandchildren she probably wanted when she read the Tarot cards for me back in 1976! I'm sure she won't be disappointed this time.

August - December, 1984, Kuwait

All too soon Rose was back in Kuwait with her new qualification which enabled her to confirm her earlier application to Kuwait University for a teaching position. She was still committed to the BC as Main Course Tutor for the Cert.TESOL which would take place in the evenings this time. So although it seemed a little disloyal, Rose had not forgotten that since September 1976 she had been paid as a local employee with no air tickets or accommodation costs, although she was well qualified. She would move on to her new job feeling the eight year relationship had been fair on both sides. The BC had been important in creating a sense of stability and security in that first part of her marriage and life in Kuwait.

Rose had applied for a teaching position directly to the Health Sciences Centre, a Department which had some autonomy within the University. The Head of Department was a British PhD holder, with an American wife, and three children. Rose had met them socially and looked forward to a new working environment. She was placed in the Allied Health Faculty, in the first year program, working with an English girl from Birmingham as course coordinator. The medical content of the teaching was challenging but intrinsically interesting to Rose, with her mother's health so damaged. She was quickly drawn into testing and assessment of learners on account of her MA dissertation and her boss's own special interest.

The five departments in the Faculty, for which the eighteen language teachers and supervisor prepared ESP materials, were Nursing, Medical Technology, Radiologic Technology, Medical Records and Physiotherapy. In order to write appropriate teaching materials teaching staff were required to meet with medical staff from the UK, the US and Sudan, which made the challenge both easier and more fun. The only visible difference between the two sets of teachers was the distinctive white coat worn by medical teachers. Parallel with the Allied Health teachers were the Medical Faculty language teachers. Periodically the two groups met with the Head of Department so social as well as professional relationships were established. The Supervisor of Medical Faculty English, Beatrice, became a close friend, as she, too, was married to an Arab.

Sadly, as life seemed to be improving for Rose, her friend Janet was diagnosed with cancer. This was very hard. Like Rose Janet had realised that a master's degree would get her a better position at Kuwait University. So she had left and spent time with her aged father, studying at an American university for her Master's. She had then begun work at Kuwait Uni and had been given accommodation. Whether Nabeel was influenced by seeing a non-smoker become a victim of cancer, or not, he gave up smoking at Xmas. Rose was amazed but pleased. He seemed to have become aware of the negative impact his smoking was having on her, causing quarrels when they went out at weekends, with Rose dressed in party clothes and long hair washed, having to sit in a smoke-filled car for the ride to the social function. In addition, he bought a couple of self help books for couples, and asked Rose to read them.

Perhaps he had noticed that she was growing away from him and starting not to care whether he smoked or not, so he stopped! Reverse psychology had worked in practice. Stop complaining about something and the other person will do what you want!

Dear Diary, Two years and my MA is finished. A new job ahead!

1985, Kuwait, Dubai, USA, UK, Oman

As soon as Xmas and New Year were over Rose began to press Nabeel to find somewhere she could bring Mum to stay. It seemed only logical to her that she should take up the rent-free flat she was entitled to as a University teacher. Rose was determined to move as soon as possible. She applied to the Housing Department, a male-dominated environment, so not without its risks. As she was married to an Arab, she had to seek special permission from her Dean to access an apartment. Since the Dean of Allied Health Sciences was a woman, and a woman who had lived independently in both the USA and the UK where she completed her two doctoral degrees, she was supportive. Rose was promised an apartment as soon as a first floor apartment was available.

Rose was pleased with how things were working out this year with work and a move on the cards for her home. However, one morning when Nabeel was driving a couple of Japanese visitors south to the oil town, Ahmadi, their lives nearly took a very dark turn. Major roads in Kuwait were three lane highways in both directions, so six lanes wide. In between was a central reservation with metal barriers. Crashes were common as American imported cars were cheap and fast and petrol (aka gas) was cheap in this oil-producing country. Young men drove like maniacs and the slogan often posted on huge billboards warned: Beware of road surprises. Rose had penned an ironic ditty on the subject:

Beware of road surprises: It'll catch you if it can.

Beware of road surprises: It's out to get you, man.

On that awful day, the road did not rise up to meet them, but a driver coming into the city in the fast lane veered onto the central reservation. The car was going so fast that it flipped over when it hit the metal barrier and landed in the fast lane in the out of town direction, right in front of Nabeel's car. His four-door sedan had a long bonnet which was completely crushed as Nabeel could do nothing but emergency brake and then slam into the other car. The three men were badly shaken and their seat belts tore into their bodies, leaving wounds and bruises, but amazingly none of them was seriously injured. They were taken to hospital to be checked over then released. Of course, Nabeel, as a 'foreigner' was then charged with causing an accident, which was ludicrous. Local lore had it that if there was a road accident involving a non-Kuwaiti and a Kuwaiti, the non-Kuwaiti would be guilty because he should not have been in the State of Kuwait! Fortunately the two Japanese were witnesses to the true situation and gave evidence which meant Nabeel was proven not guilty. But he started smoking again, even more heavily than before.

The same month, in May, Rose presented a paper at the first Language Teaching Symposium organised by Kuwait University Language Centre. She was very pleased when the paper was published in the proceedings. It described her ETC placement test design, how it fitted with language testing theory and discussed how the test had worked in practice. As for Janet, when metastatic bone cancer set in she was no longer strong enough to walk but she still had a fighting spirit. Rose bought a wheelchair and enjoyed taking her out at weekends for coffee, or shopping, or simply to sit at the beach and watch the sea. Janet engaged a fulltime housemaid, and did her best to keep up social contact even as she slowly began to fade.

Rose couldn't visit her over the summer vacation as Nabeel needed to go back to the USA for business and Rose needed to see her family. First she had an assessment to conduct in Dubai, then on to the UK where she was able to attend the christening ceremonies of her new nephew and niece. After a couple of weeks Nabeel joined her and they went first to New York, where they enjoyed a Broadway musical, <u>A Chorus Line</u>, and an evening in a jazz bar, then on to visit business friends in San Diego. After that they made a side trip to New Orleans for the jazz. They stayed in the Latin Quarter at a lovely hotel and enjoyed a long, lazy Sunday brunch jazz session, drinking the specialty Hurricane cocktail. On their way back, via the UK, Nabeel heard that Janet had died only a few days earlier. Instead of sharing this information he hid it, not realising that Rose needed to know the truth to adjust to it.

When they got back to Kuwait, and Rose learned that Janet had died she was incensed. Nabeel was only able to make up for keeping this secret by arranging for Janet's funeral and burial in the Christian cemetery in Kuwait. Rose had to process a visitor's visa for Janet's cousin, Penny, to attend the funeral, although women were not allowed to go to the burial site, according to Kuwaiti law. Unfortunately in the Ministry she experienced the dark side of bureaucratic power when a woman gets involved in a man's world. To take away the memory of this creepy encounter, and to apologise for the unnecessary secrecy Nabeel bought her a ruby ring. Despite this consolation Rose felt bereft. Janet had worked hard and was a much loved lady but life was unfair to her.

In September Nabeel and Rose were able to move into the apartment newly vacated by their friends on the first floor of one of the University apartment tower blocks. It was a great relief for Rose and she eagerly told Mum about it, hoping that she would be able to make it out to Kuwait before she became too ill to make the flight. Abu Ali and his wife were sad to see them go, but understood the issue with regard to Rose's Mum.

Another positive event that autumn was an invitation to go to Oman to induct a new assessor for the Dip. TESOL. She stayed with their old friends Justin and Lucy and enjoyed visiting the silver shops in old Muscat. She came home with many photos and some shiny souvenirs, including a Maria Teresa silver dollar, of a very happy few days. But perhaps most outstanding in the achievements of this year was the move to computers and CALL in the Unit. Rose's American colleague was an expert so after completing a DOS course, Rose had a helpful mentor to assist her with developing word processing proficiency.

Dear Diary, 1985 was a year of two halves, of good and bad events. Both Bill and John have asked me to be godmother to their new babies. I'll be able to watch their growth and progress on life's path and find consolation in their parents' joys and help them with any future tribulations.

1986, Kuwait, Egypt, Bahrein

The New Year brought plans for Mum to visit Kuwait. Nabeel had to process her visitor's visa and Rose had to arrange air tickets. Mum would stay with Bill in London before she took her flight. The winter in the UK was always hard for Mum, even in her warmly heated bungalow, so she would escape to the January/February winter sunshine in Kuwait, rather than experience the heat of summer. All went well on the flight with sympathetic airline staff helping Mum take her painkillers at regular intervals. Rose had kept Janet's wheelchair which now came in handy for Mum when they met her at the airport.

Although Mum was alone during the day, she was not far away from Rose at work on the University campus now, so Rose could pop back for lunch to check on her and take her out in the afternoon to see the sights, such as Kuwait Towers. On weekends they could make major visits, to the beach and to the shops in Fahaheel and Fintas. One of the funniest was a trip to the Jahra camel farms. Mum staggered across the sand to a pen which held a splendid camel and stood rather unsteadily for Rose to take a photograph. Mum's fair hair attracted the camel, which approached the wire fence and leaned down to nibble this substance just as Rose was taking the shot. Mum screamed and Rose ran to move her out of reach of the beast. Both were laughing as they got back into the car, a slow process with Mum's painful joints. As they prepared to drive away, Rose realised a pick up truck was parked nearby and a man in peasant type dishdasha with a cloth turban on his head was calling out to them, "love, love".

Rose turned to Mum as she started the engine, "Don't look now, but that man is saying he wants some love. I'm a bit worried about him."

"Does he want both of us, do you think?" Mum asked drily. At which Rose burst out laughing. Nevertheless she watched him in her rear mirror as he continued to follow them. When he was still behind them as they reached the first traffic light in Jahra town, Rose put the handbrake on and opened the door to get out and approach the car in front of her, which was being driven by a man in uniform, either police or army. The driver behind realised that she was about to report him and so he drove off at speed. Rose breathed a sigh of relief and got back into her car. It was a story to dine out on.

Rose planned a party for Mum to celebrate Valentine's Day at which Mum could meet all her Kuwait friends. All seemed to be going well with red paper hearts pasted on the walls and the food organised, when there was bad news from the UK. Mum's brother, one of the two who had supported her after the separation and divorce, had died. Rose and Mum were grief stricken. Uncle Alec had frequently taken them out in his car, and Aunt Marie had made and decorated Rose's wedding cake. Rose wondered if she should cancel the planned party.

"Mum, what do you want to do? Should I explain what's happened? It's not too late."

"No, dear. Uncle would not have wanted that. Carry on. I'll be home soon to grieve."

But things were never the same and Aunty found life very difficult without her 'strength and stay' afterwards as Mum, Bill and John found out after Mum's return to the UK.

That summer Rose was invited to assess a Cert. TESOL in Cairo. It was, of course, Nabeel and Rose's tenth wedding anniversary so they kept their promise to return to the country where they had spent their honeymoon. This time they would travel further up the Nile but first Rose stayed alone in a hotel in Cairo close to the British Council, funded as an assessor. She marvelled at the sight of a donkey delivering slabs of ice to the hotel on a cart. Cairo was full of amazing contrasts between ancient and modern. The assessment mode for the Certificate was described as a moderation process and was beneficial for both assessor and assessed as it was an opportunity to share approaches. The staff on the course were open and welcoming, so this occasion was an enjoyable event for Rose.

When Nabeel joined her they took a boat up the Nile to Luxor, where an Egyptian foreman in the construction side of the family company had invited them to his home for lunch. Luxor itself was fabulous to visit, but when Mahmoud joined them Rose was horrified to see that he regarded the pre-Islamic statues not as wonders but as heretic idols. So great was his contempt for these sites, which attracted both tourists and wealth to his country, that he took out his pen knife to scratch on a column. Rose tried to hold back a scream, but obviously her reaction had some impact on Mahmoud and he desisted, thankfully.

After a drive to Mahmoud's house, which was bewitchingly simple, like a Hansel and Gretel cottage, with a white cow installed on the ground floor, and the living and sleeping quarters upstairs, they were served a lunch of grilled pigeon and sweetcorn from the fields. Rose gratefully ate the latter and ignored the former. She was once again bemused when the bones and husks left after their meal were thrown out of the window - which had no glazing! Water to drink was served in an empty, rusty Crisco tin, so Rose drank as little as possible. She was ashamed of her slightly negative reaction when on leaving the foreman's wife pressed on her two small silver rings as a gift. She looked at Nabeel, instinctively wishing to refuse them, but she saw from Nabeel's eyes that she should accept. Later he told her: "Don't worry, I will make the cost of the gift up to him. His pride would have been wounded if you hadn't accepted the rings." So she had done the right thing, though she felt terrible about it. It was clear that these rings were treasured items.

The grand finale in Luxor, where they had a drink in the hotel which Agatha Christie had stayed in, The Winter Palace, was a long, challenging donkey ride to the Valley of the Kings. The route was mountainous but the donkeys were sturdy and seemed to know their way. Rose held on safely for most of the journey but on a ledge above the Temple of Hatshepsut she felt her saddle beginning to slide. Miraculously the guide noticed her imminent descent and jumped off his donkey in time to stop her hitting the floor. Gratefully she walked the rest of the way down to the Temple grounds. The tomb of Tutankhamun had only recently been opened to the public, so although

425

they had missed seeing the boy king's tomb treasures ten years earlier, they were now able to enter his tomb and see the fabulous paintings on the walls. The whole trip was amazing, and they found alabaster ashtrays and boxes in a workshop en route which they bought as souvenirs.

From Luxor they travelled on to see the sights of Aswan where they stayed on Elephant Island in the middle of the Nile. The hotel was run by the Oberoi chain, just as their Giza hotel had been. The surroundings were extraordinarily beautiful but the Pharaonic sites were out of this world. Since the building of the Aswan Dam by the Soviets the original site of the statues had been flooded. It had been a huge UNESCO funded project to move the huge treasures to their new home. From here they had plane tickets to fly to Abu Simbel further up the Nile and with more treasures to see but a fish dish for dinner ruined that plan. Rose spent most of the night in the bathroom. As there was no room service and the bar was closed Nabeel had to break in forcibly to get some *arak* to hold her intestines together.

Despite this 'medicine' she was unable to get up for the flight to Abu Simbel. Instead, they stayed an extra night on Elephant Island, returning to Cairo and Kuwait directly the next day. It had been a fantastic trip and Rose had bought some kaftans and *zills* in the Luxor market as souvenirs this time. They had made a lot of material progress over ten years, that was evident. But Rose was not satisfied at heart. She still longed for a child. Perhaps adoption would be the solution to the problem? Would Nabeel accept this? She would have to see.

Back at work her MA thesis had prepared her for work

on the Unit's placement test. The Head of Department was a testing specialist so she was fully engaged on assessment work. The students who failed tests objected strongly. One day the staff were informed that an article had been printed in the English language daily. The title was 'The butcher of Kuwait University' and the content was about the 'brutality' of the assessment process. Rose was able to counter this with an interview in which she explained that the students who graduated to work in Allied Health Sciences would be required to use English at a level of accuracy not needed in other professions. A mistake with an item such as 15 grams versus 15 milligrams of medicine could kill a patient. The point was well made and well taken. The students who objected to stringent English language tests moved to other faculties, such as Islamic Law (*Sharia*) where English language was not a requirement.

Working closely with the Head of Department on testing for placement and achievement purposes, Rose got to know his family and invited them to parties and dinners at home. Susan, his American wife, did some teaching and had three children to care for so rarely socialised. But Philip often visited on his own, attracted, it seemed to Rose, by Nabeel's business acumen. He was interested in exploiting his academic talents in a way which could set the family up with savings greater than those he could make as a professor. In the course of these visits Rose discovered that he and his wife had adopted a child. This gave Rose the ammunition she needed to work on Nabeel. Most of his friends had children, and quite young ones, so she thought he might be amenable to a new idea.

One Friday after the usual visit to the family she reminded him of their visit to Beirut and meeting Charbel and his wife and baby. Lebanon was still in the throes of civil war and it was reported that many children had lost their parents.

"Nabeel, do you think we could offer a home to a Christian orphan? We could adopt one or even two to save them from this crisis, don't you think?"

"Don't even think about it. No way. I'm not taking an unknown child into my home," he retorted.

"What on earth do you mean? All children are unknown, even those born with your own genes. They create their own selves, their own personality, character, likes and dislikes. Do you think biological children are carbon copies of their parents?" Rose tried to expand on the subject, but Nabeel shut her up.

"I told you to forget it. Adopted children bring problems."

"All children bring problems. That's the challenge of parenthood. We have to learn to cope and bring out the best in a child," she tried to continue.

"Look, your boss talks to me about his problems with his children. They aren't easy to handle, you know."

Rose gasped in astonishment. Her trump card was gone. Was this true or was Nabeel using his tricks again to manipulate her?

"Well, I can't argue about something I don't know about. I'm just very sorry to think what we could do to help the children in Lebanon. That's all."

"And that's enough. Forget it. Subject closed."

As the Head of Department had not shared any information with Rose about his children it would be embarrassing for Rose to pursue the matter, so she had to let it go. But resentment began to build on top of the disappointment. And then Nabeel launched into his own cause for resentment.

"Now let's talk about another thing. I feel embarrassed bringing business visitors to this flat. Everyone knows it is my wife's, not mine."

"Are you completely crazy? What does that matter? Do you like throwing money away? We have saved a lot and we have spent it on Mum's house and airfare. Isn't that logical?"

"No. This is the Middle East. A husband should pay for the rent. Otherwise there is no respect," Nabeel insisted.

"OK. Do what you like. But never say you spent a lot of money on me, when you have no need to. We can live here as long as I work for the University. It costs nothing and I like it."

"OK. Stop now. I'm going to look for another place to live."

Rose was not just perplexed, she was angry. The situation was crazy. She wondered again if she could leave him and live on her own, but the change of status might be difficult for her job. There were single women employed as teachers in the Units, but a divorced woman? That might not be acceptable. Plus, they had been together now for 16 years. Should she throw that away because he, an Arab man, had an Arab man's pride? Somehow she

429

had not realised that his personality was so imbued with patriarchal Arabic values. His veneer of French manners and sophistication had not prepared her for such an archaic attitude.

True to his word, Nabeel began taking Rose to look at alternative accommodation. One particular apartment still stuck in her mind. One bedroom had a heavily stained carpet. Rose mentioned how unsightly it was, at which the agent showing them around explained "That's where the last occupant killed himself." There was no need for words. They turned and walked out. Soon after that, however, a lovely single storey villa was found, on the edge of the Emir's private palace. It needed some renovation and decorating but had an open plan lounge and sitting room, two bedrooms and two bathrooms, and a large kitchen as well as a large private back garden with a lawn, trees and a paved front garden, fenced with trellis, suitable for a barbecue area. Rose had to agree that it would be very pleasant living there, on the first ring road, close to the sea and Kuwait Towers. They moved at the end of September, handing over the Uni flat to another Health Sciences teaching couple. The new house's interior was perfect for parties, and would be comfortable for Mum in future. But Rose had to put her case again.

"I don't know how I'm going to explain to Mum that you want to spend money on the rent, just to keep your pride. Really, it's a waste of money, paying rent for this place. It doesn't matter how fabulous it is. So remember what I said. You are doing this for your ego, for your business, not for me. So don't complain if I go shopping in Fintas or Fahaheel, OK?"

"OK. Enough said. I'm doing it for my ego and my business. No complaints."

In October Rose was invited to assess a Certificate course in Bahrein at the British Council. The Course Director was a woman with whom she established a friendly professional relationship. Rose enjoyed travelling independently as she had done in Cairo, and began to realise that she could indeed be as independent as she wished to be in future. Listening to music on the plane, as always obsessed with classical, pop or jazz, Rose noticed a pop song trending at the time, about a woman who picks up a guy while driving and has a one night stand in order to have the baby her husband cannot give her. The last line of the lyrics is about the 'surprise' the man gets when he meets the woman again by chance, sees her child and recognises "his own eyes".

At the time, expat Kuwaiti folk lore gossip was about rich, bored Kuwaiti young women picking up handsome young Arab men for some 'afternoon delight'. Some men professed to have had this experience, but Rose had taken it with a huge pinch of salt. Now, with her own interest piqued by this unusual pop song, she began to wonder? This was the start of her third academic year in the Uni, work she was enjoying immensely. Why was she tormenting herself with thoughts of what she could not have? Count your blessings, she told herself.

> Dear Diary,
>   A child would enrich our lives immensely. But it would also be a great responsibility and I cannot do it alone. So that's that.

431

1987, Kuwait, UK

After the usual end of year festivities, work consumed Rose's time and thoughts again. Around Easter she was called to discuss the future with her boss. She was told, to her surprise, that the current Allied Health English Language Unit Supervisor was leaving at the end of the academic year to pursue doctoral studies in the UK. The vacancy was offered to Rose, given her expertise in the assessment area. It would not involve more work, just different work. Rose was flattered, but unsure whether she wanted to take this on. After all, she had been recommended to pursue a doctoral degree, so perhaps that is where she should be concentrating her time.

Back at home she told Nabeel about the offer of promotion to Supervisor.

"OK. How do you feel about it?" he asked.

"That's the problem. I don't know. Our unit is quiet and the teachers are hard working, so it might be easy enough to handle. I just don't know if I want to do that, or to study some more."

"Oh, no. Not more study. Haven't you got enough qualifications now? I think you like being with your books more than with me," Nabeel complained.

"Come on. That's an exaggeration. You are out at work most of the week and on our only day together, Friday, we spend our free time with your family," Rose shot back.

"I know you hate my family, but I take care of yours, don't I? So is that fair?" he asked bitterly.

"Look, I'm grateful that you bought the house for Mum and that she came out here to visit last year when we moved to the University flat, but if you do the calculations on the rent we would have saved if we had stayed in the Uni apartment, then I think I have paid for the UK house, don't you? And no, I don't hate your family, I hate spending most of Friday with them instead of going to the beach on the only day off we have together."

"So what are you going to do about the job? Are you going to take it?" Nabeel asked.

"Yes, of course I am. Your actions don't seem to be logical, but mine are. It's a promotion and I'm glad of it. It won't make any difference to you and your life," Rose retorted angrily. "But first we need to throw a party for the staff who are leaving. I know you'll like that, always showing off and talking about the money you are making. But you never mention the money you are wasting, do you?"

Rose's mood was not improved by her own health and Mum's at the time. Mum had not been able to come out to visit that year as she had had two major operations since her previous visit: Her left knee and then her left hip had been replaced. Rose too was in need of specialist endodontic surgery. So Rose left for the UK as soon as her long eight-week vacation began. She had had some root canal treatment years ago in London when she was 21 but the dentist had overfilled the root with mercury amalgam and she needed to have it extracted by experts. Her Kuwait dentist had advised her to seek treatment in the USA, but it was too far to go and too expensive, with no contacts who could arrange a suitable American clinic since Rose's Aunt and Uncle in California had both passed away.

So she found herself back on Harley Street where her private dentist was also a teacher at the London Dentistry School. Unfortunately the surgery was not totally successful as it involved invasive work on the upper jaw and cheek bone. Fighting off panic at the unsuccessful outcome, she stayed with Bill and Katie during her treatment and met her new nephew who was born in January and enjoyed getting to know her god-daughter, now two years old. Travelling by taxi through London between appointments she also saw the devastation caused by the huge storm that hit the UK that year, with massive trees uprooted in London's Hyde Park.

After the dental treatment was over Rose hired a car and drove north to Mossfield. She planned to take Mum for a British vacation. She booked a lovely hotel in the Lake District and they enjoyed a week driving around to see the fabulous scenery of the lakes and moutains. But what Mum enjoyed most was being home and having hot baths every evening to ease the pain she still felt in her left leg. They spent a happy three weeks together, with John and his children visiting and Bill and Katie with theirs too. Rose wondered if she was doing the right thing returning to work in a new role, but Mum reassured her. "Don't worry about me. I've got John here and Bill in London. They look after me."

So Rose went back to Kuwait and started her new supervisory role in the Allied Health English Language

Unit. This year she took with her a pile of music videos recorded from Yorkshire Television programs. She had enjoyed catching up with the Top 10, 20 and even 100, and was looking forward to using the videos in her now regular Xmas and birthday parties. When she got back to Kuwait, Rose was surprised by Nabeel's continued generosity.

"Isn't it your 40th birthday, this year, *habibti*?" he asked.

"Yes, it is. Well done for remembering! Why do you ask?" Rose replied tartly.

"I think you need a diamond this year. You never had an engagement ring, did you?" Nabeel reminded her.

"I'd love that, but only if you're sure," Rose told him. "I know you are doing well, but I don't want to overspend on our budget."

After a visit to the gold souk, Rose became the proud owner of a 1.25 karat diamond solitaire ring, her pride and joy. Nabeel could be sure his wife was as bejewelled as his friends' wives were, though she still refused to buy designer clothing.

Dear Diary, A promotion at work but Nabeel is not supportive. With no kids at home, what am I supposed to do? Roll vine leaves? My diamond ring is my consolation prize I suppose.

1988, Kuwait, Iraq, China

This year was busy with even more work than usual. There were more EMP (English for Medical Purposes) course workbooks to revise and a curriculum review to undertake to check on achievement success and investigate those examination results which had caused so much grief to students. The English curriculum review was a massive task. In addition, Neil left Kuwait. Three years earlier he had founded a Medical and Paramedical Newsletter. It was published by Kuwait University and circulated internationally at no cost to subscribers. Rose, formerly the Assistant Editor, took over as Editor. There was a lot of work to do but having also taken over as Supervisor, Rose was able to deploy some of the teaching and office staff to support the production of the Newsletter.

In February Mum was well enough to visit the new one storey villa. In her two month stay they made a boat trip to Failaka Island at the head of the Arabian Gulf where the helpful boatmen nearly destroyed Mum's wheelchair, the first they had ever seen and did not know how to open up. Disabled people were not a common sight in Kuwait. Disability was regarded as shameful, so the disabled were hidden away in family homes. As a result, pushing a wheelchair in Kuwait City was quite a challenge: There were no ramps to wheel down onto road crossings, nor up onto the pavement (aka sidewalk). Nevertheless, Rose persisted in her daily pattern of work, then home for a late lunch, a nap/siesta and then a drive out to see something new, or just to sit by the sea.

They also made a trip by air to Bahrein where Rose had built up a steady relationship as the assessor of the BC TESOL Certificate Courses. Although Rose took lots of photos of Mum at all the well known archaeological and modern sites of Dilmun, she forgot to put a film in the camera (those were the pre-digital days) so they had no souvenirs of the trip! At home they gave barbecue lunch parties and had the pleasure of meeting Sara's parents, also out on a visit to avoid winter in the North of England. Mum was able to dine out frequently with these new friends and kept in touch with them later in the UK. Thus she was able to enjoy a very different life from hers in the UK, which she very much enjoyed.

In the background to their daily lives the war between Iraq, *Iraq al shaqiqa* (sisterly Iraq as the morning radio news reader from Baghdad proclaimed) to the north of Kuwait and Iran across the Gulf waters from Kuwait had been going on since May 1980 when Iraq invaded Iran. There had been huge loss of life on both sides, but in May 1988 it seemed that a ceasefire was in place, with a view to the war of attrition ending.

The English language supervisor at the British Council Baghdad came to Kuwait to ask if Rose, as a Dip. TESOL assessor could help two of his teachers. He came for dinner and explained to Nabeel and Rose that these two British teachers could not leave Baghdad on account of Iraqi Government restrictions and very few assessors were willing to go to Baghdad to assess. The women had passed the written examinations but needed to be assessed in their practical lessons. Rose was the obvious choice to help them complete their qualifications. Would she travel to wartorn Baghdad? Nabeel was not at all happy about the situation. "What if you get killed? Your Mum is here, what will I do if you don't come back?"

Rose was upset - she didn't want to get killed or injured but how could she refuse to help others? Mum agreed that she should go, and after all, a chance to visit Baghdad was rare.

She flew to Baghdad and while waiting at the airport for her visa to be checked at Customs she was amused to be asked by a female traveller in Arabic, how she had managed to obtain a British passport. A British passport was a golden ticket to the world, she realised. Brendan met her in Arrivals and took her to the Sheraton, where she was given a luxury room. Security seemed to be strong in the Hotel, but returning to her room after dinner with Brendan and other BC staff she was horrified to receive a phone call at 11pm from an unknown male inviting her for dinner. She lodged a chair back under the door knob and rang the reception desk to complain.

After a restless night, disturbed by the unexpected phone call, Rose ordered breakfast in her room, then went down to meet the British Council driver. At the teaching centre, she assessed two lessons, writing up her assessments in a quiet office afterwards. After lunch she had two more assessments and was able to complete her written reports. The next morning she checked out early and was driven by the BC driver to the ancient site of Babylon which was being restored by Saddam Hussein, the President. It was a beautiful historic site with winged statue guardians at the gate. She flew back to Kuwait that afternoon after spending just two nights away from home. There had been no bombs or shells and the two teachers had given more than satisfactory lessons. One of the women was in a similar situation to herself. Married to an Iraqi, she had not been able to visit her family in the UK for years on account of the war and the Government restrictions on taking money out of Iraq. Although she had family in the UK who would support her during a visit, she was too proud to ask them to do so. Rose felt glad that she'd stood up to Nabeel and gone to help these teachers achieve their practical assessments.

Back at home in the villa, Nabeel seemed to have forgotten his negative reaction to the invitation and life returned to normal. Mum told Rose very much later that Nabeel had been furious at her action and even said he would not let her come back to the house. On hearing this, Rose began to wonder if she should have taken the opportunity to revert to single status at work.

There was a sad episode the following month with Lightning, the dog. He was a stray who enjoyed chasing men on bicycles, barking incessantly. So after feeding and watering him for a few days, so that he became used to staying quietly near the house, Nabeel took him to a vet who placed him with a farmer in the Jahra area, 50 kilometres away. Rose and Nabeel felt they couldn't take on a dog because they were often away. Two days later he turned up on their doorstep. With heavy hearts, they cared for him for another few days, then tried again to place him with the farmer. This time, he either stayed voluntarily or was made to stay.

That summer Nabeel and Rose made a wonderful journey to China. They flew direct from Kuwait on CAAC (China Airways Always Crash was the joke) with rather stiff Communist air stewardesses to Beijing where they stayed in a huge hotel with massive landscape paintings on the walls. In those days bicycle was the only mode of transport for ordinary people, so the streets were choked with cyclists dressed in grey or black Mao suits. It was quite amazingly different from any other place Rose had ever been. They marvelled at the many terracotta tiled buildings in the Forbidden City, aka the Imperial Palace, with its many ornate thrones and at the entrance exquisite white marble steps carved with dragons. They astonished the locals as they drank canned beer while walking through a park where the Lotus Festival was being celebrated with a fantastic display of decorative lights. Strolling around the various installations with a beer in the warm evening air was a wonderful treat.

They visited the Summer Palace on the edge of the city with its amazing decorated walkways and bridges over the lake and wondered at the elegant marble boat built for the Last Emperor's mother. They ate genuine Peking Duck with plum sauce and pancakes, using chopsticks to Nabeel's discomfort. They walked on the Great Wall of China in the pouring rain wearing thin white plastic raincoats provided free but which made them feel like sausages. They bought Emperor and Empress silk jackets with intricate dragon and phoenix embroidery and took lots of photos.

From Beijing they flew to Xian, the ancient walled city at the start of the Silk Road. It was incredible to be in such a well preserved city. Just outside the city the famous army of Terracotta Warriors had recently been uncovered by a farmer, and were on display to tourists. Of course, they had to buy a small souvenir soldier to remember that visit. Next they went on to Suzhou, a pretty city celebrated for its beautiful gardens as well as for silk production and silk clothing. Once again, they made purchases.

After that they visited Shanghai and managed to get themselves a room in the stunning waterfront (Bund) Peace Hotel where jazz bands had played in the 1920s and '30s before the Communist era. They uncovered examples of the 'iron rice bowl' mentality of workers in Communist China which discouraged individual enterprise. The night receptionist didn't want to let them have a room until they proffered a bribe. The waiters bemoaned the laziness of their boss who was simply doing other jobs than serving customers. At the Old Teahouse they witnessed the original building, garden and bridge, for the blue and white porcelain design. Delightful!

Their next stop was the fairytale wonderland of Guilin. The topography was amazing and they made a lovely river trip. On the boat they had some fun with Chinese fashion models on a day out. Then a train to Hong Kong through kilometres of fields under intensive Cantonese agriculture to spend a night, before flying back to Kuwait feeling they had had a special time.

Sadly in their absence their lovely little renovated villa had been noticed by a Sheikha (princess) who claimed it for herself so Nabeel and Rose had to move out in

September. Fortunately they were offered an alternative residence: a large ground floor apartment with a garden in a building on the other side of Dasman Palace, closer to the sea. It was an even more elite area, with the Emir's Palace on one side and the Guest House for visiting dignitaries, such as Yasser Arafat, on the other side of the garden. Rose grew hollyhocks and marigolds and put two cane swings in the massive tree sheltering the garden beds. There were orange trees from which Rose made marmalade at harvest time. There was a huge palm tree in a deep bed next to the wide steps up to the apartment. Inside there were mirrored walls and marble floors, as well as huge rooms. It was a palace in a mini Garden of Eden so they accepted the change with good grace.

After all, this was not home. Foreigners could not purchase homes, they could only rent. So their residence would only ever be temporary in Kuwait. They needed to plan their futures elsewhere, they reminded themselves. Would their retirement residence be in Lebanon, the UK or elsewhere? Spain could be a good halfway house for them in future.

The temporary nature of their stay in Kuwait had not hindered them from continuing to adorn their home with brass and copper coffee tables, Persian carpets and brightly coloured Iraqi kilims on sofas. They had lots more furniture now, inside and outside rattan sitting suites including a bar, with high stools just as in the West. Of course they had to search for them in stores by asking for kitchen stools rather than bar stools!

"Well, your birthday is coming up and we need a housewarming party, don't you think?" Nabeel asked.

"Yes, that would be good. Shall we do a Spanish- or Chinese-themed party this year?"

"I think Spanish would be nice. Are you up to it? We've had a busy year."

"Spanish it is. This place needs a good party," Rose reassured her husband and started planning the food and designing a flamenco style top and skirt in flamboyant red satin for a tailor to make.

Meanwhile, back in the UK to cap off a very good year, John's second child, Laurel, was born in December and for Xmas Nabeel gifted Rose a brand new car: a Grand Prix sport model! Was it for her pleasure or to keep 'face' in light of his friends' criticisms, she wondered?

> Dear Diary
>   Nabeel is extremely generous at the moment but I have no idea what the state of our bank accounts is. I hope he's being sensible. I have a feeling his friends have goaded him into giving me the car. I know they used to laugh at my huge, old-fashioned 'yank tank' so maybe he's just 'keeping up with the Joneses'?

1989, Kuwait, Bahrein, Kenya

At the end of 1988 Nabeel's family had moved from the old villa which was starting to deteriorate and needed serious renovations. They had taken a large modern apartment in Salwa, a new residential suburb much further away from the city and from Nabeel and Rose. where cleaning was not such a huge task for Asma. The increased distance between their homes meant that the call to lunch on Friday could be avoided sometimes. They still had not bought a membership in a hotel beach club, which was becoming popular with expats at the time, but they managed to get to the sea often enough on Fridays to satisfy Rose's craving for sea and sun bathing on her days off.

Rose and Nabeel in their new home had some concern about security, but the neighbours presented only one small problem. The top floor was occupied by someone who came home in the early hours of the morning and fried onions for his supper. The smell was disturbing to the olfactory senses, but otherwise neighbours kept to themselves. The entrances to the other flats were completely separate and so there was no crossing paths or even sight of each other most days. Cars were parked on the street outside the garden walls quite safely, and Rose was enjoying driving her new two-door, two-tone blue Grand Prix, her Xmas present from Nabeel.

This year Mum came out for Xmas and her New Year birthday in their huge new apartment. She had her own specially made high chair for ease of access with her damaged knees and hips, and she brought with her a bag for the knitting and crochet she enjoyed doing. The family came to Nabeel's apartment this year for the festivities and Nabeel sourced the caviar from the Iranian car-wash guys who rode around on bicycles. They had also managed to smuggle in some vodka, so it was a special treat but Mum only took one sip of the chilled vodka. She enjoyed singing carols while Rose played the piano they had bought second hand while in the spacious villa. Mum was 61 this year, not old, but suffering terribly from RA. The family were very impressed with her stoicism and showered her with gifts as always. On this third visit Mum was to stay for several months, with her own residence visa. The only constraint on her stay was the type of painkillers she was taking daily. They were opioids which were not allowed to be given to outpatients. So she was limited to staying as long as she had enough painkillers.

Rose was doing well in her job although the curriculum development project had taken a lot of time and delayed the publication of the EMPN for 1988. Mum joined the team typing the copy out, so 1989's issue went out on time. Kuwait University was still publishing and mailing out copies to subscribers for free. It was a good time to be working in English for Medical Purposes. But Rose had one problem: a recurrence of the dental problem treated in Harley Street two years earlier. Rose hated dental treatment. It made her cranky. But it had to be done, nevertheless. Rose tried to compare the temporary pain she felt with Mum's permanent pain. There was no comparison. Rose had to put up and shut up.

After Mum had gone home to avoid the heat of

summer, Rose made another independent visit to Bahrein to assess the BC's Cert.TESOL course. Then in the summer holidays Nabeel and Rose went to Kenya to visit a former London college friend of his. He and his wife had stayed with Nabeel and Rose in their London apartment before their marriage. The then fiancee was now a wife with two young children, living in expatriate luxury. However, the contrast between the life lived by this old college friend and his family in a gated residence with a huge avocado tree in the lovely garden, and the people who inhabited the slum dwellings on the outskirts of Nairobi was tragic. Rose experienced the pampering of live-in servants bringing 'bed tea' in the morning, and had the thrill of visiting Lake Turkana in the far north of Kenya with Nabeel's friend piloting his own private plane, a Cessna. But she knew she could never live like that herself. The gulf between the people was intolerable to her.

Another extreme contrast presented itself on 4 June in China, when citizens and students' protests in Tianenmen Square protests against the Communist Government were violently quelled. There were tragic scenes when the army moved in with tanks against the protesters. Rose knew she preferred to avoid countries where life's natural unfairness was supported and even increased by the ruling parties. She hoped she would never experience such inhumanity herself.

Almost worse than death as a result of tyranny was the taking of individuals as hostages which had started in Beirut in 1982 and continued till 1992. 140 people of different nationalities, but mainly US and UK citizens, were kidnapped and kept in cellars and other prisons for various lengths of time. The most famous in the UK were John McCarthy and Brian Keenan, who became friends and were eventually released. Terry Waite was sent to plead for their release and was himself imprisoned and finally released in 1989. Rose thought about crossing the 'green line' and the threat to her safety she had experienced. She would never choose to live in Beirut if she could help it. Another crack had appeared below the surface of the marriage.

For Xmas Nabeel treated himself to a new car. It was a grey Mercedes four-door E Class saloon with white leather upholstery. It was so luxurious Rose was too scared to drive it very far. She simply took it down the street and back one afternoon to sample the luxury.

Dear Diary,

I count myself very lucky to be able to live in a secure, democratic society and not to have any illness as yet such as Mum's. It does give me pause for thought in case I have inherited the disease, but so far, so good. But the idea of living in wartorn Beirut is horrific to me.

January - August, 1990, Kuwait, Europe

Mum was having another joint replacement operation so didn't come out this New Year. The plan was for her to come out with Rose when Rose and Nabeel came home from a long trip to Europe in summer. They had discussed their personal financial situation and future in detail and had decided to search for a 'halfway house', a home in Europe, most probably in Spain. Rose was insisting on having a home in a more secure place than Kuwait where they could only rent property. Also, the laws on Lebanese inheritance had started to prey on her mind because should Nabeel, a heavy smoker still, die, then she would not have a secure legacy. Mum's little house in the UK was not where she saw herself spending her retirement, nor did Nabeel. But neither did she wish to be permanently located in Lebanon as a housewife. She was only in her forties and she wanted to obtain the doctoral degree she had patiently put on the side lines for the past six years. Perhaps now was the time to pursue it?

Rose was now a Senior Assessor for the Dip.TESOL, UCLES. (The RSA operation was taken over by Cambridge University Local Examinations Syndicate in 1988.) She obtained permission from the Dean of Faculty to take leave to attend an examiners meeting in London from 28 March to 1 April. After staying at Bill and Katie's to attend the meeting Rose drove up with Bill to see Mum for a couple of days before flying back to Kuwait. Sadly, she heard later that Mum had fallen over and been rescued by her neighbour. She was taken to hospital in Mossfield. Luckily Bill managed to arrange an appointment at Barts and took Mum to London. Mum was in great pain, so Bill and Katie had to get up in the night to look after her before she had yet another operation to replace her knee joint.

Having put the EMP Newsletter to bed for the year, Nabeel and Rose set off from Kuwait in July for Italy first to see their business friend Pietro again. After an enjoyable visit to Milan and Rome they moved to France where Rose looked up Josephine, her former secondary school student in her year of teaching in the South of France in the '60s. She was happily married and living with her family in Correze. It was wonderful to catch up after twenty years. Then suddenly they got bad news. Katie's father had died in the UK while Bill and Katie were on holiday with a group of friends in a chateau in the Dordogne. Would Nabeel and Rose stand in loco parentis while Bill and Katie went back to the UK for the funeral? The children were too young to understand and it would be a waste of a lovely holiday for them if they were to go back too.

So Uncle and Aunt became Mum and Dad in a chateau for a few days. It was a wonderful experience to be living in such a grand place, although the children had been warned not to mention the word 'chateau' in public, in case they were kidnapped for a ransom. There were some memorably funny moments. The first was on the beach.

Noelle noticed the small holes in the sand at the edge of the sea.

449

"What are they, Aunty?" she asked. "They're breathing holes of worms that live in the sand," explained Rose to Noelle's horror. She started screaming with fear and had to be carried back up the beach to dry sand. There were scary moments too in the chateau, as the children's bedroom wall was decorated with stuffed badger heads. Rupert couldn't sleep because of them so Rose covered them with towels. There was some relief when their parents got back to the chateau and their children.

Once Bill and Katie were back in France, Rose and Nabeel set off for Spain where they met up with Martin and Susan on the Costa del Sol. They stayed in the Lew Hoad Campo de Tennis on the outskirts of Fuengirola. The location was lovely and they looked around at several properties to buy but couldn't find one which suited them perfectly. In the end, Martin showed them a large piece of land, a 'finca', with a half-built house, a panoramic sea view and a river, which was close to his own and also to Ruby and Mark's place on the hill slopes between Fuengirola and Mijas. They would finish building the house, put in a pool and live *la dolce vita* as neighbours in future, they planned. Good friends would become good neighbours! They arranged with a real estate agent and solicitor to buy the property and on 23 July flew back from Malaga Airport to Paris, where Nabeel embarked for Kuwait, and Rose for London. The plan was to take Mum back to Kuwait on 8 August for an extended stay.

In London Rose stayed with Bill and Katie for a few days, telling them eagerly what had happened about the land. Aunt Rose enjoyed catching up again with the growing children. Both Noelle and Rupert were doing well at school. Noelle loved gymnastics, while Rupert was showing talent with music, his favourite song at the time was Brand New Key by Melanie! First Rose had optician's appointments to check on her contact lenses, then John drove Mum and his kids to London to do some sightseeing, a first for Laurel, Jill and Jasper. They travelled around by underground and overground train, which thrilled the children, and visited the Zoo, Buckingham Palace and the Tower of London, the photos showing Jasper proudly wearing his souvenir policeman's helmet. After John had taken the children home Bill organised a hire car for Rose and drove her to St.Albans to pick it up. As she drove Mum back to Mossfield, Rose updated her on the details of their holiday in Europe.

"We've found a lovely piece of land, Mum, to build a house in Spain. I feel really pleased with it. I just have to pay for the land now with our savings here when the contract comes through," Rose told her. "We're going to build a house which will be between our two homes, Lebanon and the UK. A halfway house!"

"That's great, Rose. It won't be so far for me to travel so as to be with you. I'm glad we are going back to Kuwait together. That will be so much easier for me. I'll be able to use the toilet this time!"

"I wouldn't bank on it if I were you, Mum. The toilets are really small! I don't know how people join the 'mile high club' in there!"

"What's that?"

"You don't want to know. It's rude," Rose laughed. "How far along are you with your packing for the trip to Kuwait?"

"Well, I've been lazy. I thought you could do it for me. We've still got a week, haven't we?"

"Yes, I'll be able to catch up with John and his kids for a few days. I'll give him a ring and get them to come round tomorrow. We'll drive down to Bill's on 6th August to spend a couple of nights with them before we take our flight. Let's get your suitcase out and start the packing, shall we?"

"Why don't we just make a packing list today. I'm feeling really tired and I'd love a nice bath and a rest after that. It's lovely to have you home again."

"OK. I'm just going to give Nabeel a ring. There was some news on TV about trouble between Iraq and Kuwait. He's only two hours ahead, so should be at the office now."

A phone call to the office found Nabeel at work as expected.

"Hi, hon. How was your flight yesterday?"

"All good. No problems. How are you and Mum?" Nabeel asked.

"She's fine. We're both a bit tired. But I heard something on the TV last night at Bill's about a high level meeting with Iraq about a disagreement over oil. Is everything OK?"

"Of course. They sorted it all out. No worries. Hey, I've got Ruby and Mark staying with me. They are driving out tomorrow through Saudi and on to Spain."

"Wow. That's great. I thought they'd already left. The journey will be amazing. Say hi to them when you get home. Are they cooking dinner for you?"

"I don't know. I think we'll go out. Or get some pizzas."

"OK. Bye for now. Love you." Rose signed off with a sigh of relief. All was well back in Kuwait. She could give Mum her bath and have an early night herself.

At 6pm the news on BBC was normal. No sign of trouble in Kuwait. Rose went to bed relieved and relaxed. But at 3am Mum called out to her. As usual, she had been listening to the radio during her pain-filled nights.

"Rose, Rose."

"Yes, Mum. Are you OK? Can I get you something?" Rose replied sleepily.

"They are invading Kuwait. It's on the radio. They are invading Kuwait." Mum's voice was shrill.

"OMG! No, it can't be. Are you sure?"

"Yes, I've just put my TV on. Come and look."

Together they watched as unsuspecting drivers heading to work in Kuwait City driving along the Corniche were stopped by tank commanders and made to leave their cars and go onto the beach. It was 5am Kuwait time.

Rose immediately rang Nabeel. There was no answer. Three adults had been in the house the evening before, but now, no one. Rose then rang the family home in Salwa.

"Hello, Rose. This is an early morning call. How are you?" Edouard asked.

"Edouard, the Iraqis are invading Kuwait. Kuwait City is already taken. Nabeel is not answering his phone," Rose shouted in fear and trembling.

"Oh, come on Rose. There's no problem here. Where did you get that news?"

"Edouard, it is real. It is happening now. It's on TV. You have to prepare to get out."

"Look, I'll call Nabeel. I'll ring you back. I'm sure you needn't worry." Edouard signed off abruptly, obviously not concerned at all with her news.

There was no further phone contact between Kuwait and the UK. The lines were too busy, and then they were cut. So began a time of extreme stress and uncertainty for Rose and her family. Would she ever see her husband again? What on earth was happening in Kuwait?

Dear Diary,

How can this be happening? Why have the Iraqis invaded Kuwait? What will happen to Nabeel, Ruby and Mark and our home? War has come into our lives out of the blue. It's unbelievable. The wheel of fate has turned, but in fact, it's just another example of might is right. Why are humans capable of such inhumanity to man?

August - September, 1990, UK

The first day was the worst. Watching the TV and wondering what was happening to Nabeel, his family and their friends. Rose tried to keep busy, helping Mum, doing the daily chores, even taking on some extra work in the garden. She didn't dare leave the house in case Nabeel rang. Then on the second day came a phone call from the British Embassy, Kuwait. It was Nabeel.

"Listen. I can't talk for long. The Ambassador has taken us into the premises. Ruby and Mark are here, but there isn't much food so we will have to go back to our house. We are OK. Don't worry. I'll get in touch as soon as I can."

"OK. Stay safe. Thanks for calling. Where did you all go?" Rose asked desperately.

"We had to go on the beach. We were digging holes to hide from the shells. The Kuwaitis were shelling the Iraqis on the beach road. We stayed there all day then the Embassy took us in."

"OMG. Give my love to Ruby and Mark. I love you, darling. Stay cool. Don't make trouble."

"I can't do anything against these tanks and soldiers. I have to stay put. Bye for now."

And so a long period of not knowing what exactly was happening in Kuwait began. But in Mossfield, things had to be done. First, British banks were told not to allow Kuwait residents to access their UK accounts in case they were helping finance Saddam Hussein. As if! Rose needed to return the hire car and buy another which would be long term. It could be stored in the garage if they were able to return to Kuwait at some point. But for now, there was no Kuwait. It was subsumed into Iraq as the 19th state. What would happen to their home and their precious possessions? What about her job and Nabeel's business? The future, once so certain, was now a huge question mark. Survival, staying sane, was the first objective.

"Mum, looks like we won't be going to Kuwait on the 8th! Let's concentrate on staying calm and trying not to worry. There's absolutely nothing we can do but hope. What do they say? Hope shines eternal."

Instead of returning the hire car to London, Rose arranged for it to be collected in Mossfield. She then did some research on available second hand cars and found a cheap, low mileage Ford automatic, four door saloon which would be perfect for her to drive. She made an appointment to meet the bank manager to arrange for payment despite the monetary restrictions. She had not been into the branch since she was a student, many years ago, so it was an interesting visit. The manager was understanding and as the amount required was not huge (only five thousand sterling pounds) he released her account so that she could support herself over the coming months.

Back in Kuwait, although she did not know it at the time, Nabeel had been able to go back to their home, after proving to the Republican Guard keeping watch over their elite area, that he was indeed a resident. His photo of him smoking a large cigar in a silver frame on the piano was enough proof for them. Ruby and Mark had also gone back to the house with him but as they were British, and Saddam was building up his 'human shield' defence of hostages against a possible attempt by the West to free Kuwait, it was wiser for them to go and stay with Nabeel's family in Salwa, away from the action in Kuwait City.

Knowing that Rose would need access to bank accounts in their joint names, Nabeel prepared a letter requesting the signatures to be modified to 'either/or' instead of 'both'. He also sent copies of his siblings' passports so that Rose could arrange visas for them to come to the UK if necessary. As there was no postage service the envelope was sent in the Embassy's Diplomatic Bag to the Foreign Office in London, then posted on by civil servants to Rose in Mossfield. A Gulf Support Group was formed in the UK by civilians with support from the Foreign Office for those in the UK unable to return to their expatriate homes and jobs. Mental illness became a common problem and even suicides occurred as a result of the shock of the invasion, the loss of homes and jobs and the taking of hostages.

However, personal news was slow in forthcoming. Phone lines between the UK and Kwuait were still closed and mail services were not available. The only way for news to come out was through messages carried by Palestinians who had escaped to Jordan. It seemed that Saddam Hussein had no argument against Palestinians, even buying into their anti-Israel cause to seek validity for his invasion of Kuwait. But the global coalition was building against him, and war was being threatened by the Western allies if the Iraqis did not retreat to their own country. Various diplomatic efforts were being made to persuade Saddam to release the hostages he had taken. Rose did not know what had happened to the four University teachers who had stayed behind to teach summer school for Medical and Allied Health Science students. She could only hope that they were safe and not taken hostage.

In the absence of news from Kuwait Rose kept herself busy in the garden, getting stung by wasps in her enthusiasm for digging. Mum enjoyed having her only daughter with her, and John's children found it a great novelty to have Aunty Rose at home. They took walks in the country and went to local beauty spots and a theme park for special treats. If Rose hadn't had concerns about her staff and her husband amid the talk of the impending war it would have been a happy time. She tried not to get particularly worried but focussed on the purchase of the piece of land that Martin had found for them in summer when the contract of sale came in. Once again she had to go to the bank, this time with Nabeel's letter to prove the change of signatories. She had to make a will, as was required of all purchasers of Spanish property, and so completed the purchase of a hillside property in the South of Spain with a partly built house, some land with a small river and pomegranate trees.

Of course, work did not stop for Rose, although her salary was not being paid, and as she later found out, the University had cancelled all staff contracts. Rose's team members, and those in the parallel Medical Unit were in touch with regard to their possessions, payments and the future. It was obvious that there would be no return to Kuwait until Saddam Hussein was ousted. Rose wrote to University delegates at the London Embassy listing her staff and their status, explaining that people needed to know if there were any plans to move University studies to Bahrein. Together with her colleague, Beatrice, the supervisor of the Medical Unit, she made sure there was communication about the status of the Uni but by October it was clear that there would be no going back for the academic year 9/90 - 6/91. Most teachers needed to find new jobs in order to earn a living, and so after a visit to the Embassy in London to meet the Uni representative, and to inform him about the status of the team, Rose had to settle down to life in Mossfield, hoping Nabeel would come out of Kuwait before the war which the West was threatening began.

Rose heard from their friend in Jordan that Nabeel had made a visit to Baghdad and immediately she suspected the worst. Had he planned to work at his business, paying no heed to the legality of his situation? Treachery would not endear him to the Kuwaitis and Rose did not believe Saddam could be trusted. Although there was a lot of political division in Europe and the USA about the need to free Kuwait, Rose believed there would be a war, sooner or later. It seemed clear to her that their lives in Kuwait were finished but it was obviously not so clear to her husband, who was lingering in Kuwait for some reason.

On a brighter note, there had been movement in getting the expatriate women out of Kuwait. Ruby came out with a group of Australian women but her husband, Mark, was still in hiding in the false ceiling of an apartment with other British men. There was no word about the four teachers who were still in Kuwait. Rose

459

was anxious about their fate as well as her husband's. She hoped Nabeel was helping the expats in hiding like Mark.

Dear Diary,

These are terrible days. I am very lucky that I have a home to stay in, and that I can be useful to Mum for a change. Others have no home, no jobs, and perhaps no savings or relatives to help them. I just hope Nabeel is not doing anything silly. He could be helping the Brits in hiding. I hope so.

October - December, 1990, UK, Spain

It was with relief that Rose received a message via friends in Jordan saying Nabeel would be driving to Lebanon across Saudi Arabia with his brothers and sister. After that he would be coming to London in November. Why, she wondered, did she not know how her husband's mind worked, after all these years? She had known him for 20 years but he was still unpredictable. It seemed that the Civil War in Lebanon was drawing to a close but had still not finished. Generals Aoun and Geagea were still fighting for leadership in the Christian realms and life was uncertain. Perhaps that is why the Fardan family had been delaying before they drove across the Saudi desert to their apartment in Lebanon.

After meeting Nabeel at Heathrow in London, Rose and Nabeel stayed in London at Bill and Katie's for a few days as they had been asked to meet with officials at the Foreign Office. Here Nabeel was questioned about the weaponry he had seen, and especially about the types of planes he had witnessed overhead while the Iraqis were invading Kuwait. After the interview they laughed about it.

"You know, Rose, it reminded me of the weekly confessional with the priest when I was a child. As a kind of penance or sacrifice to atone for naughty things I had done, I used to claim that I had NOT looked at a plane in the sky, a difficult thing for a child to do in the 1940s when planes were scarce and exciting to see. Now I have to try to remember the details of planes I really preferred NOT to see in case they dropped a bomb on me!"

After driving to Mossfield and staying with Mum for a while, Nabeel was smoking heavily and was clearly depressed. Rose remonstrated with him.

"Nabeel, it's no good chain smoking. You'll just make yourself sick. And it's driving Mum and me crazy, we can hardly breathe. Why don't you try chewing gum?" Rose asked him in desperation one day. "You know, we could make a trip to Spain to check on the land. I had to complete the purchase while you were still in Kuwait. It might take your mind off things."

Nabeel agreed and setting off in the little car he drove like a madman for five days, clocking up the kilometres every day, only stopping for them to eat and sleep at night and to fill up the petrol tank. In Fuengirola they visited the land and made wills with a local solicitor as the law in Spain required. However, they started arguing as the pressure for the war of liberation increased around the world. Nabeel felt Saddam was justified in his actions because he was using the Palestinian exile as an excuse for his invasion of Kuwait, to free it of the USA influence, and to reclaim the oil he believed Kuwait was stealing from the Rumaithya oil field. He even attacked Israel with Scud missiles, but fortunately the Israelis could defend themselves with Patriot missile defence shields. Of course, Rose saw through Saddam's pretence and completely disagreed with Nabeel. Their arguments were circular and never ending. It was pointless, time consuming and eventually wore away any positivity between them. Rose was tired of it. If this was to be their life in future, she didn't want it.

On a lighter note, before driving to Spain Rose had attempted to make cider from the apples in the garden. The apples were small, so cutting them up had been a long, painstaking process but while they were away in Spain the heat in the dining alcove made the brew ferment fiercely and spill over the bin! Mum was furious about her expensive fitted shag pile carpet getting stained, and rightly so! John had to throw the 'must' away! So there was no home-made cider to greet them when they got back!

But they were able to celebrate Xmas and the New Year with Mum and John for a change. Bill and Katie came up and all the children enjoyed getting together for some holiday fun. They were still at the age when they believed in Santa Claus and could be spoiled with lots of presents. Rose and Katie prepared the festive meals, so Mum was relieved of any work in the kitchen. Her 62nd birthday on January 1st was the first they had spent together in a long time.

Nabeel in particular enjoyed playing with the young children and Rose could see with chagrin that he would probably have made an excellent father if he had had the chance. Would their lives have been different if they had had the children they both wanted?

Dear Diary,

It's so sad to see Nabeel playing with the children. He seems to have forgotten the old arguments while he's involved with them. I'm glad we've had this chance to live a normal life for even a short time. Who knows what next?

1991, UK, Malaysia, Australia, Kuwait, Hong Kong

In January there was some bad news. Katie and her two children had been driving to see her siblings in Cornwall after Xmas and had had a terrible head on collision on a Dartmoor road. They were rescued from the crash site by helicopter and taken to Plymouth Hospital. Katie was treated for a broken nose in the Emergency Department, but the children had to be admitted for treatment. Noelle needed to wear a body brace for a long period of time, while Rupert needed several operations for his broken scapula. It was fortunate that these severe outcomes were not worse. It meant the start of a long legal struggle for costs against the guilty party in the accident, which added to the difficulties Bill had had to contend with in addition to caring for their mother while Rose was away in Kuwait. Rose wondered yet again why on earth she had married and gone so far away from her family?

That winter in the UK was extremely cold and miserable. Nabeel visited some of his UK principals to advise them about what they should do in the interim while Kuwait was regarded as a state of Iraq. It seemed clear the war of liberation would start, but it was not clear when or how long it would last, or what the outcome would be, since it was thought Saddam might use chemical weapons as he had done before on the Kurds in Iraq. So, the couple decided to get away from it all and go to Australia, a place Rose had long wanted to visit but had never had the leisure time to do so before. They applied for visas and made travel plans. Rose's Mum was in agreement with their leaving. She had had enough of the half-hidden arguments and the smoke created by Nabeel and his cigarettes. She waved them off as they drove down to London, planning to leave the car at Bill's while they travelled.

First they flew to Malaysia for a short holiday, meeting up with some of Nabeel's colleagues from KOC. They enjoyed visiting the street markets in Kuala Lumpur and some batik stores where they could watch the fabric design and dying process. Then Nabeel went to the Philippines to research manpower supply again. Rose flew to Brunei to stay with the former Allied Health Supervisor and his wife, their friends, Malcolm and Lina, who were married in Kuwait. Rose enjoyed catching up with the family and admired their life in tropical Brunei. Once his research was done, Nabeel flew to Kota Kina Balu to meet Rose and they visited Sarawak for a few days, but missed out on an opportunity to see *orang utans* in Brunei.

Next they flew to Sydney to make an extended tour by bus from Sydney down to Adelaide, then to the caves of Coober Peedy, up the red center, to Uluru or Ayers Rock as the non-indigenous people called that magnificent monolith. They hiked in Katherine, then went across the top to Darwin, down the East Coast, stopping in beautiful Brisbane and back to Sydney where they stayed for a few days with old friends from Kuwait, who understood the

Palestinian connection but did not support it mindlessly as Nabeel did.

So once again Nabeel and Rose argued. Just as in Spain they argued their way around Oz about who invaded Kuwait, Iraq or the USA? Rose became incensed about this ridiculous argument. She had had enough of both the politics and the marriage. She tentatively proposed a 'conscious disconnection' over a period of years in which they would try to get Nabeel a British passport and she would study in London for her Ph.D.; Nabeel paid no attention to her proposal. He seemed oblivious to the resentment which was building up between them. His only concern seemed to be the retrieval of his business and his bank funds.

One day by chance Rose saw a position advertised in a Sydney newspaper for a Senior Teacher position at Hong Kong University Language Centre. She applied for the job because she suspected she would not be employed in Kuwait for some time to come, if ever. She knew her friend Neil and some other former Kuwait colleagues had gone there and found the working conditions congenial, with accommodation and airtickets as was standard for expatriate teachers in those days.

The Gulf War began while they were in Oz and when they got back they were invited to return by the Dean of Allied Health Sciences to Kuwait in April when Saddam had been ousted. There was a rumour of ill treatment and even expulsion of Palestinians from Kuwait on account of the 'showcase' support Saddam had given their cause as an excuse for his invasion. Nevertheless, Nabeel decided to go back with Rose and with Beatrice who had also been invited to go back to the Health Science Centre. He guessed that his British wife would provide sufficient protection from any antagonism by the Kuwait Government.

The night before flying Rose had a severe, possibly psychosomatic attack of arthritis in her right knee but went back to Kuwait on crutches. Wearing a headscarf as a triangular face mask to protect herself from the filth left behind by the Republican Guard who had occupied her Departmental offices she cleaned up her area. She was able to retrieve ESP materials the Unit had produced plus her own files regarding the revised curriculum for the coming academic year, though she heard that the University would no longer employ 'foreign' supervisors. The senior positions had to be held by Kuwaitis in future. On top of the destruction wreaked by the occupying soldiers on various hotels, embassies and other institutions, the atmosphere in Kuwait City was affected by toxic clouds of smoke from the oil wells which the departing Iraqis had set alight. They had also leaked oil into the relatively pristine waters of the Gulf. The State was not simply war torn, it was being environmentally destroyed. Nabeel drove Rose to take photos of the oil wells burning and although they did not get close to the fires their clothes were permanently stained with soot which sank into the fibres and could not be washed out.

Back in the UK in July to recruit for language teachers to join the University in September Rose was surprised but pleased to receive acceptance of her application to work in Hong Kong. She called Nabeel in Kuwait to explain what was on her mind.

"Nabeel, you know I probably will not be a supervisor in future in the Uni. Don't you think it would be a good idea for me to take this job in Hong Kong? I will get accommodation and air tickets back to the UK, so if Kuwait doesn't go back to 'normal' and you can't do business there, you could leave and come to Hong Kong and look around for different types of business."

"I suppose you are right. Plus, I need to get settled here again. I'm staying with my brothers at the moment as their flat was still intact. I have to find a new flat, get a new car and sort the office out and my contracts and suppliers."

"OK. So you'll be busy. You know the oil fires are still burning too. It won't make any difference to you because you are still smoking like a chimney, so you should go back and I should leave. What do you say?"

"OK. You are right. But it's not for ever, OK?"

"Of course not, but it might be much better for me, so let's agree to wait and see. How did you say it? *Hatt n Shuuf*? And at least we won't need to go on arguing about who invaded Kuwait. I'm rather tired of that old row, aren't you?"

Nabeel laughed and agreed that she should take the job, but reluctantly. So Rose travelled by train from Mossfield to the wedding of old friend from Kuwait and future Hong Kong colleague Neil in Edinburgh. Over the weekend Rose stayed with Lucy and Justin from Kuwait and enjoyed catching up with them. She met Joan at the wedding reception. They would soon be colleagues in her new job and they are both afficionadoes of language testing, which was encouraging as this was the field Rose was thinking of focussing on for her long-dreamed-of doctoral degree.

Once back in Mossfield, Rose drove Mum to Bill and Katie's. Mum had dry eye syndrome, for which the cure was to have her tear ducts sealed at Moorfields Hospital in London. Back in Mossfield John and Rose worked on the garden. Rose bought guttering for John to install when he had time. It was good to know that he was close by to help Mum while Rose was away in Hong Kong, a journey far too long for Mum in her worsening physical condition.

In early August Rose flew back to Kuwait to report back on UK recruitment. She also submitted her resignation to the Dean, who was very disappointed but understood the stress Rose was under. Rose did not admit she was afraid her marriage was irretrievably broken by the frequent unresolved arguments, even fights, they had experienced in Australia. She suggested to Nabeel a possible permanent separation.

"Nabeel, aren't you sick of our constant rows? Don't you think we should separate, not just while I'm in Hong Kong, but perhaps for ever? We don't seem to be on the same track any more. In fact, we seem to be on parallel lines. I'm really tired of arguing and I don't see you changing. And nor will I. We just can't agree."

"Do you remember what I told you years ago? You have grown too big for your *bottines de Caroline*. You are not what you think you are," Nabeel retorted grimly.

Rose was stunned. Throughout their marriage Nabeel had used 'put downs' about her physical appearance, and worse, about her childlessness, calling her *Immishqurdum*, or 'mother of monkeys', which only he knew was his fault, not hers. Now he was attempting to belittle her again. Was she sleeping with the enemy? She said no more, knowing she was about to escape anyway.

In September she flew to Hong Kong via Dubai, staying with Beatrice and her family overnight. In Hong Kong Rose was met by Neil and stayed with him and his wife for a couple of nights before being installed in a temporary apartment by the Housing Department. She had the floor of her own apartment sanded and sealed so that she would have a lovely home after the tragedy of their beautiful Kuwait apartment and all their possessions being trashed in the invasion. She also began shopping to replace all the items lost in the invasion of Kuwait. Hong Kong's exotic street markets were her comfort zone.

At Nabeel's request Rose filled in the United Nations claims forms for the loss of their home and Nabeel's car. She agreed to spend Xmas in Beirut, taking with her new upholstery silk for the two sitting room suites which were now in Adel's flat in a Christian suburb of Beirut. The first night there was pleasant, the brothers and Asma were welcoming and Nabeel seemed thrilled. But on waking that first morning a photo in a frame that Nabeel had placed by her bed fell over. It had a message on the back, written by an Iraqi solder, with a cryptic message that chilled her spine: "I know you, but I do not love you." The implications suggested by someone who had possibly gone through all her clothes, her private papers, Nabeel's photos, and videos, were like experiencing a burglary or even a rape. She couldn't help screaming and Nabeel came to see what the problem was. She showed him the reverse of the photo.

"You do realise that someone has been through our private affairs. I feel exposed and I'm so glad I am not going back to Kuwait."

To console her Nabeel took her shopping for a festive outfit. She had lost so much weight since the invasion that all her clothes were too big. They had a pleasant night out in a night club with friends for New Year. In the apartment Rose played her own piano which the brothers had transported together with Asma's to Lebanon. After New Year she went to Kuwait to see Nabeel's new flat, and 12 small items remaining from their Kuwait home. He had bought a new Jeep in case there was another invasion and he had to flee across the desert as others did in August 1990. He also seemed rather close to his new Philippina secretary. She was married, but Nabeel told Rose:

"She's very helpful. She cuts my toenails for me. Because of my back pain."

Rose recalled the Thai massage scenario and wondered what this was about. If he had found someone else to care for him, that suited her perfectly. She'd had enough of him.

Dear Diary,
    I know Nabeel must be as sick of our arguing as I am. I wonder if he secretly thinks we

should separate? I'm glad I'll be going back to Hong Kong where I feel secure and have peace and quiet, unlike in war torn Beirut and Kuwait. There may be tornadoes over there but the ground is steady beneath me.

1992, Hong Kong, Seoul, UK, France, Kuwait, Jakarta

Back in Hong Kong Rose met Harold, a visiting American English Professor at a lunch party and began a platonic friendship, spending weekends going to concerts, plays and ballet. She was also working hard both fulltime and with Neil on an MA Social Studies language evening program and with Hong Kong British Council evening classes in the outer suburbs, taking the hovercraft to the school. Exciting times indeed, but Rose's legs were starting to hurt and spider veins were appearing on her ankles. She sometimes wondered if she was doing too much and should take it easy. She consulted a doctor who recommended an appointment with a surgeon. She had excellent accommodation, tickets and health provision as a university teacher and she had bought her own gorgeous full length curtains and matching bedspreads and sitting room upholstery. This could be a perfect new start to her own, independent life, she thought. Any medical treatment she needed would be paid for by the University.

Rose had joined the Hong Kong Action Research group on arrival and now started her own classroom research project. She was also introduced to the Hong Kong Exams Authority by Joan and wrote the Use of English paper for secondary schools in use that summer. She also helped Neil on his Social Sciences Video Project. In addition she worked on the Hong Kong English

Language Papers as a sub-editor. She was completely fulfilled in her work and enjoying a busy professional and social life. It was a huge contrast from Kuwait. For once she felt pretty, confident and full of fun. She looked forward to beginning her doctorate soon.

But meanwhile there were requests to assess the RSA Dip.TEFL practical lessons in both Hong Kong and Seoul. She spent a week in South Korea where she met up with former colleagues in Kuwait, who now had a lovely little girl. It was interesting to observe Korean culture at close quarters. Rose enjoyed visiting the exotic palaces in the city centre, and despite the language barrier and the emphasis on meat in Korean cuisine she enjoyed her time there.

Back in the UK for her summer holiday, in July John drove Mum and Rose and his three children to France for a Euro Disney package holiday. They spent the frst night at Bill's, getting up early to board the car ferry at Dover. After a night in Calais at a motel the next day they drove to Eurodisney on the outskirts of Paris. They stayed for three memorable nights in the US Wild-Western-styled hotel on site, then spent a night in a city centre hotel in sight of the Eiffel Tower. They spent the next day going up to the second stage of the Eiffel Tower and taking a *bateau mouche* trip. Although Mum was in her wheelchair, it was great fun. Little Laurel, having struggled with the concept of another country and another language at first, made her debut in the French language, and using a French 'fry', modelled smoking with panache.

After this holiday Rose had to fly to Kuwait where she spent a stormy few days with Nabeel in his new flat.

She felt distinctly uncomfortable here despite Nabeel showing off his brand new Jeep. She was also suspicious of Nabeel's relationship with his secretary. The effect of the oil fires was everywhere, a tainted, dirty atmosphere and although 90% of the fires had been put out the most difficult to extinguish were still burning. Soon Rose was back in Mossfield to take some belongings from the house and to enjoy some time out with Mum. She made an appointment at Birmingham Uni with her MA tutor on language testing, to see if she could start a doctorate with him. He was not able to take on the role, however, on account of his different workload. She also presented her research paper at Aston Uni which was then published in a book of selected proceedings from the conference.

Early in September Rose flew back to Hong Kong where for a few months she housed a Chinese MA female student she had met on the Extra Mural course. Harold had left in summer but his place was taken in September by another US professor as Visiting Fullbright Scholar. Kyle was a Shakespeare specialist. Rose developed Self Access materials with the lectures given by both these scholars, on Bram Stoker's Dracula and Emily Dickenson, the American poet.

Having bought a fax machine for the house in Mossfield, Rose installed a fax in her Hong Kong apartment so as to communicate with Mum on weekends. She and John's kids exchanged pictures they had drawn as well as written messages as the children were developing their writing skills. Mum told Rose about Laurel calling to the fax machine in Rose's Mossfield bedroom: "Come out Aunty Rose, I want to see you." It was sad but sweet.

Bill and Katie visited with the children and Kyle joined them on a long junk trip around Hong Kong Island. They enjoyed each other's company and had dinner at a restaurant on Hong Kong Island. Noelle, aged 8 was baffled by Aunt Rose's home in Hong Kong. "Are you from Hong Kong, Aunty Rose?" she asked innocently. Rose laughed. She wasn't sure where she was from any longer, but she knew she loved her life in Hong Kong.

Rose's prescribed vein operations were completed early in December. This Xmas Rose and Nabeel agreed to meet on neutral ground in the hope of avoiding sad memories of arguments in Beirut and Kuwait. Because of her health, they flew to nearby Indonesia, and stayed in a five star hotel in Jakarta where they celebrated New Year's with a late dinner and dancing in the hotel discotheque. It was almost like old times in the London Playboy Club before they were married until Nabeel questioned Rose about her life in Hong Kong. "Well, *habibti*, have you been having a good time in Hong Kong?" he asked as they prepared for bed.

"Why don't you come and see my friends, my office, and my work, and make your own judgements?" she retorted. "I've asked you to come over often enough."

"Yes, but will you tell me your little secrets if I do?" he probed salaciously.

"If I had time for secrets then I would keep them secret," she told him angrily. "I do nothing but work, and socialise in cultural settings, which are few and far between in Kuwait. I don't see why you are so keen to have me back when you obviously do not trust me."

"Better the devil you know, isn't it? I got used to you," he laughed, sharing his little joke.

Dear Diary, Nabeel infuriates me at every turn. Why am I putting up with this power game playing? I have had enough. But am I strong enough to make the break?

1993, Hong Kong, UK, USA

After the negative experience with Nabeel in Jakarta, Rose developed a deeper relationship with Kyle whose own romantic past had been extremely complicated. He gave her advice based on his own experience and offered her a refuge if she needed to get away in future. Despite the bad feeling with which the New Year holiday had left them Nabeel came to Hong Kong in March to persuade Rose to go back to Kuwait.

"You know, Rose, I'm tired of you being away from me and I want you to come back to Kuwait. By the way, I've bought a lovely flat for us in Beirut. You'll love it."

"Well, that's nice for you. But in Kuwait, have things changed? I really enjoy my professional status here. I can't imagine going back to Kuwait now. I'd like to study for a doctorate, as you know. I suppose I could start it in London, and come back to Kuwait just for the holidays. What about this? If we bought a place, a small studio apartment, near London Uni, in your name, then you could become resident in London and could get a British passport. No more visas for you to travel anywhere. Just an easy, no visa, British passport."

"Well, that's an interesting idea. Look, here's how much money I've got now, just two years after we thought we'd lost everything. You won't need to work at all." He made notes on his assets in her notebook. Rose stared at them unbelievingly. He had not lost any of his wealth.

"That would be good. My legs are still giving me trouble and although I enjoy working, I'd like to get my doctorate finished in the minimum three years."

"OK. You resign, go back to the UK, find a flat, and register for your degree."

After more discussion of the issues involved, Rose resigned, knowing that his brothers would laugh at Nabeel if she did not go back to him. Once again, she felt sorry for him. Her colleagues were surprised and expressed their dismay but also their understanding of the situation she was in. With her savings from her several lucrative jobs in Hong Kong Nabeel and Rose went shopping. They chose expensive, formal Chinese rosewood furniture for the dining and sitting room in the proposed London flat before Nabeel flew back to Kuwait.

Rose completed her work, especially the Self Access Materials she developed based on Harold's and Kyle's lectures. Then, having shipped some things back to Kuwait, including her new keyboard, she had the new furniture packed and shipped to London. In a last minute flurry, assisted by friends, she closed up her flat and flew Emirates, crying bitterly all the way on the plane back to London to the consternation of the air crew. In her heart of hearts she knew she had yet again made a terrible mistake, giving up an excellent job with optimum working conditions and remuneration, to save the 'face' of her husband who she had to admit she no longer loved. The aircrew brought her a whole box of tissues to mop up her tears. Finally, she fell asleep nursing a large scotch and soda.

Why was she so bad at making decisions concerning herself, she wondered? Under pressure she always gave in. What was wrong with her? Where had her independent spirit gone?

In London Rose stayed with Bill and Katie and started searching for a suitable studio apartment with the help of Rupert who was very good at reading the prices on the flyers from the real estate agents. He selected only the apartments within budget. The problem was the budget kept increasing. On the phone to Kuwait Nabeel escalated the purchase from a studio to a three bedroom apartment in pricey West London, for business reasons, he claimed.

After spending a month tramping the streets of London Rose finally made an offer which was accepted and asked Nabeel to transfer the money with which to buy the apartment. To her amazement, he claimed that he had to get Edouard's permission to transfer money. He wanted her to use the savings they had in the UK to make the purchase but there would have been no money left for the annual property charge for the apartment. So, fired up with a strong instinct for self-preservation, realising that Nabeel had reneged on the deal they had made, Rose finally told him she had had enough of his failure to keep his promises. The marriage was over. Of course, in retrospect she could see that had she bought the flat in her name, she would have had the money in her own hands. But Rose was not playing a game. She wanted to get away from her manipulative husband and take only what was due to her. She even hoped they could keep some sort of friendship going, on the understanding that they were no longer compatible and life would be better for both of them if they separated.

On the phone for an hour Nabeel talked to Mum, who was perplexed by the situation but who had suspected for some time that things were not right. He then flew to the UK from Kuwait to talk things through again face to face. Rose was adamant about separation but attempted to keep the relationship calm and amicable. On 4 October Nabeel flew back to Kuwait and four days later Rose flew to the USA for a trial holiday with Kyle. She enjoyed her time with him and his dog on his ranch. She realised she would avoid confrontation by staying there while she began divorce proceedings. Mum agreed because she was afraid of what Nabeel might do. Like Rose, she no longer trusted this man who had called her 'Mum' for 17 years.

As expected, back in the UK, Rose had to cope with an onslaught of telephone calls from Kuwait which increased her level of sadness and distress on making this decision after 23 years together. It caused severe psychosomatic back pain which physiotherapy could not remedy but chiropractic treatment was successful. After further discussion and warnings from Mum, who was still receiving phone calls from Kuwait, Rose went back in November to the USA for what she hoped would be the duration of the divorce. Before doing so she moved the money which was intended for her if Nabeel died, to her account in Hong Kong as she suspected that Nabeel would not agree to a divorce settlement. She told Nabeel frankly what she had done. She had not understood that honesty is not always the best policy when dealing with someone who fears being 'taken to the cleaners' by his wife, a subordinate in the marital relationship, not an equal by any means.

Dear Diary,

Why do I have to be so honest? I am a sucker for the truth, while involved with a 'machiavellian'. I need to learn the ways of the world. At least I can get out of this marriage and breathe again.

1994, USA, Hong Kong, UK

Rose attended Kyle's lectures, did some editing and private tuition and researched a potential PhD project. Back on the ranch she cared for the dog, sheltered in the basement from tornadoes and at Xmas hosted a small party with Kyle. In March Rose attended the TESOL Convention in Baltimore and met several old friends on the TESOL circuit. Over the past three months Rose had written to Nabeel and even sent him a shirt as a gift. She felt his pain and humiliation but tried to get him to understand that she would not change her mind. The fault beneath them was hers in agreeing to marry, but his too, in lying about his family's reaction to the marriage. She had agreed under pressure and the fault beneath them had erupted.

When she returned from Baltimore to find Kyle at the airport waving a fax that revealed Nabeel had managed to move the money from her account in Hong Kong to his brother's account in Kuwait, she was not surprised. That he had gone so far as to commit fraud only completed the clear picture she now had of him. She did what she had to do to re-establish her finances. She went for a job interview in Washington DC. Rose revealed to the interview board that she desperately needed the job on account of her personal circumstances and got the job she applied for. Moreover, given her CV and performance at interview she was offered an even a better one. Kyle was sad but he had his own problems and Rose was in a distrustful mood. She simply wanted to get away from relationships and find herself again.

In May she flew to London where she had to change her passport name and find an international solicitor. She then went to Hong Kong to launch an investigation into how Nabeel had managed to steal the money from her bank account. She reported the defrauding to the Commercial Crime Bureau. Despite the obvious English language errors in the letter instructing the bank to move the money to Edouard Fardan, the signature at the bottom of the letter was Rose's, given years ago in Kuwait to obtain visas to Lebanon, so Rose's claim failed. She returned to London where Kyle was due to pay a visit to the UK. In exchange for his hospitality in the USA Rose made sure she and Kyle had a pleasant holiday. Even though Kyle asked Rose to marry him she realised she had to be strong, independent and rely on herself. She started divorce proceedings but Nabeel hid his assets, especially his new apartment in Beirut, and lied about his status, pretending to be a poor, lowly employee in his brothers' firm. Rose made a final attempt to get through to him on the phone.

"I've reported you to the Hong Kong Commercial Crime Bureau. Don't you think you should give me half the money I moved to safeguard it from you? That would clear your name from Interpol's watch list. As your brothers said years ago, you are indeed a liar and a thief."

"You know, it would be cheaper to have you killed than to settle financially with you," Nabeel laughed in his usual way, sure of himself and his manipulation of the situation.

"Those are the last words you will ever speak to me. They prove you are a coward, threatening a woman who from the start of our relationship has done nothing but help you achieve your objectives. Goodbye." Rose slammed down the phone. Her marriage was over, if not yet legally, and she was determined never to see this confidence trickster again.

Epilogue

In August Rose flew to the Arabian Gulf to take up her management job in a country-wide tertiary education system. She took with her a guitar which John helped her to choose. She hoped to learn to play it in her spare time. On arrival at the airport she probably gave the impression of a carefree troubador. Along with other new colleagues she was about to start a new life which would be completely different from the life she had started after her marriage, based on a lie about the happy family she was to be welcomed into.

For a time after the discovery of the fraud her revulsion towards the man she had given so many years of her life to, made her hate to hear Arabic spoken. However, her antipathy towards the first language of the man she had married had faded. She realised her Arabic language skill was an asset which had helped her obtain this job which could re-establish her finances. She also realised that Nabeel had planned to spend all her savings on buying furniture in Hong Kong to ensure she would go back to him. When she didn't, he defrauded her.

She had several big questions on her mind: Would she be able to survive mentally and physically in this new post where she would be completely alone? Was she now on safer ground emotionally? Would her expensive solicitors manage to achieve a divorce with a satisfactory financial settlement? Should she try to seek revenge if not, given the insider knowledge she had of Nabeel's business deals?

Would Mum manage to cope with her increasing pain and disability alone? Would her friendship with Kyle continue?

Whatever the answers, they had to be accepted. Kyle had taught her one invaluable lesson: You cannot play tennis on both sides of the net. If your motives are pure and your intentions justified, then you can only act unilaterally and hope for a positive response. She would not seek financial revenge and blacken her own name in the process. She would hope for karma, and keep her own feet on solid ground. She understood in retrospect that the doubts she had had about marrying were intuitively correct, warning her, although she did not perceive it at the time, of the fault beneath the interesting but insecure landscape of their relationship.

In psychological terms as a couple they were probably co-dependent. Both had challenging childhood backgrounds, and both had inferiority complexes with regard to their looks. Rose had felt unceasing sympathy towards the Palestinian refugee but had not realised that marriage to a man who had the surface veneer of a European would involve relinquishing and renegotiating her identity as an independent woman.

Using her innate sense of personal agency she had struggled incessantly to increase her educational qualifications during their 23-year relationship. As a result, she had been able to overcome the setback of the invasion of Kuwait by finding a new job in Hong Kong, which opened the door of her marital cage. Even the defrauding of her funds had not vanquished her spirit. The decision to marry changed her life, her career and her identity but thanks to her strong sense of agency as an individual with free will she realised she had come through the dark, heavy clouds to find a silver lining in New Zealand.